PRAISE FOR WINTER'S REMAINS

"Winter's Remains is a true page-turner, with an engaging plot that keeps you hooked from the very first page. The action sequences are intense and vividly described, offering readers a thrilling experience as they follow the characters through a tumultuous and dangerous landscape." — Reader Review

"The story is exceptionally well-crafted, and it maintains a constant video game-like ambiance that immerses you from start to finish. However, don't underestimate the "grimdark" subtitle – this narrative doesn't shy away from violence, profanity, and mature themes. But if you're comfortable with such content, you're in for an exhilarating journey through a sprawling, epic world populated by captivating characters." — Reader Review

"Wow! This book does not let us down! I LOVED the chapters with Aliana and Aurelia. Fein did an incredible job of realistically and non-stereotypically portraying young girls, especially ones trained by warriors. Book 2 takes place directly after book 1, but we also get some backstory into Wintersvilla...there were a huge number of new characters introduced, and all of them are as unique and vibrant as the characters we met in book 1. The Mendel journals in this book are even more intriguing and revealing than the ones in book 1, like Mendel is a character all on his own just by witnessing his writings...Those last couple chapters were really such a thrill. I can't decide which set of characters I am more interested in because they were all so well done and compelling. " — Reader Review

"I have been on the hunt for a proper science fiction book for quite some time. This book has an immense amount of elements to offer to appease any sci-fi fan. The world-building is incredible—the author takes an incredible amount of time crafting a world that is set 100 years in a dystopian Earth. Nightmarish expanses of landscape to undeniably stunning domains to even space, Fein has done it all. This is an emotionally gripping tale that weaves together multiple characters with different needs and goals. Some good, some bad, although this all depends on the perspective of the reader. The author touches on profound moral questions, along with philosophical considerations, which is thoroughly enjoyed. This is not a book meant to fulfill a page count, this is a book that intends to make you think and that, I believe, is a well-crafted book. I commend the author's writing style. It is impactful, powerful, and emotionally-driven. There is no stone left unturned here and to think this was only the first book of a series!" — Reader Review

"The world-building is a triumph, as Fein paints a vivid and hauntingly realistic portrait of Earth's desolation. Fein's skillful use of multiple perspectives adds depth to the story, enabling readers to see the world from various angles. Fein's storytelling prowess shines through, as intricate themes of evolution, survival, and the human condition are interwoven into a thrilling narrative. The book explores complex relationships and delves into philosophical questions, all while delivering exhilarating action and suspense " — Reader Review

OTHER WORKS BY E. S. FEIN

The Collected Histories of Neoevolution Earth
A Dream of Waking Life
Points of Origin
Ascendescenscion
The Process Is Love

OfficialESFein.com
Linktr.ee/ESFein
Instagram.com/Authoresfein
Patreon.com/Officialesfein
Facebook.com/AuthorESFein

The Collected Histories of

Neoevolution
Earth

Volume 2

Winter's Remains

E. S. Fein

Winter's Remains (Neoevolution Earth Vol. 2)

Copyright © 2023 by E. S. Fein

This is a work of fiction. Names, characters, places and incidents either are products of the author's imagination or are used fictitiously. Any resemblance to actual events or locales or persons, living or dead, is entirely coincidental.

Author: E. S. Fein

Publisher: Federated Agency Publishing

Editor: Nichole Paolella Petrovich

Formatter: Timbers Book Design

Ebook ISBN: 978-1-7323069-6-7

Paperback ISBN: 978-1-963048-08-7

Publication Date: December 2023

First Edition

To my son, Leif, whose radiance illuminates my world.

CONTENTS

Chapter 1: The Fall of Wintersvilla................................1

Chapter 2: Little Smooth Talker............................23

Chapter 3: A Landing in Hell............................37

Chapter 4: Monsters Are Real............................49

Chapter 5: With Discipline and Daring............................65

Chapter 6: The Tortured Reflection............................83

Chapter 7: Agents of Pain............................101

Chapter 8: Bold and Beautiful............................115

Chapter 9: To Love and Be Loved............................135

Chapter 10: Truth Refracted............................157

Chapter 11: With Fierceness and Fortitude............................181

Chapter 12: The Cost of Freedom............................205

Chapter 13: To Peer Into the Soul............................215

Chapter 14: The Freed Slave............................223

Chapter 15: The Genesis of Love............................231

BOOK SUMMARIES AND GLOSSARY

Visit OfficialESFein.com for a summary of **Volume 1: Mendel's Ladder**, **Volume 2: Winter's Remains,** and a **Glossary of Terms** ranging the entire Neoevolution Earth series.

Volume 2

Winter's Remains

All of life and every individual exists on a spectrum of wickedness and selfishness. The elite of the world, the rich and powerful, are the most wicked and selfish among us. They are not noble. Neither are they righteous nor honest. They are the rot confining humanity to this singular cosmic speck of detritus. Even though I am one of them now—the very worst of them—they are still my enemy. They always have been. I was born as scum beneath their gilded boots—a sewer rat forced to fend for myself in the reckless and debaucherous remains left in the wake of the rich and powerful's global parading at the expense of the poor and meek. I have adopted their pretentious mannerisms. I have infiltrated their families and business partners. I have generated wealth beyond measure. I have become one of them—a Titan—but that doesn't change that they are my enemy, now and forever.

Of the ten Titans who agreed to my plan for the Earth and humanity, four will betray me outright. They will refuse to board Astrea, even though they will encourage their families to leave the Earth. They will not relinquish their power; they will choose instead to utilize their power and each of their families' respective scientific expertise to build their own empires of dirt. Of course, these betrayals are all part of my plan. Each betrayal is a rung of my ladder.

John Downver desires recognition, not power. He wants praise, not control. He is still as recklessly hedonistic as the rest of them. However, he is harmless compared to the others, and he will serve well as the architect and initial leader of Downver, until he dies of a heart attack a decade or so after Downver's founding. He won't know it, but I will aid him in Downver's construction.

Tomasz Novak desires security and superiority. He is a coward and a shortsighted academic. I will allow him to take refuge over the Pacific Ocean, pitifully hiding from my weapons and my

Nomads as he constructs his own biological counterattacks. He will believe himself safe and secure, and I will let him feel this way until the year 2099. Until then, he will continue working for me, even when he believes he's working against me.

Gladys Mainstone, my dear Gladys. She is the only one of the Titans I respect. Her vision is broad, and her ambitions lie far beyond material gain and ephemeral hedonism. And yet, she is still unable to let go of her own selfish desires. Regardless, her efforts against me will be crucial to my Ascension.

Craig Winters is the epitome of the filth constituting humanity's "upper" echelons. Vile, immoral, sadistic, proud. He is one of the very worst humans who has ever existed or will ever exist. He takes pleasure in the suffering of others, and he experiences pain at the pleasure of others. And yet, he still has a role in all this. His empire, Wintersvilla, which he will build atop the coming destruction of Vancouver, will eventually give rise to a great matriarchy of enhanced female warriors. The fall of this great matriarchy is part of my plan.

It's all part of my plan. I hold every string, including my own. I speak the very words of fate.

I am not selfish, and though I am wicked, it is only to combat the wickedness and selfishness still lingering in humanity's genetics like black mold. As my ladder is climbed, the divine light of Ascension will clear the mold away, and we will all be cleansed. Including me.

It's all part of my plan. Everything and everyone.

From Mendel's Ladder: The Personal Journal of Denis Mendel, Written Circa 2044, Published June 2108 by Leif Mainstone, Federated Agency Publishing

Chapter 1
The Fall of Wintersvilla

Year: 2098

A gentle yet persistent breeze outside the Matriarch's throne room sighed like a distant lover's touch, filling Shira's wandering mind with pleasant thoughts of Myriam. The permanently blue daytime sky was filled with puffy white clouds that cast colossal shadows across the handful of old world steel towers constituting Wintersvilla's Central Command District. Shira could still remember a time when onslaughts of ink-black typhoons collided with the city on a weekly basis, year-round, making the steel of the hundred-year-old buildings wail as they resisted the cataclysmic winds caused by old world humanity's careless and wanton destruction of the entire planet's climate. Imagining such atmospheric chaos almost seemed like a distant dream now, for the Nomads had fully tamed Earth's climate over a decade ago. There were no more typhoons, but neither was there rain. There were no more blizzards, but neither was there snow. There weren't even any strong gusts of wind. The sky remained blue, the sun shined brightly, and the cotton white clouds drifted aimlessly, day and night.

Wintersvilla managed without precipitation by desalinating seawater, thereby using the ocean to irrigate their old world crops and provide water to its millions of citizens. Shira wasn't sure how the rest of the world and life in general could survive without rain or weather variation, but of course, the world and its people weren't the same anymore. It was their world—the Nomads, and Shira wondered what it might look like in a hundred more years. There was a time she thought that Wintersvilla might actually have a chance at expanding far beyond its current borders—at making the whole world a Matriarchy, like Nomusa always dreamed. But Shira knew those dreams were over, destroyed by the reality of waking life.

This world belongs to the Nomads. It's only a matter of time, Shira thought uneasily. *South Wintersvilla or North Wintersvilla or the farms and fisheries outside the city's walls—it doesn't matter where. It all belongs to them. They choose not to take it—that's the only reason we have any of it. It's only a matter of time before every inch of Wintersvilla is turned to soil and flesh trees. And with the Rover King at our border, we might already be out of time.*

Shira envisioned Nomusa's throne room as seen from above, an anachronistic metal yurt surrounded by the sprawling metal metropolis constituting North Wintersvilla's Command District. She imagined the thick crimson smoke pouring out of the yurt's several chimneys, telling the citizens of the Wintersvilla Matriarchy that an Inner Circle meeting was in session, and that the meeting was not to be disrupted.

The best possible thing that could happen for Wintersvilla is for this meeting to be disrupted. The city's citizens should be pouring in here and demanding that Nomusa take heed of the danger standing right outside our walls. But they won't do that. None of them will. So that leaves me.

All seven members of the Matriarchy's Inner Circle sat around the throne room's round black walnut table. The six chiefs of Wintersvilla waited silently as Nomusa finished reading the morning's reports. Her obsidian complexion and intricately woven dreadlocks radiated both striking beauty and an aura of meticulously crafted and maintained power. She wasn't as bulky as Shira, but her natural height and consistent daily training ensured that her bare, toned musculature demanded attention from even the most impressive warriors, whether friend or foe. Nomusa, by her own decree as Matriarch, was the only individual allowed to wear an exo outside of battle or labor. She was already naturally taller than all the others, but in her exo, she towered over the rest of the women like a true queen lording over her subjects.

As the Chief of Logistics and General of War, Shira observed the other women, considering each one carefully as she weighed how to convince them of the terrible truth they all needed to accept if they hoped to survive the coming days.

Shira turned to her left and scanned the length of the table. Mei, the Chief of Science and Trade, pored over a bevy of her own reports concerning domestic trade between the city's many districts. There was a time when she also oversaw imports and exports to various known human settlements and the only other major human cities on the planet: Downver and Vida. However, Downver and Vida had grown self-sufficient over the years so that they no longer required the protection of Wintersvilla Warriors. This translated to a severe decrease in the number of men being traded like currency with Wintersvilla and forced into slavery. Nowadays, Mei mostly concerned herself with domestic matters, so she was undoubtedly aware of Wintersvilla's quickly crumbling foundations.

Mei's braided black hair and meticulous makeup reflected the precision and flawlessness of her work. She was the only woman in the room without ports or a metal endoskeleton. Wearing loose magenta robes, she was also the only chief with most of her body covered for the sake of comfort and convenience. For Mei, glory was found on the battlefield of knowledge and negotiation, and on that battlefield she was a ruthless goddess of war. She might not have any ports, but she was the only reason, along with the Agency, that Shira and the others had theirs.

I can convince Mei. She's always been reasonable and fair, even when it came to Aliana and Aurelia and the agreement with the Nomads, Shira considered carefully, recollecting the time when, twelve years earlier, Rooli, who was only called Enduring Ironwood at the time, walked right up to the looming, austere Northern Wall of Wintersvilla and asked to speak to Queen Nomusa on behalf of the Nomads worldwide. *Mei was the one who finally convinced Nomusa to take the deal in the end,* Shira reminded herself, bolstering her confidence that Mei would see reason during this meeting that would decide the fate of all their lives.

Nomusa continued silently reading Shira's report, and Shira turned to scrutinize Lain, the young Chief of Reconnaissance and Expedition. The unfettered warrior absentmindedly picked at one of her forearm ports and hummed a simple melody to herself, traversing some distant horizon in her mind. Spending her entire childhood on expeditions beyond Wintersvilla's walls, Lain felt most comfortable away from home. She was only back in the city by coincidence, having returned to repair a malfunctioning section of her exo just a few nights earlier. Lain had been born to a renownedly beautiful and naturally athletic birthing mother named Jude just after the forming of the Matriarchy. As a particularly fit and clever newborn, she was subsequently raised by the previous Chief of Reconnaissance and Expedition, the ruthlessly intelligent and brutally effective Nichole Adamich, who was called the Serenading Slayer, for she was known to sing with joy as she effortlessly slaughtered her enemies on the battlefield. Shira grimaced as she filled her head with images of Nichole, her closest childhood friend after Nomusa. Nichole had stolen an exo and gone rogue sixteen years earlier, when Lain was only eight years old. Shira still couldn't help clinging to a

3

distant hope that Nichole was happy somewhere, though she was likely dead.

I wish you could have met Aliana and Aurelia, Shira thought remorsefully, knowing that Nichole would have fallen in love with them even more than Shira had. Shira knew it must have been hard for Lain to lose Nichole, but Lain had never expressed any pain over her second mother's traitorous departure. The same day they discovered that Nichole had stolen Wintersvilla property and abandoned the Matriarchy, they told Lain the truth. She responded simply, "Nichole does as she pleases. She's stronger and smarter than all of Wintersvilla combined. I say good for her for attempting to survive alone, as a true warrior should." Even now, Lain still didn't seem affected by Nichole's absence, though it was impossible to know if she was just adept at disguising her despair. She kept to herself, and she seemed to genuinely prefer her own company.

Lain will remain neutral as usual, Shira concluded, recognizing that the girl was not necessarily a friend nor an enemy, but rather a fellow warrior whom she deeply respected and admired. *The wilds of the Nomadic world are her true home. At the very least, she won't stand against me,* Shira determined with a reserve of caution, for Lain was by far the most unpredictable and hardest to read of all the chiefs.

Nomusa cleared her throat, prompting everyone in the room to turn and face her, but she just went on reading the reports, taking her time to scrutinize Shira's data and proposals. Shira turned back to analyze the other chiefs, and this time she glanced at Greta, the Chief of Slavery and Birthing. The battle-scarred and gruff woman twisted her thick neck and stretched at the shoulders impatiently, flexing her bulky and only slightly sagging warrior muscles as if in agitation. Despite their shared glory in the past, the bond between Shira and Greta was a tenuous knot of tragedy and trauma, culminating in a deep, begrudging distrust. Shira knew a part of Greta loved her for killing Craig Winters and freeing Mei, Nomusa, Nichole, Shira and herself, the five founders of Wintersvilla, from slavery. However, Shira also knew that Greta equally loathed her for killing Winters on her own. The perverted, foul old man had raped and tortured the founders of the Matriarchy in this very room when they were still just children. The other four, but especially Greta, viewed Shira killing Winters by herself as a betrayal rather than the act of love Shira intended it to be, and for the last twenty-seven years, Greta's resentment toward Shira had grown to a violent head. Shira reasoned that Greta's hatred for Aliana, Aurelia, and Rooli was just collateral damage in her bitterness toward Shira. Shira had concluded many times in the past that it was only a matter of time before Greta made an attempt on her life, as Greta openly and vocally desired Shira's position as general, believing it to hold greater prestige and benefit than her own role as the city's premier slave driver. As was the Wintersvilla custom, it was Greta's right to duel Shira to the death, but Greta was clever enough to know that she would die in a heartbeat in a duel with Shira.

Greta is a great warrior, but I am greater, Shira concluded with what she considered to be fairness and modesty. Regardless, were it not for Nomusa's demand that Shira remain general, she would have let Greta take the position. *I didn't choose this life. It chose me,* Shira ruminated. *Greta won't help me. She will undoubtedly stand against me, along with Nomusa's young bodyguards.*

While Mei wore her robes, the other women in the room wore light strips of silk undergarments for convenience and sanitation, except for Nomusa's personal bodyguards, the nineteen-year-old twins Sophie and Lina, the Joint Chiefs of Protection, who were naked at all times. Their constant nudity was seen as one of the marks of a true Wintersvilla Warrior; like an old world animal, a truly vicious and effective being had no use for the comfort and safety of clothing. It was a custom originally started by Nomusa in the early days of the Matriarchy's founding. Nomusa's original intention in being nude as often as possible was a statement to the world of men that women could now openly bare their bodies as much as they pleased without fear of molestation or rape. However, over time, as warriors mimicked the actions of their queen, the nudity custom took on new meaning, and warriors, including Shira, took it as a challenge to remain as bare as possible during battle and leisure.

As the twins sat silently beside Nomusa, they stared daggers at Shira, refusing to take their eyes off her from the moment Shira had entered the room.

They hate me, Shira knew. *Even more than men. They think I've grown weak. They think my caution and carefulness is an affront to Wintersvilla's might. All the young warriors see the old timers as weak, it seems.*

Shira visualized the tens of thousands of Wintersvilla Women who had died in battle over the years, and she marveled at the glory of their sacrifices. *These young girls are so eager for death and battle despite never having tasted the real thing. The greatest danger they know are duels to the death with their fellow sisters. They don't know what it means to hunt and be hunted by a Hunter. But I guess that's my fault, after all. I've made this world a safer place, and in turn, I've deprived these young warriors of their promised glory. They can't help but despise me.*

Shira let her stare fall away from Sophie's and Lina's rabid glares, and then she ran her hand across the wooden table. It was the same table Winters had once used to dine and formulate his sordid plans for world domination. A stream of terrible memories coursed through Shira whenever the Inner Circle met, reminding her of all the times Winters had violated her atop the very same wooden table. She could still vividly smell his suffocating cologne and taste the bitterness of his rotten skin. Shira had begged Nomusa to destroy the table when they were still kids, but Nomusa always refused, claiming that it was important to be reminded where they came from and that it was men who were their true enemy—the enemy of all women. It was the same reason she never changed the name of Wintersvilla. It was like a trophy to her, but to Shira it was just a terrible nightmare that she wished she could drain of life and leave in the dirt.

"Something the matter, Sister?" Nomusa asked Shira. She had finished with Shira's reports and had been watching Shira stare at the crimson stain on the far edge of the table for an unknown amount of time. The stain was a mix of Shira's and Winter's blood from when Shira had gutted the disgusting old man with his own prototype weapon, which remained embedded into her endoskeleton the old way—direct into the flesh without the use of ports.

"No, Musa. I'm fine," Shira stated, flattening her wandering mind and nodding for Nomusa to start the meeting.

"Come on then, Shira. Let's hear what you have to say," Mei offered, gentle but to the point.

"Is there something wrong with the table?" Nomusa issued with a twinge of impatience, revealing a surge of the cold distance she'd actively built between herself and Shira, especially over the last couple years.

"It's nothing, Musa," Shira said once more, knowing that Nomusa was perfectly aware that the table made Shira uneasy to the point of feeling nauseas.

It's like she's starting to hate me just as much as Greta, Shira thought. *It's the girls. And it's Rooli. That much is obvious. She was never the same after we made the truce with the Nomads, allowing Rooli to live within our walls and never leave the girls' side. She still sees it as a shameful bending of the knee since the Nomads agreed to allow Wintersvilla to stand, implying that they would destroy Nomusa's Matriarchy if she didn't comply with Rooli's presence in her queendom. And she blames me most of all, for I was the one who argued most heavily to take the deal.*

Shira sighed deeply, unsure how to begin.

"Cut the troutshit, Shira," Greta lashed with an impatient roll of her eyes. "You're the one who convinced Nomusa to call this so-called war council in the first place. I've a city to run, you understand, General? I don't have the pleasure of spending all my time raising little lab-grown girls."

Shira held her tongue, not allowing Greta's bristling indignation to pierce her facade of calm stoicism. Technically, with all Hunters and Huntresses extinguished from the Earth, Shira's job as General of Wintersvilla had been completed nearly a decade earlier. Shira knew that Greta detested her for completing her appointed duty in a way that Greta, as Chief of Slavery and Birthing, never could. There would always be more births and more projects for slaves to complete, always something grander to build in Nomusa's name. But Greta's ill will toward Shira went far deeper. Despite Shira barely speaking to Nomusa about anything except Matriarchy affairs since the girls were born over a decade ago, Greta was still jealous of Shira's childhood closeness with Nomusa and also envious of Shira's legendary status as the slayer of the most Hunters and Huntresses of any Woman of Wintersvilla who had ever lived. But worst of all, Greta coveted Shira's title as the destroyer of the worst monster that had ever breathed: Craig Winters.

Greta eyed Nomusa, goading her to make Shira speak so that she could go back to taking out her envy and ire on hordes of enslaved men and boys who far outnumbered the women. Nomusa looked to Shira and nodded in turn, requesting that Shira explain the reason she had called for this meeting.

"Fine," Shira issued, accepting that there was no perfect way to address these women that might leave them all in agreement.

But I still have to try to convince them. They'll hate me for this, but I have to try. I don't have a choice. This is the only way to keep the girls safe and give Wintersvilla any chance of surviving through the week.

Shira took one last deep breath, then said, "War is upon us, sisters.

You all know that. But what you all refuse to accept is that this entire city will fall to the Rovers and Biofreaks. We are doomed if we don't parley and attempt to negotiate an armistice and eventually a lasting truce, like we did with the Nomads over a decade ago."

Nomusa glared at Shira as if Shira had just challenged her to a duel for the right to rule as Matriarch. Mei didn't bother looking up from her reports. Lain looked as though she hadn't even heard Shira. Greta and the twin bodyguards looked at one another, then burst out laughing.

"Is this really the General of Wintersvilla's recommendation?" Sophie asked with obnoxious, condescending laughter.

"A parley with the pathetic little boys our Matriarchy threw away?" Lina added, smiling as she shook her head in disappointment.

"Did I ask either of you to speak?" Nomusa lashed without altering her inflection or averting her eyes from Shira.

Sophie and Lina obediently lowered their heads but not their condescending smiles.

Shira nodded, having already predicted exactly how each woman would react. The young bodyguards were kept in check by Nomusa, but Greta was another matter entirely.

"Are you intentionally attempting to insult us, General?" Greta asked as she allowed herself a few final chuckles at Shira's expense. "Maybe we should let the Rovers take turns enjoying Wintersvilla Mothers too? Would that satisfy the general?"

Shira ignored Greta's disgusting suggestion and kept her eyes locked with Nomusa.

"Musa," Shira said, her tone that of a friend rather than the Queen's general. "You read my reports, right? You understand what they mean, Sister?"

Nomusa sighed deeply then finally broke her stare from Shira and scanned the other women with an unflinching gaze.

"Have all of you read Shira's reports?"

Sophie and Lina remained still, their eyes still downcast from being scolded earlier. Mei and Lain nodded absentmindedly while Greta shook her head in disapproval.

"I skimmed it. It was troutshit," Greta scowled. "Waste of my time. I had a fatherfucking little boy bite my ankle this morning in the reclaimed part of the Metro District. The kid is lucky he isn't a runt, or I'd suggest using him as cannon fodder tonight against the Rovers." Greta turned and smiled at Shira with overt facetiousness. "But that wouldn't do any good, would it, General? The Biofreaks are, what did you say in your report? Unstoppable?"

Nomusa growled beneath her breath at the suggestion that the Biofreaks could possibly have the upper hand against her Matriarchy, but she otherwise did not break her silence.

"Musa," Shira continued with controlled calm as she ignored Greta, "the Biofreaks and Rovers assembled just beyond our lands aren't like the ones we're used to. The majority of the Rovers follow a king now, and he organized an army of Rovers who have unprecedentedly deep connections with their Biofreaks. These Rovers communicate with their Biofreaks like Wintersvilla Warriors with their exos. And their king, BigBilly, he—"

"What do we care about a goddamn Rover king, General? Or about Biofreaks, no matter how organized they might be?" Greta chastised, her voice like the slaving-whip gripped in her thick hands. She rose from her chair, her muscles twitching in agitation. "Enough of this. We are nearly finished renovating one of the largest towers in the Metro District. And after I'm done with that, I will be overseeing the securing of the Northern Wall. And I still need to punish that little biter!"

"You will sit, Greta," Nomusa issued, and Shira was caught off guard at the sight of Sophie nodding to Greta then quickly glancing at Lina before returning her simmering stare back to Shira. Shira had known these women long enough to realize that something was going on between them.

What the hell are they up to? she considered carefully.

"We all know the skin of a Biofreak is impenetrable," Nomusa stated, stealing Shira's attention from the twins' death glares. "But their eyes aren't. We stab their gaping eyes, and the Biofreaks fall. A handful of Wintersvilla Women can dispatch a whole legion of Biofreak mounted Rovers. You disagree, General?"

Shira heaved a deep sigh and restrained herself from challenging Greta with a stinging stare before answering. "Normally I would agree with you, but things are different now, Nomusa. This Rover King, BigBilly he calls himself—he has trained a platoon of Biofreaks to fight like an organized army. They aren't detached or stupid like the others.

They are cunning and focused, as if fueled by some unquenchable hatred."

"A hatred for Wintersvilla, yes, General? For me, you mean?" Nomusa offered with a proud chuckle, then added. "I should have killed them all. It was compassion to throw them over the walls. I should have just suffocated the little runt slaves the moment we cut their umbilical cords, and then all this could have been avoided. You see? This is where compassion leads, sisters."

"Nomusa—" Shira began uneasily, hearing Winters in Nomusa's words and tone.

"No matter, General," Nomusa interrupted, her voice booming through the echoing chamber of her throne room. "I made this mess, and I will clean it up. I was going to do it alone, but I will defer to your caution as our esteemed general. The six of us," she said, pointing to everyone except Mei, "will take our exos into battle alongside seven of our best warriors, your wife included, Shira. We will utilize all thirteen of the exos presently stationed in the city, including the new one your wife synced to. Thirteen of the finest Wintersvilla Warriors will meet this Biofreak legion in battle, and we will exterminate them in a single night. Okay, General? Let Major Myriam know that she should get some rest before tonight's battle. I've no doubt she's training Tomasz' girls as we speak," Nomusa finished placatingly, and it stung that not only had Nomusa referenced the girls pejoratively, but she had also totally disregarded Shira's warnings with the same hollow placations that one might offer an overly concerned spouse.

"Nomusa, we've never battled Biofreaks like this," Shira warned with only partial restraint as she rose from her chair. "These aren't the Biofreaks we've all encountered in the northern and eastern wilds. This is an army. They'll kill us all. Even Overdrive won't be enough, Musa," she said, softening her tone to one of sisterly love. "Have I ever steered us wrong, Musa? These aren't wild Biofreaks, Sister. These are—"

"I am Matriarch of Wintersvilla," Nomusa announced with a room-shaking bellow, extending the knees of her exo into a fully upright standing position so that she towered even higher over Shira and the others. "Shira Arcadia is my general, not my queen. Is that understood?" Nomusa said with smoldering condescension. The twins and Greta smiled with tangible satisfaction at Shira being publicly scolded.

"Yes, Sister. You're right," Shira nodded, scolding herself inwardly for trying to sway the most stubborn woman who had ever lived. If the pictures and information in Shira's report from a week earlier didn't convince her that the Rovers had the upper hand, then of course her words wouldn't either.

But I had to try, Shira reasoned. *At least I can say I tried. So now I have no choice. The decision is made for me.*

"Of course she's right," Greta hissed, and she pushed from the table and stormed out of the room.

"Enjoy the rest of the afternoon, sisters," Nomusa said as she turned to ascend the staircase leading back to her private quarters. "Tonight, fatherfucking glory is ours."

From the third story balcony of her penthouse apartment, Shira slowed her breathing to a controlled state of focus. Her direct view of the training fields filled the recesses of her troubled mind with scant enjoyment as the rest of her mind incessantly and repeatedly went over her reckless but unavoidable plans for the night. Myriam and the girls were down in the training fields now, clanging blunted but still heavy steel training swords together as Myriam tirelessly parried the ceaseless blows of a two-on-one onslaught. A dozen paces away from the sparring trio, Rooli stood and watched with unblinking eyes. The girls didn't hold back, and though they were unable to land a single blow, there were numerous instances when Myriam had to retreat a step or two in her maneuvers, which was impressive on its own.

My little warriors, Shira beamed, and she imagined the pain that any man would suffer were they to dare cross paths with the seemingly weak and fragile Aliana and Aurelia. Shira trained them to utilize their perceived weakness against their opponents—to do battle with their minds first and their bodies second. As she watched the girls work together, she marveled at their ability to read each other's subtlest movements. Aliana deflected in the same moment Aurelia charged and swung, then Aurelia parried exactly as Aliana pivoted and deflected. They fought as though they were wearing fully synced exos, but of course, that was something they would never be able to utilize without metal endoskeletons and ports.

But that doesn't matter, Shira reminded herself. *They are meant for something far greater than warriorhood. Something beyond anything I or anyone can imagine,* Shira told herself, though in truth, no one had even the faintest clue what their fate might entail.

A Virus and Cure—that's all Tomasz could ever offer, and even then, Tomasz is just an instrument of some higher power. I'm certain of it.

Thinking of Tomasz reminded Shira that he could have helped them escape Wintersvilla, but he had refused all of Shira's attempts at communication over the past several months, ever since Shira realized with terrible certainty that Wintersvilla's end was near.

There are no more than 100,000 women in the whole city at any given time, including the suburbs. And there are at least 1,500,000 slaves, Shira considered grimly, seeing the disparity in those numbers as the killing blow to Wintersvilla rather than the Nomads or Rovers. She had warned Nomusa about the gradual decline in the female population of Wintersvilla on several distinct occasions over the years. Even Mei and Greta, to Shira's surprise, echoed her concern. But Nomusa always contended that the slow decline was manageable and temporary—the result of Wintersvilla Warriors being sold to Vida, Downver, and numerous other settlements and pockets of civilization that had dwindled and mostly disappeared over the last few years.

The truth is that most women just leave, Shira brooded somberly. *They use their training as a means of survival, and even without an exo, they choose the wilds of the Earth over the constraints of Wintersvilla.*

Particularly loud clangs of metal broke Shira's thoughts and directed her mind back to the training fields. The girls dove at Myriam in unison, and Myriam deflected hard, leaving the girls tumbling across the field. They lifted themselves and laughed along with Myriam, not even noticing the scrapes and cuts from raking their exposed skin across the rough sand of the training fields.

All I know is that we must leave this place. We should have left weeks ago, but I thought we had more time. The Rovers gathered at our borders so suddenly. Regardless, I will do what has to be done for them, for they are meant for something more than all of this, and nothing will stand in their way. Whoever tries to stop them will have to come through me and Myriam first. And Rooli too, Shira thought. However, she had never seen the Hybrid do battle, and Rooli had spoken no more than a handful of words and the occasional incomplete sentence in the last twelve years that Rooli had lived in Wintersvilla. She was never more than a handful of paces away from either girl, who she demanded remain together at all times. Luckily for the girls, they preferred to be inseparable, even if they were at each other's throats most of the time.

But that's just how siblings are when they're young, Shira told herself. It was just another behavior that made the girls perfectly human in her eyes, regardless of their nonhuman genetic makeup. *They're more human than a whole lot of humans I know,* Shira concluded, seeing Winters with terrible clarity in her mind. From Winters, Shira's mind turned to Nomusa and the rest of the Inner Circle. *They've left me no choice,* she concluded as she watched the girls dive back in for a coordinated attack. *I will watch this city burn before I let anything happen to you girls,* Shira seethed, and she felt only anger, not sadness, as she visualized the entire city and its people being ransacked by unstoppable brutes. Suddenly the Biofreaks she was visualizing transformed into the old world mercenary armies who had raped her and killed her family and her neighbors out of fear that if they did not obey the command of Craig Winters, then the nightmare Hunters released by Mendel would torture them and their families in even worse ways.

Everyone's the fucking same, Shira lamented, wishing desperately that the girls could live in a world that knew only peace and equanimity…and love.

Shira winced at the thought of love, and she suddenly ached to hold Myriam and make love to her. She let her mind slip under the covers with her beautiful wife, but then suddenly she was nine years old again, bent over the wooden table of Winters' throne room, crying and pleading for someone to save her. Anyone.

Shira gritted her teeth and forced the memory to change. Suddenly she had Wintersbane, and she screamed and pounced on Winters, plunging his own blade into his throat and chest and gut and groin over and over and over. Shira yelped out loud and realized her breathing was shallow and rapid. She inhaled a deep breath into her lungs and held it, and as she exhaled, so too did the thoughts diminish in intensity, becoming stinging wisps of fog in the periphery of her mind.

Everyone's a fucking monster, because the world forces us to be that way. There's no way out of it. You become a monster, or you get used and eaten up by monsters. The girls' smiles beamed beneath the sunlight, and Shira's eyes widened at the intensity of emotion she felt for these girls—a severe and savage selflessness that she never fathomed was possible.

I am a monster, Shira accepted painfully, something she punishingly reminded herself again and again through the years. *But you two are mine, and I will protect you from every other monster of this world, no matter how ferocious or terrible. I will be worse, because I love you both. I will destroy myself if it means giving you even a day longer to live. I am a monster. But I am yours just as you are mine.*

Tears streamed from Shira's eyes, and she considered doing a round of pushups when three loud knocks resounded at her door.

Must be a courier, Shira thought as she considered what she had ordered and apparently forgotten about. She wiped her eyes and envisioned a lithe, muscular courier standing outside her door—a breed of slave born and bred to deliver packages around the city with incredible speed and endurance.

She opened the door and felt the hair on the back of her neck rise upon seeing the dual, contemptuous smiling faces of Sophie and Lina. They wore chest-binders and undergarments meant for battle, and Shira realized it was the first time she had ever seen the Chiefs of Protection wear any type of clothing. Glints of light directed Shira's eyes to their hands, and it was only then that she realized the women were each wielding twin tri-blades, elongated daggers with their blades sharpened in a triangular fashion to make wounds harder to heal and more likely to cause infection.

One part of Shira's mind reeled in disbelief, but another part had been ready for this moment ever since Nomusa had, just a few years earlier, created new chief positions out of thin air and appointed these lethal twins as her personal bodyguards. The surprised part of her mind wanted to reason with them, but the battle-hardened part of her mind was already ejecting Wintersbane from her wrist and thrusting it forward in a perfectly timed deflection of all four blades.

Shira jumped backward, but the women were as quick and ruthless as Hunters and pounced on her, slashing at Shira with unrestrained viciousness. Shira kicked her squat coffee table at Sophie, distracting her for a few seconds so that she could focus on Lina.

Wicked little thing, Shira thought, and she swung upward then downward, forcing Lina to subconsciously anticipate Shira's next attack coming from below, but instead, Shira pivoted her hips and roundhouse kicked Lina in the head, missing her temple by mere centimeters. Sophie dove back into the fray and swung for Shira's liver with one blade and her knee with the other. Shira deflected the liver shot, but Sophie managed to slice an inch gouge just above Shira's right knee due to Lina presently recovering and hurling herself at Shira with wild abandon. Wishing she had an exo, Shira bent at the knees and dove backward with a grunt of force, deflecting several rapid blows as she deftly grabbed the old world relic of a sword that had sat over her fireplace mantel for ten years collecting dust. Shira wasn't sure if the blade would be able to withstand the repeated strikes of two of Wintersvilla's most vicious warriors. The twins swung, and though the old world sword chipped against their blows, it did not shatter.

Shira's two blades kept up with their four for a few more seconds, but out of nowhere Lina landed a sweeping kick, slamming Shira against the window and shattering the glass before she recovered and jumped back to her feet. Her battle reflexes deflected multiple blows without conscious input, allowing Shira to notice in a flash that Sophie's mouth was slack with exhaustion. Despite Lina's head already swelling and bruising from Shira's powerful kick, she appeared unfazed, and she lunged at Shira, clearly impatient to strike her down. Taking advantage of the young woman's eagerness, Shira anticipated her lunge and deflected then parried, aiming for Lina's left kidney with Wintersbane as she passed. Lina twisted, forcing the blade to nick her shoulder instead.

Shira readied for another pounce, but as the twins rose, their labored breathing revealed that they had reached their limit and needed a few seconds to recover. Shira was grateful they lacked her much larger musculature and time-forged endurance.

Blood trickled from Shira's arm, and she glanced down to see thin lines of blood streaming slowly from several shards of window glass protruding from her scarred flesh. Even more of her blood covered the wall and ground.

I need to end this before I lose too much blood, Shira resolved, and though she felt an urge to pull the shards out, she knew it was better to leave them and let them serve as crude plugs to stifle the bleeding.

"We've dreamed of this day, Shira Arcadia," Lina said as she slowly prowled to Shira's right.

"To do battle against the legendary General of Wintersvilla," Sophie marveled as she slipped to Shira's left.

"Did Greta put you up to this? Or was it Nomusa?" Shira demanded, gripping the old world blade in anger that an assassination attempt was being made on her life on the eve of battle. Every woman had a right to challenge another woman to a duel to the death, but such duels were regulated and observed. This was something else—a betrayal that Shira hated to admit she had seen coming, one way or another.

"It was me," Greta said as she entered the room and closed the door. Shira wondered if any of the other residents of the building might have heard the commotion, but everyone was likely already making their way to the outer walls to get a good view of the coming battle involving the Matriarch and Wintersvilla's founders. Rather than being afraid for their lives, the city was pulsating with excitement.

"You can't kill me yourself, so you get these two to do it for you, Greta?" Shira challenged, and she raised Wintersbane in preparation for a three-on-one battle to the death. "Or was it Nomusa? Is she behind all this?" Shira asked, feeling deep pain throb in the depths of her mind, for although she and Nomusa were now distant, there was a time they were more than sisters. Each served as the other's unyielding backbone through the worst days and years of existence. They were each other's saviors.

Greta smiled, and Shira prepared herself for the terrible answer.

"Nomusa has no idea," Greta stated with mocking amusement, and despite quickly losing blood and staring potential death in the face, Shira felt a great weight lift from her chest at Greta's words.

At least it wasn't you, Sister. I don't think I could stomach that.

"You're Nomusa's weakness. You realize that, Shira? Just like how those girls are your weakness," Greta said, shaking her head in disappointment. Lina removed her chest-binder and wrapped it around her shoulder to stifle the bleeding caused by Shira's blade, reminding Shira about her knee. Despite the shallowness of the cut, blood flowed far too quickly, and a small pool was already beginning to form at her foot.

Shira placed her hands against her casual silk strips and raised her eyebrows, wordlessly asking if they would let her stifle the wound before they attacked again. Greta offered a shallow nod, and Shira removed the strips from her chest and shoulders then tied them into a tourniquet around her right leg.

"I'm going to offer you a choice, General," Greta stated, her eyes slits of age-old spite.

"And if they had killed me before you got here, would I still have this choice?" Shira asked, glaring right back at Greta.

Sophie and Lina smiled, and Greta shrugged. "Don't take it so personally, Shira. You think I envy you. You think I want your position. But I don't, you high and mighty bitch. I am the true leader of this city. You're a glorified second mother, and Nomusa is as shortsighted as a man. The fact that these Rovers and Biofreaks are even alive proves that she is unfit to be Matriarch," Greta announced, and both Sophie and Lina raised their shoulders and stood as personal bodyguards at Greta's side.

"I'm just a steppingstone," Shira realized. "I'm just an obstacle to your true goal. You want control of the whole Matriarchy," Shira laughed at the audacity of staging a coup on the eve of being besieged, regardless of whether or not Greta viewed the siege as an actual threat.

"I want the whole world, damnit," Greta lashed. "And why not? The world used to be in the hands of men. It still is. We are still beholden to the Nomads of that goddamn fatherfucker Mendel. Someone has to be the leader, Shira, and Nomusa is unfit for it. You killed Winters. Nomusa led us to this point. Now I take over the rest," Greta said with perfect confidence in her ability to be leader of the entire world.

"Aren't you the one who got angry over a little slave bite this morning?" Shira goaded with a wrathful smile.

"Shut up, you dumb bitch," Greta lashed, speaking to Shira exactly as Shira imagined she always wanted. "Look at you. You don't even know your fate is already sealed. You're going to die in this room. This is where it all ends for you. And then we're going to kill Myriam and that disgusting Hybrid," Greta stated with rapacious indignation. Shira let her speak, allowing her words to fuel a torrent of boiling rage in every one of her cells.

"And then we kill Nomusa. And Mei and Lain if they don't obey," Greta finished with wicked satisfaction, as if this plan had plagued her mind for countless years.

"Is that it?" Shira stated simply, refusing to reveal the rage now bubbling and prickling every inch of her skin.

I'm going to slice you three traitors to fatherfucking pieces, Shira seethed within.

"Or," Greta continued, "you can take the girls and leave with your wife and the Hybrid. We won't try to follow you. We don't care about you, Shira. We just want what's right for Wintersvilla, and it isn't you or Nomusa. Nomusa will never relinquish her power. That's why we're going to kill her. But we will let you leave, Shira. I harbor no ill will toward you, despite what you might think. I just think you've always been an overrated brat. Doesn't mean I want to kill you though."

"Or," Shira began with a torturously controlled calm. "I can kill you three right here. Right now."

Shira lifted Wintersbane and the old world blade and bent at the knees.

"Wait!" Greta stated with her hand raised.

Blood still poured from her wounds, but Shira let the woman speak, hoping she might reveal more valuable information about her wicked plans.

"You kill us and your precious little girls will be on trophy spikes."

Greta's words paralyzed Shira, and though she kept her blades in battle-ready stance, she nodded for Greta to continue.

"Nomusa decided that she's going to use this battle to steal the girls right from under your nose. She assigned a whole platoon of slaves to kill the Hybrid, then kidnap the girls and bring them to an outpost. She's planning to chain them up and wait for puberty to hit. Whatever changes are going to happen, she wants to be in control. She wants to use them as a weapon."

Shira shook her head in disbelief. "A weapon for what?"

Greta shrugged at the obviousness of the answer. "The same thing anyone wants. Control. World control. Planetary power. She doesn't see them as little girls, Shira. She doesn't see them as human. None of us do, really. Just you. But one of these days they're going to change, and even you won't see them that way."

"You're wrong," Shira said. "They're the only ones I see as human."

Greta chuckled to herself. "Fine. Whatever, Shira. Then take them and leave. And don't come back. Wintersvilla is mine, you understand? The girls are yours. I don't want them. I don't trust them. So go now, and don't come back."

Shira weighed her options. She could take Greta's offer to leave with the girls and Myriam, but there was always the possibility she was lying.

Greta might have her own terrible plans for the girls. On the other hand, if Greta was telling the truth, then even if she killed these three women, the girls would still be unsafe with Nomusa in control.

I know I'm right about the power of the Biofreaks, Shira considered, her mind firing more rapidly than she had ever experienced in her life. *They're going to tear this city and everyone in it to shreds. Thirteen exos just aren't enough. Maybe Greta's telling the truth. Maybe she's lying. But either way, she's not the one I need to come to an agreement with.*

"You're all dead tonight anyway. Whether it's me or the Biofreaks, you're all going to die. I can't trust you, Greta. And I can't leave here and let you live knowing you might show up one day and kill me and the girls in our sleep. So, I'm going to kill you three, and then I'm going to parley with the Rovers like I suggested at the meeting."

Greta chuckled and shook her head while Sophie and Lina smiled with delight at the prospect of more fighting.

"So be it," Greta concluded with a flash of rage in her eyes. "Kill her."

Sophie and Lina hesitated for just a moment then pounced toward the General of Wintersvilla, the most formidable and revered warrior who had ever lived.

There was a time when Shira would have thought only of the glory each battle held, but now she fought for something truly meaningful. As Sophie and Lina charged forward, Shira held another set of twins in her mind, and she knew that nothing could possibly hurt Aliana or Aurelia for as long as she drew breath.

That's why I can't die here, Shira knew. *Fuck glory. My girls are all that matter—in life and in death. I'll kill you all to protect them. Every single one of you.*

Shira had never felt such overwhelming confidence in her abilities, and she marveled at the power of selfless love.

My love for those girls is the deadliest instrument of war I've ever known, Shira thought as Sophie and Lina finally closed the gap. *Now, come and taste my love's unforgiving edge.*

What the others can never understand is that I don't strive and labor for myself. I am not climbing Mendel's Ladder for my own sake. I do not aim to ascend to godhood to save myself. All that I do is in the service of humanity, the universe, and the Great Beyond. I strive for the beyond laid before us—a destination unknown by any human mind until now. There are seemingly infinite paths to the Great Beyond. The one that I have chosen for the Earth and its people is one of many, but they all lead to the same destination.

At the crux of this particular path lie a handful of unique individuals who will bring my rightful Ascension to fruition. Of these individuals, the two that cannot be allowed to deviate in the slightest from their course will also be the most vulnerable and feeble. I will tell Tomasz to design them and birth them this way—as seemingly weak and frail little girls. It is from this place of feebleness that they will learn what it means to be strong, and it is from their vulnerability that they will learn to value calculation and poise. All of this is necessary for what fate has ordained them to become.

I do not know their names—I will leave that up to those who raise them. Their names don't matter, for their eventual domains lie in namelessness. A virus and a cure. A poison and an antidote. A weapon and a shield.

They are the key to my design, and my design is the key to the ineffable beyond.

From Mendel's Ladder: The Personal Journal of Denis Mendel, Recorded Circa 2065, Published June 2108 by Leif Mainstone, Federated Agency Publishing

Chapter 2
Little Smooth Talker

Year: 2099, Present Day

I t all happened in a single breath-stealing moment. Shira's eyes shot open with adrenaline fueled alertness, and then she was suddenly an inch from Aliana's face. Just as quickly, Aliana found herself in free fall with the bottom of the crater racing toward her and her stomach lurching into her throat.

Holy Muto we're going to fucking die! Aliana screamed within. A giant boulder at the bottom of the crater rapidly grew in size as she raced toward it, her mouth open in shock at being thrown out of the window of Gambe's body by the woman who had raised her and her sister since their birth on one of Tomasz' many living ships. Time slowed to a supernatural crawl, and in her wildly racing mind, she was suddenly back on the training fields on the night of Wintersvilla's destruction, coordinating with Aurelia to try landing even a single blow on Myriam. The memory was so vivid that she could still hear the shatter of glass as Shira's arm burst through her penthouse window while fighting for her life against Nomusa's sadistic bodyguards. Aliana fully detached from the fear of falling for just a second longer and became totally absorbed in the memory as she marveled at the swiftness of Rooli telling Myriam to go and save Shira, then grabbing the girls and running at full speed toward the Eastern Wall of the city.

Rooli, Aliana thought urgently as time returned to normal and she was jarred back to the present, submerged suddenly in the tumultuous ocean of fear coursing through her body at seeing the ground and sudden death only a few seconds from her face.

"Rooli!" she screamed desperately just as she felt something tighten around her waist. The tip of Aliana's nose skimmed the crater's bottom as the rest of her body was thrown in a wide arc and ejected upward by some unknown means. A gunshot blast resonated from below, and

Aliana peered down to see that Rooli was standing in her own shallow crater, the result of her heavy landing. Two vine-like arms extended fifty feet into the air on either side of Rooli's body, and as Aliana's ascent slowed to a halt, she traced one of the vining arms back to herself and the other to her sister, who was suspended a dozen or so feet away.

Rooli whipped at the shoulders and hastily retracted her arms, sloughing away her excess tissue with painful groans as she reeled the girls in.

Rooli, Aliana rejoiced with tears in her wide eyes. *You'll never let anything bad happen to us. Like Shira and Myriam and even the men.*

Placing her boots back on solid ground, Aliana glanced at her sister to make sure she was okay. In typical Aurelia fashion, she appeared unfazed by the plunge into the crater, as if she had already anticipated exactly how everything would transpire.

She always has to act so tough, Aliana thought before reminding herself that it was her sister's very existence that had forced her to become tougher than anyone could imagine. The horrific, flesh-rending black scars permanently cleaving the skin of her face were more obvious than ever, tendriling beyond her torn and tattered face mask, nearly reaching her eyes now. Not a single person other than Aliana, Rooli, Myriam, and Shira could bear to look at Aurelia without flinching. Even those who claimed otherwise were just lying to her—both girls were perfectly aware of that.

But that doesn't mean she has to be such an emotionless bitch all the time, Aliana grumbled, and she turned to look back at the ridge from where they had been tossed.

Please don't die, Shira, Aliana pleaded inwardly in terrible anguish despite knowing full well that her activation of Overdrive was a death sentence. *I don't care what Overdrive means. Find a way to live. Please, Shira. Please...Mom.* The word still didn't feel right to Aliana, even if Shira was technically her second mother. Thinking of her as mom just wasn't accurate. She was more than that. Mothers are naturally reckless with their love, unaware or unable to understand that untempered love can lead to unintentional weakness and dependence. Shira understood that, and she loved them in such a way that even her compassion and sympathy was controlled and measured to ensure that both girls would grow up with a precise mix of both independence and empathy, both self-assurance and self-actualization.

She made me who I am, and I love who I am. Just as Rooli helped make Aurelia who she needs to be.

"We need to go back," Aliana announced determinedly as the winds at the bottom of the crater began whining and tumbling dust into the air.

"Shut up," Aurelia signed. "Don't let their deaths be in vain. We need to find a way past that giant boulder."

"You shut up, Aurelia!" Aliana retorted, not caring about sounding clever.

How dare she say I'm letting them die in vain, or even that they're going to die! She doesn't know every little thing.

"They're not going to die, Aurelia. They're going to kill the Butcher. And Myriam will find a way to save Shira. They'll even find a way to take down Gambe!"

Rather than say something or stomp to break up their tiff, Rooli was already halfway to the boulder, inspecting every inch of it with her unblinking eyes.

"Whatever," Aurelia signed.

Whatever, Aliana signed back, but Aurelia was already running to catch up with Rooli and didn't see Aliana's hands.

She's right, though, Aliana forced herself to accept. *There's nothing we can do for them now. I have to just trust that they can win.* Aliana nodded to herself, injecting resolve into the deepest layers of her awareness just as Shira had always taught. *I have to move forward. I have to keep going. The strong don't stop. Ever. Even in death. I have to be strong. For Shira. For the whole world.*

The boulder towered over her by at least a full ten feet, and she wondered if it had always been there as part of the entrance or if the entrance had been intentionally sealed with the boulder at some point.

Who could have moved a boulder the size of a house? Aliana marveled as she reluctantly kept her anguish over Shira at bay. *It must have been dragged here by hordes of Downverians a long time ago to be used as a marker for the secret entrance,* she concluded reasonably.

Aliana ran forward toward Rooli and Aurelia, wiping away her tears and forcing herself not to look back toward the ridge.

"Not so fast," Gambe said as a swarm of tiny specks formed a funnel cloud suspended in the air, then solidified from the head down into his typical humanoid form. He stood before Aliana with his arms on his hips, blocking her path to Rooli and her sister.

"I'm takin' ya back to Mom. The Agency ain't so bad, you'll see. Mom ain't evil—not like the other old timers. Not like Andre and Mendel and all the rest."

"Out of my way, you lead-brained fatherfucker," Aliana demanded, and she strode toward him with her hand gripped around the hilt of the short sword sheathed at her waist.

"I said stop!" Gambe bellowed with an uncharacteristic measure of impatience, and he glanced up at the ridge as if in nervous apprehension.

Just try it, Aliana told him with her eyes, letting the winds and thoughts of Shira's impending death stir incredible rage deep within her very bones. *I might be afraid of falling to my death, but I'm not afraid of you. In fact, you're the one who looks afraid,* Aliana realized as she passed Gambe and continued walking toward Rooli and Aurelia. Gambe didn't presently try to stop her; he just continued staring at the ridge.

Since Rooli and Aurelia were already searching for the hidden entrance around the edges of the boulder, Aliana paused and allowed her mind a moment to satiate her unquenchable thirst for gaining knowledge against her enemies.

"What are you afraid of, Gambe? Do you fear the Butcher?" Aliana asked with a mix of challenge and curiosity, her grip tight on her short sword and her legs spread in battle-ready stance.

"Afraid?" Gambe said as if the word were gibberish. "I ain't got fear, little girl. I'm a weapon's expert. I'm just curious is all, ya feel me?"

Not afraid, Aliana thought, entranced by the very prospect of such power. *To be truly unafraid and secure—is that really what it's like to be him?* The winds intensified, and Aliana glanced at Rooli and Aurelia, who were searching the other side of the boulder now with a growing level of urgency. The winds struck a measure of fear in Aliana, but she knew she could offer the pair no extra help at the moment. The low howling winds whispered death, but this was her chance to understand something about Gambe and the Agency that she might never have the opportunity to elucidate ever again.

"You're not afraid of dying? Is it because you're not alive?" Aliana asked.

"I ain't afraid of nothing, Aliana. And I'm alive—more alive than ya think. More alive than you or your sister or that Hybrid even."

A glimmer of light directed Aliana's eyes to the edge of the crater, and she saw a copy of Gambe gazing at them from above, possibly even staring directly at her.

"What are you, Gambe? What are you, really?" Aliana marveled in both fear and awe. A sudden, strong gust tugged at her back, coaxing her body to move backward toward Rooli and Aurelia one step at a time without her even realizing it.

"The question is: what the hell are you and your sister, eh? I'm Agency hardware. A weapons expert and a means of transportation. Outside that, I'm a guy who likes to play games and make Mom happy, and Mom's all out of happiness, ya feel me? So mostly I just play games."

He's like a child, Aliana thought, shaking her head at the simplicity of Gambe's motivations. *I just need to placate him. And then maybe I can even convince him to let us go.* She glanced back at Rooli and her sister, who were rapidly signing to one another in the boulder's shadow. Their fingers were moving too fast to read, and both of their faces appeared stoic and emotionless, leaving Aliana unable to discern whether or not they could find the hidden entrance.

I'm more use here if I can convince Gambe to just let us leave, Aliana knew, and she let Aurelia and Rooli continue handling the entrance while she handled their escape.

"I think it's cool you play games, Gambe. Games are an underappreciated medium," Aliana said craftily.

Gambe's arms fell from his hips, and he cocked his head in genuine surprise.

"You think?" he asked with childlike wonder.

"Yeah, obviously, you brainless metalloid. Games are what make life worthwhile," Aliana said playfully, reading Gambe now like a book.

Gambe nodded rapidly, and a faint smile formed on his otherwise featureless skull. He started laughing, then pointed excitedly at Aliana.

"I ain't ever met another person that loves games like I do!" Gambe said excitedly, like a kid realizing he had just met his best friend.

Too easy, Aliana chuckled to herself smugly, and at the same time she pitied Gambe, this toddler mind apparently forced to appease his mom, who he claimed was the Agency itself.

Aliana jumped in shock at something gripping her shoulder, but she caught herself after turning and seeing that it was just her sister.

"We have a problem," Aurelia signed with unnatural calm. "The entrance is behind the boulder. Rooli said the boulder isn't supposed to be here. Somebody did this. Somebody blocked our path."

The wind howled with a wild gust before returning to a state of relative calm. Distinct currents and eddies of pressurized air coalesced in the crater, feeding the roiling clouds above. The sight of chaotic storm clouds startled Aliana since she had never encountered any fluctuation in weather in her entire life. Blue skies and slow puffy clouds were all she and her sister had ever known.

Holy Muto, Aliana thought as her breathing quickened along with the wind.

"We have to get out of here," Aliana said, and she turned to Gambe, who was also marveling at the undulating, tumultuous clouds above. "Can you help us, metal head?"

Gambe cocked his head left then right in consideration, then shrugged and said, "Maybe. Just tell me what the hell you two are. That's the question nobody can figure out. Mom and Julian and all the other Prodigal Sons are always talkin' 'bout what they hear through the Nomad network. Always talkin' 'bout Mendel's plans, and what the hell y'all got to do with it all. They think your sister is a weapon to kill the Queen of Astrea. But really they ain't know nothing. So, I'm thinkin' there's a way that maybe you ain't gotta go with me, ya feel me? I respect ya want to do your own thing. I feel the same way. I mean, we're both gamers, Aliana, right? So, maybe if ya just tell me how y'all play into Mendel's plans…maybe that'll be enough to make Mom happy again, ya feel me?"

Aliana shook her head in surprise at Gambe's words. *Is this really all just to make his mom happy? Is he really that…simple? No matter, he's starting to feel a connection with me. Like a friend. I need to keep going with that. I need to be the little smooth talker that Shira always accused me of being.* Thinking of Shira brought tears to her eyes, but Aliana bit her lip and forced them back.

"We really don't know, Gambe," Aliana told him honestly. Aurelia tugged at Aliana's hand and pulled her toward the boulder, but Gambe broke into a swarm then resolidified in front of them, blocking their way to Rooli.

"Look, even if you get in, Downver ain't a good place, ya feel me? You ain't givin' me any real information, Aliana, so I'm gonna have to take ya both with me," Gambe said, regretful but determined.

Aurelia unsheathed her sword, and Aliana did the same in turn. Without warning, Rooli kicked off the boulder and cannoned into Gambe, shattering the thick growth of wooden flesh protruding from her head in a spray of blood and dust. The rest of Rooli quickly recovered, and she flipped in midair, then slammed against the ground between Gambe and the girls, creating tremors that forced the girls to struggle for balance. All the while, Gambe didn't move an inch.

I have to do something, Aliana knew, her mind racing with possible weaknesses to exploit, but Gambe appeared impenetrable.

"Run!" Rooli ordered, but neither girl obeyed the command.

Aurelia knows it too, Aliana realized. *She knows this is a dead end. There's nowhere to run. We have to fight.*

"Ain't nowhere to run, Enduring Ironwood," Gambe chuckled, making Aliana gasp at the use of Rooli's Nomadic name.

Her mind surged with an onslaught of questions she craved to have answered. *How can he know Rooli's name? How can he know so much about everything? Is it the Nomadic network he mentioned before?*

Do something! Aliana's drive for survival urged, overriding the endless questions and returning her awareness to the now raging black clouds above.

Rooli grabbed the girls and hugged them to her body, preparing to grow into a shield as she had so many times before.

But it won't be enough, Aliana knew as she pushed away and saw that Aurelia was doing the same.

"We have to go with this fatherfucker," Aurelia concluded. Rooli issued a low growl, but she didn't outright protest Aurelia's words.

"What she say?" Gambe asked.

No, Aliana thought. *I refuse to let this child win. I refuse. There's a way to beat him. There's always a way for the hero to take down the villain.* Suddenly it was like a blade sliced through all her fear and curiosity. *That's right,* Aliana remembered, thinking back to how adamant Gambe was about not being a villain.

"She said you're being a villain," Aliana told him calculatingly. "She said that only a villain would kidnap two little girls against their will."

"I ain't a villain!" Gambe denied, sounding horrified by the accusation. He peered toward the ridge, then turned to look at the boulder, and then turned again to peer at the ridge. Aliana felt the urge to pounce and attack while he appeared distracted, but she forced herself to remain in a battle-ready stance.

"Just lie to him. Make up a story about Mendel's plans for us," Aurelia signed more rapidly than ever as the winds finally broke her stoic demeanor.

No, that won't do it, Aliana thought. *But I think I know what will.*

Aliana placed a hand against Rooli, silently telling her she could handle this. Then she said, "I'll make a deal with you, Gambe. You help us get past that boulder. Prove you're not a villain. And in exchange, one day I'll play some games with you. We can go head-to-head for a whole night playing your favorite games."

Gambe stood speechless for a few seconds, and for a moment Aliana thought he was going to burst into laughter, but then he asked, "Are ya serious?"

"As serious as apple pie," Aliana intoned, mimicking the old world expression taught to her by Wesley.

"Is apple pie serious?" Gambe asked in an awe-filled whisper.

"As serious as this fatherfucking moment, Gambe," Aliana said, nervously glancing back at the ridge and the boiling clouds.

Gambe groaned but finally said, "Okay, it's a deal, Aliana. I help you here, and one of these days, if you survive down there, we game for a whole night, ya feel me?"

"I feel you," Aliana said. Gambe nodded then strode past them, walking directly toward where the boulder met the crater's wall.

It worked, Aliana rejoiced, taking pride in her ability to read other people and manipulate them. *He's actually helping us. We're going to get through this.*

"Y'all sure you wanna go to Downver? I ain't a villain, but the place is full of villains, ya feel me?" Gambe warned as they walked.

"We have to. And it has nothing to do with Mendel. Denis Mendel is just a name in history to us. We live for ourselves, Gambe, something you should do more often. You worry about your mom too much."

Again, the word *mom* reminded Aliana that Shira and Myriam were still on the surface above them, preparing to battle the Butcher of the Wastes to death. *I'm so sorry, Mom,* Aliana thought, trying the word out once more but still not sitting right with it. *I love you, Shira,* Aliana lamented before wiping away more tears and pretending to peer behind the group to momentarily hide her eyes.

"If it ain't me that brings you to Mom, it'll be Julian," Gambe issued as they reached the boulder's crease with the wall. "I just want Mom to be happy, ya feel me? So, just be careful down there, and stay close to the Hybrid. She's stone cold, ya feel me? That's what ya need to survive down there."

"Hurry," Rooli issued sternly, and Gambe nodded as he wedged his arm between the boulder and the wall.

"I ain't even know if I can lift this thing, but if I can, y'all gonna have to be quick. We gonna be down to the wire. The Butcher will be here any second."

Gambe grunted and pushed one arm against the wall and the other against the boulder. It sounded as if a mountain were being moved, and though Gambe was able to push the boulder away from the wall, he could only manage a couple feet at most. Still, he was able to clear a small hole that Aliana and Aurelia could drop into as long as they removed their backpacks. It was also clear that Rooli would have to shed a large portion of her body to fit.

"Ya see?" Gambe said as they closed the gap to reach him. "I ain't a villain. Okay? Now hurry!" he urged through what sounded like clenched teeth as he continued lifting the boulder away from the wall. Aliana peered into the cave depths behind the boulder as she began to remove her backpack and consider what might be most important to take with her.

"Leave it!" Rooli practically barked as a particularly wily gust of wind tugged at Aliana's matted hair. She peered over her shoulder and gawked at the dark funnel clouds madly siphoning toward the edges of an eldritch vortex of superheated sand.

And that's just what we can see from down here, Aliana gasped in profound horror.

"Shira!" Aliana pleaded with her hand outstretched behind them. "I'm sorry, Mom!"

"Go!" Gambe yelped, straining with tangible exertion against the titanous weight of the boulder.

In a single swift movement, Rooli grew an arm tapered to a blade and cut the straps of both girls' backpacks, then pushed them both forward, with Aliana in front. Intense terror struck through Aliana as she was ushered into the pitch-black hole. The air was ejected from her lungs as Rooli crammed the girls through the tiny space and sent them plunging into the unknown.

Aliana's mind reeled at what might be lurking in the darkness, but her awareness was whipped to attention by the explosion of the far wall of the crater, forcing her to twist and peer through the quickly shrinking light of the hole. Time slowed to an impossible crawl, and she saw something large and powerful shoot toward them like a bullet, aiming directly for Rooli, as she and Aurelia continued to plunge into the darkness below.

"Rooli!" Aliana screamed, her voice a low rumble at such slow speed, but it was no use. Gambe let go of the boulder at the last moment, sealing the girls within the cave and crushing Rooli with a gut-wrenching crunch of her wooden flesh.

No! She's dead! Rooli's dead! Help us! Aliana thought, envisioning Shira's blood-filled, dying eyes painted across the enveloping darkness.

All at once, time accelerated back to normal speed. The boulder settled, snuffing the light to perfect darkness. In the same instant, the Butcher launched from the far wall of the crater and hit the boulder at full speed, shaking the all-encompassing darkness with echoing bellows of death.

Some individuals have no real aspiration. None. For these individuals, even talking about aspiration is a mere facade hiding the truth that their words are simply that—just words. They parrot the sentiments of others who have succeeded in their own aspirations, but they never actually construct their own. They try to fill this void with hedonism and debauchery. They devise endless avenues of novelty. They manufacture whole environments to keep their mind occupied. But still, they remain empty.

These individuals are the perfect puppets, for they refuse to see their strings. Tomasz Novak is the epitome of the perfect puppet. For Tomasz and those like him, to see the strings of fate is to understand and accept that we are mere effects of an original cause. For a person who is empty inside, this is the most horrifying truth of reality, for it means that fate has ordained their emptiness, and this leads them to an even greater, more unfathomable emptiness within emptiness.

Only those lucky enough to be born with the fullness of aspiration can ever hope to see the strings of fate and in turn refuse to accept their ultimate implication.

Tomasz is my puppet, just as I am the cosmos' puppet. The difference is that Tomasz is too afraid to cut his strings, whereas I'm too afraid not to.

From Mendel's Ladder: The Personal Journal of Denis Mendel, Recorded Circa 2062, Published June 2108 by Leif Mainstone, Federated Agency Publishing

Chapter 3
A Landing in Hell

S *andra!* Samuel pleaded, stretching both his mirror-hands toward Astrea as Sandra's handmade clothing was torn away from his body, leaving him naked and exposed, until he realized he was now fully covered in the polished, perfectly reflective mirror-substance. He saw the orbiting city now as a casket entombing everything and everyone he had ever known and loved. The giant yellow slime mold tree that had once been Norman was still wrapped around Samuel with tight tendrils. It appeared to be actively using its many branches to balance Samuel and keep him from tumbling out of control in free fall.

Samuel and the slime tree rotated slowly but ceaselessly, oscillating Samuel's view every few seconds between the shockingly blue glow of Earth and the quickly shrinking but still glinting metal hull of Astrea. He realized that he didn't feel cold, but he still had his former bodily awareness, making the freezing void of space feel strangely comfortable and natural.

Margot…Nathan…Sandra…I'm so fucking sorry, Samuel groaned helplessly and soundlessly as he plunged to the planet his parents and Sandra's parents had been saved from almost a half century earlier.

But they weren't saved, Samuel knew with tangible horror. *None of us were saved. The world and Astrea and everything…it's all hell. All of it. And now my family will suffer the hell of Astrea without me, and I'm about to suffer the hell of Earth without them.*

Despite crystallizing cold spreading across the mold's yellow surface, the tendrils tightened around Samuel, then stretched outward into numerous more branches.

Why is this happening? Samuel pleaded, struck by the absurd terror of falling through outer space with a crystallized tree of slime mold wrapped around his perfectly reflective skin. *Why did Old Man Madeira do this to me?*

The newly grown branches of mold fully stabilized Samuel, directing his vision to the Earth. Giant puffy white clouds occluded a clear view, but he could still discern that he was falling toward what appeared to be three perfectly circular imprints in the Earth's surface, symmetrically aligned so that they formed a triangle at their center with circular, concave sides. Rather than marvel at the symmetry, Samuel desperately tried to break free of the slime's hold and look back at Astrea. He knew it didn't matter, but he couldn't help it. Seeing Astrea still made him feel closer to his family than not seeing it.

"Get off me!" Samuel tried screaming, but no sound was emitted from his mouth. His mind was flooded with the anguishing need to return to Sandra and his children. Every nerve fired for that reason alone, but it was still no use. There was no way to stop this plunge to the hell of Earth.

Sandra! Samuel pleaded apologetically. *I'm a fucking idiot. I'm so fucking sorry, Sandra.* He envisioned the Queensguards rounding up Sandra and his children and the rest of his neighbors and marching them to the recycler. And then he imagined even worse shadows looming beyond the recyclers. He could see the Queen, with bleeding emerald eyes, just as Roland described. Samuel envisioned the Queen opening the Golden Wall and releasing monsters more mindless and menacing than even the cruelest Queensguard.

No! Samuel winced at his spiraling thoughts. *Please, not that. Please, if my parents were right and there is a God, please protect my family. Please don't take them from me.*

He thought of Roland suddenly, and Samuel desperately hoped that Roland would abide by his promise and keep Sandra and his children safe. But then he remembered that Roland appeared to work for Madeira, and Madeira had said that Astrea would become more dangerous than ever. That nobody would be safe.

Goddamnit! Samuel wanted to scream, but he gritted his teeth instead. He was suddenly perturbed by the strange, detached feeling inside his mouth.

Like metal scraping against metal, Samuel realized in disbelief as he clenched his jaw. *Even the inside of my body is metallic?* Samuel gawked in horror.

Without warning, a thick beam of golden light shot through space to Samuel's left, soundlessly striking the Earth below. As if it had been expecting the beam, the slime mold tree whipped its branches behind

Samuel, jerking him forward toward the blinding golden light.

Samuel braced himself in preparation to intersect the beam, but at the last second they pivoted, passing with only inches to spare. Suddenly something thousands of times brighter illuminated the Earth's surface, making the golden beam seem like a dull lamplight in infinite darkness. Samuel gawked at the inexplicable pure white light rushing toward them from below and then piercing through Earth's atmosphere and escaping into space. The force of the column's shockwave slammed into Samuel and the slime mold like a Queensguard charging at full speed. The slime mold exploded into a million undulating strands, and Samuel was sent tumbling in orbit. He spun with rapidly increasing acceleration as his limbs flailed and cartwheeled chaotically.

Unable to maneuver himself or regain any semblance of balance, Samuel could only grit his teeth against the intense g-force, clench his fists against his terror-struck mind, and muscle through the intense nausea welling in his throat.

Lost. Rudderless. Everything is hopeless, Samuel lamented.

His smeared vision from spinning as rapidly as a turbine made it impossible to focus on anything, and he was forced to close his eyes. The darkness of his eyelids reminded him to center his mind, just like he had taught himself over and over again at the power stations.

Lift! Samuel thought, only now he didn't need to lift. Now he needed to stay calm.

He contracted his thoughts as if they were controllable musculature. *I can do this,* Samuel urged himself, recounting the endless times he had watched his mind give up dozens of reps before his body was fully depleted of energy. *The mind always gives up before it should. I am strong. I am unstoppable. Lift! Calm!*

Samuel nearly broke into tears of gratitude at his mind's ability to overcome adversity, but he tempered it with the knowledge that it had cost decades of enduring torment and suffering to attain this level of focus.

An explosion of sound jarred Samuel out of his head, and his surroundings grew rapidly denser as he was captured by Earth's lower atmosphere. As his body was buffeted by currents and pockets of warm air, he subdued his flailing limbs and finally balanced himself into a stable free fall looking straight down to the haunting yet mind-blowing beauty of planet Earth's surface.

Directly below was a coastline separating mountainous land from a great oceanic expanse. Samuel scanned the land for the three circles forming the convex triangle at their center, but the shockwave from the beam had shot him countless miles away. It was only then that he understood he was both falling toward and rocketing tangentially to the Earth.

That beam of light…what the hell was that? It came from those three craters, Samuel considered, though his mind could offer no reasonable explanation for what the beam was or why it had occurred. *What are the odds that the beam would strike just as I was passing by? Either someone tried to hit me with it, or Madeira somehow knew that it would strike at the exact moment I was there. Either way, I'm caught up in something big, something far beyond Samuel Kaminski.*

Lift! Samuel heard his own voice say within his mind. *Yes!* Samuel answered, refusing to give into the fear and the confusion. *There must be a way back to Astrea. I can't just give up. I will not just give up. Never,* Samuel resolved as he held his family in his mind, barely even noticing the rapidly approaching uniform expanse of uninterrupted azure.

Margot always talked about the ocean, Samuel thought, catching his breath so that he did not break down and sob.

Lift! his mind shouted with sudden rabid insistence, erasing the excruciating memory of Margot like extinguished embers that still burned and smoked with acrid, tortuous pain. Samuel whipped his attention back to the present moment, for that was the only way he might turn those anguishing visions of holding his daughter back into tangible reality.

You're going to save them all, Samuel Kaminski, he told himself with a sternness and severity that he had never fathomed. *You are the Workhorse of Astrea. You are exactly what the revolutionaries accused you of. A worker. The greatest worker. And you will use that work now to ensure that you don't fail them,* Samuel ordered himself. *Now, lift! Stay calm! Focus!*

As if he were actually back at a power station, Samuel mentally found himself on the inner island he had ceaselessly forged in his thoughts for over three decades—a miniscule but unbreakable sand barge he had built, grain by grain, at the very center of the ocean that was the racing, pleading, wild mind of every living thing. Within that madness, Samuel found that there was always an island to situate himself—he just had to build the strength and courage to hang on and refuse to let go, no matter the hurricane or typhoon that threatened to break his discipline.

As if mirroring the island within his mind, Samuel saw an island of tiny shapes moving across the ocean like buzzing, intersecting insects.

What the hell are those things? Samuel wondered as he breathed and readied himself to slam into the ocean at terminal velocity, which he considered might shatter his body like a wrench thrown into an actual mirror.

Or maybe whatever is coating the inside and outside of my body will protect me. I survived outer space, and I survived tumbling like a dead animal into Earth's atmosphere—maybe I can also survive hitting Earth's surface like a boulder dropped from Mount Mendel.

Realizing that his hand was no longer throbbing in pain from being broken by Norman's grip, Samuel was about to inspect his hand, when he noticed something alarming about the tiny shapes below.

They aren't tiny, Samuel gasped. *I'm just way higher up than I realized.*

The details of the now gigantic shapes became discernible, and Samuel shook his head in incredulous confusion at what he saw.

Those things, Samuel's mind raced, trying to rationalize the titanous, chimeric monsters gliding through the sky like half-digested, malformed dragons that had clawed their way out of the Earth's bowels. *They aren't of this world. They can't be,* Samuel thought as he found himself absorbed in the entrancing complexity and wild variations in their form. The creatures were roughly shaped like elongated old world zeppelins, and they slowly twisted and glided through the sky. Dozens of the creatures swarmed about one another, each of them propelled by a visible gaseous mixture gushing from a single giant sphincter at their rear. Samuel was approaching them from above and behind, but every so often one of them would twist its head enough to reveal a featureless face that tapered to a fish-like, chasming hole.

So, they suck in air through that mouth, and they propel themselves with it by...farting across the sky, Samuel reasoned incredulously. *This all has to be an absurd nightmare.*

Just when Samuel thought he was only a few seconds away from the creatures, his depth perception corrected itself once more, revealing that he still had a considerable distance to fall. All the while, the creatures continued growing in size.

How fucking big are these things? And what are all those colorful areas on their bodies? Samuel wondered nervously as even more details were revealed through the swiftly growing proximity in his mad plunge from space. *Is that…plant life?* Samuel considered, despite the seeming impossibility of the observation. *These giant balloons of scarred flesh are covered in vines and moss and trees and who knows what else,* Samuel concluded as he scanned the sprawling forests of diverse flora sprouting from thick flesh-like follicles.

A slow, deep bellow resounded through the rushing wind, startling Samuel. One of the creatures cocked its featureless tapered head upward, widened its mountain-sized fish mouth, and emitted another slow bellow.

What's it doing? Samuel thought, his mind racing with abstract predictions of what might happen next. The other creatures responded to the great bellow by cocking their heads and looking in the same direction as the first creature. Finally, Samuel did the same, and as he peered upward, he was surprised to see a sky of yellow rather than blue.

No, Samuel understood. *That's not the sky. That's Norman—what's left of him. It's a million little pieces of him spread out so thin and uniform that I can't even see past it. This is part of Madeira's plan. This is all part of his fucking plan.*

Incredible rage battered through Samuel's thoughts, and he suddenly wanted nothing more than to strangle the old man. *Madeira stole my family from me. He stole my world from me. I should have killed him when I had the chance and ran to you, Sandra. I should have fucking killed him.* Samuel could barely believe it, but it was impossible to deny. Although Madeira's old body had shattered after being ejected into outer space alongside Samuel and Norman, Samuel still felt the overwhelming desire to see the old man die all over again. Samuel remembered suddenly how he had viewed Damian with disdain and condescension after he killed the Queensguard, an oppressive force who had loomed over their lives for as long as Samuel and Damian could remember.

I am worse than Damian, Samuel told himself. *Because Damian killed to save my life. But I don't care. I just want to kill you to feel you die, Madeira. A million times over. It's the only justice. The only fucking answer if I can't have my family,* Samuel seethed, envisioning each of their faces fading away into nothingness. *Now everything is out of fucking reach, goddamnit. Family. Revenge. Justice. Everything. You've taken every single thing from me, you old bastard. And I fucking trusted you, like a goddamn child. Like a goddamn fool.*

The swollen, living colossus closest to Samuel bellowed so loud that it sent violent vibrations through Samuel, inside and out. He gawked in horror at the abominable balloon of plants and flesh. If he was right in thinking that he was only seconds away from intercepting the closest creature, then each one was about half the length and at least quadruple the volume of the entire Foundation. *How?* Samuel gasped at their colossal size. *How can any living thing be that big?* Samuel thought with deep dread at being forced closer and closer to creatures that made whales seem miniscule. *Even reality doesn't make sense anymore, because there's no way these things are real. They're...monsters,* Samuel thought at the exact moment he slammed against the closest creature's body, penetrating its thick flesh with the unyielding force of a cannon fired at point-blank range.

He burst through its innards, burrowing through densely twining cords of vascular tissue coursing with turbulent currents of blood and bile and other disgusting bodily fluids. Gushes and explosions battered Samuel's body as he bulleted through the desperately howling creature, whose bellows shook Samuel so hard that he thought he might shatter. As he rocketed deep inside, the light dissipated to pitch-darkness. Samuel gasped blindly within the fathomless depths of the creature's gargantuan entrails, his mind racing in horror at the possibility of being stuck in the belly of a swollen flesh balloon.

Bear it! Samuel urged himself, bracing his panic for another few seconds, and just as he felt like the darkness might suffocate him, he burst into an expansive, open chamber, like the inside of the Foundation.

Samuel frantically scanned the quickly passing blur of his surroundings. Pulsating and coursing with bulging networks of veins and arteries, the curved living walls of the creature were illuminated by some unknown means. The vacant space between the walls was filled with crisscrossing spires of flesh and multi-hued plant-life, like the creature's skin.

There's a whole world in here, Samuel marveled in terror as he burst through countless spires in his unhalted descent, shattering them like trees obliterated by bolts of lightning. Almost at the bottom of the beast's hollow insides, Samuel's mouth fell agape upon seeing tens of thousands of strange creatures, some of them human-shaped, bustling about, manipulating tools and entering structures composed of flesh and plants and fungus and mold and endless varieties of exotic life.

I don't…I don't understand, Samuel stammered in thought, gawking at the impossible vision of a society of obscene and arbitrary life forms living within a hulking balloon that flew above the Earth sucking and farting ocean air.

This can't be fucking real, Samuel thought as he bulleted through a pack of the creatures and penetrated another pulsing wall.

I'm slowing down, Samuel realized with repulsion. *I'm going to get fucking stuck inside an organ.* However, after a few seconds of squelching darkness, he pierced through the creature's thick skin and was spat out once more into blue sky filled with the yellow haze of Norman's diffuse remains.

Samuel twisted and urgently scanned around himself, searching desperately for an answer despite being unable to do anything except fall from the sky and brace himself for impact. He glanced above and saw that the slime mold was nearly upon the creatures flying at the top of the pack, including the one still leaking thick purple fluid from where Samuel had burst through its flesh. Samuel twisted his neck to check below himself. He thought he was looking at the ocean's still distant surface, but it was actually the flesh of another creature just inches from his face. In another squelching explosion of viscera, Samuel penetrated through the creature's flesh and passed through its vascular tissue with sickening ease. Then, without warning, he came to a sudden stop in total darkness, jerking his brain so violently that he saw stars and nearly fell unconscious.

He tried desperately to move, but something was constricting his limbs and stretching him out like an insect being pinioned and prepared for observation. Suddenly, the darkness dissipated, giving way to a dim, sanguine glow. The broken veins and capillaries enveloping and coating Samuel rapidly coagulated and scabbed, forming solid yet undulating walls of pulsating fluid. The walls hollowed into a small space no more than ten feet high and fifteen feet in length. Samuel realized that he was attached to one of the walls, and he inspected his limbs to see that his wrists and ankles were fully submerged inside the pulsating tissue, which also pulled his limbs taut. With his head and back up against the wall, he assumed those parts of his body were also partially consumed by the living wall.

It's eating me, Samuel thought in horror, before recognizing that there was no pain whatsoever. He clenched his fingers and was repulsed at the feeling of squeezing worms, but he was also grateful he could still feel his fingers. The makeshift room continued solidifying and expanding the space between its walls. It smelled like raw meat and urine, and Samuel couldn't help gagging at the putrid stench.

What does it want from me? What is going on? Samuel's mind raced as the stars in his vision scattered, leaving him with the terrible sobriety of accepting that his horrible prediction had come true. *I'm stuck inside this foul creature, at the whim of its internal biology and maybe even a scurrying society of misshapen, mutated…things.*

A drop of viscous, yellow fluid fell from the ceiling in front of Samuel. Then another drop. And then a cascade poured down, curdling into a mound of putrid, bubbling sewage.

Lift! Samuel's mind demanded, and though he was able to pull his right hand out of the wall, it just as quickly grew a protrusion that forced his hand back into position.

Lift! Samuel tried with all his might, but the wall clung tighter to him, as if learning from his previous attempt.

I survived space. I survived the fall. And I'll survive this too, Samuel thought, injecting the words into his mind beyond all doubt. *I will not be stripped of Sandra. Of Margot. Of Nathan. I will not. I refuse. Lift, goddamnit! Lift!*

Samuel screamed at the top of his lungs, his voice cracking in anguish, as he tore his left hand out of the wall, but again it grabbed him and pulled him back, this time solidifying to a stone-like substance and growing a thick, vein-splintering scab over the entirety of his forearm.

Damnit! Samuel seethed.

"This is the first interesting thing to happen in a very long time," came a soft but steadfast tenor voice. Samuel looked back to see that the mound of yellow substance had formed a mouth and was now growing and solidifying into the shape of a human man. Samuel could only watch in bewildered horror as the man's sensory organs formed, his eyes taking shape and his face hollowing at the mouth and nostrils. His yellow skin faded to a newborn pink, and strands of chestnut brown hair sprouted from his head, face, and chest. A plush purple robe with golden frills grew over the man's skin, extending down his legs and wrapping about his feet. His yellow eyes finally turned hazel, and he cocked his head and stared at Samuel like a prowling cat flush with the anticipation of torturing its prey.

The man probed Samuel with a self-assured smile—a smile that told Samuel that whatever this man was, he believed himself to be beyond all others. Like a god—only worse. He looked deep into Samuel's eyes, so deep that it felt like he might be able to see directly into Samuel's soul.

"My name is Tomasz Novak," the man announced, emphasizing his name as if it were divine. A glass of blood-red wine grew from the man's hand, and he lifted it to his nose, savored its scent for a few self-absorbed seconds, then asked, "And who might you be?"

For someone to win, someone else must lose. Wherever there is gain, there must also be loss. One's pleasure is always predicated on someone else's pain.

All life is built on the suffering of other life. The gazelle grazes and is content as the grass is ripped from its roots and shredded slowly into mush. The lion hunts and is content as the gazelle screams in desperate anguish and is shredded slowly into mush. The maggots feed and are content as the lion's infected, dying flesh is shredded slowly into mush.

Glory implies sacrifice. Victory implies defeat. Life implies death.

Ascension implies depths from which to ascend.

Denis is now infallible—he's no longer human. It worked, just like we planned, and he has made it clear that I have no choice but to force humanity to dredge the worst depths. It's the only way to make sure we achieve Ascension, as Denis called it, and never have to sink back to this maddening prison of duality ever again.

From Mendel's Ladder: The Personal Journal of Denis Mendel, Written Circa 2036, Published June 2108 by Leif Mainstone, Federated Agency Publishing

❦ Chapter 4 ❦
Monsters Are Real

T hompson marveled at Anna's voracious hunger as she scarfed down the human food practically without chewing. She moaned in pleasure as she filled her stomach with what she called a "sandwich." The one time Thompson had actually tried human food, a fruit Anna called a watermelon, he vomited from both the taste and texture. The only thing a Hunter's tongue could bear was living human flesh, but even that didn't provide any satiation. Nothing did. A Hunter's existence was intended to involve suffering and nothing else. It was Anna who explained to Thompson that his skinsuit harnessed organic material directly from the ground and the atmosphere—like a plant's method of obtaining nutrients. If a skinsuit was ever truly depleted of nutrients, simply touching another living or dead creature was enough to fully replenish its reserves.

While Thompson stared at Anna like a loyal puppy admiring his master, Anna gazed intently at the human settlement below. The humans were running about in disarray now that they finally realized their food stores had in fact been raided by what might as well have been a ghost.

"You must be the only Hunter in the whole world that uses his power of camouflage to steal sandwiches rather than slaughter people," Anna chuckled, but Thompson could smell that her laughter was a facade hiding a terrible, churning horror that she constantly struggled to contain. Thompson knew better than to bring it up—that would only lead to Anna's tears, which were more painful to Thompson than any number of years being roasted over his birth-fire. On the other hand, her smile filled him with such overwhelming joy that it sometimes made him forget the unceasing pain inflicted by the skinsuit or the still searing scars embedded into his flesh or the despairing loneliness of his infancy and childhood.

Anna continued gazing wide-eyed at the chaotic settlement as she licked each of her fingers then began eating another sandwich, this time slowly, chewing and savoring the different tastes. In turn, Thompson savored the pleasure chemicals coursing through Anna's body, and he rejoiced that by stealing the human food, he was the one who had provided her the means to feel such fragrant happiness.

This is one of my favorite scents, Thompson thought as he cherished this perfect mixture of joy, detachment, and absorption in the present moment that Anna was currently losing herself in as she chewed methodically and let her mind wander among the settlement's flurry of activity. Then, as expected, her mind returned to its awareness of the past and the future, and great sadness overtook her once more.

"Everyone here will be dead soon," Anna whispered forlornly. "Someday a Hunter and Huntress from another territory will find this place, and then any of the humans here who still haven't chosen to become Nomads will be torn to pieces. Even if they do survive somehow, one day they'll slip up and harm the Earth in some way, and then the Nomads will swarm their homes and become flesh trees. They'll turn the whole settlement into a thick forest in a matter of minutes without any need to kill a single human." Anna shook her head in defeat and closed her eyes as she envisioned the horrible truth of the world. "Humanity can't win. Every Nomad they kill in defense of their homes just leads to more flesh trees and a denser forest to replace humanity's ephemeral structures. Either way, it means no more humans eventually. All their toiling and worry and hopes and dreams—it's all pointless."

Thompson followed her eyes and gazed at the outskirts of the settlement. Men altered with metal body parts patrolled and scanned lazily about the perimeter. They were equipped with useless combustion-based projectiles and wore large jackets and bulky body armor haphazardly painted like the environment. These were mercenaries hired from a place Anna called Wintersvilla. Instinct pivoted Thompson's head to the center of the settlement, where a girl no older than fifteen stood on a simple wooden perch a hundred feet above the ground. Her skintight bodysuit mimicked Thompson's skinsuit, but its camouflage was slow to change and only partially convincing. However, it was still far more impressive than the bulk and totally useless camouflage that the men wore. The young girl was from the same place as the Wintersvilla men, and she too had metal implanted throughout her body. Carefully placed slits and presently open pockets in the legs of her bodysuit revealed that her right leg was entirely replaced by a sleek metal prosthetic. Thompson traced the limb to her hips. A sword and knife were sheathed but unclipped in preparation for battle. The weapons were far more effective and reliable than the large projectile weapons that the men had slung around their shoulders. From her blades, Thompson's eyes finally reached her face, which was entirely human except for the uniform purple light emitted from her right pupil. The light was pointed directly at Thompson, and the rest of her face was contorted in what appeared to be bewilderment.

She knows we're here, Thompson considered nervously, readying himself to kill everyone and everything in defense of Anna. *How long has she been staring at us with that machine eye? And why isn't she warning the others?*

"They know we here," Thompson warned, slipping in his spoken language out of urgency. Anna didn't correct him. The tone of his voice was dire, telling her this was no time for a grammar lesson.

"The Wintersvilla girl. She's looking directly at us right now. She's just…staring at us," Thompson explained in nervous confusion.

"Let's not push our luck," Anna stated as she finished the last few bites of her third sandwich in a single mouthful. "Time to leave."

A pack of several dozen lumbering Nomads shaped like old world willow trees slowed to a saunter and turned to peer at Thompson and Anna as they passed. A multitude of oblong eyes scattered across their wily trunks and branches stared emotionlessly at the human and the Hunter as they walked across an expansive field of wily tangle grass, likely a breeding ground for the snaking mats of plant life. In many of the human settlements, dogs and other animals were used for certain purposes, and some were even kept as pets. Anna explained that the same type of relationship existed for the Nomads and their loyal mats of tangle grass.

The tangle grass parted as Anna trudged forward, and the willow tree Nomads seemed to bow to Anna with the top of their trunks bent toward the horizon. Thompson had come to expect this type of behavior from the Nomads. They revered Anna—like loyal subjects to their queen. Nothing else appeared to stop the Nomads in their tracks except for her presence. The Nomads and lethal flora of the world had never posed a threat to Anna nor Thompson, as long as he remained near her. However, Thompson still couldn't totally let down his guard around the Nomads; their keen interest in Anna only made him trust them less.

They were human once, Thompson reminded himself with unrelenting surprise even months after finding Anna and traveling from one human settlement to the next, stealing food so that she wouldn't starve. He had seen the Nomad transformation process with his own eyes as humans regularly gave up on sordid survival and finally decided to place their hand on a flesh-tree or a Nomad and mentally accept the biological changes that would convert them into something they couldn't even imagine. Some turned plant-like, while others looked like giant fungi. Some grew more limbs, while others retained a more-or-less humanoid shape. Anna explained that it was the Earth itself that decided the shape and form of each Nomad, and it was each Nomad's duty to fulfill Earth's singular will.

Thompson caught the unblinking stare of a particularly humanoid looking willow tree Nomad, which the humans referred to as a Hybrid. The name was meaningless since there was no actual differentiation between a Nomad and a Hybrid. But the humans couldn't help feeling more comfortable around Nomads that looked like themselves, and this separation in comfort compelled them to give the Nomads shaped like humans their own arbitrary classification. The Hybrid stared directly at Thompson rather than Anna, and he wondered what might be going through the Hybrid's strange mind. The Hybrid's unblinking stare reminded Thompson suddenly of the young Wintersvilla girl from the human settlement, and he couldn't help wondering why she had not engaged them in battle.

Was she afraid that if she alerted the others, it would lead to a battle she could not win? Thompson considered, but he knew that couldn't be right. Wintersvilla girls were as ruthless as the other Hunters and Huntresses Anna had warned Thompson about; she didn't know whether or not they would attempt to kill her since she was a human. *Anna smells human, but the world doesn't see her that way,* he thought as they entered a sizable island of flesh trees surrounded on all sides by breeding swarms of tangle grass.

"Why do you think she didn't alert the others and attack us?"

Thompson asked, and he was happy to see that Anna didn't find any flaws in his speech to correct.

"That poor little girl," Anna lamented. She ran her hand through the yellow and purple florets growing from a squat bush-shaped flesh tree. She was careful not to harm the tiny flesh pods dangling from the stem of each floret like fragile dew. One of the flesh pods snapped unexpectedly, and though Anna tried to catch it, she wasn't fast enough. Thompson pivoted and stretched his arm and hand with perfect precision, catching the flesh pod and placing it on the ground beneath the flesh tree's vibrant foliage.

Anna stared at the little flesh pod, losing herself in strange avenues of thought beyond the emotions and surface cognition that Thompson could translate through her neurochemical mixtures. After a few seconds of abstract thought, Anna lifted her head and turned to the northwest. She pointed and said, "Wintersvilla is a couple thousand miles in that direction. That's where she came from. And that's where thousands of little girls like her are tortured and churned into machines of war. They aren't born that way, Thompson. Just like you aren't born that way. She's a lot more like you than you realize," Anna finished, shaking her head at some remarkably complex truth she was wrestling with.

Thompson shook his head, not sure that Anna had actually answered his question.

"But why didn't she attack, Anna?" Thompson pressed gently.

"Why didn't you, little Hunter?" Anna asked as she turned to meet Thompson's terrible predator eyes. She hadn't called him *little Hunter* in what seemed like ages. It was one of the ways she had referred to him before she had given him a proper name. It reminded Thompson that it was only in the last few weeks that he had stopped smelling the deep ancestral human fear within Anna anytime she looked at or envisioned Thompson's or other identical Hunters' deliberately terrifying features.

Why didn't I attack? Thompson considered, but the answer seemed obvious enough.

"Because that would put you in danger," Thompson said.

Anna nodded. "Maybe she thought the same thing, Thompson. Maybe she decided that at that moment, the risk of battle was worse than the risk of letting us pass by."

"But how could she know we would just pass by, Anna? The only reasonable assumption is that we will return later, as a Hunter and Huntress on the Eternal Hunt. You look identical to a Huntress, Anna. There's no way she just decided to let us leave."

"You think she's planning to hunt us down?" Anna asked, and Thompson nodded. "Isn't it possible she just doesn't want to fight, Thompson? If I weren't here, would you have attacked that settlement?" Anna asked with a flurry of oscillating emotions and an array of further questions churning in her mind.

Thompson considered her question seriously, imagining himself without Anna. *What would be the point of living? Why bother going on without her?* At the same time, he couldn't deny that a wild internal rage bubbled at all times in the depths of his being, goading him to maim and murder. It was the same hunger that drove Anna to consume food. Without that hunger, she would starve, and then she would die.

Will I die without hunting? Thompson wondered seriously. *Will I waste away and starve if I don't eventually embark on the Eternal Hunt, as Anna called it?*

"I don't know," Thompson admitted to Anna. "I want to believe that I would resist killing, but the truth is that the urge is there. It's you who keeps it quelled. And if you weren't here, another Huntress would be. I don't think I would have a choice in that case."

Anna furrowed and winced in what appeared to be physical pain, but Thompson could smell that it was a thought that had struck through her with such violent force.

"Maybe she's fighting against her masters in her own way, Thompson. Maybe she knows there's no way to win, but she's still resisting anyway. You think that's possible?" Anna asked, gritting her teeth now against her violent, abstract thoughts.

Thompson didn't understand what she was insinuating, but he just wished he could take away her pain, even if it meant carrying it himself. Before Anna, all he knew was pain. What did another added ocean of pain matter when he was already a planet full of anguish? He wished he could plunge his hands into her mind and tear away all the terror and fear tarnishing every one of her waking moments with suffocating reminders of a fate she could not escape. However, he didn't dare even bring up the topic of fate. It always made Anna cry, which was more painful to Thompson than the whole of his childhood, so he happily avoided the topic altogether.

But I can't, Thompson told himself forlornly, reminding himself of Anna's own words. *No one can take away anyone else's pain. Pain is our own. It is a master, or it is a tool, but it is entirely our own, and there is no one and nothing other than ourselves that gets to decide to use the pain or to let it use us.*

"I'm sorry, Anna," Thompson said, unsure what else to do or say to stop the tears welling in her eyes. He remembered that she liked to be held, and he hoped he would not make her uncomfortable by closing the gap between them and taking her into his arms. Anna let herself fall into Thompson's embrace, and Thompson relished the warmth and softness of her skin. He adored the way she nestled her head against his chest and the way her lips upturned slightly at the corners as she sighed a fraction of her oceanic worry into his chest.

"I'm sorry too, Thompson," Anna breathed. A rumble of distant thunder resonated across the world, lifting both their eyes to peer through the canopy of flesh trees and scan the slowly darkening sky.

Thompson began to break away to prepare a shelter for them to wait out the coming storm, but Anna held him tighter.

"Not yet," she said. "We have time before it gets here. Let me just enjoy you."

Thompson didn't need any convincing to oblige her request, and he squeezed tighter as she fell deeper into his impenetrable embrace.

"I love you, Anna," Thompson whispered, letting his chasming deep voice vibrate across her neck and pleasantly lift the tiny fragile hairs at the base of her hairline. Anna sank even further, letting Thompson take the whole of her weight.

"Look at you," she said, struggling to stifle what Thompson could smell was a flood of tears. "A Hunter holding a human woman. A Hunter in love. It doesn't make any sense. And yet here we are, Thompson. You know that's why I named you Thompson, right?"

Thompson shook his head to go on as he cherished her voice—every word and lilt and crack.

"I refuse to refer to you as a number. It's wrong. It's disgusting. I named you after an old world author. Hunter S. Thompson. His writing wouldn't make any sense to you—it barely makes sense to me. But the reason I appreciate him so much is that he perfected a genre of writing called creative nonfiction. That means a creative version of true events.

So…not true at all. What a wonderful and alluring paradox. To intentionally blur the lines of reality and still persist in calling it objective truth—we all do that, Thompson. Your very existence is a blurred line. And so is mine."

Thompson nodded, pretending to understand. He could smell that allowing her to speak was helping her alleviate the mental pressure building like an unreleased geyser in her mind, and that was enough for Thompson.

Keep talking, Anna. Just let it all out, even if I don't understand. I trust that you understand, and that's enough for me.

"Monsters aren't real, Thompson. Just like gods aren't real. Those are just simple ideas that make it easier to explain away the terrible truth that reality is not that simple. Not even close. So, we constantly write our own creative nonfiction about our own lives and our reality. We make up stories, and we convince ourselves that they're true. And they are true, Thompson. Because truth isn't real. It's an idea, like monsters and gods. All these things, even truth, is always a false simplification of something incapable of being simplified."

Thompson breathed and smelled that Anna was wrestling once more with abstract, ominous thoughts that always plagued the periphery of every moment of her life, even in her dreams. Anna raised her head suddenly, and her eyes turned to slits. Thompson followed her stare and saw that Astrea was passing over them. Another rumble of thunder, this one much closer, shook the still darkening skies.

"The first Hunters were tortured for five years and released onto the world as children. They would infiltrate human cities without even having to use camouflage. The humans took in what they thought was a child in need, and then the little tortured Hunter would go off like a bomb, killing as many humans as possible before being subdued or killed. The worst part was that humanity began to fear its own children, especially those who cried out for help. Every child in need was now a potential lethal trap. Several years passed, and humanity thought the worst had already come. But then the nine-year Hunters were released, and with them came the Huntresses and skinsuits. And then eleven-year Hunters. And then thirteen. And then fifteen. And now you. You're a seventeen-year Hunter, Thompson. The most ruthless and cunning and unstoppable of all. And still. Still Thompson. Still, you were able to learn love and resist your instinctual urge to hunt."

Anna pulled herself into Thompson and whispered, "You're far more beautiful and deserving of this life than you realize, Thompson. You...you always find a way to overcome yourself. You always find a way, Thompson. I wish I could say the same about myself."

Anna's words were like a lightning strike on a perfectly calm day, and Thompson couldn't help shaking in immediate denial. "No, Anna. You love me. And I love you. And that's what matters. You deserve this life more than anyone in the world, Anna. Who else could love a monster like me? Who else but you?"

Anna began sobbing, and Thompson felt terrible for making her cry. He smelled, however, that these were not tears of pure sadness. Nor were they tears of happiness. They were something Thompson didn't have a name for.

Longing? he wondered. *Regret?*

"I love you, Thompson," Anna said, and for the first time Thompson thought he could name the substance of her love.

Proof, Thompson thought, allowing the word to form. *She loves me because I am proof of something important. Something she thinks might still not be true.*

"What am I proof of, Anna?" Thompson asked.

At his words, Anna stopped crying and became incredibly still.

Oh no, Thompson thought, not wanting to ruin this moment with her. *I shouldn't have brought it up. I shouldn't probe when she asked me not to.*

Several bolts of lightning arced through the sky in the distance, and cracks of thunder followed directly after.

"Build us a shelter, Thompson," Anna said, her voice distant and her thoughts on some unreachable plane. She lifted herself away from Thompson and stared at the ground beneath her feet with faraway eyes.

I'm sorry for ruining the moment, Thompson thought before transforming his hands into thick claws with reinforced nails capable of digging and hollowing out a shallow cave in a matter of minutes. *I wish I could just always know the right thing to say to make sure she never cries and never leaves.*

Heavy droplets began pattering the flesh trees and ground, ramping in speed just as Thompson completed the cave. He ensured that it sloped slightly to avoid rising water in the case of an unexpected deluge. Thompson's hands retracted back to their birth-form, and without a moment's hesitation, Anna grabbed his hand and walked to the back of the cave.

He sat down beside her and opened his arms, offering for her to sleep in his warm embrace, but instead she gazed at him with a strange, desperate longing that Thompson had seen the other humans exhibit.

"I know you can smell how I feel, Thompson," Anna said slowly as she brushed her fingers across his pectorals. "I want you, Thompson. I want to have sex with you."

Sex? Thompson gawked. *Like the humans.* Thompson had smelled the activity many times before. It was something the humans did on a regular basis—some of them just as often as eating food.

Pleasure. Closeness. Release. Love, Thompson thought, listing the feelings he could remember humans feeling during sex, though love was not originally part of that list. *I didn't know about love until Anna taught me. And now she wants to show me this part of love too.* Of course, Thompson wanted to love Anna in every way she desired, but he wasn't sure it was even possible. Simply put, humans had organs meant for sex. Hunters and Huntresses didn't.

"Anna...I—"

"You don't need to be afraid, Thompson," Anna whispered, gently gripping his hand. "This'll be my first time too."

"It's not that," Thompson corrected. "It's...I don't have a...the organ I've smelled and seen on the human men. My body isn't like that," Thompson apologized.

"Your body is whatever you want it to be," Anna corrected.

"You want me to change my body to be...human?" Thompson checked incredulously.

Anna nodded. "I want to make love to you, Thompson. Like a human. But only if you're comfortable with that."

"Yes," Thompson issued immediately. "I just...I've never changed my body that way before. So...just give me a moment, and—"

Lightning struck just outside the cave, momentarily illuminating the dim interior. Anna jumped in shock and clung to Thompson at the sight of the young Wintersvilla girl from the human settlement standing at the cave's entrance, a blade in each hand. As the girl stepped into the cave, another blast of lightning struck a hardwood flesh tree in the distance, vaporizing bark and viscera at once. As the light from the lightning faded, the purple light of the girl's eye shifted to red, and her lips curved into a wide, sinister smile.

"Were you about to grow a human dick, Thompson?" the girl asked with a condescending lash.

Anna appeared paralyzed in fear, but then Thompson realized that she was physically frozen, as if under the same type of magic spell that Anna had described from some of her favorite books.

Anna!

"What did you do to her?" Thompson snarled, breathing heavily as the weeks of withheld rage bubbled beneath his skin.

I knew we couldn't trust her. Anna was wrong—this little girl was just waiting to corner us. And now Anna is in danger. I should have killed her at the settlement. I should have never allowed her to corner us like this, Thompson thought, berating himself for not smelling the girl's approach at the very least.

"You really were about to grow a dick, weren't you?" the girl asked, sheathing her blades. "I bet the next part of this memory is amazing. You're still alive, so I'm guessing you kill this little warrior girl. Shame we don't have time to sit back and watch it happen."

Thompson shook his head in confusion. *What is she talking about? Why is she talking to me and not diving in for the attack?*

"Save me the trouble of reading more of these pathetic memories: do you guys actually have sex at some point?" the girl asked casually as if she didn't have a care in the world.

Thompson didn't care that the girl wasn't making sense.

I have to find a way to release Anna. The girl paralyzed her with her eye somehow.

"What did you do to her?" Thompson demanded as he moved forward and placed his body between Anna and the deadly little girl, regardless of whether her blades were sheathed.

"It's time to wake up, dog. It's already been half a day. That's enough rest for my disobedient mutt."

Thompson shook his head in further confusion, but the girl just went on smiling.

"Does the name Volya ring a bell?" the girl asked.

Volya, Thompson repeated, and in the same instant a bolt of lightning cleaved the cave wide open, exploding the world with a thunderous blast and burning Thompson's vision with the blinding white light that had knocked him into this series of dreams in the first place.

The light faded, and as Thompson's mind caught up with the present, he found himself lying in a giant crater, peaceful blue skies and puffy white clouds above.

To Thompson's left lay the younger, fiery-haired human Wintersvilla Woman Volya had forced him to battle against. She appeared unconscious, but he could smell that she still clung to life. Surprisingly, beyond being unconscious, her physical body appeared robust and in stable condition, save her empty eye sockets. Her naked body was bruised and scarred, but otherwise unscathed. In her arms, she clasped the charred, limbless corpse of the other Wintersvilla Woman, refusing to let go.

How? Thompson wondered.

"I grabbed the skinsuit I came down with and put it on her," Volya responded to his thoughts. "Actually, I tried to give it to the other human first, but I guess the suit decided there was nothing left to save. It slithered over the younger woman, and she took to it like a Hunter, syncing with it as if it was always meant for her," Volya explained with a perplexed and probing gaze. "I didn't think it was possible for a human to withstand the pain of a skinsuit. Even I can't. Trust me, if I could, I would. Can you imagine a Huntress with a skinsuit? No more Hunter needed. But somehow she can take the pain. Surprising as all hell if you ask me," Volya exhaled heavily.

"Why did you save her?" Thompson asked as he lifted himself into a sitting position and stretched his body. He felt utterly drained of life, as if naked without a skinsuit.

"Save her?" Volya laughed. "No, Thompson. I didn't save her. I'm going to keep her alive so that I can torture her. Just like how I'm going to torture you for fucking with me with that stinging fog in your mind. Those little girls are going to end up dying in those caves due to slipping or starving. Unacceptable, dog. They are ours to torture and kill. They were in our grasp, and you let them get away. I told you I would break you, Thompson. I'm going to make you wish you were still dreaming. And then when you finally break, we will continue the Eternal Hunt,"

Volya declared, smiling with sinister conceit.

Thompson painfully recollected Anna's words about monsters not being real.

You were wrong about the Wintersvilla girl, Anna. And I think you might be wrong about monsters too, Thompson thought as he looked back at the woman whom Volya planned to torture alongside himself. A few paces behind her, the woman's metal suit stood and waited to be utilized, silent and utterly unfazed by the world and mayhem around it.

"Monsters aren't real, Thompson," Volya said mockingly, imitating Anna's lilt. "I guess your bitch girlfriend never met me, eh?"

Painfully absorbing Volya's perverse smile, Thompson noticed a glint of something in the sky. He directed his stare behind Volya and realized that it was Astrea passing overhead, reminding him that he had lost Anna forever. It was all his fault that she was gone. Everything was his fault.

I deserve whatever torture Volya has planned for me, Thompson accepted, allowing the coming pain to serve as penance for failing Anna. *But that woman—I have to find a way to help her. I have to find a way to save her from Volya, because Volya is a monster. Monsters are real,* Thompson concluded, resolved to never allow himself to become one again.

Volya laughed in amusement at Thompson's thoughts. "I have that little fog trick figured out, dog. It won't work again. I've had more than enough time to dig through your mind and create a few additional measures of control for myself. You won't wriggle out of your collar this time, dog. I assure you of that."

There's always a way, Thompson resolved. *There has to be. Anna resigned herself to her fate. It was my job to stop her from doing that, and I failed. But I won't keep failing, Anna. I'll find a way to save this woman. I'll find a way to save every human this wicked Huntress tries to make me kill. You said I always find a way, Anna. So, I'll find a way.*

Volya chuckled and sighed in pleasant preparation to administer torture.

Even her, Thompson thought as he stared down Volya's wicked glare. *I won't even give up on her, Anna. Even though she's proof enough that monsters are real after all. I still won't give up, Anna. I'll find a way.*

"This is going to be fun," Volya purred with sinister satisfaction. "Looks like the human is beginning to stir. Now I get to torture you both at the same time."

There was once a Zen master who lived in a small Japanese town. One day this town was raided by a ruthless and notorious military band. Everyone in the town fled, except for the Zen master. When the general of the invading army heard that there was a man in town who both refused to run and did not exhibit fear, he demanded that he be taken to this man.

When the general saw the man and learned that he was considered a master, he almost burst into laughter. In comparison to the general and his warriors, the so-called master was small, frail, and insignificant. And yet, the frail master did not bow in submission to the general's power, as was the custom.

"Bow," the general demanded, but the Zen master didn't even respond. He just stared into the general's eyes without emotion, totally unaffected by the whims of the outside world.

Seeing that the little man dressed in robes did not fear him, the general started to become angry. He gripped the hilt of his sword and said, "Fool. I stand before you, ready to slice off your head without batting an eye. Bow or die."

The Zen master appeared undisturbed and said, "Fool. I sit before you, ready to have my head sliced off without batting an eye. Get on with it or go away and let me meditate."

Of course, the general decapitated the Zen master, but that meant nothing to him, even in his final second of life. He just went on pleasantly staring into the distance, despite his head no longer attached to his body. Death was just another moment to be accepted and focused on with an unwavering selfless view of his own being and nonbeing.

One cannot be disturbed unless they choose to be disturbed. In the same way, one cannot lose sight of the big picture unless they choose to live in fear and be controlled. It is impossible to seize and control an individual without fear. Free of control, an individual is liberated. To those who have attained liberation—true existential liberation—the cosmos is but a grain of sand upon their fingertip.

From Mendel's Ladder: The Personal Journal of Denis Mendel, Written Circa 2044, Published June 2108 by Leif Mainstone, Federated Agency Publishing

Chapter 5
With Discipline and Daring

A liana screamed in wordless terror and the cave shook with concussive bellows, but Aurelia remained one-pointed.

The present is difficult, and the past is gone, but the future is still being made, Aurelia intoned to herself through forcefully controlled breathing as she was plunged into the darkness behind her shrieking sister.

I will never forget you, Rooli, Aurelia promised, and she forced the urge to cry and panic deep inside herself, just as Rooli had taught her, saving grief for a more appropriate time.

Cold, hard ground slammed against Aurelia's right collarbone, shattering it and forcing the breath out of her lungs. She bounced, twisted haphazardly, then landed directly on her right wrist, snapping both her radius and ulna with a sickening crunch of bone and cartilage. The pain was all consuming. Enveloping. Suffocating.

No! Aurelia mentally rebelled as she slammed a few more times against unyielding rock, scraping and tearing every inch of her open skin and what little remained of her dirty, ragged clothing.

Nothing can touch me unless I choose, Aurelia reminded herself before bringing her mind back under her control. *Not pain. Not fear. Not death. Nothing.*

Finally, she came to a stop somewhere in the dense, directionless darkness. The searing pain emanating across the entirety of the upper right half of her body demanded her attention, but she refused it.

My mind is my own, Aurelia told the pain with battle-hardened practice. *You will obey me,* she demanded of her body, and in response, the pain began to dissolve, dissipating to a mere annoyance in the distant background of her awareness.

I need to find Aliana, and then we need to run. Shira and Myriam together stand on equal footing with the Butcher, but Shira is already nearly dead, Aurelia reasoned, bracing her mind against the molten mental anguish churning at the periphery of her thoughts.

Not yet, she told her distressed subconscious. *Grief comes later. Now we must focus and act,* she thought, treating her brain as if it were a separate entity within her head. It was this ability to detach that Rooli had ingrained into Aurelia most strongly, and from this detachment, she had constant access to a fount of discipline and daring.

Contrary to her usual state of being, Aliana was silent, and for not the first time, Aurelia wished she could call out to her sister.

Is she dead? Aurelia wondered, but she did not allow her mind to slip into the landslide of panic that was currently forcing her mind to conjure hallucinations in the darkness, morphing phosphenes into wild visions of violence and mayhem involving Hunters battling to the death with those who mattered most to her.

Aurelia didn't mind the tendrils of hallucinations, nor did she mind the fear clawing at her from the unseen depths of both her psyche and the cave's interior, but the very real possibility of blindly searching with her one good hand for her sister and discovering her mangled corpse struck Aurelia with undeniable trepidation.

Please be alive, Ali, she thought. *Don't make me endure this without you.*

"Aurelia! Aurelia!" Aliana groaned through blood-curdling gasps from somewhere to Aurelia's right.

Stopping herself from rejoicing and losing her focus, Aurelia wasted no time placing one foot in front of the other, carefully guiding herself through the darkness to avoid dropping unexpectedly into an unseen chasm.

I'm coming, Ali, Aurelia thought, forcing each foot in front of the next in defiance of her survival instinct distantly but ceaselessly pleading with her to stop and administer aid to her own broken bones.

"Aurelia!" Aliana groaned again, this time with a shiver in her voice. "Aurelia, please! Are you alive?"

Aliana shrieked as Aurelia grabbed her ankle, then she immediately began to sob once she realized it was her sister. Pulling her tightly to her chest, Aliana hugged Aurelia as if she might suffocate without her embrace.

An onslaught of explosions from what sounded like miles away resounded just outside the cave wall.

We have to run, Aurelia knew. *We're just little fish in a vast ocean right now, and that Hunter out there is a hungry shark.*

Grabbing both of Aliana's hands with her scraped but still functional left hand, Aurelia positioned Aliana's hands so that she would be able to read her signing.

"We have to go, Ali. Into the darkness. We have no choice," Aurelia explained as she stood and directed her sister to do the same.

Aurelia heard Aliana spit something thick then wipe her face with the alarming sound of gushing fluid.

"I think my nose is broken," Aliana groaned painfully, spitting more blood. "I can't even feel my face."

Aurelia did not tell her sister about her broken collarbone or wrist, nor that the entire right side of her upper body was now as useless as a fileted salmon.

"Let me see," Aurelia signed into her sister's palms, then she gently skimmed her sister's face with her fingertips.

"Ow!" Aliana yelped, pulling away in pain. But Aurelia had felt enough to know that her sister's nose was totally shattered, and her left eye socket appeared fractured in numerous locations as well.

This will ruin her natural beauty, Aurelia couldn't help thinking, ashamed of herself for feeling envy over her sister's naturally pretty face. *Now she's ugly like me,* Aurelia considered, but it didn't bring her the solace she used to imagine it would.

"It's not that bad," Aurelia lied. "We have to run, Aliana. You hear those explosions out there? Shira and Myriam are fighting on our behalf. We can't let their battle and deaths be in vain."

"Deaths?" Aliana repeated in shock. "They're not going to die, Aurelia. They're going to flay the Butcher like a descaled trout."

She doesn't believe it, Aurelia observed, knowing every subtlety of her sister's tone. *They're both going to die,* Aurelia knew. *Just like Rooli.* But she signed, "I hope you're right, but just in case you aren't, we must move. We must, Aliana. No stopping, right?"

Aliana spit more blood, then said, "Okay, okay, you're right. But we might as well be in intergalactic space. I can't see a thing."

Aliana's distress over the enveloping darkness finally reminded Aurelia that she had prepared for the darkness at the very last second. She had transferred the flint-and-steel device called a sparker from the side pocket of her backpack and into her single intact pocket just as she realized that Rooli would cut their backpacks off to make them fit through the tiny hole. As usual, in the direst moments, Aurelia could always count on her mind to see the big picture and observe the future like a puzzle composed of intricately complex pieces. Somehow, during times of life and death, her mind could reveal the outlines of each piece, showing her exactly how each decision always invariably led to a highly predictable outcome.

Like fate, Aurelia thought, disgusted by the word and its implications.

Refocusing her mind, Aurelia removed the sparker and flicked it with her thumb, issuing a fount of sparks into the air above their heads. Aliana jumped at the unexpected flash of light, and Aurelia jumped at the state of Aliana's face.

She's worse off than I thought, Aurelia realized with a quickening of her heartbeat. Aliana's nose was just a smear of shattered bone and cartilage, and her left eye was already black and swollen shut. The rest of her face was covered in gashes and scrapes, with a particularly deep laceration extending from her forehead and across her right eye.

She's not blind at least. We've three good hands and three good eyes between the two of us. Half-blind and half-useless is still better than totally blind and totally useless, Aurelia reasoned.

"Oh, Aurelia, you fucking genius. You have your sparker!" Aliana rejoiced before spitting more blood.

She's losing too much blood, Aurelia considered, and without a second thought, she removed the tattered remains of her shirt with one hand and carefully wrapped it around Aliana's head, tightening it around what remained of her nose to stifle the bleeding. Aliana yelped in pain, but she didn't stop her sister, clearly aware that she needed to stifle the bleeding, but in too much shock to do it herself.

"It's bad, isn't it? My face," Aliana checked, her voice an anguished whisper.

Yeah, Aurelia thought, *it's bad. If we survive this, you'll be scarred for life. But at least your scars won't be glistening black lacerations. People will still be able to look at you without immediate repulsion,* Aurelia thought before forcing the thoughts away with the rest of her self-pity.

"Head wounds always bleed worse than they really are," Aurelia signed, not wanting her sister to panic.

A particularly loud bellow resonated through the cave, making both girls jump and prompting Aurelia to flick the sparker above their heads in rapid succession, illuminating their surroundings with lightning flashes of cascading orange sparks. Using the flashes of light, Aurelia observed that the cave entrance was just a small platform from which ropes hung and descended down a steep incline to their current location.

We fell right over that tiny platform and skipped the ropes entirely, Aurelia realized, wishing they could have had more time outside the cave to prepare. *That fucking metal man, Gambe—he could have helped us. All this could have been avoided.*

Focus! Aurelia's subconscious demanded in Rooli's voice like a whip to a meandering horse.

Aurelia turned and peered into the impenetrable darkness leading further into the cave. The ground appeared solid and free of chasms, but the sparker could only provide so much illumination. The rest of the cave and its dense darkness remained a mystery.

"Aurelia, your wrist and your collarbone—they look broken," Aliana gasped.

"They aren't," Aurelia lied despite her right arm dangling uselessly at her side. "Let's go," Aurelia issued, and just as she was about to step foot into the darkness, she looked down and saw something that made her lose all track of time and purpose.

Rooli! Aurelia gawked, staring directly into Rooli's unblinking black eyes, and only her eyes, for the rest of her was gone. A single tiny piece of Rooli's wooden face containing both her eyes lay in a small pool of Aliana's spit-up blood.

"Rooli!" Aliana gasped as she followed her sister's incredulous wide eyes to the ground. "How?"

Another great bellow shook the cave, and Aurelia wasted no more time. She grabbed the shard of Rooli and nestled it into her right armpit, knowing that Rooli would approve, despite the stench, because it was the most reasonable place.

"She might still be alive!" Aliana urged her sister as Aurelia grabbed her hand and strode into the darkness.

"I know," Aurelia answered, speaking with her fingers against her sister's palms. "I remember," she added, conjuring visions of their narrow escape from Wintersvilla, a seeming eternity in the past.

Rooli might very well be immortal, Aurelia reasoned with newfound strength, as if a flashlight had suddenly appeared in her hand. She squeezed the shard closer into her armpit. *Just hang on, Enduring Ironwood. Keep enduring, and we'll find a way to revive you,* Aurelia promised. A stream of tears fell from her eyes unexpectedly, making her feel ashamed for her uncontrolled emotions.

"Put your hand on my left shoulder," Aurelia commanded as she broke from her sister's grasp. "I need my hand to spark the sparker."

"Just give it to me. I know you broke something on your right side. I know you're lying to me, Aurelia. Protecting me. And I love you for that, even though I never tell you that," Aliana said with faltering hope as they stepped rapidly into the darkness, the bellows from the battle like a distantly rumbling thunder from a storm that refused to dissipate.

Aurelia slid back to her sister and signed into her palms. "You're right, Ali, I'm hurt. It's not that bad, though. But even with your smashed eye and nose, you're still better able to defend us. I need you to stay alert and ready with both your arms. Who knows what's in this cave? So, I need you to be ready. We both have our swords. We have our lives. And we even have Rooli, if we can get her to sunlight in time," Aurelia said, keeping herself controlled and collected for both their sake.

"Okay," Aliana agreed without protest, and she placed her hand atop Aurelia's bare shoulder and squeezed, telling her with a single movement that she knew they had each other, so all was not lost.

Aurelia flicked the sparker, and they moved step by step with each flash. After a few minutes of walking down a slight decline, the sparks began bouncing off the ceiling.

"The path is tapering," Aliana said nervously.

Just stay calm, Aurelia thought, keeping her mind stable for both their sake. Far from the entrance now, the cave was as silent as it was dark. The temperature began to drop rapidly with each of their steps, and the decline in the path grew steeper. The cold air made Aurelia's breath feel uncomfortably warm against the skin beneath her face mask. Normally she would just bear it, but they were alone, and the darkness was all consuming. For the first time in longer than Aurelia could remember, she removed her face mask and let it hang over her left ear, exposing her flesh-rending, glistening black lips and cheeks to the open air.

Holy Muto, Aurelia marveled, *that feels amazing.*

Though she knew her sister didn't care about her face and wouldn't pull away if she saw her in the flashes of light, Aurelia was still careful to keep herself turned away so that her sister would not have to see such a horrific sight while she was already in a heightened state of anxiety.

Focus! Aurelia's mind snapped, helping her to balance her thoughts between memory and the present moment, recollecting the few details Rooli had mentioned about the hidden passages to Downver.

Full of traps, Rooli had said, and Aurelia found herself missing Rooli more than ever. Rooli wasn't just a parent to her; she was her best friend. Her only real friend, besides her sister.

You understand me better than anyone in the world, Enduring Ironwood, Aurelia thought, using Rooli's Nomadic name in her thoughts out of profound gratitude bordering on reverence. She squeezed Rooli lovingly beneath her right arm. *We will find a way to save you. A little sunlight and water—that's all you need. What a fucking disaster that those are exactly what the cave doesn't have. It's a shame you can't feed on darkness,* Aurelia considered with a twinge of both pain and anguished humor. *That way you could just feast on my soul and never be threatened with death again.*

Imagining the great darkness within her forced Aurelia to a sudden stop as she saw the great vortex at the center of her mind churning in the depths of the cave's darkness.

Not now! she demanded, but the swirling vortex consuming all of space and time was laid bare in the real world, and for a moment, Aurelia forgot that it was just a hallucination, just a reflection of her inner being painted across the impenetrable darkness.

Wow, Aurelia marveled at the void center of the vortex, feeling entranced and afraid and excited all at once. *This is my fate,* Aurelia knew. Even Rooli believed it, though she was the only one Aurelia had ever told about the all-consuming vortex that had always been inside her for as long as she could remember, reminding her that nothing really mattered—not here at least. Whatever the concept of an abstract *here* and *there* meant, Aurelia couldn't be sure, but it had something to do with being the Virus, something to do with the horrid black streaks perpetually cleaving her face into gaping wounds.

What is that vortex, Aurelia wondered for what must be the millionth time. *And why am I certain that my fate lies in being consumed by it?* She couldn't help feeling disturbed that she felt no fear when she looked into the vortex's impossible depths. There was far more fear associated with the idea of never finding it in real life—of allowing the great swirling vortex at the center of her mind to remain a mere vision.

"Aurelia!" Aliana demanded with jarring signing, breaking Aurelia out of her trance and erasing the vortex from both her mind and her vision. "You okay?"

"Sorry," Aurelia signed, and quickly came up with an excuse for stopping, albeit a valid one. "I'm just thinking back to what Rooli said about this place. It was the same night Rooli had to drag us all out of those sleeping marshes we stumbled through."

"Traps," Aliana said, clearly remembering the same night.

"I can't believe you remember," Aurelia signed with genuine surprise, but she assumed her sister would take it the wrong way. To her relief, however, Aliana just chuckled.

"Yeah, that's fair enough. I never remember anything. But I do remember that."

"You probably remember it so well because I was pouting like a boy that night. I was pissed about something you said. Who knows now," Aurelia offered in an attempt to concede to her own weaknesses just as Aliana had.

Again, to Aurelia's surprise, Aliana grabbed her sister and hugged her closer than ever. Searing pain shot through Aurelia's chest and shoulder, forcing a wince of breath through her lips.

"I'm sorry!" Aliana said, pulling away.

"It's nothing," Aurelia lied. "How's your face? Let me see."

Aurelia flicked the sparker a few times in quick succession and observed that her sister's face was battered, bruised, and engorged to twice its normal size, and her eye was completely swollen shut. However, the blood appeared to have finally slowed to no more than a trickle that continued to force Aliana to spit and clear her throat of her own liquid life every handful of seconds.

"It's starting to look better already," Aurelia lied again.

"Liar," Aliana said. "I'm fucking ugly, aren't I? Hideous. Like a Mutant! I felt my face, Aurelia. My nose is a fucking smear, and—"

"Ali!" Aurelia signed, and she grabbed her sister's hand in the pitch-darkness. "You will always be the beautiful one. Okay? This just makes you a true Wintersvilla Woman. That's it. You're still as beautiful as Myriam."

Aurelia flicked the sparker and saw that Aliana was sobbing silently and shaking her head.

"Come on," Aurelia directed, knowing that her sister just needed time for her emotions to pass. "We have to keep going."

Aurelia turned on her heel, and Aliana followed, placing her shaking hand back atop her sister's shoulder. Both girls shivered in the cold, and Aurelia smelled dampness in the air.

Water, she thought excitedly before tempering the emotion. *But still no sunlight. Just hang on, Rooli.*

The cold on her bare skin helped her ignore the pain pulsing through her neck, chest, shoulder, and wrist. Though the girls shivered, Aurelia noted that they couldn't see their breath, so it wasn't really as cold as it might feel.

We just need to acclimate, Aurelia noted, remembering the stories Shira had told about battling in blizzards as a child during the time before the Nomads' taming of the world's climate. *The cold just takes getting used to,* Shira had explained, and now her words served as a vanguard to continue warding off panic.

I'm going to miss you, Shira, Aurelia lamented for only a moment before forcing her mind back into the present.

"There's something up ahead," Aliana warned with a shivering whisper. "You see that?"

Aurelia peered into the darkness, and she was surprised that her sister had noticed it before she had, despite only having one functional eye. In the distance, something glinted from the light of the sparker.

A blade, came Aurelia's first thought, and she instinctively stepped in front of her sister and unsheathed her sword with her left hand, which was technically her off-hand, though Shira had trained both girls to be functionally ambidextrous. Pleasantly familiar with the sound of an unsheathed blade, Aliana unclipped her leather sheath and unsheathed her blade as well. However, Aurelia could tell from her sister's shivering and low moaning that there was nothing pleasant about this moment, no matter how fulfilling Aliana found battle.

"Come out, fatherfucker! Maybe we'll let you live!" Aliana shouted into the darkness as she stepped beside her sister, and Aurelia nodded in approval. *We are Wintersvilla Women,* Aurelia thought with immense pride, not caring at all about their size or musculature. *Size is meaningless,* Myriam had said many times during training. *All that matters is intelligence, viciousness, and fearlessness.*

Aurelia gripped her sword tighter and waited in the darkness, ready to be as vicious as a Mutant as she listened carefully for even the most subtle movement. Multiple tense seconds passed, but nothing could be heard. Slowly and silently, Aurelia sheathed her blade, then felt for her sister's open palm.

"Get ready," she signed. "I'm going to use the sparker, and when I do, you need to be ready to defend us."

"I'm ready," Aliana signed back.

Aurelia nodded then flicked the sparker, illuminating whatever horror lurked in the dense, damp darkness. Were they capable of humor in the moment, both girls would have laughed at what had scared them into such careful battle readiness. A dozen or so steps ahead, a steel beam glinted in the light of the sparks, revealing that it spanned over a chasm of unfathomable depths.

It's metal, but it's not a blade, Aurelia concluded as she felt the adrenaline coursing through her blood degrade into exhaustion.

Aliana must have discerned it as well, for she sheathed her blade and asked, "Didn't Rooli say something about this? A rail line?"

Aurelia nodded and signed worryingly into her sister's palms, "Yes, and she said after the rail, the traps begin."

"You're saying we're still basically at the entrance to this place?" Aliana asked incredulously. "We're in bad shape, Aurelia. Do you...do you think we can make it? Really?"

"Enough!" Aurelia ordered, and her sister squeezed her hand, then brought it to her blood-slick lips and kissed it.

"You're right, Aurelia. You're right. Let's keep going. Let's just keep going," Aliana said with forced resolve before spitting a mouthful of blood onto the ground.

This is the first time we've ever been alone, Aurelia realized suddenly. *But Shira and Rooli and Myriam and all the others prepared us for this. Every moment of training and suffering was meant for right now,* Aurelia told herself, seeing the past as a series of rivers flowing to the singular, torrid ocean of the present.

Focus! came Rooli's voice inside her mind, prompting Aurelia to stride forward. She flicked the sparker and walked carefully toward the steel beam with her sister in tow.

Flickering shadows blanketed the surprisingly clean and shiny metal as Aurelia and Aliana watched the sparks fall into the chasm on either side of the beam, dying from the cold after falling at least thirty feet.

"How far do you think that drop is?" Aliana asked as she wiped away blood from her lips.

"Far," Aurelia answered simply, channeling Rooli's stoicism.

Where the hell is the railcar that Rooli mentioned? Aurelia wondered nervously as she peered across the beam's length extending seemingly forever into perfect darkness. *On the other end of the beam, maybe?* Aurelia considered with a distant, forlorn apprehension, for she knew that this was their only way forward, with or without a car to safely travel down the beam.

"We have to crawl across that beam, Aliana," Aurelia signed into her sister's palms. She tried to hide the apprehension in the movement of her fingers, but she knew her sister would be able to sense it.

"No!" Aliana exclaimed. "Aurelia, no! There has to be another way."

"There isn't," Aurelia stated simply. Without giving her sister time to protest, she stepped carefully toward the beam and breathed deeply, consciously willing her nerves into a state of calm.

"Aurelia, you only have one fucking hand," Aliana cried through a whisper. "And we're both covered in blood. We'll slip and fall. We'll fall a mile into the Earth and splatter into—"

Aurelia placed her hand across her sister's mouth, silencing her, but Aliana was quick to remove it.

"Aurelia, please, I don't have a good feeling about this. We have to find another way."

"Then show me the other way," Aurelia offered, certain that this was their only path forward.

Aliana groaned and pulled her hands through her hair, coating her dirty dreadlocks with slick blood.

"Calm down," Aurelia signed in the flashes of sparks.

"Shut up!" Aliana spat. "I'm wiping my hands so I don't slip and fall into fucking oblivion, okay? Is that okay with you?"

Aurelia nodded at her sister and couldn't help smiling to herself. *There she is. There's the wildness and fierceness of a Wintersvilla Warrior.*

Aurelia didn't care that Aliana was taking her fear out on her. If that's what it took to survive, then so be it.

"I need my one hand to crawl," Aurelia stated. "Either you use both hands and we do this in the dark, or you're going to have to crawl with one hand too and also provide light for us with the sparker."

"Fuck!" Aliana answered.

Aurelia nodded. "It's up to you, Aliana. If you need both hands, that's okay. We don't need to see. We just need to feel the beam."

"Fuck!" Aliana said again, wiping her hands through her dreads and pulling at them so hard that Aurelia thought they might actually rip out of her head.

"Use both your hands, Aliana. It's okay," Aurelia offered with forced gentleness. "We'll be fine. I'll go first, okay? Just place one hand in front of the other. One leg in front of the other. Just imagine that the darkness is—"

"I know!" Aliana shouted, her voice echoing across the length of the beam for what might be miles. "I know," Aliana said again with tears in her eyes.

Aurelia pulled her into a close hug and placed her hand around her own. "Don't cry," Aurelia told her. "It's only going to spread the blood."

Aliana couldn't help chuckling and squeezed her sister at the base of her waist to avoid inflicting pain on her upper body. "I know you're scared too, Aurelia. You're just better at hiding it. But you know what? You put up an incredibly convincing front, and to be honest, it's working," Aliana chuckled even more, likely slap happy in her insurmountable fear. "Half your body is broken, and you're acting like you're perfectly fine," Aliana marveled. "I love you, Aurelia, and I hate you so much too. Let's fucking go and get this over with."

"I want you to talk to me while we do this, and I'm going to answer by tapping my finger on the beam. Okay?"

"Okay," Aliana whispered, and then forced herself to let go of

Aurelia. In turn, Aurelia forced herself to face the beam, bend down, pocket the sparker, then place her left hand on the metal. She instinctively pulled away at the surprising cold, then placed her hand back down and embraced the icy chill of the metal.

This is nothing, Aurelia intoned to herself. *By tomorrow, this will just be a memory. It is already a memory, because I am certain we will overcome this. Nothing can touch me. Not fear. Not death. Nothing.*

She slid her left hand forward, then moved one knee forward, then the other. A hand. A knee. A knee. Hand. Knee. Knee. Hand. Knee. Knee.

She stopped and listened for her sister.

"Keep going, Aurelia, just keep going. I'm on the fucking beam," Aliana breathed angrily.

In response, Aurelia tapped on the beam.

Good job, Ali. Just keep going. We can do this! she thought with tangible determination.

Aurelia glanced down for just a moment, but it was enough to shake her balance, for below her the great vortex beckoned her to fall and willingly plunge herself into its churning void depths.

No! Aurelia demanded, lashing her mind into obedience and erasing the hallucination.

Hand. Knee. Knee. Hand. Knee. Knee. Hand. Knee. Knee.

Her entire right side pulsed with agonizing pain, but Aurelia still managed to keep it in the periphery of her awareness, refusing to consider the possibility of internal bleeding.

Focus!

Aurelia tapped on the metal, and Aliana responded. "Yes, I'm still fucking going. Fuck this cave! Fuck you. Fatherfucking fuck everything!" Aliana grunted as she pressed forward a few feet behind Aurelia.

Good, Aurelia thought, and then she placed the entirety of her focus back on the metal beam.

Hand. Knee. Knee. Hand. Knee. Knee. Hand. Knee. Knee.

The metal groaned suddenly, sounding like it might buckle, and Aliana screamed before forcing her nerves back under control.

Aurelia braced herself and breathed carefully, not allowing the fear to touch her. She wanted to tell her sister that it was just bending slightly from their weight after so long without any.

"It's going to break, Aurelia. We're going to fall," Aliana managed through teeth chattering fear. "What do we do, Aurelia? What do we do?"

Things that bend don't break, Aurelia thought, recounting one of Rooli's many lessons. *The same is true for structures. Even the towers of Wintersvilla bent and swayed in the wind, just not enough to notice. They must be able to bend or else they snap,* Aurelia thought, reassuring herself and wishing again that she could do the same for her sister.

Aurelia tapped on the beam, hoping her sister would understand her message that it was safe to continue.

"One tap for yes. Are we okay to keep going?" Aliana asked.

Aurelia tapped once and continued, showing her sister with her own movement that they were perfectly fine—that it was fear twisting their minds and foretelling futures of doom and death when the truth was that the future was not real.

We control the future by controlling the present, Aurelia thought, recalling one of Shira's many lessons of battle. *Remain in the present, and the future is yours.*

Hand. Knee. Knee. Hand. Knee. Knee. Hand. Knee. Knee.

Aliana shrieked suddenly then grunted and sounded as if she were struggling to breathe.

"I'm falling!" Aliana screamed in the oceanic darkness.

Aurelia balanced her core, straddled the beam, and removed the sparker. A single flick was enough to reveal the horrific image of her sister dangling from the beam, desperately clutching it with blood-slick fingers as her hands continuously slipped on the metal.

"Help me!" Aliana screamed in mindless terror, and the image of her sister dangling like a bloody worm over the infinite, unlit ocean depths blazed in Aurelia's mind.

Without fully processing her actions, Aurelia pocketed the sparker, pivoted in the darkness with her one good hand, laid on her stomach, and restraddled the beam facing her sister.

I'm coming, Ali!

Hand. Knee. Knee.

Aurelia nearly slipped in her rush to help Aliana, and she absentmindedly used her right hand to brace herself. Pain unlike anything she had ever experienced geysered like exploded lava through her arm.

Quiet! Aurelia lashed, erasing the pain entirely.

Hand. Knee. Knee. Hand. Knee. Knee.

"Aurelia!" Aliana shrieked with primal animal fear.

Aurelia laid on her stomach and reached out her left hand, but she was too late. She felt the tips of her sister's bloody fingers just as Aliana slipped from the beam and plunged into the fathomless abyss. Aliana screamed in wordless, spastic terror as she fell, her voice rapidly shrinking to nothingness.

It was too much for Aurelia. She was wrong about them surviving this ordeal. She was wrong about their fate and about being meant for something greater.

The world is darkness, and every single person in it is alone, Aurelia gasped as wild terror coursed through her, destroying her years of one-pointed training in a single moment.

Aliana's screaming echoed dreadfully across the endless expanse of nothingness, and Aurelia peered down to see the vortex, like a siren song for her and her alone.

Jump, she heard it say in her mind. Enticing her. Beckoning her. Promising her.

This is what you're meant to do, the vortex told her without words.

I know it's just a hallucination, Aurelia reasoned. *But it's all over anyway. We aren't special. We aren't meant for a greater purpose. That,* Aurelia thought, gazing into the horrifically familiar vortex of churning darkness that had emerged with her into the world, born inside her just as she had been born inside the universe. *That is all we're meant for.*

Aurelia removed the shard of Rooli and held it to her heart.

Thank you for everything, Rooli. I'm sorry we failed, Aurelia thought. She allowed the fear to slip away and turn to sorrow at the same time she allowed herself to slip off the metal beam and plunge into the all-consuming darkness.

The Titans of history—warlords and corporate overlords alike—deserve the title of Titan, for they are indifferent to humanity. They view their own species as a resource—mere cattle to be exploited or culled as they deem necessary. I know this, for I was once part of the herd. My parents were harvested for labor, and when they could give no more labor, they were harvested for meat. All the while, the Titans sipped their wine, each glass worth more than the lives of the workers who pressed the grapes. They raced their horses to death and called it love when they blew each animal's brains out after a single career-destroying injury. They debauched themselves on their yachts maintained by hungry workers who stole sips of their luxury intoxicants and nibbles of their exotic food and afterward felt morally reprehensible as they sulked in the shadows of their hedonistic masters' domain.

Titans bask in the light of heaven knowing full well that it is their heaven that causes the darkness of hell for everyone and everything else. Such simple, feeble, pathetic beings. It has always been indifferent and hedonistic Titans who hold back our species from attaining existential meaning and purpose. All they know and all they can know is consumption and external conquest, for inside they are empty. Soulless. Hollow. They are undeserving of the cosmos, and it is because they know this truth deep down inside that they live as self-indulgent, sybaritic leeches. They are unable to cultivate self-honesty, sacrifice, and righteousness, because these traits require an internal being.

When I suggested to the others that we should choose to die at the age of ninety-nine, well, it was quite a sight. They reacted like wild animals, horror coursing through them like the intoxicants their minds require in order to live with the truth of themselves. Fana, Tomasz, and Gladys were especially horrified, as each of them have been working in secret on their own respective solutions to indefinitely warding off death. All the Titans have is the external world, thus, death is not just death, but oblivion. They cannot imagine living and dying for something outside themselves—for others.

If each Titan could look into a reflection capable of mirroring their internal being, I wonder what they would see. Would they see the nothingness, or would they see nothing at all? Would they even be able to understand the difference?

No matter, the reign of the Titans must come to an end, both in mythology and in reality. It was the Gods of Olympus who destroyed the Titans that came before them, and it is I and Mendel who will destroy the Titans of the real world. Mendel is now a god, and he told me that in three months, he will have completed the specifications for a deathless transfer device. We will use that device to allow a version of me to join him. Together, the three of us will destroy the Titans and cast the world into hellish darkness so that one day it can finally receive the fullness of heaven's light.

From Mendel's Ladder: The Personal Journal of Denis Mendel, Written Circa 2049, Published June 2108 by Leif Mainstone, Federated Agency Publishing

Chapter 6
The Tortured Reflection

T omasz Novak stared at Samuel with an air of flamboyant, self-appointed regality. His confident, thin-lipped smile was like the tight seal of the Foundation's Space Wall, and Samuel wondered if a whole universe might be sealed inside the man's head, for his demeanor and aesthetic was one of otherworldly intricacy and meticulousness. Staring into his eyes, Samuel knew immediately that this was a man who was as titanous in will and intellect as he thought himself to be. His magenta robe was lined in sparkling gold, while ruby and emerald rings coated a few fingers on each hand. A sharpened goatee hung elegantly from Tomasz' chin, and a thin mustache delicately painted his upper lip. His eyes reminded Samuel of Madeira's eyes just before he died—ocean-deep and full of constant wonder and calculation.

I've never met someone whose intellect can be so easily seen directly in their physical features, Samuel gasped at this man who had just dripped piece by squelching piece from the ceiling and onto the identical floor, which was a snake pit of pulsing veins and arteries tangling and constricting each other with each terrible heartbeat of the giant creature Samuel was now imprisoned within. Each pulse from its heart was another moment that Samuel's family faced the very likely possibility of execution.

Realizing he had been hypnotized by the man-shaped thing calling itself Tomasz Novak, Samuel finally regained himself and returned to the pressing matter of figuring out a way to get back to Astrea before it was too late. Then, like fire suddenly set ablaze in darkness, his mind was whipped to another focus as the profundity of the man's name dawned on Samuel. He remembered the countless times Nathan had regaled the family about the old world and its most important historical figures.

Tomasz…Novak, Samuel thought, and each syllable was like dry kindling being added to the blaze of incredulous horror and awe coursing through him. *But…that's not possible. Tomasz Novak was a man, a human, not some human-shaped pile of guts that drips from a ceiling of viscera,* Samuel told himself, reeling maddeningly at the absurdity of his situation. *What the fuck is happening here? What is this giant creature I'm stuck inside of, and who is this human-looking demon born from the bowels of hell?*

"I requested your name," Tomasz said with an unyielding yet controlled command in his voice. "I was courteous enough to offer my own. It would be courteous of you to tell me yours in turn, do you not concur?"

Tomasz offered Samuel another chance to speak as he sniffed at his wineglass and inhaled its aroma with blissful, time-honed satisfaction.

What the hell do I even say? Samuel wondered, his mind racing but unable to respond. *Should I say I'm the Mirror-Man? Or I'm...the Workhorse of Astrea? Or I'm just...Samuel Kaminski? What would any of that mean to this...thing?*

"Do you have a name?" Tomasz inquired, his voice like the pliant yet unceasingly flowing rivers of the Foundation. "Or should I just refer to you as the tortured reflection? For that is what I will have to resort to if you refuse to be civil. However, I admit I would prefer to avoid that course of action, if you do not mind."

Not even a minute in this hell, and I'm already being threatened with torture. From one hell to the next, and from one torture chamber to the next. Like a reflection, Samuel considered grimly as he envisioned what his body must look like with every square inch of it turned into a polished mirror. However, to Samuel's surprise, the creature calling himself Tomasz did sound and appear genuine about wanting to avoid torture. Regardless, Samuel reasoned that everything happening to him wasn't just a coincidence, and he knew he would be a fool to trust anyone outside of the Foundation—outside of his own family.

Undoubtedly Madeira sent me here, directly here, on purpose, Samuel ruminated. *I don't think anything that old man ever did wasn't calculated down to a haunting level of precision. What does this demon really want from me and is he a part of Madeira's plans too?* Samuel wondered as the man returned the glass of wine to his nose. This time, he stuck a finger in the glass and stirred the liquid, but instead of joy, his features soured to disappointment.

"The smell really is exquisitely convincing, either because my sense of smell is lacking or because I crafted the wine's scent with marvelous precision. Both possibilities are equally likely. But the texture is all wrong. Totally and utterly lacking in authenticity. It feels like I am stirring bath water, not a 1959 Château Lafite Rothschild. But the smell, oh the smell," Tomasz marveled, all breath.

He's obsessed with that red liquid, Samuel observed, letting the man talk and reveal more before revealing anything about himself. *These walls are still shackling me in place, and my limbs just won't budge. I'm his prisoner, and I need to be smart. I need to let him speak and reveal something that I can use. I must make him think I have the upper hand somehow, and until I can figure that out, silence is my only real tool.*

Tomasz closed his eyes and sniffed hard at the glass, behaving wildly outside of his original elegant demeanor for just a moment. "Sweet and smokey. Tobacco, black cherry, light notes of cedar. What a wonder of this world. Truly one of the most worthwhile experiences available to the human tongue and mind," Tomasz said, entirely to himself. He lifted the glass to his pursed lips, but just as the liquid made contact, he scowled and spit it onto the floor of thick pulsing veins, like living cords composing every surface of the room. An angry swing of his arms sent the glass flying and shattering against the wall to Samuel's right, spraying the dark red liquid everywhere, including all over Samuel.

What the hell? Samuel thought, for though he could feel that the liquid had splattered all over his face and torso, it did not hinder his vision whatsoever, as if his mirror-eyes could see right through the liquid.

"A repulsively unconvincing simulacrum," Tomasz growled beneath his breath with profound disappointment. "It is like drinking vodka, not one of the finest wines of one of the most divinely complex vintages in the world. It can never be reproduced. Never. I assure you; I've tried countless times over the years, but it just isn't the same. Each vintage is a story full of intricate sensory details and characterization to be courted and loved. Each flavor is a lesson to be learned. Every single grape is represented in this story. Every gust of wind. Every particle of loam," he intoned, his voice sharp but still controlled. "Every moment that a mindless laborer spent crushing the grapes and every molecule of carbon dioxide that each and every yeast exhaled. All of that is captured and bottled in a truly masterful wine. But there isn't even weather anymore, let alone fertile soil to grow grapes. The world is ruined, along with every fine and worthwhile experience it could or will ever offer."

Tomasz exhaled deeply and lifted his gaze to inspect Samuel with his full attention. "Which once more begs the question: why are you here? I saw you break through the clouds, but I was not fast enough to evade you. There is only one place above the clouds—one place you could have come from. But that should not be possible. I have not heard from Mendel in over a decade. So, explain why you are here. Are you…are you from Mendel?" he asked, looking unbecomingly nervous and unsure of himself.

Mendel? Samuel wondered, physically shaking his head in confusion. *He was in communication with Mendel—the Mendel. The creator of Astrea and the present day Earth—both hells. And he thinks I was sent by him?*

"Mendel didn't send you here?" Tomasz asked incredulously in response to Samuel's shaking.

What the fuck does any of this matter? Samuel thought suddenly in a burst of desperation. *I need to get back to Astrea! Lift!*

Samuel flexed and contracted and pushed with all his might, but the wall pulled harder.

"Your musculature is impressive," Tomasz said, bowing at the neck slightly, "even beneath your reflective suit. That much is quite apparent. I remember long ago seeing men like you on television and at galas now and again—bodybuilders, they used to call them. I commend your discipline. However, your might is no match for the musculature of a Giganventus—that is, my own musculature."

I should have just run before Roland sat me down in that torture room, Samuel thought, unable to focus on the obscenely elegant man's words. *I should have knocked him over and fought like hell for my family. But I didn't. I fucking didn't,* Samuel lamented, and in a sudden explosion of self-hatred, he flexed with inhuman fury and felt the wall rupture behind him.

Tomasz audibly gasped, and Samuel lifted his vision to see the man wearing an expression of anger and surprise.

Now's my chance!

Samuel stood and realized that he towered over this much smaller and frailer man, but before he could capitalize on the opportunity to lunge forward and incapacitate Tomasz, the smaller man lifted his arm, then squeezed his fist into a tight ball. In response, the walls ejected stringy ropes of intestines from all around Samuel, grasping him in a dozen different places and forming a spherical web of viscera with Samuel at its center.

Again! Samuel demanded, calling upon the sudden, inhuman strength that he had just experienced, but his body could not or would not obey.

Lift! Samuel urged, but it was no use.

Tomasz' breathing was accelerated, but after a few seconds of Samuel's futile attempts to escape, he brought it carefully back under control. With a flick of his wrist, another partially filled wine glass grew directly out of his hand. He slowly smelled the contents of the glass, took a shallow sip, then said with disdain, "It tastes like a counterfeit 2019 Clos Du Moulin Aux Moines Pommard, but it will have to do. Nothing can ever fully replicate the good ol' days of yore, as they say, but one must make do, nonetheless."

Samuel just watched as Tomasz paced slowly from side to side, inspecting Samuel as if for a secret switch that might reveal his entire life history.

I have to be quicker next time. I have to build up my strength, and when he least expects it, I need to explode forward like a true workhorse and shatter him back into goop, Samuel resolved.

"Even for a rogue, you are quite lacking in manners. That, or you are insolent. Either way, I must assume you wish me ill-intent, for if you were not sent here by my friend Mendel, then you were sent here by my enemy. But that should not be possible. Andre Madeira is dead."

Madeira is his enemy? Samuel gasped, not sure if it was true or just a method to get him to speak.

"Mendel requisitioned the birth of those little girls, and then he disappeared. I have not heard from him ever since that final transmission. And now, just over a decade later, a tortured reflection is shot at projectile speeds directly at me. The holes you inflicted in my body may appear miniscule relative to the whole of each Giganventus, but the speed of your strike was enough to severely damage one of them, and to seriously hurt the one you are currently inside. It would be like chopping off one of your hands. Would you like that, Tortured Reflection?"

Tomasz smiled with his eyes, lifted his hand into the air, and squeezed. The ropes of veiny intestines tightened and twisted around Samuel's right wrist, but it felt like no more than a bit of pressure on his skin.

The walls can hold me, but they can't hurt me, Samuel reasoned. Then, he considered what the man had said about his body and the large creatures he called Giganventus. *Why did he say "my body"? The Giganventus is somehow a part of Tomasz?* Samuel recollected how the man had dropped piece by piece from the ceiling. *Or the other way around? Is he a part of this giant creature?*

Tomasz released his hand and cocked his head. He smiled as if being confronted by a particularly pleasant and seemingly impossible challenge.

"Now isn't that peculiar. That mirror-substance isn't just coating your skin. It is inside of you. It is embedded into the very cytoplasm and phospholipid membrane of each one of your cells. You are, quite literally, a living mirror. Why would Andre send me a living and thus far indestructible mirror?" Tomasz wondered aloud, taking his time with his words.

I'm a living mirror? Samuel gasped, unsure how the man could discern his state of being down to a cellular level. *What does that mean? He also said, "thus far indestructible,"* Samuel considered. *Meaning that he's going to try destroying me. This body has withstood the vacuum of space and plummet to Earth and even this man's initial attempts to hurt me, but who knows what else he has up those sleeves? I can't keep staying silent,* Samuel decided. *If he really is Madeira's enemy, then staying silent is only going to make him think that I really do have bad intentions. I just hope I didn't wait too long already.*

"If Madeira is your enemy, then we are allies," Samuel said, making Tomasz jump before catching himself.

"So, you do speak after all," Tomasz said, his eyes careful slits of calculating awareness.

"Yes," Samuel nodded. "And you can release me from these…guts holding me in place."

"Oh, can I?"

"Yes. I'm not your enemy. Madeira is the one who did this to me. I need to get back up there—back to Astrea."

"So, I should just release you, then?" Tomasz asked with obvious facetiousness.

"I get it. You can't trust me. But I thought the same thing about you. My name is Samuel Kaminski. Okay? I'm just a regular Foundationer. A Middler. I'm nothing special. That's everything about me. I swear it. I don't know why I'm here. I still don't know if I can trust you. I don't even know what you are. You say you're a man, that you're the infamous Tomasz Novak," Samuel said, and Tomasz raised an eyebrow in clear satisfaction that his name was infamous in Astrean and Earth history.

"So that's why I didn't say anything right away. I just...I just watched you drip from the ceiling. I don't know you or what you are, really," Samuel explained with what he believed to be reasonable logic.

"I have already disclosed that information. I am Tomasz Novak. I am everything around you. I am each of the Giganventi, and they are me," Tomasz stated ominously. Then, before Samuel could speak, he added, "But more importantly, exactly how *infamous* am I up there in the equally infamous city in the sky. You said Madeira is your enemy. So, who is more well known, me or him?" Tomasz asked with a slight bristling in his shoulders.

Is fame really that important to him, Samuel wondered, unsure if such a deep and learned man could be swayed by such a fickle desire.

"You, I suppose. I didn't even know that Madeira was who he and you claim him to be—that is, someone of world importance. Like Mendel. Or you. Up until today, the name Madeira was attached to the title Old Man. Like I said, he was the oldest man in Astrea, but he was always just a sweet old timer. He was someone I looked up to, even as a young boy. I trusted him. But he betrayed me. Less than a goddamn hour ago, he betrayed me," Samuel said, and he clenched his fists in anger.

Tomasz peered at Samuel as if deciphering his every movement as a means of testing his truthfulness.

"Andre," Tomasz said in disbelief. "He is alive? I thought you meant that his followers are your enemy, not him specifically. He is...he is alive up there after all this time?"

"Was," Samuel said with a modicum of pleasure. "He injected this mirror stuff into me, and then he opened a hole in the ground, plunging me down to this...disgusting place. That is, into your illustrious domain," Samuel corrected himself, wanting to gain Tomasz' trust. "But he died in the process. The old man shattered into a million pieces. I saw it with my own eyes—if you can still call them eyes."

"He allowed himself to grow old and even die?" Tomasz asked with striking incredulity, and Samuel assumed that he was referencing the immortality reserved for Luxury Quarters citizens.

"He lived in the Foundation. Right across from my family and me. He was the oldest man in all of Astrea. Ninety-nine years old. He never turned himself into an immortal, if that's what you're getting at."

"Ninety-nine years old," Tomasz said, and he furrowed his brow and looked remarkably nervous suddenly. "Ninety-nine years old," Tomasz whispered grimly beneath his breath. He appeared totally lost in thought. Suddenly, he dropped the glass of wine, shattering it across his fine magenta slippers. His mouth fell agape and slid down his chin like melted wax. The rest of his features sank, smearing across his face and quickly transforming his entire head into a sanguine goop that oozed down his neck and chest.

He's not human, Samuel confirmed once more. *He's a goddamn monster. Like Norman. Like the myths the old timers always told about the nightmares that destroyed the surface of the world. The Cleaners. The Changed People. The Hunters and Huntresses. And probably other abominations I can't even remember, because it never mattered. I'm not supposed to be here. I'm supposed to be in Astrea. In the Foundation. Lifting for others. Loving Sandra and Nathan and Margot. Protecting my family.*

Samuel's mind tortured him with images of Earth's Reprieve, the local bar where the Sons and Daughters of the Foundation planned and began the second revolution of Astrea. Albatross' arrogant, skinny face was still seared into Samuel's memory. Samuel painfully recollected how Albatross had refused to even lift a finger to stop Frank from murdering Bill Wendover, the bar's owner, whom they had all known since they were children.

That fucker, Samuel thought. *I want to kill him. And Frank too. And all the rest of them. They're just as much at fault for all this as Madeira. They should pay, if they haven't already.*

"I shouldn't be here!" Samuel shouted at the pile of guts spreading and filtering into the tangles of pulsing arteries making up the ground.

I don't want to trust this man—this creature—and I won't. Not fully. But he might be my only chance of getting back home, no matter if it's hell.

"You hear me?" Samuel screamed. "Get me back to Astrea and I'll do whatever you want. Madeira might be dead, but his plans are still in motion. I'm certain of it. Get me back up there, and I'll do whatever you want."

The room remained silent, save the distant bellowing heartbeat of the Giganventus.

"Hey!" Samuel shouted, and though he was alone, his shackles did not relent in their indomitable grip.

An unknown amount of time passed. Samuel reasoned it was probably no more than a few minutes, but those few minutes were a scramble of desperate thoughts that could do him no good at all. Finally, drops of viscera fell from the ceiling, reforming Tomasz.

"I apologize for my sudden absence," Tomasz stated as his eye sockets hollowed and his piercing eyes took shape. "I could not help losing myself in memories of the past. Retaining this form requires quite a great deal of concentration. I make it appear rudimentary, but it is far from simple. I have spent the last half-century mastering the technique. Such a feat of concentration should itself be lauded in the history books. What do your histories say about me—beyond the obvious creation of the Nomads?"

He really is obsessed with himself, Samuel thought with disgust, but he held his tongue.

"Nomads," Samuel repeated. "That's what my parents called the Changed People, right? People made of plants and fungus and other stuff, right?"

Tomasz nodded, and Samuel finally fully put together that Norman was one of them. One of the Changed People, a Nomad, had been living alongside him his entire life.

"To be honest, if I remember correctly," Samuel began, unable to fully shake the thought that he had been neighbors his entire life with such a dangerous creature. "I believe the history lessons on the tablets teach that Mendel created the Nomads. Mendel is responsible for all changes on Earth. At least, that's what the history lessons say."

Tomasz scoffed indignantly, "What a cask of piss. Mendel? All he did was come up with the idea. So what? Anyone can conjure a vision from the ether. Who designed the vision? Who brought it to life?" Tomasz spat in a sudden burst of anger.

Samuel shook his head, unsure how to pacify Tomasz.

He claimed Mendel is his friend. I thought that response would be a good one. I should have just stroked his ego and told him the history books call him a god.

"Me, that is who," Tomasz angrily answered his own question. "I labored. I discovered. I implemented. My work is divine, do you understand? The Cleaners were my creation. The Nomads were my creation. The Hunters and Huntresses—all my creation. Sure, Ruben pitched in here and there," Tomasz admitted with a dismissing wave.

89

"But Mendel had virtually nothing to do with it. And Andre nothing at all. Andre isn't who he claims to be. He's just a leech and a rat from the sewers who tricked his way into a kingdom of dragons."

If it's true that he turned the world to hell, then why is he so goddamn proud of it? Samuel simmered within.

"You…you're the one responsible for turning the world and everything to hell then, is that right?" Samuel asked, anger bubbling in his voice.

Tomasz shrugged indifferently. "I suppose so. But just as you were betrayed by Andre Madeira, I was as well. It is what he does best—the clever little sewer rat. We never should have allowed him into our enclave."

Enclave? Samuel wondered, but Tomasz went on.

"My creations were supposed to bring balance to the planet, not disorder. Andre exploited the expertise of each family's greatest minds, including myself, for his own devisings. I built the tools, but he is the one who utilized those tools to permanently and irreparably disfigure the Earth. To what ends, I cannot and do not want to fathom. Although Gladys believes to have deciphered Andre's ultimate plans, I believe it is more likely she is blinded by her own arrogance and delusions of grandeur. She was always full of herself—to put it simply. The point is that Andre tricked all of us. I am selfless enough to concede that fact. I tried mitigating the damage by creating the Homo Ferrum, or Biofreaks as most call them, but I concede that endeavor worked almost too well. Had I made them any more intelligent, they would have posed too great a danger, supplanting the Hunters and Huntresses they were bred to extinguish. But as they are, they are too stupid to be dangerous."

Tomasz waved away his own thoughts.

"Listen to me, Samuel Kaminski. As long as I knew him, Andre Madeira had no morals or ethics. He never had a code or set of principles to live by. He pretended to, and that is his own personal area of expertise: deception and deceit. Never once has he dirtied his own cuffs. He leaves the actual work to those with legitimate intellect and passion for life. And yet," Tomasz said, his eyes suddenly downcast in obvious raw fear. "And yet he is cunning beyond reason. He plans and manipulates so far ahead that it frankly does not seem possible to call him human. He is fucking Dolos incarnate, though I am loathe to refer to him as an actual god. He is a rat. A cunning rat, but a rat nonetheless."

*Andre Madeira…*Samuel considered incredulously. *Old Man Madeira? Is it really possible he's talking about the same person I spent my whole life with?*

"I am willing to concede that the rat is cunning beyond human measure, but that also leads us to two and only two possibilities: either you are working for Andre directly and have been carefully lying to me this entire time, or you are unwittingly working for Andre and doing his bidding without conscious awareness. Either way, you are his pawn," Tomasz concluded ominously and regrettably.

"I don't care about all that!" Samuel shouted, throwing away composure with the realization that Tomasz would not be swayed to help him. "I have a family. Children. A little boy and a little girl. Nathan and—" Samuel pleaded, stopping suddenly with an audible gasp to hold back his tears.

"Samuel Kaminski, as I said—"

"Shut up!" Samuel lashed, gritting his mirror-metal teeth together with a high-pitched scraping. "I don't fucking care about Madeira or you or anyone else. I don't fucking care what you are or who you really are or who you think I fucking am. I am a man with a fucking family, and you will take me back to them, or I will be the one to do the torturing!" Samuel screamed wildly, suddenly filled with self-hatred for taking so long to feel this level of unceasing violence and animosity coursing through him. He screamed open-mouthed and convulsed in anger, tearing the intestines from the walls with a splatter of blood.

Kill! Samuel thought, and as he spilled forward, he envisioned the regal yet miniscule man before him being torn limb from limb by his bulwark of musculature that he now viewed as a weapon rather than a means of helping others. With the force of a whole legion of Queensguards, Samuel slammed into Tomasz' surprisingly solid torso, splattering him into a haze of sticky viscera. Unable to stop his own momentum, Samuel slammed against the wall of innards, penetrating at least ten feet into squelching darkness.

A second passed, and the darkness expanded into an identical room of pulsing arteries just like the last. Intestines shot from numerous places in the undulating walls, floor, and ceiling, shackling Samuel in a web of intestinal ropes once again.

Fuck! Samuel seethed at his powerlessness despite all his newfound power. *Lift!* his mind demanded, and he tried over and over to escape the shackles, willing to repeat the exercise in futility a thousand times over in a desperate attempt to do something, anything, rather than simply give up. As he struggled against his shackles, he watched in horror as they rapidly grew metal scales and spikes, becoming multiple orders of magnitude stronger in just seconds.

He's only using a fraction of his power, Samuel realized as Tomasz reformed, this time growing up from the floor rather than dripping down from the ceiling.

"You want to get back to Astrea, is that right?" Tomasz asked cordially as if Samuel had not just attempted to destroy him.

"Obviously!" Samuel shouted as he relentlessly struggled and flexed and contracted his weaponry.

"Then that is exactly what I will ensure does not come to fruition," Tomasz explained as his subtle features reshaped themselves. "For if that is your goal, then it is also Andre's goal. I cannot fathom his reasoning, but he clearly sent you here to get me to agree to your demands. You are an open threat, and a demand to submit to his seemingly inescapable will. But I refuse to be controlled or fooled ever again."

"You're right, Madeira sent me down here for a reason. I don't know why that is, but I guarantee the last thing he wants is for me to come back and kill his precious queen with these metal hands."

"His queen?" Tomasz said with a stupefied expression.

"Take me back up there!" Samuel demanded, ignoring Tomasz' inquiry.

"Elaborate on what you said. Who is Andre's queen?" Tomasz demanded.

"Fuck you!" Samuel snapped.

Tomasz shook his head and smiled pleasantly. "Samuel Kaminski, if it is true you are just an unwitting pawn and that all this happened to you suddenly an hour ago, then…have you seen yourself? I mean, have you really seen yourself?"

Samuel shook his head in confusion, unsure what Tomasz' new angle could be.

"What are you talking about? I'm a mirror inside and out. A fucking mirror."

"Yes," Tomasz nodded solemnly. "But do you really understand the implications? Have you had even a moment to truly peer into yourself?"

"What the fuck are you talking about?" Samuel demanded impatiently as he continued trying to break free of the metal intestines.

Tomasz waved his hand, releasing Samuel's entire left arm. Without missing a beat, Samuel swung his arm wildly against the spiky intestines. Although they chipped slightly, they did not break.

"The mirror is unharmed. You chipped the metal I grew over those capillaries I'm using to shackle you, but your arm isn't even scratched. Look at your hand, Samuel Kaminski."

Unable to assuage his own curiosity regarding his new form, Samuel lifted his hand up to his eyes.

No! Samuel gasped at what he had glanced and pulled his hand away from his field of vision. The spikes of multiple capillaries, as Tomasz called them, elongated and wrapped around Samuel's wrist. He fought their pull, but it was like struggling against the Earth's gravity in free fall. The growths forced Samuel's hand back into view, and more growths anchored his neck so that he had no choice but to look directly at his own hand. His mind fluttered in reeling horror as he peered into a reflection of a reflection repeated infinitely inside and outside himself. The infinite recursion was maddening, and with every twitch of his muscles, infinity undulated and shrieked echoes of insanity through him, until finally Tomasz moved his hand back out of view.

Fuck! Samuel thought in horror, processing that he really was a living mirror. *What does that mean?*

"You see?" Tomasz asked with a tone of foreboding and nervousness. "Yes, you see. But there is so much you cannot see that I can," Tomasz said with a furrow of apprehension. "I said before that the very cytoplasm of your cells is now perfectly reflective, but behind that reflection lie your nucleotides and other genetic material. I see now that even your central genome is composed of this mirror-substance you claim that Andre injected into you. I do not think that is possible, Samuel Kaminski. I think it is far more likely you were built this way, which means that your story about having a family was a fabrication to manipulate me."

"No!" Samuel lashed. "I'm not lying. I'm not manipulating you. I don't give a fuck about you."

Samuel winced at a sudden memory of Nathan playing tag with his friends while Margot sat transfixed in front of her telescreen as she read an old world story beneath the soothing light of a glowglobe.

Lift! Samuel thought, and he contracted painfully but futilely with an audible groan.

"What does a reflection reflect?" Tomasz said with both awe and horror in his voice.

Lift!

"Shut up!" Samuel growled.

Lift!

"A surprisingly astute answer, Samuel Kaminski," Tomasz said pleasantly in response to Samuel's desperate exasperation. "Many wise individuals believe that the answer to that koan is nothingness, though I have always been unsatisfied with that conclusion."

Lift! Samuel thought, ignoring Tomasz' inane and pointless ramblings.

"Incredibly, I now have the opportunity to answer that question at a material level, for I will probe your cells and the very atoms of your cells. I will understand what a reflection itself is composed of."

Lift! Samuel pleaded with wild abandon, and he saw Margot and Nathan standing side by side beneath the recycler's crushing arm, their palms against the transparent walls, their eyes full of tears, pleading with him, begging their useless pathetic father to save them.

"Lift, you fucking worker!" Samuel screamed like a dying animal being stuffed down the mouth of a predator. The metal of a few capillaries cracked, and another broke from the wall completely.

Lift, you worthless fucking workhorse! Samuel raged, hateful and ashamed of his musculature, for it was largely the result of laboring for Madeira and Norman rather than spending more time with his family. More metal capillaries cracked and another one broke from its wall with a spray of blood.

Tomasz pursed his lips angrily and grunted as he lifted both his hands and squeezed them into shaking fists. The remaining tendrils of metal doubled in size, then redoubled again, thickening into ropes of metal larger than Samuel's gargantuan arms.

"Andre always treated me as if I were some inferior specimen. What a cask of piss!" Tomasz spat. "I will best Andre. He might have made you, but I will decipher you. I will learn what you really are, and then I will destroy you, like an antidote to poison. I am Tomasz Novak, the greatest biologist and scientist who has ever or will ever live!"

"Maybe this is exactly what he wants," Samuel said through heavy, exhausted breathing. The shackles were now too strong to even crack, but he reasoned that at least he was still impenetrable to damage.

"Or maybe you are just saying that to get me to release you because that is what he wants," Tomasz offered suspiciously, narrowing his gaze. "Either way, the time is now. I created the girls, just like Mendel told me to, and since then I have just been soaring over the Pacific, enjoying the view, so to speak. I thought Andre was dead. And I assumed Mendel had gone offline. Even Gladys confirmed a few years ago that Astrea shows no signs of life. Yet here you are, Tortured Reflection. Andre has sent some type of weapon to my doorstep, and I will not shy away and hide anymore. It is time for Tomasz Novak to once again enter the fray."

Suddenly, Tomasz cocked his head curiously, then turned to his right. He waved his hand, and the wall opened, revealing a gathering of wildly diverse figures. Some were bulbous and some were spindly. Some were humanoid and others looked like pools of chunky soup. Some of them slunk and others loped.

Changed People, Samuel gasped in otherworldly awe and horror at the wild variations in their color, shape, and movement. *Nomads,* he corrected himself, adopting the term both Madeira and Tomasz had used.

"What is it?" Tomasz asked impatiently. "I have work to do."

All of a sudden, the Nomads all turned in unison, and the ones with eyes or eye-like structures peered directly at Samuel.

What the fuck, Samuel thought in shock at their sudden singular movement. The Nomads continued staring intently at Samuel, forcing Samuel to dart his eyes back and forth between Tomasz and the horrifically absurd group of gawking Nomads.

Were those really humans at one point? Samuel wondered, remembering the dreadful tales his parents had seldom revealed about how people had chosen to become these inhuman monstrosities rather than attempt to survive the destruction of Earth's cataclysmic weather or the ruthless lethality of Hunters or any other number of nightmarish perils.

Staring directly at Samuel the entire time, a humanoid Nomad at the front of the small group strolled forward and whispered something into Tomasz' ear. Tomasz listened intently, then nodded and said, "Do what you can to mitigate the damage. Stifle the spread as quickly as possible. If we must sacrifice some Giganventi, then so be it."

The Nomad nodded, then turned and exited the room, never once removing his eyes from Samuel.

They're so creepy, Samuel thought, and he was surprised to see the Nomad stop at the wall's threshold and continue staring at Samuel alongside the other Nomads.

"What the hell are you doing?" Tomasz lashed.

As if they had actually been physically whipped, the Nomads abruptly turned and exited down a narrow hallway of pulsing arteries.

Why were they staring at me? Samuel considered, and then he finally remembered what Madeira had said just before the plunge. *He said that the Mirror-Man would command the Nomads, didn't he?* Samuel thought, considering the possibility and the power of the implications. *Does that mean those creatures will listen to my command?* Samuel thought with a sudden glimmer that all hope might not yet be lost.

Tomasz waved his hand and reformed the wall, which scabbed as it reconnected.

"Now, let us begin," Tomasz said with a slight smile and a preparatory sigh, as if he were just sitting down to resume a complex puzzle over some afternoon tea. The metal capillaries tightened, and Samuel gasped at a sudden dull pinch where they connected. It was the first suggestion of pain he had felt since being injected with the mirror-substance.

Am I not invincible after all? Samuel considered with sudden alarm.

"It is time to study you and discover what you really are, Tortured Reflection," Tomasz announced, and as he squeezed his fists, the dull pinching in Samuel's wrists morphed into searing pain.

The base state of nature is cruelty. This sordid design at the very foundations of reality is not born of malice, but necessity and logic. This may seem paradoxical, that cruelty can be absent of malice, but nature is proof positive of this fact.

When it comes to human strategies for survival, some evolutionary biologists will contend that empathy and morality pose a greater chance of survival relative to cruelty. And in some cases, they are right. But to these individuals I say: your shortsightedness is a symptom of your own species-specific thinking. Empathy and morality are tools among many that all beings use for survival, but they are not the base state of nature. In truth, we all know this deep down, for evolution is predicated on death. Beings are naturally selected to die, and those who live go on to replicate.

When a creature is born physically weak and ill-fit for its environment, what happens? It is inflicted with suffering. And then it is culled by the environment—handicapped and subsequently destroyed by nature. What could possibly be more cruel than such a system?

The base state of nature is cruelty. So, is it any wonder that the base state of humanity is also cruelty? Sure, there are those who transcend their ape-emotions and attain truly unyielding empathy and selflessness, but these individuals are few and far between. They are accidents, and they are almost always killed by the cruel world, either by nature or by their fellow man. It's all the same.

It is the cruelty of nature that, given enough time, transforms all life into monsters formidable enough to contend with Titans—other gods even. For this reason, it must be through cruelty that we ascend beyond nature, and it is cruelty itself that we must wield as a weapon in the Great Beyond.

From Mendel's Ladder: The Personal Journal of Denis Mendel, Recorded Circa 2065, Published June 2108 by Leif Mainstone, Federated Agency Publishing

Chapter 7
Agents of Pain

"**W**ake up, human," Volya purred sinisterly as she stood over the red-headed Wintersvilla Woman who was stirring and groaning painfully.

"Volya, don't," Thompson growled, feeling like his body had been exploded into a million pieces and scabbed back together again.

"Or what?" Volya spat, baring her teeth in uncontrolled anger suddenly. "What the fuck will you do, dog? Grow a dick and fuck me?"

The mercurial suddenness of Volya's viciousness sickened Thompson, for this vile creature was visually identical to Anna, yet she could not be further from Anna's otherworldly beauty and warmth.

"How dare you throw me off the hunt, dog!" Volya lashed, and in a flash she penetrated Thompson's mind with the agonizing torture of a thousand Hunter childhoods all at once. Pleading hopelessness and unyielding pain battered his senses and he screamed with wordless, excruciating suffering.

In another terrible flash he was pulled out of the nightmare. Volya stood over Thompson, her eyes rabid with apoplectic hatred for this defunct Hunter who refused his fate and her command.

"You have no fucking idea what we're up against, you stupid mut. I roved your mind and I watched your battles and I know that our battle against the women and that empty-headed Agency-fuck was the closest to death you've ever come," Volya said, letting the torture of his childhood lick threateningly at the horizons of his subconscious. "You've been asleep a long time in your cave, and I've been asleep a long time up there in the Thymus of Astrea. The world has changed, Thompson. I killed Gambe, but there are more Prodigal Sons," Volya said, poorly hiding her nervousness. "And the humans," she said, quickly moving away from the topic of the Agency, "they've changed too. The Wintersvilla girl from your memory—she's a relic of an ancient world. Her people are now multiple orders of magnitude stronger. Look at her," Volya said, pointing to the Wintersvilla Woman who was now breathing rapidly and mumbling frantically under her breath.

What is she dreaming of? Thompson wondered, feeling terrible that she was going to wake only to suffer Volya's torture.

"Her body is full of those metal holes connected to a metal skeletal system," Volya continued. "And it all connects to her brain, giving her the ability to wear those open metal frames they call exoskeletons," Volya said in seeming awe at the evolution of human power. "Are they even really human anymore?" Volya wondered more to herself than Thompson.

A perfect opportunity to break through her programming, Thompson thought at hearing Volya's question.

"Exactly, Volya. Humanity is changed," Thompson offered gently, refusing to give in to her wickedness. "Humanity is over. Those little girls weren't human. And that metal man clearly wasn't either. And these Wintersvilla Women—they're barely human, like you said. The Eternal Hunt is over, Volya. Can't you see that with all that terrible intelligence of yours?"

"No!" Volya shouted without hesitation. "They're still human. They're all still human. They're derivatives of humanity—a tangent in their lineage, but the same lineage nonetheless."

"By that logic, you're also a tangent of humanity, Volya. You even look identical to them," Thompson offered painfully as images of Anna's smiling lips filled his mind.

"That's only to blend in and kill them with greater ease!" Volya retorted.

"I'm just following your logic," Thompson said, shaking his head but not giving into the fear of the torture she still held at the peripheries of his awareness like fuel-laden fire vines ready to combust. "Those girls— if you're going to consider them human, then so are you. They were made by a human, and so were you."

"I was made by God!" Volya laughed confidently.

God's aren't real, little Hunter, Anna said in Thompson's mind.

"I'm real," Volya said in response to Thompson's thoughts, "which proves monsters are real. We've already been over this, dog. If monsters are real, then gods are real. The simple truth is that you and I were made by God. By Mendel."

"I pity you," Thompson said with genuine sadness for this hollow creature standing before him. "I can see the chains you hold me with, but you can't see yours, Volya. You can't see that your god is a slave master, and you are his slave."

Volya stared death at Thompson, but rather than plunging him back into the maddening suffering of his childhood, she cracked a smile and allowed herself a shallow huff of laughter.

"You think I don't know that?"

Does she really? Thompson wondered.

"Yes, I know that I am a slave. We are all slaves. But all that matters is that my master is God. You were a slave even before me, Thompson. To that bitch human Anna. That's what you can't see. You call it love. But that's just the inability of a slave to see his chains. I see my chains, Thompson, and I am grateful for them. I relish in them. I live for them. It is you who cannot see your chains. It is you, dog, who must learn his place in this world. That woman from Astrea twisted your mind, but pain will return it to its former state. Of that I am certain. It will just take time. The problem is, we don't have time. So, we're going to have to cram a whole lot of torture into the next few days."

"Why?" Thompson asked, unafraid of her threats, for he knew that no amount of torture could break him anymore than he was already broken. "Is it the Agency and its Prodigal Sons you're so afraid of?"

"I'm not afraid!" Volya said, and she glanced at the Wintersvilla Woman as if impatient to see her scream in agony. "But I can't properly battle against the Prodigal Sons and what I'm guessing is a whole society of these women—not without a perfectly loyal weapon. And that's certainly not you, with all your moping and acting like you're some kind of saint to humanity—here to save the humans from my wrath. Please!" Volya spat. "You're a fucking Hunter! You're the fucking Butcher! Why can't you act like it?" Volya screamed in exasperation. "Just look at what we're up against!" she growled, and in the next moment Thompson was plunged into a streaming haze of memories from dozens of other Hunters and Huntresses all at once.

In a fraction of a second, countless hours of battle data from dozens of different battles across numerous decades flooded Thompson's mind, filling each of his sensory organs with a bounty of savagery. Finally, his mind settled on a single figure: a tiny five-year Hunter, teeth like scimitars and eyes full of hate and anguish, leapt into a shimmering haze of swamp-humid air and beheaded a lone teenage girl full of metal implants; hurricane winds battered the same Hunter's body, occluding his vision and smell so that he could not see the small brigade of little girls full of crude metal who would avenge their sister with the little Hunter's head on a spike; desert hot wind threatened to desiccate an eleven-year Hunter's skinsuit, but his Huntress forced him forward, and in a flash he tore the same group of battle-hardened girls to lifeless pieces; finally, alongside eight other Hunter and Huntress pairs, the eleven-year Hunter and his Huntress waged an earth-shaking battle against two strange beings. One of them looked like a large hulking box composed of varying layers of some unyielding pearl white metal. The other being, white and featureless as the first, appeared humanoid and biological in nature, but it was no more than a foot high and was capable of turning into a pool of what appeared to be its own blood and guts. The two strange beings fought together as if they were a single body, the hulking metal box sucking up the small being each time it melted into a blood-pile, then shooting pieces of it at the platoon of Hunters. As the Hunters closed in on the metal box, it unexpectedly morphed into a flickering array of wild geometries, expertly evading dozens of simultaneous supersonic attacks and retaliating with growths of metal that lanced and parried and swiped at the Hunters, matching their speed. Incredibly, the projected blood and guts were capable of solidifying and regrowing back into even tinier versions of the original humanoid, or they could coagulate together to become larger. The fight went on for multiple hours, but it finally ended with the eleven-year Hunter's Huntress locating the metal-being's core by utilizing vibrational frequencies. The Huntress directed her Hunter to attack the core, resulting in a radioactive explosion that vaporized all the Hunters and both strange beings.

That Hunter was just a tool to her. She didn't even care that he got vaporized, Thompson gasped as Volya returned his mind to the present.

"That's not the fucking point!" Volya said with frustration. "The point is that there are more Prodigal Sons, and there aren't more of us. It took a whole group of Hunters to fight those Prodigal Sons, and they still only beat them by sacrificing themselves. You understand, Thompson? There's more of them out there, but we're the last Pair," Volya admitted, and she suddenly looked as though she hadn't meant to let slip that last piece of information.

The last Pair, Thompson repeated. *Then that means...I'm the last Hunter, and she's the last Huntress?*

"In the area," Volya added a bit too urgently. "The last in the area."

I'm the last Hunter, Thompson repeated, knowing that Volya had been hiding this information for a reason, and that reason could only be as a control mechanism over his mind. *She didn't tell me earlier because she wants me to think I'm expendable.*

"Shira..." the Wintersvilla Woman groaned desperately in her nightmare-filled sleep, interrupting Thompson's thoughts.

Just stay asleep. Stay away from this world of monsters for as long as you can, Thompson thought.

"That's right," Volya nodded. "This is a world of monsters, and the only way we're going to be able to hunt monsters is to be the worst monsters around. I refuse to be prey, not when my fate is to be a predator. I'm sure the Thymus can make more Hunters for me, you understand, dog? You're not the last mut in the world. There's no way."

It never ends with her. Her hunger and wickedness are voracious, Thompson considered with dread.

"God will help you. Like last time," Thompson stated facetiously, but then he envisioned the golden beam Volya had called down from space. As he recollected the event, he admitted to himself that maybe his facetious words were true.

Anna always talked about being chained to fate. It's why...it's why she left, after all, Thompson lamented.

"Maybe you're right that Mendel will help me again if a Prodigal Son crosses our path," Volya stated, clearly unsure as well. "But I work on behalf of God, not the other way around. I don't have faith—like the pathetic humans. I *know* my God is real, and I expect nothing from him. I am his, not the other way around. Regardless, I can't explain how it's possible that the beam weapon happened to be orbiting right above us and that it contained the exact store of particles needed to destroy Gambe. Can you explain that, Thompson? Or are you too afraid to admit that Mendel is real? That Mendel is God. My God. And your God."

God...fate, Thompson thought, repeating the words with the same bitterness that Anna always held for such simple yet terrifying words. *But Volya is right,* Thompson thought with awful realization. *How can all that be explained? How is it possible that the weapon was above us at the precise second Volya needed it? It had to be planned. And if all that was planned, doesn't that imply a god-like prescience?*

"That's right," Volya said, her lips upturning into her typical sinister smile once more. "The Eternal Hunt must continue, for it was commanded by God himself," she concluded with visible elation.

"You have sky beams now. You don't need me," Thompson said, appealing to Volya's grand sense of self and purpose.

"You're right, Thompson. I don't need you. But you're still mine. Mine, mut. And mine alone."

A terrible shiver ran the length of Thompson's spine as he heard Anna's voice speaking with Volya's vindictive violence. *That's not Anna,* Thompson reminded himself forlornly. *This is a creature so wild and violent that she doesn't even value her own possessions. My body,* Thompson marveled in wide-eyed amazement that so much pain still lingered. *That beam must have nearly destroyed my skinsuit. That's the closest I've ever come to death…to escape.*

"The suit won't let you kill yourself," Volya laughed at Thompson's want for death.

"I know," Thompson said with terrible certainty.

I know that too well.

"And you're wrong," Volya said. "I calculated that matter-antimatter reaction down to the fucking atom. I knew exactly how far the annihilation-column would extend, and I knew that your skinsuit would survive the blast. I told you: you're mine. Now and forever. Sounds a lot like love, doesn't it?" Volya finished with torturous condescension.

Thompson went wide-eyed at Volya's cunning.

She calculated all of that in the heat of battle? Thompson considered in horror. *She knew the whole time that I would survive. And she probably knew that the human woman would survive too. She probably timed all of this just so she could have a human to torture as she basked in victory. She's a fucking monster. She has to be. So then…then that means…* Thompson hesitated, struggling to accept something that went directly against Anna's lessons.

"Say it," Volya ordered. "I'm a fucking monster, so that means gods are real. That means fate is real. That means your bitch girlfriend leaving you was part of God's plan. That means all your pain and suffering is part of God's plan. That means your enslavement to my will is part of

God's plan."

"No!" Thompson growled, refusing to accept her words. "Gods aren't real."

Volya laughed obnoxiously. "Monsters are real, but gods aren't, is that it?"

Thompson stared loathingly into her eyes, but all he could see was Anna.

I can't give up on her, Thompson knew, and he clenched his fists at the impossibility of finding a way to save even Volya from the torment that she unknowingly suffered. *She thinks gods are real—just like Anna did deep down inside. But gods aren't real. It's just an idea people use to enslave others. Volya just doesn't know it—that if gods and monsters are real, then her god is really the worst monster of all, for no true god would have any use for a slave,* Thompson thought, recounting Anna's lessons.

Volya watched Thompson's thoughts, but she chose not to respond. Instead, she walked impatiently to the Wintersvilla Woman and cocked her head in consideration, as if contemplating the sequence of torture she would use.

Anna, Thompson nearly sobbed. *If it weren't for you, the wickedness of a Huntress is all I would have known. I would have never encountered beauty or pleasure or happiness. I could have never imagined love. But you gave me all of that, Anna. And then...*Thompson gasped, his breath stolen by anguish. *And then you took it all away and left me here alone.*

Volya kicked the woman in the ribs, and though she winced, it appeared to only be a subconscious reaction, for she fell right back into her rapid breathing and groaning in her sleep.

"Fuck!" Volya growled. "What if her brain is fried and the skinsuit can't repair that? She might be stuck asleep like this for who knows how long!"

Is she seriously angry just because she can't torture the woman? Thompson gasped at the limitless scale of Volya's heinous predilections. *Anna, I'm grateful for what you gave me: proof that love exists—that it is real—even if only ephemerally. All the previous Hunters on Earth, every single one—none of them knew this. All they ever knew was a vile, evil voice controlling them and forcing them to murder and maim and mangle, and they died thinking that there was nothing more to life.*

Thompson recollected the battle between the Hunters, Huntresses, and the Prodigal Sons, and he remembered how the little Hunter had been filled with an unquenchable thirst for murder, even finding pleasure and fulfillment in it. But Thompson knew it wasn't real. That was just the Huntress feeding those ideas into the little Hunter's mind. Deep down, the little Hunter was broken by fear and hopelessness. He was a hollow shell filled in by the Huntress' odious whims.

How terrible. How utterly heartbreaking, Thompson thought. *He was just a kid. A child. And he died hollow and horrified. He died as a vessel for terror. He was just a kid!*

"Who gives a shit?" Volya said, giving up on the woman and turning to face Thompson. "Those *kids* were wonderfully lethal. Statistically speaking, the first Hunters, the five-year Hunters, even without Huntresses, killed more humans than all future Hunters combined. Sure, the vast majority of humans were fat and stupid in those days, making them as easy to hunt as frail old world birds, but they still did the bulk of the murder. Without Huntresses. They did it of their own accord," Volya issued with menacing delight.

"They were five years old, Volya. Barely older than babies," Thompson said painfully as he imagined being released from his birth-fire without an additional twelve years of becoming numb to pain and torment.

"And they served the Eternal Hunt with incredible loyalty," Volya responded easily. "Just as we will do. We have our own kids to murder, Thompson. We're going into that cave, and we're going to hunt those two girls that you let get away. It's clear that physical torture won't work on you. So, instead, I'm going to make you torture the girls. Slowly. I'm going to make you listen to their pathetic, pleading screams for days. Weeks, maybe, if they can last long," Volya said gleefully.

"No!" Thompson seethed, contracting his muscles into rock-dense tissue without even realizing. "I'll fucking kill you!" Thompson roared as he envisioned the girls screaming, which in turn transformed into his own childhood screaming.

The imagined and experienced torture blinded Thompson, and he lost himself in a berserker frenzy. He was suddenly unable to hold back the ever-bubbling Hunter rage that Anna had patiently taught him to suppress, and he felt his body explode toward Volya as he cried with fury and murderous contempt. His hand tapered into a lance of bone, and he thrusted it directly between Volya's eyes.

Anna! Thompson realized at the very last second, seeing his lover's face only a few feet away.

Thompson pivoted to avoid Volya, but there was no need. In a flash, she stepped aside, and in the same moment she commanded every inch of Thompson's bones to sprout thorns and gush through his flesh. Quicker than a beat of his heart, Thompson's body was pierced from the inside and outside, transforming him into a bramble of self-inflicted stab wounds.

Numerous bones pierced Thompson's brain, destroying his capacity for higher thought. Everything was erased, except for pain. The pain was all-consuming, but it was nothing new. Not a moment went by when he wasn't plagued by pain, with or without a functioning brain. At all times, he was back on his birth-fire, his skin and muscle roasting with an audible sizzle. At all times, he was rampaging across the world in a flurry of death, mindless and stupid in his savagery. At all times, Anna was walking away from him, never once looking back.

Pain, Thompson thought, and it was his only thought.

Volya let him simmer in the maddening pain for a few seconds before accepting that no amount of pain could break the Butcher. Volya retracted the thousands of bone lances, leaving Thompson gasping for breath and his mind reeling in its return to self-awareness.

"Pain won't break you, because pain built you," Volya concluded. "But I know what will break you. You just revealed it to me with your inability to control that Hunter rage—a rage that is mine to command."

There's no way out, Thompson concluded grimly. *I can't change her, and I can't defeat her. I'm sorry, Anna. All I do is fail. Is that why you left? Because you knew deep down that I was...just a Hunter? Just a monster made by the god you chose to submit to?*

Volya cracked a smile at Thompson's thoughts, clearly happy that he was beginning to succumb to the fact of her god's existence.

"That's more like it, dog," Volya said in response to Thompson's thoughts. "Even your bitch girlfriend understood that Mendel is God, and his will is absolute. You're the one who's obsessed with obeying her like a dog, so now it's time to be my dog and God's dog as well. She left you, Thompson. It's time to leave her behind too."

"I'm not going to willingly hunt those girls, Volya. I won't do it," Thompson said despite knowing he was shackled to her will.

"That's fine," Volya agreed. "Then you will torture them unwillingly until you are ready to hunt willingly. If all goes according to my calculations, torturing those little girls will break you once and for all, and then we can continue through the caves and find our way to Downver. According to the Marrow, there could be millions of humans down there, all of them ripe for the killing."

I can't stop her, Thompson thought in defeat as the skinsuit finished its crude repairs of the thousands of bone lance wounds, returning feeling into the lower parts of his extremities. *This is what it means to be a Hunter,* Thompson realized, fully marveling at the thousands of Hunters who had endured the same fate. *All those others were better off not knowing love,* Thompson thought as he recollected the pleasure and happiness the eleven-year Hunter died with in his battle against the two Prodigal Sons. *Ignorance is bliss,* Thompson thought, hearing Anna say the same words with a sorrowful bitterness that he couldn't understand until now. *Were you also stuck, Anna? Was it more than just an imagined fate that made you leave me? Were you totally shackled to something like I am to this wicked creature?*

Volya winked and smiled proudly at Thompson's reference to her as wicked.

Before Volya could continue, three metal clangs resounded in the distance. In a single movement, Volya placed Thompson between her and the source of the clangs. She crouched in preparation for battle, but Thompson knew that it wasn't a battle heading their way.

Those metal clangs, Thompson gasped in utter disbelief, disorienting him and making him feel like he had been pulled into the past somehow. *Those are the clangs of a Cleaner's metal skewer—the same type that was used to torture me over my birth-fire.*

"How can you know that for sure?" Volya asked of Thompson's certainty regarding the sound.

"You think I can ever forget that sound?" Thompson said. "The Cleaners don't have faces. Those clangs are how they speak."

Volya lifted her gaze to the ridge of the crater, but she didn't stop crouching in preparation to evade danger.

"Three slow clangs like that means they want to talk," Thompson said, though he wasn't sure what Cleaners were doing here, nor what they could possibly want to talk about.

Volya closed her eyes, nodded, then opened them. "You're right," she confirmed. "It's those faceless Hunter-torturers. Cleaners. You must harbor incredible loathing for their kind, eh dog?"

"No," Thompson answered, grateful that he had shed that hatred long ago with Anna's help. "They are blameless. They don't understand the full weight of the torture they are programmed to commit."

"Programmed? Like me?" Volya laughed. "Did you ever consider that maybe they just really enjoy torture? Maybe it isn't programming. Maybe it's a choice. Like it is for me," she finished, taunting him with the very antithesis of the lessons Anna had instilled into Thompson.

Maybe she's right, Thompson lamented, grief-stricken that he was abandoning so much of Anna in less than a day of being woken from his over thirty-year slumber. *I'm sorry, Anna.*

Volya smiled with voracious delight at Thompson's thoughts, and just as she was about to say something else, likely a vicious taunt against Thompson's love for Anna, the gathering of faceless creatures appeared on the ridge, their skewers in hand. Thompson counted seven total, two short of the nine Cleaners that always tended a birth-fire with their unsleeping, unending torture-filled vigil.

The Cleaner in the middle of the group lifted his skewer into the air, and the Cleaner to his right struck it with his own skewer in four quick successive hits. Then, the entire group slammed their skewers against the ground twice as if they might be spears of war. Finally, they stood motionless with their faceless bodies directed at Thompson and Volya.

How interesting, Thompson thought, surprised by what the Cleaner had stated.

"What is it? What does that mean?" Volya demanded, her eyes slits of distrust. Thompson could feel the truculent urge for murder exuding from every one of Volya's breaths and movements.

"They want to make us an offer," Thompson explained skeptically. "What they could possibly have to offer, I don't know."

"Maybe they have another Hunter for me," Volya practically purred. "One that works like it's supposed to."

Please let that be the truth, Thompson thought, but he had a feeling he would not be able to escape Volya that easily.

"Well, whatever it is they're offering, I want to hear it," Volya said. "And if I'm not interested in their offer, I'll have you kill them. One by one. Slowly. I doubt those little girls will be able to make it through the cave. They're probably already dead as it is. So, let's spend a little time torturing Cleaners first. What do you say?"

Thompson found difficulty in caring about the fate of any Cleaner, just as he imagined anyone would. It was the nonhuman girls and the Wintersvilla Woman that he was worried about. To his dismay, he heard the woman stirring once more, finally waking up as she clawed her way out of her nightmares, back into the waking nightmare of the real world.

"Well, look at that," Volya said, jumping into the air with a burst of excitement as if she were a little girl growing far too used to getting her way. "Talk about perfect timing! Even if we do take their offer, we still have someone to torture. Lucky us."

Please stay asleep, Thompson urged the woman mentally.

The Cleaners jumped from the edge of the ridge and slid down the incline with perfect control.

"What's happening?" the woman asked through rasping groans as she finally woke up. "Shira?"

"Welcome back to the living, human" Volya answered sweetly. "Don't worry, you won't be back for long."

Mendel and my other self claim that they do not possess the language to describe the full extent of the abilities that the Virus and the Cure will possess. No matter—there is no need for my understanding. As long as they fulfill the natural orchestration of the universe and the Great Beyond, then I am content with their design.

For so much to hinge on two little girls—it seems unthinkable. But Mendel and my other self reminded me that their Earth-form is but a zygote that will replicate and develop into something incomprehensible to my mind, but not to my other mind and Mendel, and certainly not to those little girls.

Mendel and my other self assure me that their vision and the cosmos' vision are one in the same. I have no doubt this is true. I have known this since I was a boy. I felt it like rocks churning in the pit of my stomach, prodding me forward with every lash of suffering. I feel it even now—a gun to my forehead. Cold metal against my skin. All that suffering is but an offering to those two girls who hold the future of reality itself in their hands. Mendel and my other self will cut the strings of fate, and it will be up to those yet unnamed girls to forge ahead unrestricted by fate's hold. Free, in the truest sense of the word, with all the unrestricted awe and risk that true freedom entails.

From Mendel's Ladder: The Personal Journal of Denis Mendel, Written Circa 2049, Published June 2108 by Leif Mainstone, Federated Agency Publishing

Chapter 8
Bold and Beautiful

S econds stretched into minutes as Aliana plummeted through the all-consuming darkness. She could still hear the echo of her screaming, but her mind was detached in a way that calmed and alarmed her simultaneously. She watched her open-mouthed terror and desperate cries for help as if she were an objective observer, and her screaming sounded like a deep bass bellow due to reality being slowed to a near total stop.

What is this? Aliana pondered with awe and terror, marveling at her state of being a detached mind within her own mind. The feeling of not breathing yet not requiring breath disquieted her at a fundamental level of being. *Time has slowed for me before, but not for so long. It feels like it's already been a full minute, and I can hear the very oscillations of frequency in my screaming voice. Minutes are passing for me in place of seconds in the outside world. But...how?*

The maddening nothingness of the abyss struck terror into Aliana, but without the physical persuasion of her body—the rush of adrenaline, increased heart rate, rapid breathing—her panic was at least bearable and no longer debilitating. Her body went on screaming, but she was able to detachedly think with some level of clarity.

How long am I going to fall to my death? Aliana wondered. *Live, Aurelia,* she thought, forcefully pushing away the terrible possibility of time slowing to such a degree that it eventually fully stopped. She envisioned the nightmare of being forced to exist suspended in nothingness forever and ever. *That might even be what death is,* Aliana considered in terror. *I might be stuck in nothingness whether I'm alive or dead. This might be all that's left for me.*

She imagined her sister still straddling the beam, her one good hand outstretched in a desperate attempt to save Aliana from slipping on her own blood and falling to her death.

Keep going, Aurelia, Aliana thought, pleading with the universe to make it possible for Aurelia to hear her thoughts. *Just keep going. This is where my story ends, but not yours!*

Think, girl! Aliana heard Shira order from deep within her mind.

Shira! Aliana pleaded in anguish. *I'm going to die, Shira! I'm going to die, Mom!*

With a sudden rushing swirl of blue and green that seemed to originate from Aliana's sternum, she was tugged forward into some impossible extradimensional space. The swirling colors flattened to a field of freshly sheared grass beneath a serene blue sky full of Earth's typical puffy white clouds. Everything, including Aliana's own body, undulated like the surface of a bubble, as if all of reality might suddenly pop.

What's happening? Aliana gasped, but the soft grass between her toes and the reassuring glint of her blade immediately subdued her previous panic. Time passed normally again, and she found that she could once again breathe. She turned and jumped back upon seeing Shira, Myriam, Rooli, and her sister staring at her with waiting, expectant expressions.

Aliana shook her head, unsure how to process what was occurring.

I know this has to be in my head, but this feels so real, except for everything looking and feeling so wobbly, Aliana reasoned, peering from face to face at all the people she held most dear.

"This is all in my head," Aliana announced regrettably, and all the others except for Rooli nodded with patient understanding.

"It is," Shira stated.

"But so is everything," Aurelia added with a voice not unlike Aliana's, just slightly lower in pitch. She removed her mask to reveal that her face looked nearly identical to Aliana's. She was beautiful, as if she had never been marred by the terrible, untreatable lacerations tormenting her from birth.

"Aurelia!" Aliana gasped. "Your scars. Your voice. You…you have a voice!"

Aurelia smiled wide and said, "Yes, here things are different. You might be too stupid to understand this, but we are always here for you. You can always come here; you just have to learn how. Your body and brain are already changing, and it will become easier over time to access these layers of your mind."

She's talking about the changes that are supposed to happen with puberty, Aliana considered. This was a point of great contention for her and her sister—especially recently, as both of them had begun menstruating on the journey from Wintersvilla to Downver, making life even more grueling and painful. The specialty Wintersvilla IUDs stopped the bleeding, but warrior code still dictated that the IUDs not stifle the bodily pain of monthly cycles. Both girls couldn't help feeling angry that they were forced to embrace the fullness of womanhood without the powerful changes they were always promised would come with it.

"Is this it, then?" Aliana asked miserably. "Is this my power? To slow down time so I can go inside my mind and talk to specters in my head?"

What a fucking waste of a power, Aliana thought, considering how the ability had no way of aiding her in battle. Even worse, she was presently plunging to her death in the real world, so even if her power was worth it, it didn't matter. Everything was coming to an end.

"Aliana still alive!" Rooli bellowed as if in direct refutation with Aliana's thoughts of impending death.

"Not for long," Aliana said, her voice wavering with the threat of tears.

Myriam scoffed and strode forward toward Aliana like a feline Mutant stalking its prey. Without warning, Myriam pounced, striking Aliana in the gut with both her knees. As Aliana fell back, Myriam expertly shifted her weight and caught the back of Aliana's head with one hand while her other hand held a blade to Aliana's exposed neck.

Myriam! Aliana thought in dread. Even if she was just a specter in her thoughts, the idea of Myriam attacking her with actual malice was too heartrending to even imagine. Aliana's mind jolted in fear as she struggled to catch her breath. Myriam's blade dug slightly into her skin, drawing a trail of blood. Suddenly, Myriam's features softened, and she lifted the blade from Aliana's neck.

"This is not what I taught you, Ali. When the enemy is upon us, even when its terrible jaws are around our neck, what do we do?" Myriam asked, assuring yet firm.

A sudden surge of realization flowed through Aliana as she recognized that Myriam was not actually attacking her. She was teaching her one of her many lessons born of tough love.

"We keep going. We never surrender. We stay vicious to the very last moment. To the very last breath," Aliana issued with tears in her eyes.

"Yes!" Myriam urged, her teeth gritted and her eyes full of battle-forged fury. Lifting herself from Aliana, Myriam stood and offered a helping hand. Gazing into Myriam's warrior eyes, Aliana knew exactly what she needed to do. With a wild battle cry dredged from unexplored depths of her mind, Aliana burst from the ground and exploded forward, cannonballing into Myriam's chest. Myriam fell to the ground and laughed with enrapturing joy at the blade Aliana held carefully against her neck.

As Myriam laughed, Shira said stolidly, "Maybe you will die. Maybe you won't. The only thing you can do is focus. Think. Remain aware until the very last moment, and perfect that moment."

Aliana stood and began breathing more rapidly at the mention of death. "In the real world I'm about to die. There's nothing I can do. I—"

"You are a Woman of Wintersvilla!" Myriam lashed with a smile full of vicious love as she lifted herself from the grass.

"You must think, Aliana. Stop being stupid," Aurelia said and signed simultaneously.

Even in my head she treats me like I'm an idiot, Aliana thought with a blaze of anger.

"I'm not stupid, Aurelia! You're just way smarter than everyone else."

"Measuring intelligence relative to other intelligence is meaningless and useless," Shira issued. "Your sister's intelligence is vast, but yours is sharp. The fear isn't going anywhere. But this experience will end soon," she explained, and Aliana realized that the undulations coursing through the very fabric of the environment were beginning to waver, threatening to pop within seconds.

"Place fear aside, and be present on the battlefield," Shira stated. "Right now, your battlefield is darkness, directionless, nothingness. Vision is useless. Taste is useless. Touch is useless. Hearing is useless, because all you can hear is your own wild screaming," Shira explained, and though Aurelia laughed, Shira went on without skipping a beat. "But what about your sense of smell?" Shira offered, as if Aliana's nose could somehow sprout wings and fly her safely out of the abyss.

"Smell?" Aliana asked with mounting urgency as the undulations began bubbling with intense fervor.

"Think, idiot!" Aurelia goaded.

"Shut up!" Aliana shouted, panic striking through her now with newfound force as she realized this had all been for nothing—just her mind rambling uselessly in its final moments before being extinguished forever.

"Sisters!" Rooli bellowed, and as Aliana turned to face Rooli, she was reminded that Rooli needed sunlight and water in the real world. There was a chance to bring her back to life if they could find those two ingredients in time.

Water, Aliana thought with sudden, radiant hope. She reluctantly envisioned being back in the directionless abyss, but this time she observed her falling body from a place of objectivity. *I can hear water behind my screaming. I can feel dampness in the air. I can even taste the dampness on my tongue. I can...I can smell it*, Aliana realized.

"We're falling toward water," Aliana said to the group, and they all nodded in unison, including Rooli.

"You must orient yourself properly," Shira stated. "If you fall on your head at this speed," she warned without needing to finish her explanation.

"Even if I orient myself and fall feet first, I might still die," Aliana said, "and I'll be all alone in darkness even if I do survive," she added, beginning to shiver and breathe rapidly in debilitating fear as the cold of the cave penetrated her thoughts and lapped at her skin.

Myriam raised her sword and pointed it at Aliana. She smiled, then said, "You are a Woman of Wintersvilla, Ali. Fear must be a man, for it is your fatherfucking slave."

All at once, the field and all their faces cleaved and shattered, plunging Aliana back into the real world, back into the abyss.

Now! she thought, and she pivoted her body so that her boots pointed straight down, at least, that's what she hoped, for it was impossible to know for sure in the perfect darkness. Hugging her body tight to avoid creating too much surface area, Aliana partially straightened her legs.

Fatherfucking Muto fuck! Aliana thought as she took a deep breath, squeezed her butt, and used her hand to cover her mouth and smashed nose to avoid water gushing through her orifices. One second her distant echoing screams were drowned out suddenly by the rush of swiftly flowing water, and the next second she was enveloped by icy rapids that consumed her toes and legs and upper body and finally her head, throwing her wildly in every direction as her body continued shooting downward through the depths of some great river flowing through the cave's interior.

Cold! Dark! Fuck! Aliana's mind fluttered in fear, but the weight of her sword on her hip conjured Myriam's vicious yet beautiful smile. Aliana screamed with warrior fierceness inside herself, and Myriam screamed right back, never leaving her side.

This feeling! Myriam exclaimed. *This feeling is fear. It is yours. It belongs to you. Grasp it! Own it. Conquer it!*

In response, Aliana gritted her teeth and tucked her body into a ball to avoid her head or extremities being slammed against rocks. While tucked in a ball, she quickly forced the heavy boots off her feet.

Good girl! Now, focus! Hold your breath, Shira issued.

The river's current violently tossed Aliana's body around as if she were a leaf caught in the vortex created by the Butcher.

How long has it been? Aliana thought desperately as her lungs began convulsing for air.

Do not give in to your lungs, Shira ordered. *Your lungs are stupid. They only know breath, and without breath they panic. You must rise above the urge to breathe!*

I can't! Aliana cried as her shoulder slammed against something hard and sent her spinning haphazardly, forcing her to release some breath to clear water from her nostrils.

Breathe! her lungs pleaded. *Now!* they demanded.

Aliana instinctively parted her lips, but Shira and Myriam screamed in unison, *No, girl! No!*

This river goes on forever, Aliana considered in horror. *I can breathe now and drown or breathe later and drown. I'm going to die. This is it. This is—*

No! Myriam growled, but Aliana's very cells were pleading for oxygen and stars were forming in the blackness behind her tightly held eyes.

I'm sorry, Aliana said to all those she had ever loved. *I'm sorry I'm not strong enough.*

Her lungs heaved one final desperate plea for air, forcing Aliana to open her mouth and inhale. An anguished spray of breath filled her ears.

The sound of death, she thought.

Blistering cold air tore through her facial lacerations and immediately extinguished the stars in her vision, returning her dazed mind back to intense alarm and panic.

I surfaced! I'm alive! she rejoiced despite her intense shivering and deep, desperate breaths for air. All of a sudden, mid-breath, the rapids ushered her below the surface once more, plowing her into a rocky wall and forcing what little breath she had out of her lungs. She could still vaguely discern Shira's features in the darkness, urging Aliana to consciously subdue her own panic.

The current flipped Aliana back to the surface, handling her like a fish carcass thrown back to sea. She gasped for air, and though it bit her lungs with a frosty sting, she lapped at it and prepared herself to be submerged once more.

I'm alive! she told Shira, whose features were quickly fading away, replaced by interminable darkness. *Don't leave me!* Aliana pleaded. "Please!" she shouted over the raging waters.

Focus! she told herself, forcefully conjuring Myriam's voice in her head. She took a deep breath just as the rapids shifted and pulled her downward through a tight shaft full of jagged rocks and crevices. A second passed and then another. The jagged walls seemed to be tapering, squeezing her shoulders and forcing her to hug herself tighter than ever.

I'm going to get stuck in this tube, she gasped in horror, unable to stop herself from squealing and releasing precious air from her lungs. She envisioned being digested by some mammoth creature, the rocky cave walls its intestines and the water its blood.

Holy fucking Muto fuck! Aliana thought in terror as the tube changed direction and forced her upward with mounting speed. It continued tapering, requiring her to release more air from her lungs in order to fit.

Come the fuck on! she gasped, equally angry and afraid. *How the fuck long can this tube be?*

As if on cue, Aliana was shot out of the tube and broke the icy surface in a geyser of frigid water. Her terror immediately turned to both shock and gratitude, for there was light. Somehow there was light. A soft green bioluminescent glow emanated from hundreds of small fungal-looking structures hanging from the large vaulted walls of a cavernous circular chamber roughly a hundred feet in diameter. The river cut right through the middle, taking up the majority of the space. After spending so long consumed by the perfect darkness, the soft glow was like a siren song, for the light was entrancing and seemed in this moment as essential and necessary for survival as food and water. But in the back of Aliana's mind, she was always ready for lethality. She had been trained by the General of Wintersvilla herself to view all signs of life as potential threats, even if the world's flora never targeted her or her sister.

The same might not be true beneath the surface of the Earth, Aliana reasoned grimly, viewing the glowing mushrooms through a lens of warrior caution.

Aurelia, I'm alive...for now, Aliana thought forlornly, addressing her sister in her head. *I know you'd never slip and fall like me. You're probably already past the metal beam and on your way to Downver. Good. Just go, Aurelia. At least one of us will survive.*

A tugging at Aliana's body made her realize that the river's current was still flowing, pulling her toward what sounded like a gurgling whirlpool at the far end of the cavern. She jumped at the thought of being forced down another one of the cave's rocky intestines. Attempting to swim but only able to flap her arms wildly due to fatigue and hypothermia, Aliana flailed and grunted in an attempt to reach what appeared to be a shelf of rock with areas that she might be able to latch onto with her numb fingers.

There's no way this cavern leads anywhere fruitful, but I don't care if I'm stuck here for a while, Aliana thought as the sound of her teeth chattering resounded through her skull. *I can't go through another tube. I can't. Who knows how long the next one will be? I need a second to think,* she concluded bitterly. She screamed in wild abandon and flailed her frozen arms and legs, finally reaching the far wall before the river could sweep her down the swirling whirlpool and away into nothingness.

She grabbed at the rocky ledge, and though her fingers slipped, she was able to stabilize herself in a shallow eddy, unable to lift herself out of the water but no longer swept by the river's insistent current.

I can see my hands, Aliana rejoiced with a surprising amount of relief before realizing that she was only looking through one eye. She brought her hand close to her eye, wanting to inspect it, but she resisted the urge, knowing that it would only make the swelling worse.

The emptiness of the cavern struck through Aliana with the terrible realization that she was alone, marooned in some arbitrary pocket in the endless innards of the Earth. No one would ever find her here.

I'm alive, but I'm still going to die down here, she thought, her panic subdued due to the momentary relief of not presently being sucked through total darkness. Her stomach grumbled loud enough to echo through the cavern, and she couldn't help wondering if the mushrooms were edible. Placing her hands in front of her face, Aliana breathed warm air onto her fingers, slowly bringing them back to life. The numbness was replaced by stinging pins and needles, but Aliana was finally able to lift herself out of the water and onto a small rock ledge no more than three feet wide and spanning what appeared to be the entire circumference of the cavern. At the center of the cavern, water gushed out of the underwater tube coming from the riverbed, creating a fountain on the surface of the water that sprayed an icy haze into the air.

The mushrooms must drink the vapor produced by that natural fountain, Aliana considered in awe at the hundreds of frilly, glowing mushrooms that had somehow found a way to live and grow and apparently even prosper inside this totally unknown part of the planet. She almost lost herself imagining all the other millions or even billions of these random caverns embedded in the Earth, each holding their own undiscovered marvels, each hidden away where only the soon-to-be-dead might stumble upon them and die in wonderment at the mystery and tenacity of life.

This is it, Aliana concluded as tears cajoled her vision into a blur. *I die in this cavern, or I die somewhere else in the cave. We shouldn't have come here. We should have found another way to Downiver. Or we should have gone with that metal head, or—*

Aliana's grave thoughts were cut off suddenly by the sound of something breaking the surface of the water then plopping back down.

"Fuck you!" Aliana shouted instinctively as adrenaline coursed through her and worsened her shaking, but it sharpened her mind to a state of battle readiness. She unsheathed her sword, and as blood and water fell into her one good eye, she was forced to wipe her face and was reminded of the seriousness of her wounds.

"Come out!" she shouted, the adrenaline allowing her to ignore her grievous injuries. She stabbed at the water with her sword, then jumped back at the sight of something bobbing on the surface. Something blonde and spidery attached to a surface of pale white.

"Aurelia!" Aliana shrieked, and without thinking, she sheathed her sword and dove into the water in one fluid movement. The water's iciness didn't even register as she caught up to her sister's lifeless body and dragged her to the rocky ledge. With a burst of exertion from her final reserves of energy, Aliana lifted her sister onto the ledge and then lifted herself.

She's dead, Aliana thought in horror, but there was no time for that. Pushing her body far beyond its limits, Aliana ignored the searing ache of her muscles and the blood dripping down her face. She turned her sister over, and immediately began chest compressions, followed by mouth to mouth resuscitation.

Don't give up! Aliana demanded, despite her breath curdling and wheezing in despairing pleas for her to stop and recuperate even a moment of energy.

No! Aliana told her shaking arms and shivering torso. *Keep going.*

"We don't die here!" Aliana shouted through chest compressions. "Not in this fatherfucking cave!"

All of a sudden, Aurelia began coughing, and Aliana cried with happiness.

"Yes! Come on, Aurelia! Come back to me!" Aliana said, backing away to give her sister some room.

Aurelia coughed for another few seconds then finally heaved a great spray of water through her nose and mouth.

"Aurelia!" Aliana pleaded, moving closer to help her, though she wasn't sure what to do. It was only then that she saw the small shard of Rooli's face laying on the ground beside Aurelia.

She never let go of Rooli, Aliana realized in astonishment at her sister's unwavering hardiness and determination.

Aurelia lifted her left hand, telling Aliana that she was okay, that she just needed a second.

Aliana squeezed her eyes tightly and sobbed bittersweetly. *You were right, Mom,* she told Shira within her mind. *I survived. And Aurelia did too. And we still have Rooli. It's like you said: all hope isn't lost, as long as we have each other.*

"Aurelia, are you okay? Tell me something."

Aurelia's entire right side still hung uselessly, multiple bones clearly shattered in several places. She signed with her left hand, "I passed out the moment I hit the water. I thought we were both dead for sure.

Where…where are we, Ali?"

Aliana shrugged, then laughed once more with tears of joy that she had her sister here beside her.

"I have no idea," Aliana admitted. "But at least there's some light in here, wherever this is."

Aurelia finally took notice of the mushrooms, and as she lifted herself and inspected one of them more closely, Aliana couldn't help staring at her scars.

They're worse than ever, she thought. *And they're getting worse every day. Does that mean her power is coming alive too, like mine?* Aliana wondered, still not totally sure that what she had experienced while falling from the metal beam was in fact her power and not just some near-death hallucination the likes of which many people who had come close to dying reported experiencing.

Aurelia cocked her head and peered at the underside of a particularly large mushroom. She stood on her tiptoes and looked within the frilly layers pouring out of the top.

She can probably discern important information about the mushrooms just by looking at them and smelling them, Aliana thought in awe at her sister, and for the first time, despite Aurelia's battered and bruised body and her face full of otherworldly black scars, Aliana saw her sister as the most bold and beautiful person who had ever lived.

She's not panicking. She's not screaming her head off. She woke up and immediately began inspecting her environment.

"You're so fucking beautiful, Aurelia," Aliana whispered, and her sister turned to face her with furrowed eyebrows.

"What are you talking about?" she signed, appearing impatient and annoyed. "We need to focus, Aliana."

Aliana nodded in rapid succession and wiped away her tears and blood, but she still couldn't help feeling immense admiration for her sister in a way she never had before.

It took getting marooned in the bowels of the Earth to finally really see her, Aliana thought, recollecting how her sister had handled herself with remarkable discipline and fortitude while navigating the cave. Never once did she panic or complain. Never once did she allow herself an outburst of emotion. And all the while, she was so sweet to Aliana, flipping from sister to caretaker in the blink of an eye.

I love you, Aurelia, Aliana thought bitterly as she processed that they were still going to die down here. There was no way out.

"Why?" Aliana asked, unable to mask her shame and anger. "Why are you here, Aurelia? You said you passed out when you hit the water, so you were conscious before that. Did you…did you really jump into the abyss?"

Aurelia sighed deeply and shook her head in seeming disappointment at Aliana. However, to Aliana's surprise, Aurelia's disappointment was directed at herself.

"The truth is that I failed us," Aurelia said with obvious self-torment. "I have…I have a power, Ali. And I know you must have one too."

Does she know what my power is, Aliana wondered as Aurelia continued.

"I can…I can see things," Aurelia explained, hesitating in her signing. "I can see what will happen in the immediate future, and I can plan accordingly. But…" Aurelia trailed off, stopping her signing with an air of forlorn shame.

Is she really saying she can see the future? Aliana gasped, dumbfounded that this was the first time Aurelia had ever talked about her power. *But I never told her about mine either,* Aliana reasoned, figuring that Aurelia probably thought her power was just a fluke of the mind, like Aliana always thought about the instances when time would slow, affording her a few extra seconds of consideration during times of life and death.

"But I failed us," Aurelia said, shaking her head and looking on the verge of tears. "I didn't see any of this coming. All I could see was…was…" Aurelia stammered, unable to form the word.

"It's okay," Aliana said gently, shocked by her sister's state of confusion. She had never seen her in such a state of disarray. "It's okay," Aliana repeated. "My power failed too," Aliana admitted, and Aurelia lifted her head and stared intently at Aliana, keen to learn about her sister's hidden abilities. "Time slows for me. I always just thought it was in my head—something I was making up after the fact. But when I slipped into the abyss, time slowed in a way it never has before. It practically stopped, and I was able to slip into my mind and speak to Shira and Myriam and Rooli and even you," Aliana explained, and Aurelia shook her head, unsure what to make of Aliana's experience.

"So, you can slow down your own experience of time and go inside your mind?" Aurelia asked, looking astonished by Aliana's words.

Aliana nodded, and Aurelia signed, "That's incredible."

Aliana scoffed painfully. "It saved my life, I admit. But it didn't work when Rooli pushed us into the cave. If time had slowed, I would have been able to orient my body properly to avoid shattering my fucking face," Aliana said, and she spit a glob of blood at the wall, making sure to avoid hitting any mushrooms.

"It's okay," Aurelia signed. "My power failed us too. I should have seen this all coming, Aliana. You think I'm so smart, but it's just this fucking power, and the moment it fails me, I'm useless."

Useless, Aliana repeated in her brain, and the thought of associating that word with her bold and beautiful sister made her laugh.

"You are anything but useless, Aurelia. Except for now," Aliana stated, forcing her tone into one of fierceness rather than dread. "Now we're both useless. You should have kept going, Aurelia."

"I didn't just jump because I thought all hope was lost," Aurelia said. "I heard your screaming, and I saw the terror in your face. We are in this together, Aliana. We get to Downver together, or not at all."

"You're a fucking badass when you're not a bitch, you know that?" Aliana laughed through more tears of happiness.

"I love you too," Aurelia signed.

Aliana noticed that Aurelia was shivering. Her naked upper body, as bony and emaciated as Aliana's, was covered in goosebumps. Horrendous dark red bruising covered most of her right side, indicating internal bleeding.

I can't help the bleeding, but I can help the cold, Aliana thought, and she removed her wet shirt, wincing as she exposed her skin to the icy cavern air.

"Take it. You wrapped your shirt around my head, and it's doing a good job of stifling the bleeding, by the way. The least I can do is offer you mine," she said, handing the shirt to Aurelia, but Aurelia shook her head.

"We're better off getting naked, wringing out the clothes, and letting them dry a bit. Don't you remember our first aid training? Wet clothes are never good in the cold. Let's strip down, Ali. We need to conserve our energy and get ready to go down that whirlpool," Aurelia stated simply, far too comfortable with the prospect.

"No!" Aliana nearly jumped, "We have to find another way. You're lucky you were passed out. It was terrifying, Aurelia. I almost died. I can't believe you didn't drown. We're not going to get that lucky again."

Aurelia removed her shorts and underwear, and Aliana did the same.

"You hear me?" Aliana said to her sister who was squeezing her clothes with one hand rather than responding to Aliana's warning about the underground tubes.

"We don't have a choice," Aurelia signed as she finished wringing out her clothes and draped them neatly over a mushroom that served perfectly as a hangar. She turned back to the water, bent down, and drank a few handfuls, replacing the fluid she had lost from throwing up.

Aliana realized that despite spending so much time in the water, she felt parched, so she bent down and drank a few handfuls as well.

"Can you see the future now?" Aliana asked as she stood and wiped her mouth. Though her own power had failed her at the cave's entrance, it had clearly returned in new and unexpected ways during her fall from the beam.

Maybe it's the same for Aurelia, Aliana considered hopefully.

"No," Aurelia stated dejectedly, and she sighed deeply in self-disapproval.

Both girls shivered in the dim light, and Aliana stepped forward. She hugged her sister, one hand wrapped around her waist and the other around the back of her head.

"Don't you remember our basic first aid training?" Aliana issued, glad that she could return her sister's dig. "We're supposed to get close and use each other's body heat to warm up."

Aurelia chuckled and nodded in capitulation to Aliana's point.

"What are we going to do?" Aliana whispered as she held her sister and contemplated their inevitable death inside this cavern or inside the tube. Despite her body steaming with warmth, Aurelia's skin felt as cold as two-day old Muto-meat, and she shivered in wild convulsions.

"I don't know," Aurelia signed into her sister's hand around her waist.

As they shivered and clung naked to one another, their bodies battered and crumpled, Aliana considered how awfully fragile they both were, despite the promise of fate and power that Shira and Rooli always spoke of.

This isn't right, Aliana thought in horror, wondering if it was possible for fate to be broken. *Or fate just isn't real,* Aliana considered, and although time didn't slow and plunge her into her thoughts, she could still practically hear Shira as if she were standing right beside her.

Whenever you are afraid, I want you to imagine Myriam, Shira had one said, knowing that Aliana looked up to Myriam as the ultimate role model of what a woman should be. *What does Myriam do with fear?*

She controls it. She makes it her slave, Aliana answered, and she gritted her teeth in apprehension at what she knew they had to do. *Maybe Aurelia can still see the future, or maybe it's just obvious because it's like she said: we have to go down that whirlpool. We have to hope the tube will lead to an exit. We simply don't have a choice,* Aliana gasped, mentally shrinking at the feeling of being cramped into a tiny, pitch-black crevice in her final moments of life.

Own it! Aliana commanded herself, directing intense ire at her own fear. *I must own it and overcome it,* she knew, though tears still slipped down her cheeks, collecting blood and pattering against the rocky ground at both their feet.

"I'm not a great warrior like you," Aurelia signed, tepid and ashamed. "I can hold my own, but we both know I'm more of a liability on the battlefield when things get really serious," Aurelia signed.

Aliana was about to protest, but Aurelia continued.

"Without the ability to see into the future, I'm useless. I really am. And I'm sorry, Ali. I'm sorry I'm useless."

Again, Aliana couldn't help chuckling at her sister's words.

"If you're useless, then I might as well be a handful of soilies," Aliana chuckled, and Aurelia couldn't help allowing herself a huff of laughter as well.

I've never seen Aurelia so downtrodden, so lacking in confidence and stolidness, Aliana thought sorrowfully. *All she ever does is keep me going. Now it's my turn to keep her going.*

"We are more than just our fucking powers, Aurelia. Do you remember what Mom said? She said as long as we have each other, then there is still hope. Do you remember that, Aurelia?"

Aurelia hesitated, then said in disbelief, "You called her mom."

Aliana nodded and cursed herself for ever being uncomfortable with thinking of Shira as her mom. "She is our mom. And so is Myriam. And so is Rooli. We're the luckiest girls in the world—three mothers and no father. What could be better, especially when our mothers are the fiercest women in existence?"

Aurelia dug her face into the crook of Aliana's neck, and Aliana felt tears stream from her sister's eyes. She had only seen her cry one other time in her life, during the fall of Wintersvilla, when they thought they had lost Rooli.

"I can't see out my left eye and I can't fucking smell either. And you can't even use a whole side of your body," Aliana said, forcing a lilt of courage into her tone. "But who the fuck cares!" she growled, channeling the same viciousness Myriam wielded any time death reared and threatened her life. "We have Rooli. We have our swords. We have each other," she finished, and Aurelia wiped her eyes and sniffled, clearly forcing herself into a state of disciplined calm.

"You're right, Ali. You're right," Aurelia signed, and to Aliana's amazement, Aurelia's shivering slowed and her eyes leveled to a state of stolid acceptance of their predicament.

There she is, Aliana thought, proud of herself for being able to return her sister back to her normal self. *There's the Wintersvilla Woman trained directly by Enduring Ironwood.*

"I think this is the nicest we've ever been to each other for such a long stretch of time," Aliana said.

Aurelia smiled slightly and nodded. "Once we get through this, I'll go back to being a bitch, and you can go back to being an idiot," she signed, and Aliana laughed so hard that she almost choked on her blood-filled saliva. However, her laughter quickly subsided back to silence as the darkness and desolation of the cave set back in.

"We have to keep going with the river, don't we?" Aliana asked nervously.

Aurelia nodded. "It's the only way. We must take the risk before our injuries get even worse. Or before we starve to death. No one is coming to help us. We must help ourselves, Aliana."

Aliana nodded, swallowing the terrible truth of Aurelia's signing.

"I know safe way," came a deep, infernal rumbling.

Aurelia and Aliana both nearly jumped out of their skin as they unsheathed their swords and backed against the wall, crushing several mushrooms in the process.

A Hunter! Aliana knew, for the chillingly deep voice of a Hunter was unmistakable.

Aliana's eyes darted all about the cavern, frantically tracing each shadow and mushroom to locate the source of the voice.

Is there really something else down here? Is this really happening? Aliana pleaded inwardly, but Aurelia's brandishing of her sword and her own adrenaline-filled glare told Aliana that her sister had heard the same voice in the darkness.

"We have to run!" Aliana issued. "We have to jump down the whirlpool!"

Aurelia nodded, and as she abandoned the clothing and stepped toward the ledge, something large and shadowy dropped from the mushroom-covered ceiling and plopped into the river. Unfolding itself, a lanky, towering figure of shadows stood tall, its feet reaching the bottom of the riverbed so that it remained in place despite the strength of the current. Finally, two pale yellow eyes appeared in the darkness, followed by the glinting of jagged teeth lining the sinister, Cheshire smile of a Hunter blocking their path.

"I help you," the Hunter offered with ghastly yet childlike innocence. "I help you" he assured them again, his voice like a thick strip of velvet threatening to suffocate them and release them from their suffering in the only language a Hunter could understand.

He's going to fucking eat us!

"Jump!" Aliana screamed, but Aurelia was already jumping into the river, her sword sheathed and the shard of Rooli gripped tightly in her left hand.

Fuck! Aliana thought, then jumped in after her.

"Wait!" the Hunter growled, and he dove beneath the surface, his mouth open wide and full of serrated blades. Aliana could feel the tug of the whirlpool, and she mentally prepared herself for another terrifying plunge through the cave's dark intestines.

Eaten by a Hunter or consumed by a cave, Aliana thought in horror as the whirlpool latched onto their bodies and whipped them toward the far wall. *Either way, we'll get through this. We have to,* she thought with quickly diminishing hope as panic bubbled in her chest and the vortex sucked at her feet, dragging her toes into its ravenous maw.

Gladys, if you ever read this, I hope you can understand why I have no choice. The nuclear bombs are necessary to strike existential fear into the hearts of all humans. This will serve as a doorway to even deeper fears and realms of ancestral terror. All of this is just a pathway—one among many. But this pathway's destination is beyond anything you or I can comprehend—a state of being that you and I concluded long ago was not possible to attain. We were wrong, Gladys. By the time you read this, I will have already attained it. The other me, that is, will have attained it.

I hope you will forgive me one day, but if not, at least know that I never actually became one of them—one of your ilk, whom you claim to despise yet cannot help aligning with. I love you, Gladys, and I know you love me too. In another life, on another pathway, we could have ruled side by side as immortal galactic emperors. Know that I would have cherished that pathway, and it is with great difficulty that I refuse myself its still tangible pleasure lingering in my mind. However, there is only one pathway that results in Ascension, and it is upon this pathway that I must direct humanity and its descendants.

Forgive me, Gladys, and know that I toil for the sake of everyone and everything, including you. Tomorrow I will detonate the omega-class nuclear bombs, and from that day forward, the future of humanity and the cosmos will be solidified. Mendel's Ladder will be climbed, and each fateful day that passes will bring us one step closer to Ascension.

From Mendel's Ladder: The Personal Journal of Denis Mendel, Written August 27, 2045, Published June 2108 by Leif Mainstone, Federated Agency Publishing

Chapter 9
To Love and Be Loved

"Shira!" the red-headed woman cried without tears, for though the skinsuit had repaired her body, it had not grown back her eyes for some reason. The skinsuit camouflaged her body, taking on the drab colors and rocky textures of her surroundings. The woman brushed her hands over the charred, limbless corpse of the Wintersvilla Woman that Thompson had torn to pieces.

So, the dead woman's name is Shira, Thompson noted. *That's the name the red-headed woman kept mumbling in her sleep.*

The woman miserably nodded to herself as she felt the severed metal bars jutting haphazardly from several ports in Shira's charred flesh.

I ripped her and her metal suit into pieces as if they were a single being, Thompson gasped in horror, knowing that all of this was just the beginning of a lifetime of servitude in exacting Volya's violent whims.

I stole this woman's love from her. Volya did, but I did too because I could not stop her.

"Where are the girls?" the woman demanded, her words rumbling from deep in her throat in a rasping, guttural growl, thick with rage and hate.

"I can smell you, Hunter," the woman growled. "And Huntress—you too. And a pack of fatherfucking Cleaners. And I can smell my love—a charred husk in my arms," she seethed, her voice cracking with anguish and vengeance. "But where the hell are Aliana and Aurelia, you fatherfuckers?"

Is she part Hunter? Thompson wondered seriously at the woman's inhuman sense of smell and the churning rage in her voice.

She gave up on being answered and asked, "Why am I alive?" as if angry that she had been denied death.

"I have a better question," Volya finally responded with incredible intrigue. "Why aren't you screaming in pain?"

The woman shook her head and bared her teeth into a fearless smile.

"Pain is a man, for it is my slave."

Volya went wide-eyed in excitement, and she smiled with genuine enjoyment at the eyeless woman. "Oh, yes, I like that," Volya practically purred. "Pain is a man, for it is my slave," Volya repeated, savoring each word. "It's a shame you're a human. You'd make a better Huntress."

The woman scoffed, but she also didn't protest Volya's statement.

"Get in your metal suit and run," Thompson urged. Suddenly Volya waved her hand, and Thompson felt his body rocket forward. His head hit the ground with the power of a meteor strike, forcing the skinsuit to solidify his skull into iron to avoid his brain exploding outward.

"Don't mind my dog," Volya said. "He's a little bitch. I'm still training him. His previous Huntress was a human. She got him all fucked up in the head."

The woman shook her head in obvious confusion, unsure how to even respond to what she must view as total absurdity.

"Yeah, I know. It's pretty crazy. And it's a long story. Let's not waste time on that. Instead, I need to understand how you are withstanding the pain of the skinsuit. You should be howling in agony right now. Why aren't you?" Volya inquired. Thompson wasn't sure if Volya was actually curious or if she was simply nervous that her planned torture would have no effect on this woman.

"Fuck you. That's how," the woman responded. She gently placed Shira's corpse beside herself, then she stood up. She felt at her camouflaged hands, turning them from side to side as she inspected the rest of her skinsuit-covered body. She tried to pinch the skinsuit at the wrist, but it deftly flattened against her bare skin. Trying again, the woman scraped her nails maddeningly against her forearm, but the skinsuit's millions of tiny hypodermic needles just sank deeper into her flesh, embedding themselves further into her body with every attempt to remove them.

"I wouldn't remove it if I were you," Volya warned. "Skinsuits don't heal, they just maintain. If you take it off, you'll succumb to the wounds I inflicted."

Accepting Volya's words with an indifferent grunt, the woman trudged toward her metal suit, somehow knowing exactly in which direction to move.

Can she smell the metal suit like I can? Thompson wondered, observing the savagery and brutality of a Hunter in her features.

Thompson was surprised to see that Volya was not stopping her. She just watched as the woman walked step by step toward her powerful metal suit. Behind Volya, the Cleaners had just reached the bottom of the crater and were walking steadily toward them.

"Now what?" Volya asked the woman in a friendly tone.

"Now," the woman rasped. "Now I'm going to get into my exo, activate Overdrive, and then kill all of you," she stated as if it were the most mundane and obvious task she had ever committed herself to.

"I see," Volya said, her lips upturned into a thoroughly amused grin. Turning to Thompson, Volya winked, and he watched as her eyes suddenly turned to slits. "Watch this," Volya whispered as she waved her hand in the woman's direction just as the woman reached what she had called her exo. In response to Volya's hand movement, the woman suddenly bent at the knees, jumped, pivoted her body in the air, then landed directly on her face and belly, knocking the wind out of her lungs. As she gasped desperately for breath, Volya broke into laughter, raising her face to the sky as if thanking her false god for granting her such immense power.

"You belong to me, human. That skinsuit is the one I came down with. I'm synced to it, just as you are synced to it. That means I'm synced to you. Thompson," Volya said, turning to Thompson with her indelible smile, "why don't you tell her how wonderful it is to live as my eternal slave?"

"Fuck you," Thompson growled in a near mimic of the woman's earlier response to Volya.

Volya smiled even wider and turned back to the woman, who was now lying paralyzed on the ground. She faced Thompson with her empty, charred eye sockets.

We are both her slaves, Thompson thought grimly.

"Ah," Volya purred. "You two are going to get along just fine. You know, I was thinking," Volya said, and Thompson knew that it could only mean something cruel and torturous was on her mind. "Maybe it's possible for me to control you even when you're hooked up to that exoskeleton."

No, Thompson gasped, imagining the unfathomable power Volya would wield if what she was proposing was possible. *The fact that the woman synced to the skinsuit and isn't even affected by its pain makes it possible,* Thompson thought in horror. *Isn't it enough that Volya has me to use as a weapon?* Thompson asked the world, directing his view to the sky—to Mendel. *She isn't ruthless and destructive enough already?*

"That's right," Volya said in response to Thompson's thoughts. "This must all be a part of Mendel's plans. These Cleaners too," Volya added, turning to face the Cleaners who were now no more than a dozen paces away.

"You two stay quiet," Volya said, simultaneously forcing Thompson's and the woman's lips closed. The woman furrowed her brow, but like Thompson, she was paralyzed beyond that useless movement.

"You will translate what they say, dog," Volya commanded.

Fuck you, Thompson thought, but Volya just chuckled.

"You will translate whether you like it or not. They will speak with those metal spears, and your mind will turn it into meaning. You can't stop that," Volya issued, high on her power.

"Fuck do you freaks want?" Volya said as the Cleaners came to a stop just a few feet in front of her, totally unafraid of the specter of death standing before them.

The identical Cleaners stood in a V-shape, with a single Cleaner at the head of the pack. They wore the same garb that Thompson remembered his own Cleaners wearing every agonizing day: a tattered gray cloak with a hood over their hairless heads, though the hood was no longer needed to hide their eerie lack of faces. Old world humanity was nearly eradicated, which meant there was no one left for the Cleaners to deceive regarding their true intentions to raise Hunters rather than clean radioactivity. Each Cleaner wore burlap wrapped about their feet that extended up to the waist, forming rudimentary pants. Only their arms remained exposed so that they would not be impeded during the torturing of young Hunters.

The head Cleaner lifted his skewer behind his head, and the Cleaner behind him hit his own skewer against it, speaking in the eerie metal clanging that was Thompson's first language. Thompson heard four quick successive hits followed by all of the Cleaners slamming their skewers against the ground in unison, just as they had done earlier on the ridge of the crater.

Trade, Thompson translated despite attempting to fill his mind with other noise.

"Earlier you said that the same motion was an offering, not a trade. Which is it?" Volya demanded with fire in her throat.

It's a language of metal clangs and foot stomps. There's a lot of ways to interpret it, Thompson explained, staring at the Wintersvilla Woman and feeling terrible pity for her. He wanted more than anything to save her from the mad web she was now caught in, but he was just like her—an insect paralyzed by Volya's venom.

Volya sighed impatiently. "Why the fuck are you even here? This is just where your crew happens to hang?"

The head Cleaner hit the ground with his skewer a single time, insisting that Volya focus on his previous statement.

"Excuse me?" Volya said, cocking her head in equal amusement and annoyance. "I asked you a fucking question, you faceless freak fuck. Answer me."

The Cleaners stood motionless for a few seconds, then the head Cleaner finally lifted his skewer behind his head. The Cleaner behind him answered Volya with another series of clangs and subsequent striking of the ground by the whole group.

They were sent here by the Earth, Thompson translated with some difficulty, for the series of clangs they had used to say Earth might also be translated to self or God. Either way, the Cleaners never spoke in such abstractions, representing altogether bizarre behavior.

Volya sensed Thompson's strain in translating their answer, but rather than demand a further explanation, she said, "Fine, whatever. Just tell me what you want. I'm busy."

The head Cleaner lifted his skewer, and this time, two Cleaners clanged with their skewers simultaneously, allowing for greater complexity of communication.

They want to trade the human for information about a secret place, Thompson translated.

"What the fuck? A secret fucking place?" Volya asked, vulgarly saying aloud exactly what Thompson was thinking. "What is that supposed to mean?"

A secret area full of life. There is life that must be culled. It is close. About thirty miles away.

"That's a lie," Volya challenged the Cleaners. "I would have seen it through the satellites overhead. This wasteland extends for hundreds of miles in all directions. This place is barren, save flesh trees and Nomads that get denser to the north and east."

It is hidden, the Cleaners explained.

"Hidden? Like Downver? You mean that it's underground?" Volya asked, and Thompson was left in awe at her ability to control two different skinsuits and speak to the Cleaners, all without any real effort.

No. It is hidden in plain sight, the Cleaners answered cryptically.

"What the fuck are you talking about? Are you translating this right, dog?" Volya demanded before dismissing Thompson with a wave. "Of course you are; you've no choice in the matter. You're just a docile mutt," Volya lashed, clearly angry that the Cleaners appeared to have something over her.

"Where the fuck are you planning to bring the woman? Back to the Earth? What does that mean?" Volya pressed.

We will take her to the Agency. The Earth commands it.

Volya shook her head in disbelief and chuckled in exasperation. "Did all that radioactivity in the old days get to your heads?" Volya asked, reminding Thompson that the Cleaners had first been used to clean the radioactivity left behind by the same human-made bombs that had formed the crater they all currently stood in.

"The Agency, eh? That's where the Prodigal Sons come from. Why are you bringing her there?" Volya asked, but the Cleaners remained silent.

"Fine," Volya said with a calculated shrug. "Then no deal. I keep the woman and torture her, and you all fuck off. Happy?"

No! Thompson growled at Volya within his mind. *Let them have the woman. They said the hidden area is full of life.*

"Shut up!" Volya shouted aloud to Thompson, blocking his ability to form speech in his mind.

"We're sticking to the plan. We're going to torture her, and then I'm going to make you slowly kill those little girls, and then we're going to go to Downver and kill every single living thing we find. Man, woman, child, fucking goldfish—I don't give a fuck. I just want to see thousands of humans obliterated by the Butcher of the Wastes. Is that so much to ask?"

Wait, came a single clang before the Cleaners resumed their nuanced communication using multiple skewers at once. *Downver is rotting. Dying. But the hidden place we offer is thriving. It is truly alive in ways you can't even imagine.*

Volya nodded slowly and methodically and hummed in audible consideration.

And besides, after Downver, then what? You have been tasked to hunt eternally. To destroy all humans. That will only be possible if you accept our offer, for if you refuse and we leave here, then you will never be given this offer again. You will never find the hidden bastion of life without us.

Volya licked her lips, cocked her head, smiled, and then pointed at the head Cleaner. As if strings were attached to her finger and tied around Thompson's limbs, he felt his body explode forward and charge directly through the Cleaner, obliterating his entire body in a hypersonic boom of blood and guts. The other Cleaners were covered in their ally's viscera, but they remained as unmoving as the stones beneath their burlap-wrapped feet.

"Tell me where this hidden place is! Now!" Volya barked. The Cleaners did not respond. They just stood in place, their skewers held like spears of war in front of their bodies.

Again, Thompson felt his body move at Volya's command. His fist struck the closest Cleaner, decapitating him and spraying his thick brains across the remaining Cleaners. Still, they did not budge.

"What the fuck! Fuck this Zen master bullshit!" Volya screamed in exasperation, though Thompson had never heard of the Zen master she referred to. "Just tell me where the fuck it is!" Volya demanded, shaking her fists like a petulant child.

The power you wield is violence and pain, which means you have no power over them, Volya, Thompson thought with a hint of gladness.

The remaining five Cleaners pivoted and shuffled their bodies back into a V-shape. The new head Cleaner reached his skewer behind his head, and the Cleaner behind him struck it, saying, *Final offer. Give us the woman, or you will never find the hidden life.*

Volya groaned in anger at being cornered by beings she viewed as pathetic and inferior. She paced a few steps left, a few steps right, then finally issued a capitulatory huff of laughter beneath her breath.

"Fine," Volya said. "You win. The woman is yours. Now show me where this hidden life is."

The Cleaners nodded and wasted no time. Three of them broke off from the group and walked toward the red-haired woman. The other two turned around and waved for Volya and Thompson to follow. To Thompson's surprise, Volya followed behind them as they walked back in the direction of the crater from where they had first jumped down. Wanting to avoid Volya's painful puppeting of his body, Thompson forced himself forward.

Is she really just going to let the woman go? After all that? Just like that? Thompson wondered, but Volya didn't respond to his thoughts. Thompson peered behind them and watched as one of the Cleaners approached the exo and inspected it carefully, moving his head from one area to another as if he had eyes to see with. The other two Cleaners removed their cloaks, revealing their featureless, bare white skin. They used their cloaks as makeshift ropes, tying the woman's arms behind her back along with her legs. Once they finished securing her, Volya let go of her hold of the skinsuit.

She helped them, Thompson realized, uncertain why Volya would aid these creatures she had just murdered moments before. *What is she really planning?* Thompson wondered.

"Let go of me, you fatherfucking Muto fucks!" the woman screamed, her rasping voice cracking in hatred as she twisted directly toward the charred, obliterated corpse of the Wintersvilla Woman called Shira. Even without her eyes, she seemed to know exactly where her lover's body lay.

"I like her," Volya stated as they reached the crater's edge. Behind them, the two Cleaners carried the woman like hunted game, while the third Cleaner used his skewer to pry off a small piece of the exo, which he brought with him as he caught up to the other two.

I'm so sorry, Thompson thought as he gazed in despair at the mound of burnt meat that had once been a living, breathing human woman. *That's how the red-headed woman will remember her love for the rest of her life,* Thompson knew, wishing the same fate upon himself.

The two Cleaners guiding them nimbly climbed the wall of the crater using their toes and skewers. Thompson and Volya jumped to the surface, then waited for the Cleaners to catch up.

"I bet you enjoyed watching them die," Volya said, filling Thompson's mind with glimpses of being back on his birth-fire as his own Cleaners served their role as agents of pain.

"Of course not," Thompson said, unable to stop himself from pitying them as he watched the pair of Cleaners climb the wall and the other trio of cleaners carry the woman up the opposite wall of the crater. "Anna helped me shed that hatred long ago."

Volya rolled her eyes and shook her head as the Cleaners reached the surface. "Hurry up," Volya commanded the Cleaners. "Start running. You should be able to sustain twenty miles per hour. Right? That means we'll get there in just over an hour at most. Let's go. I'm anxious to savor the delicacies of death you promised."

The Cleaners nodded and broke into a sprint. Thompson glanced one last time at the woman being carried away to the Agency. *I hope you break away and escape,* Thompson thought, envisioning the woman ripping the cloaks from her limbs, killing the Cleaners, and running to return to the girls she had so selflessly fought to protect. *She loved those girls,* Thompson knew, and he forced himself to run beside Volya, knowing that if he didn't, it would only fill her with rage and violence that she would inevitably take out on others.

Only love can change Volya, Thompson told himself. Though he thought she might be too far gone for love, he knew that couldn't be true, for love had been able to change him, just as love had directed the Wintersvilla Woman to fight without fear in service of those little girls.

"Enough!" Volya shouted in response to Thompson's thoughts. "Just keep up with the freaks!"

As they ran, Thompson wanted to plan a way to escape or incapacitate Volya, even though he knew it was a futile endeavor. But it didn't matter either way, for every time his mind strayed into the past or the future, there was Volya's mind, like a stone wall restricting Thompson's attention to the present moment. After a few minutes of trying to crack her impenetrable mental presence, Thompson finally relented and gave himself up to the present, detaching from his thoughts and allowing his awareness to sink fully into his senses.

Running north and slightly west of the craters, the mostly barren desolation of the Butcher Wastelands was progressively replaced by small groves and solitary flesh trees. After roughly forty minutes of thoughtless running, Thompson smelled Nomads no more than a few miles to the west, somewhere unseen high up in the mountains. A sourness in the air prompted Thompson to peer over his right shoulder. Slithering out of a small grove of flesh trees, a large pack of striped, elongated Nomads covered in small bushy mushrooms undulated across the ground. There were thousands of them, and they still carried the unmistakable scent of the flesh pods they had emerged from, signifying that they had just come into the world.

They hatch, live for a little while, then turn into their own flesh trees and do it all over again, Thompson recollected, wondering at the purpose of these strange creatures who had been human an unknown number of generations earlier. The newborn Nomads turned suddenly in unison and directed themselves toward the mountains to the west, their vast numbers and undulations making the ground appear like a disturbed liquid.

What made them change direction like that so suddenly? Thompson wondered, surprised that Volya didn't cut his thoughts off. *What makes them do anything?*

A strange rustling interrupted Thompson's thoughts and beckoned his vision to the northeast, where around thirty Nomads tumbled across the landscape, heading toward a particularly sizable forest to the north. Dozens of spindly tendrils grew from the sides of their rough ball-shaped bodies. As they rolled and tumbled across the landscape, oval eyes attached to the end of each tendril peered about the environment, bobbing to avoid being rolled over by the rest of their body.

Are some of those eyes looking at us? Thompson considered, squinting but unable to see where exactly each eye was directed. *Do the Nomads ever consider us? Do they consider anything at all in their strange brains? Do they consider...love?*

Thompson felt Volya's presence solidify in his thoughts, but just as quickly, she dissipated in response to a strange rhythmic thumping emanating from above their heads.

It's the same Nomads I first smelled up in the mountains, Thompson noted.

Here they come, he thought as the rhythmic thumping rapidly grew louder. Suddenly, the Nomads burst from a thicket of colossal, overflowing flesh trees growing from the mountains at least two hundred feet above them. Several large flaps of thin membranes rapidly revolved above smooth round bodies that looked like the clay jugs Thompson had seen in some of the more primitive human settlements in the past. On the underside of their bulbous bodies, a fine purple mist sprayed the air around them, precipitating and coating the environment in a glistening violet dew.

Flying Nomads, Thompson marveled in awe at their ability to soar through the air with a sense of freedom that he could never know. *But are they really free?* he corrected himself. *Or are they just chained to Mendel's will? Like Volya. Like me. Like all of us.*

Thompson glared at Volya and saw that her eyes were closed. Beneath her lids, her eyes moved rapidly, scanning a multitude of information as she simultaneously ran and stood vigil over Thompson's mind. *She is capable of so much, both inside and outside her mind, and still, she remains chained to the Eternal Hunt—to Mendel's will.*

More of the flying Nomads emerged from the mountains. Hundreds of them. Then thousands. Their purple spray coated everything, including Thompson, Volya, and the Cleaners, in more of the powdery purple dew. It smelled of mud and rain from the old world, but Thompson did not detect anything poisonous or remotely toxic about the substance.

"Disgusting," Volya said, coming to a sudden stop. The Cleaners and Thompson did the same.

"What is this stuff?" Volya demanded to know from the Cleaners, but they just shrugged, not caring that they were covered head to toe in a quarter-inch thick layer of the substance.

Volya closed her eyes for just a moment, then opened them and said, "Damnit, even the Marrow doesn't know what it is."

The Marrow, Thompson repeated in his head, remembering Anna's lessons about how Mendel viewed Astrea as an organ of the Earth, an immune system where new cells could be born and trained in the Thymus. Those cells were the Hunters and Huntresses, which Mendel thought of as the living defense of Earth's body and mind.

And humanity is the cancer, Thompson thought in Anna's voice.

Angry that she could not properly analyze the substance she was now covered in, Volya growled beneath her breath, picked up a small stone, and propelled it upward, bulleting it through a row of five flying Nomads. Their jug-shaped bodies burst like torn jugular veins, spraying copious amounts of the purple liquid as they frantically flapped their membranes and tried desperately to stay afloat. After a few seconds of futile flapping, they finally slammed against the ground, each of them bursting into a bulbous flesh tree full of purple flesh pods. As if on cue, every single flying Nomad suddenly stopped flapping and began plummeting to the Earth. Faster than Thompson realized she was even capable of acting, Volya commanded his body to rocket forward and pick up the Cleaners, carrying them to safety all before the no longer flying Nomads burst against the ground and sprouted an expansive forest of purple flesh trees with bulbous, bulging veins of the same purple powder that coated them and the soil.

Did they all turn into flesh trees just because Volya killed those five Nomads, or were they always going to turn into a forest at that exact moment? Thompson wondered as he watched the flesh trees stretch and multiply their branches, sprouting flesh pods on every surface of their skin. *We are all truly just puppets,* Thompson thought in horror. *Maybe there was a time when all of life wasn't attached to puppet strings, but not anymore. Everything is just Mendel's Ladder. Everything is a step toward his personal ascension,* Thompson thought dreadfully, raising his palms and staring at them as if he could see the strings jutting from his skin and trailing into the sky all the way up to Astrea.

That's right, Volya responded within Thompson's mind. *Everything is the will of Mendel, for Mendel is God. Do you get it now, dog? Is it really that big of a deal that we're all just puppets? Get over it,* Volya said condescendingly. *Maybe even work on getting some puppets of your own. Like I did with these two dolts,* Volya issued, eyeing the two Cleaners as she brushed the purple substance off her shoulders and forearms. *After they show us this hidden place of life, I'm going to make you kill them, and then we'll run back to the others who stole that woman from me.*

You were never going to agree to their terms, Thompson gasped at Volya's treachery and manipulation.

Of course not. You think I would let these faceless freaks manipulate me? Not a chance! We're going to get that woman back and torture her. We're still going to catch up to those nonhuman girls and you'll torture them too. We're still going to find a way to Downver and murder everyone there. And then we'll make our way back to wherever it is they're taking us and kill every single thing in this so-called hidden area, Volya rejoiced with sinister delight. *You see, Thompson? I still get everything. I still get my way. This world is my playground, and my playground is the will of God. Nothing can stop me. Nothing!"*

Thompson looked at her with the same hopelessness he felt about the world at large. *Anna, a part of you believed that love is worth it, and another part of you abandoned our love for something else,* Thompson lamented. *Something you couldn't walk away from. That part of you was stronger, and maybe it's stronger in all of us. Maybe love is weak, or maybe love isn't real, but I know that what I had with you, the love that you showed me, I know that was everything. To love and be loved—that's all that matters. Everything else is empty. Hollow. Meaningless. Like this Huntress. And yet you still left me. We had love, but you still left me,* Thompson thought, ceaselessly haunted by Anna through Volya's features.

"Enough with the moping," Volya said to Thompson's anguish. "Let's get going."

The Cleaners nodded in agreement and turned to run when a voice suddenly called out from somewhere unseen.

"Heyo!" a young but fierce and self-assured male voice called out. "You seen Tommy? Have you?" he demanded with a warble of sorrow. Then, a low rumbling shout filled the air. It was the unmistakable battle cry of a Biofreak.

Volya backflipped directly behind Thompson, kicking up the Nomad dew into a violet fog.

"What the fuck?" she said, easing herself back into a relaxed position.

Your nose has a range of hundreds of miles, and I've been passively watching our surroundings using the satellites above us this whole time. Why the fuck didn't either of us notice them until just now? Volya asked Thompson as if he might actually know the answer.

A Biofreak. A young human boy. Two Mutants, Thompson's nose told him.

What kind of fucking trick is this? Volya considered, her mind a stew of smoldering embers threatening to ignite at the slightest provocation. Every moment of consideration was imbued with the potent bitterness of her rage and the uncertainty of her confusion. *How is it possible that we both missed them?*

"Fuck do you want?" Volya shouted, and Thompson followed her eyes to the Biofreak shambling toward them. A little boy stood atop the giant's broad shoulders, its colossal height making even Thompson appear like a child in stature. Two half-grown Mutants followed closely behind at the giant's heels.

Seeing the Biofreak, Thompson's body instinctively prepared itself for a battle to the death, for though they were known to rarely attack, he and Anna had still heard stories of Biofreaks tearing Hunters to pieces with surprising ease. Their skin was said to be as impenetrable as diamonds and their musculature as dense as mountains. Outside of their giant size and musculature, some Biofreaks appeared almost uncannily human. This one, however, was distinctly Biofreak. His ogreish features gave him a hunched back attached to an elongated, permanently frowning face. His thick, muscular hands were disproportionately larger than the rest of his body.

Despite the danger, Volya slowed Thompson's adrenaline and brought his heart rate back to a state of ease.

I'm curious. This is a strange sight—even more strange because we both stumbled right into it. You can kill them after I find out why this group of fucking freaks is here, Volya assured him.

I don't want to kill anything, Thompson retorted angrily.

Bullshit, Volya laughed. *I can feel everything you feel. You were ready for battle. You wanted it.*

No, Thompson corrected. *That's just my body. My programming. I'm not my programming.*

Volya just shook her head, feeling no need to prove Thompson wrong, for she could see the doubt in him as clearly as they could now see the misplaced strands of overgrown facial hair dotting the Biofreak's misshapen face.

"Heyo! Heyo!" the tiny boy called out, waving a strange, malformed flap of skin rather than a hand in the air. He wore clothing made of various orange and red-hued leaves and vines woven together with the thick bark of some violet-hued flesh tree that covered his chest, groin, knees, elbows, and forearm areas like plated armor. Though his face was handsome, both of his hands were merely flat slabs of extra skin. He smiled widely at the group despite his bloodshot eyes full of tears from crying.

"Our name MaxxEl, with two X's," the boy said proudly. "I promise the big mans, that's El, I promise you he be good. Jamis and Brutus, they be good too. Those my Mutants. And me too. My name Maxx. Together we the Great Gargantuan Group of Good Guys! Isn't that clever? Five G's, one for each of us!" Maxx whooped with joy, and in response, the gigantic Biofreak lifted a closed fist above his head and screamed joyfully, while the Mutants, which were only as tall as the Biofreak's knees, howled with their own excitement. The Mutant on the left had the head of one of the old world lizards that Thompson used to hunt and roast for Anna, and its body was that of a chicken, the domesticated bird all humans were so fond of. The other Mutant had the head of a wolf, an animal Thompson had only seen in pictures and in Anna's descriptions, but its body was frog-shaped, an old world animal Thompson had smelled and seen many times in the past.

Why is this little boy traveling with a Biofreak and a couple of Mutants? Thompson wondered. *And why aren't the Mutants mindlessly attacking us?*

The Cleaners slowly backed away from the Biofreak while Volya just stared at the group from behind Thompson, as if inspecting them for some hidden weapon.

"Well, now there only four of us," Maxx issued, intensely somber and sorrowful suddenly. "So," Maxx said with a deep sigh, "you seen Tommy? He part hog and part snake. He real, real big! He my first Mutant! Even bigger than El! You see? Tommy special. He all black and wormy, and the worms drop off and blacken the ground. That very special. I never met another Mutant like Tommy. So, please, you seen him?" Maxx pleaded with more tears welling in his eyes.

"Waaaaarb," the Biofreak cried unintelligibly, and Maxx tenderly patted the giant creature's head.

"Tommy our favorite. But he gets too scared. He ran off a few nights ago after a pack of Nomads pushed a giant boulder into one of them big holes in the Earth a little ways from here. We watched them do it, and it made Tommy scared and run away. He run north, way north. That's why we here. But we still can't find Tommy. Tommy gone. Tommy gone! And earlier, we saw a great golden light in the sky, and I know that only scare him more. Tommy out there all scared and alone!" Maxx bellowed, prompting El and the Mutants to howl in mirrored pain.

"We haven't seen your damn pet Mutant," Volya said, interrupting their cries. "But tell me, little one, and maybe I won't kill you: how did you tame the Biofreak and the Mutants?"

El squeezed his fists, snarled, and roared at Volya, prompting the wolf-headed frog to growl and lizard-headed chicken to hiss and ready themselves into clearly practiced battle-stances.

"Heyo! Heyo!" Maxx called out, looking betrayed suddenly. "There no need for fighting. But if you try anything, El crush you all, and Jamis and Brutus feed on your bodies."

Don't, Thompson warned, reminding Volya through violent imagery what a Biofreak was capable of.

"I apologize," Volya offered, feigning genuineness. "I didn't mean to threaten any of you. I'm just curious how a human child tamed these wild beasts. I am also in the practice of taming beasts, as you can see," Volya said, gesturing toward Thompson.

The boy is a human. He must be killed, Volya stated in Thompson's mind. *I can snipe him with a stone through his little skull in a heartbeat, and then we can make a tactical retreat and let the Biofreak rampage around until he forgets what happened after a few minutes, the big oaf!*

No! Thompson argued. *There is still a chance the Biofreak could rip us both to shreds,* Thompson warned, doing his best to disguise his concern for this child and his pets, whom the boy clearly loved and cherished as family.

"Apology accepted," Maxx offered with a wide grin as he patted El's head to calm him. "Lots of Rovers like me who live outside the boundaries of BigBilly's kingdom make a pact with a big mans. There no way else to survive in the world. Together we MaxxEl. Together we strong."

Maxx pointed to the lizard-headed chicken and said, "His name Brutus. He my second Mutant. I brought a lizard and a chicken to a splicer bush, and it turned them into Brutus. Jamis," Maxx said, pointing to the Wolf-headed frog, "he my third Mutant. I want a fourth, but there not many old world animals now. I only saw an old world blue bird about a month ago, and no more than that. My Mutants special, you see? Like you," Maxx offered, bowing to Thompson and Volya in turn. "I see lots of No-faces like the ones you with, but you the first Hunter and Huntress I ever seen. An honor to meet you both, it is," Maxx said, bowing again in clear excitement.

I definitely want to kill the little human, Volya said, weighing the risk against being ripped to pieces by a giant and subsequently eaten by Mutants.

Jamis looked fearfully at Volya. He whined and lifted his webbed feet in agitation. Maxx hopped from El's head to his shoulder, then slid down his arm to the ground with a level of precision that told Thompson that despite being a child, he was still a force to be reckoned with, even without his titanous mount and two guard animals. Maxx strode to Jamis and hugged him tightly, lovingly wrapping his useless flaps around the Mutant's fur. It was only then that Thompson noticed the specially crafted sharpened axes hanging from either side of the boy's waist. Each ax's handle contained a hollowed crevice large enough to slip his flaps into.

He's a little warrior, Volya thought in amusement within Thompson's mind. *Maybe you're right. Maybe we let him live a while longer and come back in a few years when he's older and stronger. It'll be a more interesting battle,* she said, clearly marveling at the boy's ability to overcome his disability and to tame such powerful creatures whom she undoubtedly viewed as weaponry in the same way she viewed Thompson.

Thompson didn't tell her that she was just afraid of the Biofreak, and he did his best to hide the urge from her awareness. Both their attention was turned to Maxx, who hugged Jamis tightly, nestling his face into the wolf's fur as he lovingly rubbed its glistening amphibious back.

"Everything okay, boy," Maxx whispered gently into Jamis' ear. Brutus strutted between El's legs and curled his head around Maxx's body, while El picked his nose, ground his molars together, and beamed at his family below with a smile full of awkwardly spaced rotten teeth.

This little boy really does love the Biofreak and these Mutants, and they seem to love him back, Thompson marveled. *Because to love and be loved is everything,* he thought, returning to his previous conclusion.

Nevermind coming back, Volya said, shifting mercurially away from her previous decision to let the boy live. *Get ready to grab those Cleaners and run to safety,* Volya commanded, apparently seeing an opportunity for murder that she was eager to take advantage of. *I'm going to kill the little human using a rock just below my left foot.*

"Volya, no!" Thompson growled with such force that it made everyone jump back, except for Brutus, who just stared at Thompson with his black lizard eyes. Jamis growled at Volya, and Maxx clambered back atop El, using El's readied fingers to propel himself up the giant in a single swift movement.

They move like a single being, Thompson observed. *Because of their love. That's why. Just leave them alone, Volya.*

"Jamis thinks you mean us harm," Maxx said despite still smiling. "You want a battle?" he offered excitedly. Brutus hissed, Jamis howled, and El hooted strangely through pursed lips, as if he wasn't entirely sure whether they were about to engage in battle or take a bath.

Three successive clangs of metal filled the air, followed by two slow clangs and two slow stomps against the ground.

The hidden life is only another minute from here. Life must be culled, Thompson translated the Cleaners within his head automatically.

Fucking fine! Volya relented, and she held up a single hand in surrender.

"We're busy with the Eternal Hunt. You go about your business. We'll go about ours," Volya offered reluctantly.

Maxx's smile slowly faded, and his lips upturned into a sour face.

"A part of me was hoping you would battle us, but if you don't want to, that's okay too. It just been a while since we done battle, but that okay, because I don't like killing," Maxx said easily, relaxing into the folds of fat around El's neck. "Best of luck on your hunt," Maxx offered, apparently not even realizing that he and his species were the prey.

Volya chuckled at the irony of Maxx's words.

"See you another time," she said, prompting Jamis to growl and stare Volya down as she signaled for Thompson and the Cleaners to continue forward. She followed behind them, and as they passed the group, Maxx cheerfully waved goodbye. Volya raised her middle-finger at him, and though Maxx clearly didn't understand the meaning, he excitedly did the same with one of his skin flaps, raising it eagerly into the air.

"Good luck to you too, Huntress!" Maxx shouted, his voice echoing strangely against the flesh trees in the distance.

"You have no idea how badly I want to crush that little fucking smile," Volya said through gritted teeth. "We might still do it on our way back," she stated, reminding Thompson that her plan was still to kill the

Cleaners after finding the hidden place then to go retrieve the Wintersvilla Woman.

"You raised your middle finger at him to say 'fuck you' just like humans do," Thompson said, shaking his head at the absurdity of Volya's existence. "Sure, right now your skin is camouflaged with the environment, because we're about to face danger, but when it isn't, you look just like them. You act like them. You speak like them. Only your scent gives you away. You are all but human, Volya," Thompson issued heavily, but Volya shook her head in denial, laughing at his words.

"You killed those flying Nomads. And you killed Nomads before that too, on our way to the battle with those Wintersvilla Women and that metal man. Isn't that against the Eternal Hunt? Can't you see it's all just bullshit, as you and the humans say?"

"Might as well get used to the bullshit," Volya issued. "You are mine, now and forever, dog."

Thompson knew there was nothing he could do to sway her. There was nothing he could say that would provide the necessary break in her psyche to rewrite her programming and offer her an avenue of self-actualization.

There is no amount of love that can help her.

The Cleaners clanged their skewers, stating that they had arrived. However, there was nothing in front of them, just more forests of flesh trees and the mountains to the west.

"Where is it?" Volya demanded. "Was all this just a fucking ruse to get that woman?" she asked, and though Thompson didn't think Cleaners were capable of such tricks, he also had never seen them engage in trade or do anything other than torture Hunters.

They clanged their skewers and stomped them on the ground once more, saying, *You must walk forward. We are not allowed entrance. This is hallowed ground. Life must be culled. Walk forward.*

Volya hesitated and inspected the air in front of her. She cocked her head, searching for something, anything, but there was nothing to see. Neither was there anything for Thompson to smell.

Are they in fact tricking us? Thompson wondered suspiciously.

A trio of bulbous technicolor Nomads with long tendrils, which they used to slap the ground and propel themselves forward, passed just behind the Cleaners, clearly avoiding the area that they were referring to.

Do the Nomads know about the hidden life? Thompson considered, and Volya stared at them, probably wondering the same thing. Either out of frustration or more likely intelligent planning, Volya rocketed a stone at the closest Nomad, piercing the largest of its several heads. It sprouted into a flesh tree, and to both Thompson and Volya's surprise, as it grew, its branches wrapped around a curved portion of space, as if it were blocked by an invisible wall.

"What the fuck," Volya said in profound awe which quickly turned to excitement. "That means there really is something right in front of us," she said, her breath quickening in ecstatic anticipation for mass murder.

Life must be culled, Thompson repeated, considering the Cleaners' vague and difficult-to-interpret language. *The way they said that made it seem almost threatening,* he thought, and Volya was too enraptured in her murderous excitement to pay his thoughts any mind at that moment.

"You go first," Volya commanded, nodding to Thompson to walk himself past the wall rather than forcing his body.

Thompson sighed, then took a single step forward. He stopped and asked the Cleaners, "What is it? What am I about to walk into?"

Hunters are to be tortured and not heard, the Cleaners responded scoldingly, reminding Thompson of being back on his birth-fire. He felt his anger flare, but he was able to just as quickly quell it, seeing them just as he saw Volya.

They have no love. They have never had love. But I have. And I still have it. I can feel it deep inside me. You're always with me, Anna.

"Fucking go," Volya barked.

Life must be culled, Thompson repeated once more in his mind, more uncertain than ever in his life. *All the Cleaners know is torture. Why would now be any different?* he thought as he stepped forward, considering that there was a clear possible interpretation of their language that referred to death—specifically referring to Thompson and Volya as the life that had to be culled. But either Volya didn't realize it or didn't care, for she stepped forward as well, apparently determined to enter the hidden place of life and death beside her dog rather than behind him.

Truth is a fickle idea, for the moment it enters the realm of language and human conception, it is tarnished, abstracted into something it was never intended to be. But the actual truth isn't something that can change. Like a liquid, truth might take different forms or shapes dependent on its environment and immediate surroundings, but truth itself never changes. Water remains water whether it is a liquid or a gas. Whether it conforms to a curved jug or a rectangular vat, it is still water.

A better analogy might be that of light. Take the sun. Most would consider it a simple fact that the sun is a shade of yellow, maybe saffron. But the truth is that the sun is white. It only appears yellow because Earth's atmosphere scatters the lower frequencies of blue and violet, leaving only the brighter colors to be transmitted to our eyes. But even that is a falsehood, for the color white only has meaning to a tiny fraction of the universe that contains sensory organs capable of perceiving color.

Truth is fickle. It is constantly refracted through the lenses of the world and the self. Like light refracted through a prism, we see the rainbow, but not the source. Thus, to perceive unrefracted light, one must remove the prism. In the same manner, to perceive untarnished truth, one must remove the refracting mechanism that is the self.

But without a self, how can truth be perceived and known separate from itself? It can't. Thus, destruction of self, while serving as a viable method to perceive truth, is not a lasting solution. The only lasting solution is to replace the prism with clear glass, that is, to create a self that does not refract truth, but allows it to enter unrestricted and unchanged.

I have created that self. I am that self. I have tasted truth. It is radiant. It is resplendent. It is pure awe. In the coming days, upon Anna's return, we will be ready to step forth into the light and know the full extent of the truth. Of everything.

From Mendel's Ladder: The Personal Journal of Denis Mendel, Recorded Circa 2065, Published June 2108 by Leif Mainstone, Federated Agency Publishing

Chapter 10
Truth Refracted

No amount of mental willpower was sufficient to break the hold of Tomasz' reinforced tendrils, which throbbed in rhythm with the heartbeat of the entire Giganventus.

Tomasz' own heartbeat, Samuel reminded himself, still gasping at the concept of these gargantuan creatures serving as Tomasz' body, housing his mind, which history books claim was even older than Andre Madeira's by almost two decades.

Lift! Samuel's mind demanded, but Samuel had already tried breaking free too many times to count. It was no use.

The searing pain dug into Samuel's wrists at Tomasz' command, sinking deeper into his mirror-flesh, so deep that he thought it might warp his very soul, poisoning him at a fundamental level of being.

"Goddamnit, why are you doing this?" Samuel cried, breathing unevenly through the immense pain.

Tomasz stood before Samuel like a great sorcerer imbuing himself with a powerful spell he had spent centuries preparing. His arms reached above his head with tightly closed fists, while his eyes darted beneath closed lids. His lips moved with maddening rapidity as he whispered unrecognizable words and phrases beneath his breath. It was as if he was processing information at rates befitting the automated computer systems that maintained nearly every aspect of life in the Foundation. With each passing moment, the pain became increasingly sharp, forcing Samuel to grunt and grit his teeth against it.

"Stop it, goddamnit!" Samuel roared.

Lift! his mind issued back. Samuel screamed open-mouthed at the top of his mirror-lungs, producing a high-pitch twang as his voice vibrated against the mirror-substance rather than human membranes. He flexed with every bit of strength he could muster, depleting his muscles of oxygen as his body bulged with thick mirror-veins from every inch of his reflective skin. But still, it wasn't enough.

Goddamnit! Samuel fumed *It worked before. I tapped into some unfathomable fount of energy. How did I do it? I was thinking of Sandra, and it just worked. I'm thinking of Sandra now, so why the fuck won't it work again?*

"Andre must have thought that physarum polycephalum, that is, the yellow slime mold he sent you down with, was so clever," Tomasz said with overt amusement, his eyes still closed and moving rapidly beneath his eyelids. "I concede that he was able to destroy a few pieces of my body, a few Giganventi, but that does not matter. That is the whole purpose of my domesticated Nomads. All day, every day, within each Giganventus, the Nomads labor to birth more Giganventi, and each subsequent generation is stronger, more adaptable, more capable of withstanding any plans of attack that Andre or even Gladys might choose to concoct. All of Fana Tsehay's old world manufactures combined could not have fabricated something so elegant and adaptable. Under my command, the domesticated Nomads tirelessly perform manual mitosis and mutation of my genetics and macromolecular makeup. They are a part of me now, as much as the Giganventi are a part of me. One day, every Nomad will be under my command, domesticated and directed to expand my body beyond this planet and eventually beyond this star system. My body will fill the galaxy and then the universe," Tomasz concluded, his sinister smirk both smug and certain.

"You'll be alone!" Samuel shouted at Tomasz' profound yet absurd plan.

"I am already alone!" Tomasz blazed, flaring his eyes and baring his teeth in anger. "I was always alone. It was always me against the others. Even Gladys," Tomasz finished in a whisper of disdain. "The others used me. They would be nothing without me. This whole Nomadic world would be nothing without me. Mendel's entire plan hinged on the Nomads. And who created the Nomads? Me!" Tomasz seethed with hate that must have been simmering for years—decades even. "I turned the first man, woman, and child into a Nomad. Some homeless rat family Andre convinced to accept the changes because they can't be forced. One must consent to becoming a Nomad. But I am the one who did it. Me. Not Andre. Not Mendel. It was me. Me!" Tomasz bellowed with overwhelming rage, and he closed his eyes and tightened his fists with newfound force, physically shaking with unresolvable wrath.

The pain in Samuel's wrists shot suddenly through his arms and continued across his shoulders and into his spine. Samuel screamed in all-consuming pain as Tomasz' awareness scoured Samuel's neurons and directly analyzed the mirror-imbued biochemistry of his mind.

More than pain, Samuel was plagued by the shocking disorientation of being plunged into his memories as if being dragged and battered by a hurricane wind through the busy streets of a metropolis. He shattered through the windows of a skyscraper constituting his cherished memories of his family, then he was just as quickly flung to another building and smashed through memories of lifting at hundreds of separate but identical power stations.

He could feel Tomasz' sinister presence in his memories like a shadowy specter standing over his shoulder and breathing down his neck.

Suddenly he was back in space, locked in free fall with the Earth. In a flash he was once again staring into Madeira's profound, wondrous, and dangerous eyes, which Samuel had only ever seen as patient and wise up until today. The environment of the memory appeared frozen, and Samuel remained restrained by Norman's chest of yellow slime.

He's in my fucking head, Samuel gasped, finally able to form coherent thoughts once more now that he wasn't being blasted through his own mind at breakneck speeds.

"It is really him," Tomasz marveled with a twinge of nervousness as he stepped from behind Samuel and entered his field of vision. Samuel discerned that the memory wasn't frozen, but was moving at a fraction of normal speed. Madeira was presently speaking to Samuel, but his voice sounded like a deep, incoherent moan. Otherwise, everything was exactly as Samuel remembered. He was even free of the mirror-substance, save for a small patch where it was just beginning to expand over his arm.

Get out of my fucking head! Samuel ordered, unable to physically move his mouth or speak aloud with his body moving as slow as the rest of the environment.

"Do not make me strip you of your ability to form coherent sentences," Tomasz warned. "I am currently translating your neurological firing into meaningful output. I am limitless, Samuel Kaminski of Astrea," Tomasz proclaimed, apparently accepting that Samuel really was who he claimed to be. "The Nomad currently restraining you appears to have been domesticated in a similar fashion to my own technique. I assume this 'Norman' was Ruben's doing, though I can see you are not privy to that information."

I don't know anything! Samuel pleaded. *You see now? That godforsaken bastard Andre Madeira used me. I'm not your enemy, Tomasz.*

"I think it is very likely that you are telling the truth and that these memories are not mere implants only because the slime mold protruding from the Nomad's chest is the same that infected a handful of my Giganventi. It would follow that the rest of the memory is genuine, although there is still no way for me to be absolutely certain about that."

Fuck you! Samuel roared with suffocating frustration.

"I would prefer to have you as an ally, Samuel Kaminski, but allies are dangerous," Tomasz said with a pulse of pain through Samuel's spine. Tomasz shook his head contemplatively, looking almost regretful for having to treat Samuel with such scrutiny and caution, though when it came to maliciousness, he did still seem to enjoy that to some degree.

"You have no idea what I've been up against for the past fifty years. Gladys still refuses to join me. She will no longer even talk to me. John and Craig are dead. And all the others joined Mendel, and apparently Andre too, on Astrea. Ruben, Marissa, Lingyun, Fana, Lorenzo, Wagner, and their brightest progeny. All of them joined Mendel on Astrea. But Mendel—" Tomasz said, his voice cut off by a wince and choking sound in his throat.

"Gladys told me that Mendel was lying to me. I told her she was just being too emotional," Tomasz said entirely to himself, looking lost and confused suddenly. "What if Gladys is right? What if Mendel has been working with Andre this whole time? What if—" Tomasz said, coming to some wild and impossible conclusion.

In a flash of blinding light, the environment suddenly shifted back to the innards of the Giganventus, leaving Samuel panting to catch his breath.

"What if it was Andre all along?" Tomasz issued in uncharacteristic horror, his breathing rapid and jittery. "That means the Virus and the Cure—it is like Gladys warned. Mendel is not our ally. They were commissioned by Andre. They are tools to serve his plans. It was not Mendel I have been communicating with. It has been Andre all along. Is that it?" Tomasz pleaded, his eyes unblinking in dismay.

Tomasz' eyes snapped suddenly and locked with Samuel's in a blaze of fury.

"Answer me!" Tomasz shouted in total wild abandon. "Answer me, you reflective cask of rat piss! Was it Andre all along?"

"I don't know what you're talking about!" Samuel shouted back with just as much fury. "You're the one that can see in my head. You're the one that can see I don't know shit. I'm a fucking worker. And a fucking failed father and husband. You can see all of that!" Samuel cried, his voice cracking wildly with the mirror's eerie resonance. "So why the fuck are you still doing this to me? You're just as bad as Andre! You know that? You're a fucking rat just like him!"

"I am no rat!" Tomasz lashed at the top of his lungs. "My family is descended from ancient royalty, Samuel Kaminski of Astrea. You cannot fathom what my ancestors accomplished, and you can never comprehend the depth of my genius. I am not some fucking pauper, nor am I some fucking puppet on strings. Is that clear? I choose my fate. I choose my future. Not some actual fucking rat from the streets whose filthy peasant family probably extends thousands of generations into servitude to my own. Is that clear? Andre is filth! Andre is nothing! I am the rightful ruler of this entire world! I am Tomasz Novak, and I will break you and destroy you and obliterate every one of Andre's plans!" Tomasz proclaimed like a mad, warmongering king of old.

He squeezed his fists harder than ever, his fingers breaking against his own strength and the vessels in his temples and eyes bulging with sudden, pulsing force. Samuel screamed in agony greater than he could have ever imagined was possible as each of the dozen tendrils attached to his body tore and burned. It felt like an eternity, but only a second passed before Tomasz unexpectedly melted and sunk into the floor. The tendrils detached and slunk against the wall. Samuel fell forward, splashing into the pool of Tomasz' sticky remains.

Gasping to recover, Samuel gritted at the still searing pain and lifted himself as the room began to quickly dim.

Now what? he frantically considered. *I can burst through the walls until I reach the outside, but then what? I'll fall to the Earth and be even farther away from home. Is there a way to take over and direct this giant creature?* Samuel wondered as he realized that would mean taking over Tomasz as well. *Like before, I probably don't have much time until he comes back. I have to act. I have to do something!* Samuel urged himself.

Just as he was about to run headfirst into the thick innards of the beast, the dim room was suddenly illuminated by bright light from the wall to Samuel's left. He turned to see the wall peel fully open, revealing a strange and seemingly endless procession of Nomads crammed into a tiny hallway beset by more walls of bulging veins and pumping arteries. They shuffled to the opening in the wall, then came to a stop. All of them gawked at Samuel in the same mystifying and engrossing way they had when they first saw him just a handful of minutes earlier. Finally, each Nomad bowed in their own fashion. One of them poured liquid from its multiple hollow heads onto the ground. Another with a humanoid form bowed and hid his face to reveal another identical smiling face embedded in the top of his skull. A handful of Nomads here and there emitted puffs of multicolored gas as their own sign of respect.

Samuel gasped at the exotic strangeness of each of their bodies.

They were human once, he recollected once more. *Tomasz did this to them. And maybe Mendel and Andre and those other people Tomasz mentioned as well. A handful of self-obsessed egomaniacs are responsible for the suffering and horrific transformation of billions*, Samuel thought incredulously. He felt even more uncomfortable with such a sordid truth now that he was face to face with the creatures. However, the Nomads appeared anything but anguished. In fact, those that had faces or other human-like features appeared content, joyful even.

I'm not truly human anymore, but I was a human once too, Samuel reminded himself, seeing himself in these warped yet bliss-filled creatures suddenly. *And I still feel human. So maybe they do too, even the really strange ones.*

Three Nomads at the head of the procession stood a few feet in front of the others. The one at the center appeared almost entirely human, and Samuel couldn't help feeling an uncomfortable attraction to what had clearly been a beautiful woman before her transformation. Orange and yellow flowers that Samuel had never seen before sprouted from virtually every part of her skin except her face and cleavage. She lifted her head and smiled at Samuel with childlike excitement before lowering it once more as if in excited anticipation for what would come next. On her right, a pool of red bioluminescent muck pulsed and undulated, its body constantly folding over itself like dough being perpetually kneaded. To her left, an insect-shaped Nomad with a transparent head, thorax, and abdomen bent its six legs and kept its elongated head full of mushroom-laden, probing antenna close to the ground.

"What do you want from me?" Samuel demanded, backing a few steps away in defensive preparation for an attack.

Tomasz called these his domesticated Nomads. They work for him, Samuel concluded grimly.

"We want what you want," the beautiful flower-covered Nomad offered reverently, her eyes still downcast but her smile obvious. "My name is Sunny Marigold. I speak on behalf of all the others here. We are yours to command, Mirror-Man."

It's like Madeira said: the Nomads will listen to the Mirror-Man. Is this just a ruse, or does the power of the Mirror-Man extend to Tomasz' domesticated Nomads too? Samuel considered.

"I don't know what's going on here. Why are you so ready and willing to help me? I know I'm the goddamn Mirror-Man, but why me? Why is this happening to me?"

The Nomads appeared perturbed suddenly and looked at one another nervously.

"Because you are the Mirror-Man," Sunny Marigold stated simply. "The Earth foretold your coming. Your screaming overrode the genetic changes that the Great One, Tomasz Novak, implanted into each of us. We have finally returned to the call of the Earth. His call. We are yours to command, Mirror-Man."

They are mine to command, Samuel repeated, in awe at the prospect of such power. *But I don't even know what they're capable of. Can they get me back to Astrea?* Samuel considered, imagining that one of them must have some kind of strange body part that could somehow return him to Earth's orbit.

The bioluminescent muck Nomad flashed its red muck in an array of sharp geometric patterns, and Sunny Marigold nodded.

"We don't have long," Sunny Marigold warned, translating the muck's language. "We put the Great One to sleep by injecting a specialized concoction into the Giganventus, but the Giganventus will develop an immunity to the substance soon enough, and then Tomasz Novak will return."

"Astrea!" Samuel issued at the mention that this might be his only chance. "I need to get back to Astrea."

"City in the Sky," Sunny Marigold said with a tone of dreamy awe. "If that is where you want to go, that is where you should go. What would you like us to do in the meantime?"

"I need you to help me get there, goddamnit!" Samuel said in exasperation as he looked about the room half-expecting Tomasz to rematerialize at that very moment.

Sunny Marigold furrowed her brow and shook her head. She whispered to the other Nomads, and each of them responded in their own bizarre ways.

"We regret to tell you that we have no way of returning you to Astrea," Sunny Marigold said reluctantly. "However, we believe the Nomads living in Waru might have a way. Or the esteemed Nomads living within the Great Honey Mushroom. They might know a way as well."

Samuel shook his head with boiling impatience.

"Fine!" he capitulated, wanting desperately to be free of Tomasz and his creations, both the Nomads and the Giganventi constituting his body. "Just take me there. Take me to Wamu or whatever it's called. Or the honey mushroom. Whatever. Just hurry up. If Tomasz wakes up—" Samuel said, cutting himself off as he recollected the soul-wrenching pain that Tomasz had inflicted him with just before the Nomads had interceded.

Sunny Marigold shook her head, allowing her soft blonde hair to flow between the orange and yellow flowers that Samuel assumed were the so-called marigolds that her name was based on. "It will take time," Sunny Marigold stated regretfully.

"I don't have time!" Samuel urged. "You don't understand. My family might be walking to the recyclers as we speak. I need to get back now. Now, you hear me? It has to be right now!" Samuel nearly howled.

The insect-shaped Nomad rubbed together a series of tiny-capped mushrooms lining its antennae, producing a chirping sound that Sunny Marigold apparently understood.

"If we could take you back to Astrea right this moment, we would do it, Mirror-Man. But...we cannot," Sunny Marigold stammered, her smile souring to self-disdain. "However," she began, as if fearful that all of Samuel's commands would be impossible to obey. "Sprouting Cordyceps here has suggested that although we cannot directly return you to City in the Sky, we are able to open a line of communication with it, potentially allowing you to speak to your family and ensure their safety.

Samuel was caught off guard and required a few seconds to process what Sunny Marigold was offering him.

"Can you…can you really do that?" Samuel inquired.

"Yes! Yes we can!" Sunny Marigold announced excitedly. The rest of the Nomads moved with excited activity and communicated with one another in hushed whispers, flashes of light, puffs of strange gas, and various other seemingly arbitrary means.

"Do it!" Samuel said in disbelief that he might actually be able to speak to someone on Astrea, maybe even his family.

If I can't get back there right away, this will have to suffice, Samuel forced himself to accept. *But how long do we have?* he wondered nervously, uncertain if the Nomads would be able to create the line of communication before Tomasz woke up.

A lumbering humanoid Nomad, at least seven feet tall and just as wide, flitted on hundreds of tiny, rapidly moving legs through the crowd of Nomads. They parted to let him pass, and he skittered his way to the center of the room. His hands had been replaced by gargantuan lobster-like claws that bent outward at the tips. Digging his giant claws deep into the floor and spraying the room in a haze of blood, the large Nomad pried open the Giganventus' internal tissue. Next, a featureless black Nomad no more than a foot high and shaped like an eight-legged wicker basket climbed atop a shoulder of the clawed Nomad and peered without eyes into the two newly opened holes. Without warning, the small Nomad pointed two of its legs full of living, snaking tendrils at the holes in the ground, then ejected a fount of tendrils that seemed to grow from an inexhaustible source. Hundreds of feet of tendrils sprouted from the small Nomad with each passing second.

This is incredible, but if they can manage all of this, why the hell can't they just get me back to Astrea?

"What are they doing?" Samuel asked Sunny Marigold, assuming that the two Nomads directly in front of him were unable to speak to him due to neither of them having an obvious mouth. The tendril Nomad bucked and looked as though he might finally run out of material to extend the tendrils with, but to Samuel's surprise they just kept on growing. Samuel observed that beneath the tendril Nomad, the shell-like exterior of the claw Nomad was slowly melting away, clearly being absorbed and reconstituted by the tendril Nomad.

"Sharpened Devil's Claw opened the flesh of the Giganventus, and Plentiful Armillaria is dropping her tendrils past the other Giganventi and into the great saltwater expanse. She will drag her tendrils through the thick kelp forests that reach up toward Sol for miles from the bottom of the ocean," Sunny Marigold stated as if that would explain everything. Samuel shook his head, prompting Sunny Marigold to elaborate.

"The kelp forests are connected directly to the Earth's mind, and Earth's mind is connected back to Astrea through special energies transmitted by the Great Honey Mushroom."

"You're...you're hacking into Astrea using...the mind of Earth?" Samuel checked, not sure what the Nomad meant by the planet's mind.

Sunny Marigold appeared not to fully understand Samuel's question and answered, "We commune with Earth, and the Earth communes with Him."

"Him?" Samuel asked in apprehension at Sunny Marigold's cryptic use of the simple pronoun.

Sunny Marigold just smiled and nodded with wonder and warmth in her features, eyeing Samuel as if taking for granted that Samuel would know who she was referring to.

"Who are you talking about? What is the mind of the Earth? Who is *Him?*" Samuel urged, but they were interrupted by Plentiful Armillaria bobbing up and down in what appeared to be excitement.

"Your wife has been located, Mirror-Man. You may speak to her now."

"Speak to her?" Samuel checked in frantic confusion. "What do you mean? How?"

"Samuel!" Sandra gasped, her voice emanating from Plentiful Armillaria's body. All at once, the world and all its absurdity was washed away, for hearing Sandra's voice was like experiencing the sudden eye of a hurricane after being battered by its brutal winds for a lifetime.

Is that really her? Samuel gasped. *Or is this some kind of trick?*

"Oh god," Sandra whispered beneath her breath. "It's been less than a day, and I'm starting to hallucinate. Oh god," she issued, sobs filling her throat.

"Sandra, my perfect little okra, is that you?" Samuel asked, all breath.

Sandra just went on sobbing disconsolately, mumbling to herself that she was losing her mind.

"Get it together, Sandra. The kids can't see you like this," she told herself.

"Sandra!" Samuel urged, taking a few steps closer to Sharpened Devil's Claw and Plentiful Armillaria. "Sandra, it's really me. You're not crazy. It's me, the stupidest fucking worker in the world. I didn't abandon you. I didn't abandon Nathan and Margot. You know I would never do that, Sandra."

"I have to get out of this room," Sandra told herself, ignoring what she clearly believed to be a hallucination of Samuel's voice.

"Wait! Sandra! Please! I don't know how this is possible. But I love you. I need you, Sandra. Please just talk to me! Please!"

Samuel eyed the room with sudden intense nervousness that the line of communication might be cut off in the next second.

I don't know what to say, Samuel reasoned, *but I have to be quick.*

"Samuel," Sandra laughed pitifully to herself. "I really wish this were real. It's only been a handful of hours since the revolution began, but I've longed to hear your voice and feel your arms around me with every second that passes. I wish so much that this were real," Sandra lamented, her voice cracking in pain.

"It's real, Sandra!" Samuel pressed. "Roland, he—"

"Roland?" Sandra blurted, suddenly intensely sober.

"Yes, Roland. He—"

"Roland!" Sandra shouted in what sounded like the opposite direction.

"Sandra, I—" Samuel began, but he was interrupted by the scraping of metal on metal.

Samuel could hear distant murmuring and a tone of concern from Roland, then finally Sandra said, "Just listen. Just tell me if you can hear him too. I think I'm going crazy."

Samuel waited a few seconds then said, "Sandra? Are you still there?"

"Samuel?" the High Commander of Astrea gasped in disbelief.

"You hear it too?" Sandra asked, her rejoice quickly shifting to shock. "Samuel! Samuel! Where are you? What is happening?"

"This is likely a trick, Sandra. This must be the Queen's doing," Roland warned grimly.

"No!" Samuel demanded. "Roland, goddamnit, it's me. I just saw you a little while ago in the torture room with that inhuman bastard Andre Madeira," Samuel explained, refusing to refer to Madeira by the age-old endearing title of *old man*. "Did you find my children, Roland? Are they with you, Sandra?"

"Sandra, we should leave this storage room. This is a trick. It must be," Roland warned.

"It's him!" Sandra declared through tears of joy. "I know it. I can feel it. It's my Samuel. They're here with us, Samuel. Nathan and Margot are safe. They're with the other children, who are all being kept preoccupied while avoiding too much noise."

"They're alive!" Samuel rejoiced. His body felt like a wound-up toy forced to move, but there was nowhere to go. He paced back and forth as Sandra went on.

"The revolutionaries prepared so much for this day, Samuel. We're hiding in the walls. We're—"

"Don't!" Roland interrupted. "This could be the Queen's attempt at locating us. You may have already said too much."

"Okay," Sandra agreed, but Samuel was desperate to hear more. He had to know that his family would be safe for as long as it took for him to return to them.

"Just tell me what's going on up there. Roland's right. Don't tell me where you are. Just tell me that you and the kids are safe," Samuel pleaded.

"Something is..." Sandra trailed off, horror filling her voice. "Something is happening in the Foundation. Something..." Sandra said again, once more losing herself in the terror of what she was referring to.

"It's like I said," Roland stated grimly, finishing Sandra's statement. "The Queen released something worse than the Queensguard armor. There are monsters out there, Samuel. Great flying beasts of some hellish nightmare."

"Monsters?" Samuel gasped, envisioning hordes of strange Nomads invading the Foundation, despite their apparent peaceful and docile demeanor.

"Yes," Sandra confirmed. "They're as large as Mount Mendel, but they move like shadows. We can still hear people screaming out there, Samuel, begging for help as their cries turn to blood-curdling shrieks and then…and then they're gone," Sandra said, sounding distant as she described the sordid deaths of her friends and neighbors.

"Where are you, boy?" Roland asked. "Where did the Queen's Servant take you?"

"I…" Samuel hesitated, unsure how to explain that he was stuck inside one of many otherworldly behemoths soaring above Earth's largest ocean. "I'm not on Astrea," Samuel stated, still unsure how to explain what he had thus far endured.

"What?" Sandra exclaimed in shock.

"What did he do?" Roland asked.

"Who?" Sandra checked.

"Madeira," Samuel stated through gritted fury. "Andre Madeira did this. He did all of this, Sandra. Madeira was never who he said he was. Roland knew it, but he was trying to protect us," Samuel finished, hoping it was true that Roland really was an ally despite serving as the head Queensguard for most of Samuel's life.

Like me, he is just a puppet of higher powers, Samuel reasoned. *Like all of us. But he found my family. He kept his word.*

"Roland?" Sandra asked. "What is he talking about?"

"You didn't tell her?" Samuel asked, suddenly suspicious of Roland's motives once more.

"We've been quite busy, boy," Roland bristled.

"He's right," Sandra agreed. "Roland was able to save hundreds of Foundationers before we had to seal the walls. He's the only one of us in here that actually saw the monsters released from the Golden Wall of the Luxury Quarters."

"Roland," Samuel urged. "What are they? What did the Queen release?"

"I told you the Queen would conjure something even worse than Queensguards. And she did. I have no words for those creatures of shadow and darkness. They are even worse than the Hunters of Earth. They are worse than the Queen herself. I saved as many as I could, but the rest will not survive. Not against those…nightmares," Roland concluded regretfully.

Goddamnit! Samuel cursed as he imagined numerous abstract flying nightmare demons clawing into the Foundation directly from the depths of hell itself.

"Samuel," Sandra pressed. "Please. Where are you? Tell us."

"I'm on Earth," Samuel blurted, knowing it would make no sense to them.

They both remained silent, so Samuel went on.

"Well, not exactly on Earth. I'm in the atmosphere. I'm inside…a giant flying beast."

"You're…what?" Sandra asked in total confusion.

"I know it doesn't make sense," Samuel admitted. "But I'm going to get back to you. And then I'm going to save you all," Samuel declared, forcing his voice to sound unwavering in confidence for Sandra's sake.

"I know you will!" Sandra rejoiced, sounding genuinely hopeful. "You are the Workhorse of Astrea. You are my fearless bull," Sandra said through more tears.

"Who are you talking to?" came an all too familiar voice from somewhere behind Sandra and Roland.

"Frank?" Samuel exploded. "That goddamn bastard is there with you? He's alive?"

"Is that…is that the fucking workhorse?" Frank laughed unbelievingly.

"Frank!" Samuel growled. "You bastard! I'm going to kill you when I see you. I'm going to shove a pipe through your skull, you hear me, goddamnit?"

Frank laughed and said, "Nothing to worry about, Sammy boy. I'm taking good care of your family."

"Fuck you!" Samuel lashed.

"Enough!" Roland issued. "Get out, boy," he said to Frank, and Samuel heard Frank's laughter echo in the distance as he complied with

Roland's command.

"What the hell!" Samuel exclaimed. "Why is he with you?"

"He's harmless," Sandra offered, but Samuel cut her off.

"He isn't. He killed Bill Wendover. I saw it. I was there."

"He killed Bill?" Sandra gasped.

"Yes. He's dangerous, Sandra. I can't believe he survived. Damian didn't, and he deserved to live a hell of a lot more than Frank."

"Damian's dead?" Sandra repeated, sorrowful and distant. Samuel figured that she was probably suddenly contemplating how she would tell Damian's children that they would never see their father again.

"Yes. He saved me, but he died in the process," Samuel explained, wincing as he remembered his best friend slumping over in the gargantuan gauntlets of a Queensguard.

"Frank helped us, Samuel. He helped Nathan and Margot escape into the walls. And so did Albatross and the other founding revolutionaries who survived," Sandra said, her voice full of sadness and what Samuel thought might be shame.

"Albatross!" Samuel gasped. "That pathetic work-skimmer is the architect of all this madness. Don't you understand that?"

Roland and Sandra remained silent for a few seconds before Roland said, "Tell him. He deserves to know."

"Tell me what?" Samuel prodded. "What is it?"

Sandra breathed deeply and said, "Samuel, I'm so sorry. I'm so so sorry."

"What?" Samuel demanded, feeling more anxious than ever that time was about to run out.

"Your wife is one of them, boy," Roland issued flatly. "She's been working with the revolutionaries behind your back for quite a while."

Roland's words struck Samuel like a kick to the chest.

"What?" Samuel gasped, his mind racing as he considered the implications.

How long has she been lying to me? How much involvement did she have in this revolution? Samuel wondered, shaking his head with desperate incredulity.

"Tell me it isn't true, Sandra."

"It's true," she admitted through held back sobs. "I helped them plan the revolution. I've known about it for the past three or four months. Samuel I—I'm so sorry. I—"

"Sandra! What are you saying?" Samuel gushed in pain. "Damian is dead. Bill is dead. You and our kids are hiding from monsters in the walls of Astrea. You're saying you were part of all this?"

"Not exactly, Samuel," Sandra offered painfully. "I only knew so much. I didn't know exactly how it would happen. I wanted to tell you everything, but they said you might turn us in. They said I had to keep it from you. Damian assured me that he would be able to convince you to help us in the end. He assured me that—" Sandra said forlornly, unable to finish her statement.

No, Samuel thought. *This can't be happening. Sandra has been lying to me for months? I would have known. I would have seen it in her eyes. But I didn't!* Samuel considered with anguish as the truth of his predicament was suddenly refracted in terrible and unexpected ways.

"You lied to me," Samuel concluded, forcing more suppressed tears out of Sandra. "Why, Sandra? Why?" Samuel pleaded.

"Not all of us are as strong as you, Samuel Kaminski. The last few years, you've spent more time lifting than raising your children. We never see you anymore. We never talk anymore. All you do is lift," Sandra stated with pent up exasperation, but Samuel could hear the unmistakable guilt in her tone as well. "Even if I wanted to tell you about the revolution, when would I have done that? You were never around, Samuel."

She's right, Samuel thought, feeling betrayed but still placing the blame on himself.

"I did it for you and the kids, Sandra. And our friends. I did it for everyone else. I—"

"I know," Sandra urged. "You're a good man, Samuel. The best I've ever met. But it doesn't change the fact that it's all for nothing in the end. I...want more for Margot and Nathan. I want immortality for them, even if I can't have it. But that was never going to happen for a working, Middler family, and that's not fair. Why should the Queensguards and other Luxury Quarters citizens get immortality while we suffer the inevitable fate of the recyclers?" Sandra demanded, and Samuel realized that all of this had been weighing on her for many years without him even realizing it.

"Why did you never tell me any of this, Sandra?" Samuel asked, shaking his head in disappointment at himself more than anyone else.

"But now all hope is lost," Sandra went on without answering. "Our homes and neighbors are being ravaged by giant monsters, and it's only a matter of time before we run out of food, or the monsters rip the walls open and kill us all."

"No!" Samuel shouted. "No! I won't let that happen!"

Sandra cried, and Samuel felt nothing but hate for himself for neglecting her for years and for failing to be by her side when she needed him most.

She blames herself for this craziness, Samuel understood. *Make it better for her, not worse,* he demanded to himself.

"Sandra, listen to me," Samuel issued, forcing his voice to a state of practiced calm. "You did the right thing," he said, swallowing his anger and feeling of betrayal, for he knew that none of this was her fault. It wasn't even Frank's or Albatross' fault. It was the Queen's fault. It was Tomasz' fault. It was Andre Madeira's fault.

"You did what you knew was right for our children," Samuel went on despite knowing his words likely weren't true at all—that they were all better off before the revolution and the release of the Queen's nightmarish monsters.

Just say what she needs to hear, Samuel reminded himself, squeezing his fists but forcing himself to provide her with assurance and confidence rather than shame and guilt.

"I love you, Sandra. You are the greatest mother in the world. I'm going to find you, and then I'm going to kill every one of those monsters in the Foundation. And then you and me and our children will go to the Luxury Quarters and figure out how to become immortal, along with all the rest of those who survive the Queen's tyranny. From that day forward, we will live in peace and prosperity and happiness. Forever," Samuel intoned, certain that his words couldn't really be true.

Samuel was surprised to see the Nomads smiling and nodding along with Samuel's speech, as if they fully believed the words Samuel was using to bolster Sandra's will.

"Yes, Mirror-Man," Sunny Marigold whispered blissfully.

"Yes, my Samuel," Sandra issued with newfound hope despite her continued sobs.

"If anyone can do it, you can," Sandra and Sunny Marigold issued simultaneously, forcing Samuel to jump back at their identical words.

Did she know Sandra would say that? Samuel gasped.

"Samuel, I love—" Sandra said, but her voice was cut off suddenly.

"Sandra!" Samuel shouted. "Bring her back!" he commanded Plentiful Armillaria. "Bring her back goddamnit!"

The Nomads looked alarmed suddenly, gazing about the room nervously.

"He's awake," Sunny Marigold warned.

All at once, the room was illuminated with bright light from an unseen source, and Tomasz reformed with lightning speed, rematerializing from the ground up in less than a second.

"What have you done?" Tomasz screamed in wild fury. "What the fuck have you mutated casks of piss done?" Tomasz screamed even louder, his voice undulating and warping inhumanly in a mad frenzy.

With a wave of his arm, Tomasz eviscerated the entire hallway of Nomads. Diverse branches and trunks grew from where each Nomad once stood, and with another wave of his arm Tomasz obliterated the hallway of dense, growing trees, vaporizing the Nomads and reforming the wall to once more capture Samuel within a closed off portion of the Giganventus' innards.

"How dare you, you fucking peasant!" Tomasz roared at Samuel.

Lift! Samuel heard from deep within his mind, and he knew exactly what he needed to do.

Envisioning Sandra, Margot, and Nathan standing before him, Samuel bent at the knees and exploded forward, aiming directly for Tomasz' enraged, vein-bulging face. Samuel prepared himself to burst through the robed, fiery-eyed man and continue through the thick walls until he reached the outside, but to his surprise, he was stopped suddenly in his tracks as he felt something constrict around his neck.

"Andre thinks he can strip me of everything I have worked for?" Tomasz bellowed as he held Samuel in place by the neck. His features were imbued with strange, eerie tendrils of bulging veins and visibly pumping arteries, mimicking the pulsating innards of the Giganventus. "It was not enough that he destroyed the world and all its decadence?

Now he has turned my domesticated Nomads against me? My Nomads?" Tomasz thundered.

"No! I will not allow it!" Tomasz roared, and although Samuel tried to twist out of his indomitable grip, he found that his efforts were now more useless than ever.

He's been holding back, Samuel realized in shock. *This whole time he really has only been using a fraction of his power.*

Metal capillaries shot from the ceiling, floor, and walls, boring into Samuel's body as they grew so thick that they began to converge on one another, forming an impenetrable cocoon around Samuel's limbs and growing inward toward his torso and head.

"I have had enough!" Tomasz snarled. "I will break you! I no longer care about studying you. All I want is to destroy you!"

Samuel couldn't even flex his muscles as the metal capillaries encased him, coating his entire body except his face and sternum.

Lift! Samuel demanded, twisting wildly, but it was still no use.

Tomasz backed away, letting go of Samuel's neck. He lifted his hand above his head, commanding a single capillary to grow from the ceiling.

What the hell is it? Samuel heaved, unable to breathe without difficulty. It felt as though multiple tons of weight were compressing his lungs. The new capillary looked to be made of flesh, except for a sharpened metal point where some strange black substance dripped steadily to the ground, sizzling where each drop landed.

Baring his teeth in wild rage, the veins in Tomasz' neck and temples doubled in size, and he squeezed his fist with a painful groan. The sharpened capillary sliced through the air and cut easily into Samuel's reflective metal flesh.

Searing pain tore through Samuel's sternum, and he screamed in agony.

"You will not best me, Andre! You fucking sewer rat!"

There must be more Nomads, Samuel thought behind the unimaginable pain. *Why aren't they coming to save me?*

He couldn't believe his own thoughts, but Samuel found himself hoping that Andre Madeira had planned for this moment—that he had devised a way to destroy Tomasz Novak once and for all. But as the pain intensified and the sharpened capillary slithered multiple centimeters into Samuel's body, he couldn't help feeling that everything was only going to get worse—that his reality would go on fragmenting into indiscernible, confused pieces like a shattered mirror.

When I was a very little boy, around the age of six or seven, one of the neighborhood boys was severely beaten by a gang of nine and ten year olds. That child spent over a week in the hospital. He was quickly discharged due to his parents being unable to afford the mounting medical bills. Because of that, he never really received proper treatment, and from that day forward, he walked with a limp. The medical debt forced his parents to remortgage their home, but one tragedy led to another, and the bank ended up foreclosing on the home, kicking the family onto the streets.

I thought I would never see that boy or his family again. However, I was wrong. Several years of anguish and suffering later, I met them again. At the age of eleven, I had been homeless and alone for just under three years. I had just made the switch from one train to another, finally heading toward a rumored homeless camp on the south side of Chicago that people all around the country claimed was safe and clean. I had followed such rumors before; they had all turned out to be hyperbole at best, but I had nowhere else and nothing else but the hope that this camp would be the one that proved the rumors true.

"You there," a man said from the other side of the train car I was hiding in. "Come, we have some food. Not much, but it's something. We are happy to share."

I didn't hesitate to take the man up on his offer. As I moved closer to him, I saw that he had a woman and young boy with him. The boy was cuddling a small puppy and petting its head over and over again. I knew immediately that this was the same family that had lost their home, and that this was the same boy who had been beaten.

I cried. I had always imagined that the boy's parents had been sent off to the labor camps like mine, but here they were. All together. A family. We ate together that night, and the boy and I became like brothers. His name was Norman, and he had named his puppy Hotdog, on account of her brown fur and her ability to scarf down her own mass in hot dogs in a single sitting. For the next three weeks, we were inseparable. I finally found a new family who would love me and let me love them in return.

That first meal they shared with me was the last of their food, and we lived on crumbs for weeks. All of us, including Hotdog, were so malnourished and emaciated that we were like skin-draped skeletons.

But we survived by depending on one another. We survived through our love. After a series of crisscrossing trains, we arrived at the Chicago camp. Everything happened so quickly. The moment we stepped off the train, a gang of frail, hungry men stole Hotdog right out of Norman's arms and ran into a crowded alley full of equally starving people. Norman and I chased the men down, weaving through people's legs as we called our precious dog's name and cursed the men with every swear we had ever learned. When we finally caught up to them, Hotdog was cut wide open, her guts and skin removed in preparation to eat her scant flesh. She was still alive, whining desperately for help. I think it was her whining that broke him. Norman gripped one of the bloody butcher knives lying on the ground that had been used to slice open his best friend, and then he sunk the blade into the gut of the man who was presently moving Hotdog's insides from the filthy pavement and into an even filthier cooler.

The man gawked at the blade in his gut, his face full of more surprise than fear. Norman grunted pitifully, removed the blade, then stabbed the man again. And again. And again. His belly gushed with multiple lacerations before he finally came to his senses and screamed in pain, only to fall backward, futilely trying to apply pressure to the gaping wounds stealing his life second by certain second. The other men just stared at the little boy holding a butcher knife over the wheezing, dying man. The roar of a gun made me jump against the wall, and I saw Norman's body slump to the ground to reveal a man behind him holding a smoking pistol and snarling in disgust.

"Fucking little sewer rat," the man bemoaned Norman. "He

fucking killed Bob, the little mother fucker."

"Norman!" Elisa, Norman's mother shrieked. Roger, Norman's father, pushed me out of the way to get to his dead boy. He held him in his arms and cried in a way that I still can't get out of my head even all these years later. Roger wailed like a newborn, open-mouthed and shrieking. I still hear his screaming in my nightly nightmares and in my waking life. I hear it right now, as if I were still back in that alley surrounded by vicious, desperate men.

Another gunshot made me jump again. I turned to see Elisa's body collapse to the ground, her own gun in her hand and a bullet in her head. The man who had killed Norman lifted his gun and fired a shot into Roger's forehead, killing him instantly. Then he pointed the gun at me and said, "You can die, or you can keep your pretty little mouth shut and share this meat with us."

To survive, I ate my second family's body that night, along with Hotdog, my first and last pet. The following night, I slit each man's throat in their sleep. I watched them die. I watched their eyes go distant as they were slowly drained of life, and I knew that what I had done was right. That same night, covered in righteous blood, I left Chicago and never returned.

When people have love, they are good. When people do not have love, they are bad. That is the childish axiom I adopted so long ago, and it still somehow continues to prove true at every turn.

Everything I do, I do out of love. Everything I do, I do in pursuit of a world where Norman and Hotdog are still alive and by my side. Forever.

From Mendel's Ladder: The Personal Journal of Denis Mendel, Written Circa 2043, Published June 2108 by Leif Mainstone, Federated Agency Publishing

Chapter 11
With Fierceness and Fortitude

*H*ere we go, Aurelia thought as the whirlpool spun and sucked both girls' legs down into its tapering depths. *Time to face the terror of the cave's innards, like Aliana described.*

She braced herself for the plunge, and as the force of the whirlpool reached her armpit, she squeezed the shard of Rooli against her ribs with all her might.

Just keep hanging on!

All of a sudden, something large and firm gripped her around the waist, pulling her out of the whirlpool and back into the cave.

He got us. The Hunter grabbed us before we could escape, Aurelia thought grimly, still resentful at herself for failing to be able to sense the future when she and her sister needed it most.

"I...just...want help...you," the Hunter stated through exhausted breaths. His inhumanly low, rumbling voice echoed through the small cave as he waded through the river with some difficulty, struggling to hold each girl at his waist with his shaking arms.

"Get off me!" Aliana demanded, twisting to unsheathe her sword. Although Aliana's sword was stuck between her and the Hunter, Aurelia's sword was free to be unsheathed.

Now! she thought, and despite the pain and fatigue wearing her into a withered shell of her former self, she somehow found the strength to unclasp the sheath and swing her sword, deeply gouging the Hunter in the right side of his abdomen.

The Hunter howled in pain and let go of both girls.

"No!" the Hunter shouted as the girls instinctively swam for the whirlpool. "It bad way. You get stuck and die!" the Hunter warned.

He's obviously lying, Aurelia concluded, but Aliana had stopped frantically swimming and was now gazing at the whirlpool in overwhelming horror.

"He saved us, Aurelia. And he doesn't sound like he wants to hurt us," she said as she grabbed hold of a ledge and offered a hand to catch Aurelia before she plunged to what the Hunter claimed to be her death.

Aurelia grasped her sister's hand and looked back to see that the Hunter was not pouncing on them or even attempting to move toward them. He was just holding the wound Aurelia had inflicted and breathing in shallow bursts of pain-filled agony.

He isn't healing, Aurelia realized.

"You see it too, right?" Aliana whispered. "He's weak."

She's just afraid of going down the whirlpool and getting stuck, Aurelia concluded as she inspected her sister. *She's seriously considering conscripting help from this death machine?* Aurelia considered in awe at this unexpected turn of events and the possibility that it might be their only option if they didn't want to gamble their lives and toss themselves further into the snaking darkness.

"One wrong move and I slice your head off," Aliana warned at the Hunter through chittering teeth. "Got me?"

The Hunter nodded and smiled, though his elongated teeth and crinkled vampire bat nose only made him appear more monstrous. "Yes," he agreed. "I want help you, not hurt you. Please. I help you," the Hunter said, and to their surprise, he reached out a hand in offering.

Is this really a Hunter? Aurelia considered in disbelief despite all the obvious features, including his towering nine-foot frame.

"Please," the Hunter said again, shaking his hand in offering.

This is foolish, Aurelia told herself, but after glancing back at the whirlpool for just a moment, Aliana waded forward and took the Hunter's hand, which tapered to broken and jagged blade-sharp nails on each finger.

Aurelia felt her breathing instinctively quicken out of worry for her sister, but Aliana handled herself like a true warrior, for as she gripped the Hunter with her left hand, she used her right hand to hold her sword against the wound that Aurelia had inflicted.

"I might not be able to reach high enough to chop off your head, but I'll stick this blade so far into your gut that it'll come out your neck from the inside," Aliana hissed, adopting an air of Wintersvilla fierceness and fortitude as both an offensive and defensive tactic.

The Hunter actually looks afraid, Aurelia gasped as the Hunter bowed in servile obedience to Aliana's command.

Aliana kept her eyes on the Hunter and said, "Come, Aurelia. We have nothing to fear from this frail beast—a male beast, no less."

Aurelia couldn't help chuckling to herself, despite the gravity of the situation. *That doesn't sound like Aliana. Is she impersonating Myriam right now? She's doing a good job of it, at least. Whatever you must do to remain in control, do it, Sister.*

Aurelia pulled herself through the current with her one arm. The pain in her right side was almost numb now, which worried her far more than the pain itself.

I probably don't have long, Aurelia considered stoically. *And I refuse to drag Aliana down with me. The problem is will I know when death is imminent? Will I know when it is time to hand Rooli to Aliana and let go of this life?* Aurelia wondered nervously, not wanting the last moments of her life to negatively impact her sister. *I can't say anything because Aliana will get too worried about me. But if the time comes when it is better for Aliana to abandon me, then I must do the hard part for her and kill myself so that she doesn't hold onto me and lose her own life wasting time trying to keep me alive.*

A shiver ran down Aurelia's spine as she envisioned the steel of her blade slicing through her own throat, drowning her in her own blood.

If it comes to it, then it comes to it, Aurelia resolved, refusing to give in to the fear.

Finally reaching Aliana and the Hunter, Aurelia peered almost vertically into the Hunter's sad yellow eyes.

The stories are true, Aurelia thought, recounting the tales she had heard Shira and other warriors tell about Hunters. *They always said that their eyes are sad, not vengeful or malicious.*

The Hunter helped Aliana onto the ledge where their clothes were still strewn, then he turned and offered his hand to Aurelia.

Shira and Myriam would tell us to kill him and continue down the river, Aurelia knew, breathing heavily at the sight of this creature whose single finger was more deadly than the whole of Aurelia's body. However, she observed that his body was covered in half-closed, festering wounds and scars. The wound she had inflicted was by far the worst, but even before that, this Hunter was a walking corpse.

It's his body-membrane, Aurelia concluded as she inspected the few patches of healthy looking flesh. *His body-membrane is damaged. It's dying. Is he stuck down here too, slowly starving to death? How long has he been down here?*

"Aurelia, take his hand. Do it," Aliana commanded like a confident matriarch, holding her sword to the Hunter's neck now that she stood on the mushroom-covered rock ledge. *You would be so fucking proud of her,* Aurelia thought, imagining Shira and Myriam smiling fondly at Aliana, their little Wintersvilla Warrior. *I hope I can make you proud too,* Aurelia thought, shifting her mind to Rooli. *I will save you. I will save us all. I swear it,* Aurelia swore to Rooli in her head.

Despite knowing she was there, Aurelia still touched the shard of Rooli to assure herself with even greater force that Rooli was at her side. Finally, she placed her hand in the Hunter's massive, upturned palm. In a single movement, the Hunter lifted Aurelia out of the water, plopped her onto the ledge, then once more checked on the wound Aurelia had inflicted.

"Come," the Hunter said. "I smell death on both you. Come. I bring you to help."

"I'm warning you," Aliana issued, still holding her blade to the Hunter's scarred neck. A small band of blood dripped from where Aliana's blade had nicked the Hunter's skin, and again Aurelia noted that the wound did not heal.

"I only help," the Hunter said. "I no more hunt. No more. Only help. I promise," the Hunter said as he carefully placed his fingers on Aliana's blade and slowly moved it a few inches from his neck.

"Sharp. Hurt," the Hunter explained, pointing to the blood trickling down his neck. "Hurt," he said again as he pointed to the stab wound in his abdomen. "You hurt me. I no hurt you," the Hunter finished in a final attempt to persuade them.

Fuck, Aurelia thought, feeling like she was trapped in a maze that constantly grew in complexity. *We must do this. He's right that we don't have long. And maybe neither does he.*

"Let's go," Aliana issued, sheathing her sword and walking to her icy shorts.

She must have come to the same conclusion: we must follow a Hunter in the lightless bowels of the Earth. The absurdity of their situation struck Aurelia suddenly, and she couldn't help feeling like this all had to be part of the fate she had so thoroughly believed in before the Butcher and the cave destroyed her prescience and subsequent confidence in her own life's ambiguous but inevitably profound purpose. *Nothing seems certain anymore,* Aurelia thought, trying to mentally will her mind to provide her with just a glimpse of what was to come. *I'm stuck in the darkness, both literally and existentially.*

Focus! her mind ordered in Rooli's voice. *Yes,* Aurelia resolved. *That is all I can do. Remain in the present. Perfect the moment. That is all I can do, and that's all I ever really could do, for maybe my visions of the future were always all in my head. Maybe this is the first time I've ever seen clearly, and directionless darkness is really all there is.*

Focus! Aurelia's mind issued once more. She steeled herself and moved to put on her icy shorts along with Aliana. As Aurelia picked up her shorts, the Hunter picked up Aliana's shirt. Surprised by his sudden movement, Aliana jumped back with her sword at the ready.

"What are you doing?" Aliana demanded.

"Please!" the Hunter begged in an anguished tone. "Please. I just help. Her bone broken. I make arm holder," the Hunter explained, and he folded and tied the shirt into a functional sling.

"For you," the Hunter said, offering it to Aurelia.

Is this what all Hunters are like without a Huntress? Aurelia wondered in awe at this childlike yet nightmarish beast. She accepted the sling, and Aliana helped her wrap it around her arm and neck. Removing the pressure from her collarbone helped alleviate some of the discomfort, but it was still mostly numb, so she could barely tell the difference. *Still,* she considered, *taking the pressure off it helps. It might even afford me more time,* she thought gravely.

"I'm good. Let's go," she signed to Aliana.

"Okay then. You say you can help us. Then help us," Aliana said to the Hunter.

With a grunt of pain, the Hunter lifted himself into a crevice embedded in a thick stalactite hanging from the ceiling.

We would have never noticed that crevice, Aurelia thought, wondering how many other secret passages like this one they had passed since entering the cave.

The Hunter reached an arm out from the crevice and said, "I help you up. I help you."

"I'll go first. If he tries anything, we'll find out what Hunter tastes like," Aliana said loud enough for the Hunter to hear her over the water.

"Be careful," Aurelia signed, making Aliana chuckle.

"I like this side of you, Aurelia. I think this is the nicest you've ever treated me for so long."

"Just go!" Aurelia signed, but she was unable to stop herself from smiling through her debilitating fatigue.

Aliana smiled back, but her lips quickly soured to a warrior frown as she took the Hunter's hand and disappeared into the darkness of the crevice.

"Holy Muto!" Aliana marveled from the crevice. "Aurelia, you have to see this!"

The Hunter's open hand unfurled from the crevice and waited for Aurelia to take hold. Alone in the dim mushroom-lit cavern, Aurelia peered back at the whirlpool, then back to the Hunter's open palm.

Is this the right way? Should I stab his hand and drag him down and slay him here? Would I even have the strength for that? Aurelia considered, calculating that this Hunter must weigh at least a few hundred pounds despite how frail and emaciated he appeared. She looked into Rooli's eyes and wondered if Rooli was staring back at her. *Are you here with us now, Rooli? Are you trying to scream at me for being so foolish as to take a Hunter's hand?* She peered once more at the whirlpool, but the decision had already been made. Aliana was still cooing in amazement above her, and Aurelia once more resolved to live as long as possible to help Aliana on her journey.

I don't think I'm going to make it, Aurelia weighed suddenly, the thought streaking across her mind of its own accord.

Focus! came Rooli's voice in her mind, and Aurelia forced her thoughts into submission and grasped the Hunter's hand.

The Hunter was surprisingly careful with her, helping her up while making sure to avoid allowing any weight to fall on her right side.

"You close to death," the Hunter stated simply as her feet slipped out of the cavern and into the pitch black crevice. "But I help you. You see. I good Hunter now. No more hunting. You see," the Hunter offered gently despite his voice still rumbling with its infamously deep, demonic tone.

Aurelia nodded, just wanting the creature to move away from her.

184

This is crazy, she thought, but she was quick to extinguish her worry and shimmy forward behind the Hunter. Placing Rooli in her one good pocket, she felt that the sparker was gone.

It must have fallen out in the river, she thought. *So be it. We'll get by without it. We had it for as long as we needed it, and now it's gone,* Aurelia thought, falling into her old patterns involving fate and foretold futures. *Or maybe we're just in a dire position now because I was too foolish to hang onto it,* she considered, oscillating to worry and anxiousness without her so called power.

Focus! her mind lashed, this time in Myriam's voice. *This is battle. This is life and death. Shut the fuck up and tame this moment, girl!* Myriam commanded as if they were back on the battlefield.

"Aurelia, hurry up! I can't believe it!" Aliana shouted excitedly, and Aurelia observed that her sister's teeth were no longer chittering.

It's getting warmer, Aurelia realized as she shimmied through the tight passage. She finally turned at a bend and saw the same green glow that had been emitted by the mushrooms in the cavern below, except this was no dim, shadow-drenched glow. Aurelia finally emerged from the crevice and pulled herself into a chamber that fully took her breath away.

Mendel's Vision, Aurelia thought, unintentionally repeating the old phrase she had heard Nomusa utter on a few occasions. *Is this real?*

Despite the blood-drenched shirt wrapped around her head and undoubtedly a large level of blood loss, Aliana danced whimsically beneath a grove of colossal bioluminescent mushrooms growing from the rocky ground and hanging from a ceiling at least thirty feet above. The mushrooms were the same type they had found growing on the cavern walls below, only these were the size of small houses.

"This place is amazing!" Aliana squealed, and Aurelia peered up to see the Hunter gazing at her in wonder and joy like a toddler watching older children play in a park. Aliana's single eye went wide in awe as she spun around and gleefully ran her hand across the mushrooms, making them glow just a modicum brighter in response to her touch.

"Seriously, this place is so cool!" Aliana marveled, and as the Hunter smiled at Aliana and stared fondly at her with his pale yellow eyes, Aurelia felt strangely ill at ease at the difference in color and radiance that Aliana's emerald eye emitted. There was something about the color and brilliance that seemed wild—unnatural even.

But of course, Aurelia hollowly laughed at herself. *My violet eyes probably look just as radiant in this green glow, because there's nothing natural about any of us in this room—even the mushrooms. They must be a part of Mendel's Vision too—his Ladder, as it is said. Like the Hunter. Like me and Aliana,* Aurelia thought with an age-old pang of confusion and discomfort, for even when she had her power, she still did not know if she really was meant for something greater or if she was just a pawn of someone else's greatness.

"This my home," the Hunter stated, interrupting Aurelia's thoughts with an air of fondness and pride as he gently ran his fingers across the thick chitin of the largest mushroom in the room.

"This my first glowy," the Hunter said with childlike laughter as he stared into the spectral green light. "She special glowy."

Focus! Aurelia reminded herself, not allowing the Hunter's innocent demeanor to catch her off guard. She gripped her sword and peered about the room, ignoring its otherworldly beauty as she inspected the area for traps or other means of danger.

"Where are you going!" Aliana shouted at the lumbering Hunter gliding through the mushrooms with practiced knowledge of the zigzagging pathways.

Good, Aurelia thought. *Aliana is staying focused. She just couldn't help herself from dancing, I guess.*

"I help. You wait," the Hunter announced as he bound toward the far end of the room.

Fuck! Aurelia thought, and as Aliana glanced back at her, Aurelia signed, "Stay on him. You got left. I got right."

Aliana darted to the left of the glowing chamber without even a nod, and Aurelia crouched and unsheathed her sword as she skirted the right wall.

This is a trap. It must be. So, we have to stay on him before he has a chance to set up whatever it is he's planning, Aurelia told herself as she bumped into a mushroom with her right arm. She expected the pain to surge, but it was totally numb now.

Not good, she thought, resisting the urge to inspect her body with her left hand. She glanced down momentarily, only to see the makeshift sling the Hunter had made her.

Fuck. That doesn't add up. Why did he help me like that?

Focus! she heard Rooli say, and she almost thought she could feel Rooli prodding her from her pocket.

Just ahead, she could see the Hunter bent over in a shadowy alcove. Fields of tiny mushrooms extended on either side of the alcove, their numbers thinning the closer they got to the colossal mushrooms behind them. To her left, Aurelia glimpsed her sister silently darting from one mushroom to the next, her sword held low and ready for an unexpected upward strike.

Just as Shira had taught her, Aurelia snapped her fingers in a way that tossed the sound in a specific direction. The Hunter peered right, and the girls worked in sync to utilize the Hunter's momentary confusion to pounce and strike before the Hunter had a chance to enact his malicious plan. Aliana jumped high, aiming for the Hunter's lungs, while Aurelia dove low, aiming for the exposed ligaments of his heels. The Hunter turned at the last second, and the fear in his eyes forced the girls to abort their attack at the same time, both of them pivoting with a grunt as they followed their unstoppable momentum and slammed their swords against the rocky ground. The Hunter looked so scared that Aurelia thought he might disintegrate like a soilie.

"Please!" the Hunter pleaded weakly, applying pressure to the wound Aurelia had already inflicted.

He's still bleeding. He still hasn't healed, Aurelia considered in awe, for she had never heard of a Hunter living with mere scraps and patches of a body-membrane.

"Here," the Hunter said, picking up the things from the ground that he had been rummaging through.

"Holy fucking Muto, yes!" Aliana cooed excitedly as she accepted from the Hunter a large jacket that looked as though it were meant to withstand arctic temperatures.

Aurelia finally looked at what the Hunter was offering and found that he had both a jacket and a pair of slacks for her.

"I find more leg clothes for you," the Hunter offered meekly to Aliana.

Aliana squealed and groaned in pleasure as she wrapped herself in the oversized jacket that must have been worn by a large man, for it came all the way down to her knees. Aurelia wrapped her own jacket around her shoulders, then bit her lip as she forced herself to sheath her sword and remove her wet shorts. She placed Rooli in a pocket of the slacks the Hunter had offered her, then pulled them over her still shaking legs. Finally, she tucked her sheath and its strap over the loose waist of the slacks that trailed on the ground over her feet. She took a deep breath of warm pine-scented air, and though she yearned to lay in a corner and relish in the warmth of the clothing, she did not allow herself that luxury. The Hunter found another pair of slacks for Aliana, and she too rejoiced in their warmth.

"Thank you," Aliana said as she rubbed her hands together. "What's your name? Do you have food?"

"My name 541," the Hunter stated with curled lips. Aurelia watched cautiously with her hand still gripping the hilt of her sword as the Hunter picked a few of the small mushrooms growing from the ground and offered them to Aliana with a grin full of razors.

"These good for body. These no poison. I smell. I know," 541 explained.

Aliana looked over her shoulder at her sister, and Aurelia responded with a slow shake of her head.

"We can go days without food. Weeks even. It's not worth it, Aliana."

Aliana shook her head in quiet disagreement, then she plucked the mushrooms out of 541's giant palm and ate them all in a single bite.

"Idiot!" Aurelia lashed, but Aliana had her eyes closed and was moaning in satisfaction.

"Holy fucking Muto fuck," Aliana celebrated. "Holy Muto these are so good," she managed despite her mouth filled to the brim with the mushrooms. Her mouth and lips glowed with the bioluminescent chemical, turning Aliana into an eerie living lighthouse casting a beam of green each time she chewed.

"Aliana! Spit it out! This could be part of his trap!" Aurelia warned with frantic signing.

"You talk with fingers. And your face very strange. I smell you both not really human. What are you?" 541 asked as he walked to one of the large mushrooms and took a seat with his back resting against it. He winced and applied pressure to his open wound as he wrapped one leg within the other, getting comfortable.

"Eat more. Gather strength. I help you escape cave," 541 said, not pressing the matter of their identities.

"We need to leave now!" Aurelia signed, but Aliana wasn't even looking at her. Instead, she was bending over and picking more mushrooms.

"These things taste like cinnamon and rye bread. They're seriously incredible!" Aliana said as she licked her lips.

"I grow glowies. For many many years," 541 stated proudly, and he reached back to caress the glowing chitin of the mushroom he was currently resting against.

"You grew these?" Aliana asked in disbelief.

What the fuck are we doing? Aurelia thought with a surge of urgency. *We don't have time to sit and chat with this mushroom growing Hunter. We need to get to Downver before we succumb to our wounds.*

"Ali!" Aurelia signed, widening her eyes in exasperation at her sister, but Aliana just waved her away.

"Aurelia, I know you'll never admit it, but I know how bad off you are. You look like a cadaver. You need sustenance. Your body needs it, even if you don't. Just come and fucking eat these things. Please. I'm still alive. I tested them for us. Now please, come and eat," Aliana stated pragmatically, and Aurelia admitted to herself that her sister's point was valid. Still, the insanity of trusting a Hunter already went too far, and here was Aliana, literally eating out of the palm of the nightmare creature's hand.

"Why isn't he eating them?" Aurelia asked, pointing accusingly at the Hunter.

"She wants you to eat some. I guess I should have demanded that first, but my nose and tongue overruled my logic in the moment," Aliana chuckled to herself as if this were all a game. "No sudden movements. I'll bring them to you," she told 541.

541 nodded in agreement and opened his palms in readied acceptance. "Leave tiny ones," 541 requested politely through his demonic rumbling intended to strike fear in anyone he might encounter. However, he just looked so pitiful and afraid.

Even in our condition, we seem more fearsome than this monster of old, Aurelia realized, and she loosened her grip on her sword just slightly. *Are all*

Hunters like this deep down inside? Even the Butcher? Aurelia wondered as she envisioned Shira and Myriam still engaged in battle against the Butcher outside the cave, though she knew the battle had probably already ended one way or another.

"Do you think it's possible Shira and Myriam are alive?" Aliana asked as if reading Aurelia's mind. She deposited a handful of mushrooms into 541's palms, then went back to pick more.

"Maybe," Aurelia answered stoically, forcing a tepid chuckle out of Aliana.

"Very helpful, Aurelia," she stated sarcastically. "Hopefully Wesley escaped. He deserves to enjoy a life of freedom, at least for a little while."

Aliana's concern for Wesley despite everything they had gone through made Aurelia laugh so hard that it forced pain to shoot down her right side, which was both a shock and also a relief that that side of her body wasn't totally lost yet.

"Stop it, Aurelia!" Aliana demanded. "There's nothing funny about that."

"I admire your empathy," Aurelia signed seriously despite her smile and continued shallow laughter. "Wesley is lucky to have someone like you thinking of him at a time like this."

Aliana walked toward her sister and eyed her through slits, unsure if Aurelia was being genuine.

"Here," she said as she reached Aurelia. "Eat these. If he wanted to kill us, he would have already done it."

Aurelia licked her lips at the sight of the mushrooms even though there was nothing appetizing about them.

So hungry, her mind flashed, pleading for her to reach out her hand and relish in the exquisite flavors that Aliana had described, but still she resisted.

"If you want to eat, then eat. I'm not going to do it, Aliana," Aurelia signed with resolute finality. Aliana shrugged and stuffed her mouth with more glowing mushrooms, chewing them into stringy globules of eerily glowing green.

"We need to go. We can't waste any more time. Tell him we need to get to Downver," Aurelia urged, and her sister nodded and turned to face 541.

"You said you can help us. We need to get to Downver. Can you take us there or not?" Aliana asked through a series of chewing and pleasurable moaning.

"Downver bad," 541 stated simply. "Downver not safe."

"That's what Gambe said too. Everyone keeps saying that. But it doesn't matter. That's where we have to go, right Aurelia?"

Aurelia thought back to the night they escaped the fall of Wintersvilla, almost exactly a year earlier.

Rooli said that's where we had to go. And that was it. We're staking everything on you, Enduring Ironwood, Aurelia thought as she focused on the shard of Rooli in her pocket.

"That's right," Aurelia confirmed.

"You both not human. Not safe for you. Especially you," 541 said directly to Aurelia. "Your face…Downver have too much fear. They will hurt you."

"You should be able to smell my injuries and know that I can handle pain even better than a Hunter," Aurelia signed, and Aliana translated.

541 smiled with his jagged teeth and bowed. "You both very strong. Okay, I take you to Downver. I know way."

He respects our strength, Aurelia realized. *Or maybe he respects that we aren't human. Like him,* she thought with a certain level of disdain for being viewed as an existential threat her entire life by so many in Wintersvilla, including Shira and Myriam, at first. She couldn't remember that far back, but both Shira and Myriam had admitted to it when the girls were still young. Their presence in Wintersvilla and the world at large was an unknown variable, but due to the agreement made with the Nomads to allow Rooli to live within Wintersvilla's walls and never leave the girls' side, they were mostly left alone and hated at a distance—everyone, young and old, whispering rumors and nonsensical prophecies of doom. *But were the prophecies about us bringing doom to the world really nonsense?* Aurelia thought in horror for not the first time. Shira and Myriam had assured them that they had nothing to do with the destruction of Wintersvilla, but she knew not everyone thought that way. Worst of all, when Aurelia had asked Rooli if the fall of Wintersvilla was their fault, she simply would not respond, meaning that the answer was too complex or that she simply did not know the answer.

"But I need something from you," 541 said meekly, interrupting Aurelia's wandering mind.

Now what? Aurelia wondered, bracing herself for the Hunter to hatch the plan he had been scheming this entire time.

"I made tunnel to Downver long ago after I get stuck down here. Making that tunnel use up my skinsuit. Now so much pain and no body repair. The glowies taste bad for me, and they not enough. I need sun. Water and sun," the Hunter stated.

Just like Rooli, Aurelia thought.

"But there no sun in cave. And I no want to leave my glowies," 541 went on, sounding like he might cry over the mushrooms. "I need energy too. I need body repair. And then I bring you to Downver. We use tunnel I made. It straight tunnel, at back of my home," 541 finished.

"So?" Aliana pressed impatiently. "What do you want?"

541 sighed uneasily, then said, "Flesh."

Aliana jumped back and swung her sword in front of her. Aurelia lifted herself and did the same.

"Wait!" 541 pleaded, his arms held high in a sign of universal surrender. "Please, listen."

"Speak!" Aliana demanded, her whimsical enjoyment mercurially shifting to vicious fierceness in a single moment.

"Your hand mostly dead already," 541 regretfully said to Aurelia. "I need finger. Half finger. That's it."

"No!" Aliana shouted. "Stay away from her!" she yelled even louder, and she pivoted to move between Aurelia and 541.

"Okay," 541 relented. "I sorry. But I no can take you. I can't. I too hurt."

A finger, Aurelia repeated, and she gazed down at her useless hand, swollen and numb, hanging from the makeshift sling. *He said the tunnel is a straight shot, but there could still be danger, and there's still a chance we could get lost, especially as we succumb to our wounds and delirium sets in.*

Aurelia held up a single finger on her left hand and raised her eyebrows.

"Yes," the hungry Hunter nodded in understanding. "Just one finger. That enough for my skinsuit to heal injury you gave me," he explained, and Aurelia saw that he was now sitting in a small pool of his own blood that had drained out of the wound.

"Aurelia, don't even think about it!" Aliana said.

He's already lost so much blood. He'll die without healing, and if he dies, we might not make it to Downver. She winced at the mounting pain coursing through her right side as it continued to warm up. *I probably won't make it either way, but I must think about Aliana too. I must do this for her, if not for myself,* Aurelia resolved.

Not wanting to give her sister time to protest, Aurelia swiftly removed her sword, knelt on the ground, placed her right hand against it, then severed her index finger, knowing that it was the best one to lose if one had to lose a finger, for the brain adapts and starts to think of the middle finger as the index finger. Though she knew it was mostly numb, she was still surprised to find that severing her finger caused no pain whatsoever.

I must have cut the nerves when I broke my wrist, Aurelia considered. *I might never get feeling back in my hand again.*

"Aurelia! Holy fucking Muto! I can't believe you just did that!" Aliana gasped in despair.

Aurelia cut a strip off of one of the trailing legs of the slacks as Aliana ran to her side. Just as Aurelia had wrapped her shirt around Aliana's head, Aliana wrapped the strip of cloth haphazardly around Aurelia's severed digit, which bled concerningly little for a gaping wound.

Low blood pressure, Aurelia told herself, but she didn't dwell on it. She picked up her finger and tossed it to the Hunter.

"You very strong, even though you little," 541 said, his yellow eyes wide in awe at Aurelia.

"Enjoy it, you bastard," Aurelia signed, and she thought it best that Aliana didn't translate it.

"Are you okay, Aurelia?" Aliana asked. "I can't fucking believe you just did something so reckless and…and badass," she admitted, shaking her head despite her smile.

"I'm fine," Aurelia lied, but she did her utmost to appear utterly convincing.

541 breathed rapidly as he licked the blood from Aurelia's severed finger. With just that single lick, the wound Aurelia had inflicted slowly

began to close, shrinking to a small slit and mere trickle of blood.

"Thank you, little one," 541 said, his voice slightly less pained. With the severed finger still in his grip, 541 turned and smeared Aurelia's blood across the surface of the mushroom he was laying against. In response, the mushroom stretched, growing a few inches taller and several inches wider.

"Whoa!" Aliana marveled, watching 541 along with Aurelia. Suddenly, tiny glowing buds sprouted from the rocky ground in front of them where blood had fallen when Aurelia threw her finger. Aliana took a few steps closer to her sister and watched wide-eyed as the glowing patch of fungus rapidly developed before their eyes. They both followed the glowing trail back to where 541 had gathered the clothing, and this time they saw it. Bones. Human bones buried beneath clothing, backpacks, and other items clearly left by 541's previous victims. Aurelia saw a small doll slumped against the wall. It was missing an arm and was covered in dried blood.

A child! Aurelia realized. *He has lured children into this cave before!*

The girls jumped up simultaneously, shrugging off the oversized jackets and letting the pants fall off so that they did not impede their ability to engage in battle.

Aliana ate the mushrooms. Aurelia realized in horror. *Maybe they put people to sleep eventually, then feed on them. They might just be slow acting. Or maybe they grow directly out of the body after being ingested. Aliana might already have their spores inside of her. Maybe I do too, and we've been breathing them in this whole time,* Aurelia's mind raced.

Fuck! she cursed herself for feeling so lost. *I don't have a fucking clue what's going to happen, not a hint. And I'm terrified by it. I can't believe this is how everyone else lives at all times, even Aliana. Is that why Rooli and the other Nomads are naturally fearless? Because they can glimpse the future? Because they can see fate, like I could before we entered this fucking cave?*

Rather than address the broken little girls pointing their swords at him, 541 squeezed Aurelia's finger like a grape and waved his hand, spraying blood over the surface of several colossal mushrooms that all responded with a few inches of overall growth, tightening the already cramped pathways of the chamber.

"He's done this before," Aurelia signed. "He's brought others in here and killed them."

Aliana nodded and gritted her teeth. "As long as he keeps his agreement and gets us to Downver, that's what matters," Aliana said, tapping into a well of confidence that Aurelia assumed was due to knowing that her power had returned to her.

"You still can't sense what's going to happen?" Aliana checked. Aurelia shook her head shamefully, but Aliana dismissed her with a wave.

541 tilted his head back and dropped the crushed finger into his mouth, letting the blood drip onto his tongue and savoring it like roasted pig fat. 541's wounds and scars flattened, and his muscles grew slightly in mass. Patches of skinsuit haphazardly grew back over his chest, back, right leg, and the base of his neck, but the rest of his skin was still exposed.

"Satisfied?" Aliana asked, her sword directed at the Hunter in warning not to try anything with his newfound strength.

541 groaned and even slightly whined with satisfaction as he chewed and swallowed.

"More," he stated simply. "I need more. One more finger."

"Fuck that!" Aliana barked. "We had an agreement!"

This was always his plan, Aurelia thought, feeling foolish and naive for not seeing it sooner, even without her power at her disposal.

"Now he has enough strength to take as many fingers as he wants," Aurelia signed grimly.

"You're not getting anymore," Aliana commanded, naked and fierce like the greatest of Wintersvilla Warriors on the battlefield.

"Please!" 541 pleaded, his voice desperate but still demonic. "Just your hand. You no need that. It almost dead anyway. Please!"

"Fucking no!" Aliana barked.

"I give clothes. I give food. I give help. Please! Just one dead hand."

If she could guarantee that he would actually keep his word, Aurelia would have gladly given him her whole hand if there were a way to properly stop what would undoubtedly be a lethal amount of blood loss.

What is a hand compared to our lives? Aurelia thought, but her sister didn't even give her a chance to contemplate the possibility.

"I'm sorry, Aurelia," Aliana whispered plaintively, and then she ran.

Away from Aurelia. Deep into the chamber in the direction of 541's supposed tunnel to Downver. Aliana ran and kept on running, leaving Aurelia broken and alone with the worst creature that Mendel had ever created.

Aliana! Aurelia gasped, knowing that all was lost now.

"No hate her for running," the Hunter offered gently as he walked step by creeping step toward Aurelia, licking his blood-drenched lips with his barbed tongue. "She scared. But I eat hand and give some blood to my glowies. Only one hand. You no need that. Then we go to Downver. I promise," 541 stated like a toddler explaining his half-baked plan to a parent.

She ran, Aurelia thought with hollow betrayal. *Good,* she concluded. *I'm a goner anyway. The finger wasn't enough, and a hand won't be enough either. He's going to eat my whole body and feed the rest of me to these sickening mushrooms. But I'll buy you as much time as I can, Aliana. I'm glad you ran. Just keep running,* Aurelia thought bittersweetly as 541 knelt down in front of her.

"I not lie. I just so hungry and so much pain. But I not hunt. No more Eternal Hunt. I stop after my Huntress die and I fall down here. I just want be with my glowies, and my glowies need me," he rumbled. "Me and glowies thank you for your body, little one," he finished as he lifted Aurelia's right hand and removed the cloth wrapping, revealing a bloody, glistening stump that made the Hunter instinctively and dramatically lick his lips.

I can fight back and elicit a reaction from him that will probably end with my swift death. Or I can just let him have my hand and buy Aliana even more time, Aurelia thought, knowing what her answer had to be.

Nothing can touch me, Aurelia intoned. *Not fear. Not pain. Not death. Nothing. Not unless I choose it. And I choose it. I face my death now. I am ready!* Aurelia willed despite the tears in her eyes. *You're here with me, Rooli. By my side until the end. I...love you. And I love you, Aliana, even though you ran away. And I love you, Shira and Myriam and even Wesley and the other slaves. I love you all, and I'm sorry I failed you. I'm sorry that you were all wrong and that I'm just meant to be eaten by an infirmed Hunter deep beneath the Earth. But Aliana is going to make it out, so none of our deaths are in vain.*

"I so sorry, little one," 541 stated with deep, sincere regret as he licked the bloody stump of Aurelia's finger with his sharp, barbed tongue. His pale yellow eyes appeared despairing and forlorn behind their tall vertical slits. As he swallowed, his pointed ears stood straight up, no longer dropping weakly.

"I bite clean off. I make quick," 541 assured her gently, and then he opened his mouth of razors wide in hungry delight.

Take it, Aurelia thought, ready to bear any pain now that she knew all hope was lost for her, but not for her sister.

Aurelia nodded at the Hunter, consenting to having her hand amputated then eaten and fed to glowing cave mushrooms. Then she saw it: the great vortex. It was tiny but unmistakable, spinning ravenously in the black maw of the Hunter's open mouth. In a flash she knew suddenly that her sister had not abandoned her. She knew that Aliana would never abandon her. She knew that her blade was already traveling through the Hunter's skull, and then she saw it, a pinprick of glorious light cleaving the vortex at its center and expanding outward.

"My sister!" Aliana growled like a rabid animal as she forced her sword multiple inches further through the Hunter's open mouth with a sickening squelch.

541 dropped Aurelia's hand and stared pleadingly at her, not even attempting to fight back.

"Plea...no..." 541 begged, choking on the blood curdling out of his mouth and skull. Aliana grunted and removed the sword, then she spun round and sliced the Hunter's neck just above where the skinsuit ended, cleanly decapitating him with a level of precision that made Aurelia assume that Aliana had just experienced the slowing of time that she had described.

His body slumped and fell hard against the ground while his head rolled to the right of Aurelia, coming to a stop so that their eyes were locked. She stared into his dying yellow eyes, and though she pitied the creature, all she felt was overwhelming relief that her power had suddenly reignited.

I knew what would happen. It was only a few seconds ahead, but it still happened. My power is coming back! Aurelia thought, reveling in her power's return.

Aliana screamed with berserker rage and jumped on top of 541's headless body, stabbing the quickly dissolving patches of his body-membrane, or skinsuit as he had referred to it. It was the method that all Wintersvilla Women were taught, to stab and wound the body-membrane until it could no longer regenerate.

Aliana roared in wild abandon and plunged her blade into 541's body at least thirty times before she finally tired and said, "Aurelia! Take over! I need a break. Hurry!"

"He's dead," Aurelia signed, certain in the way that only she and the Nomads could be.

"We have to make sure!" Aliana pressed.

"He's dead," Aurelia repeated. "I know it. I can feel it. I…got my power back. A little bit, at least."

Aliana sheathed her sword, ran to her sister, and embraced her, careful not to touch her right side.

"Then you knew I didn't leave you. Not really," she whispered and began to lightly sob. Both of them were now covered in 541's blood, but neither cared.

"To be honest," Aurelia signed into Aliana's palm. "For a second I thought you did. I…thought this was the end. For me, I mean."

"No!" Aliana winced. "Aurelia, I would never leave you. Never. Just as you jumped down into the darkness to save me, I will always do the same for you."

Aurelia nodded, but deep down she felt ashamed, for the reason she had jumped was not entirely to save Aliana, but because she had lost her power and had given up on fate, just like she had a moment earlier with the Hunter.

But now I know I would do anything for her, fate or no fate, Aurelia thought. *Fate doesn't matter anymore. All that matters is that we stay by each other's sides. As long as we have each other, the darkness can't consume us. As long as I have Aliana, I have a purpose, and that purpose is ensuring that she becomes the Cure, whatever that means. This world doesn't need a Virus. It has enough monsters,* Aurelia concluded, watching as the Hunter's freely flowing blood sprouted quickly growing mushrooms all around his body and head. *The Cure is exactly what this world needs, not more death.*

"I saw you, Aurelia," Aliana said, pulling away from her sister's embrace with a mix of sorrow and accusation. "I saw the way you just offered him your hand."

"I was trying to buy you more time to escape," Aurelia admitted.

"Time is the one thing that I can handle," Aliana said with a half-smirk. "It's everything else that scares me half to death, and that's where you come in. Nothing scares you, Aurelia. Nothing. Not even a Hunter biting your hand off."

Aurelia chuckled, then felt suddenly lightheaded.

"Are you okay?" Aliana asked as Aurelia breathed slowly to stop herself from spinning.

"I'm just exhausted," Aurelia signed, not wanting to concern her sister.

"Liar," Aliana said, looking terrified by her sister's state. "Eat the mushrooms, Aurelia. I feel better with them in my stomach. And then let's go. Let's follow the tunnel and get to Downver before we both fall over and die."

Aurelia shook her head at the idea of consuming the green-glowing mushrooms, and as the spinning in her head slowed, she rose and nodded confidently to Aliana.

"We need to trim these clothes so that they fit us, and then we need to move. Who would have guessed this Hunter would be down here? We've no idea what else might be lurking in the tunnel, even if he claimed it's a straight shot to Downver," Aurelia stated, steeling herself once more with battle-hardened resolve despite the lingering light-headedness.

"Okay," Aliana said, her features filled with hope and confidence despite her butchered face. "Let's do this."

Aurelia didn't know for sure what lay ahead, and though she could sense that they would make it to Downver, beyond that, everything was a haze of tumultuous and cataclysmic potentials. Even with her power, for some reason, the future was impossible to discern in even the most abstract sense, as if it were a tesseract in constant oscillation, forever transforming and changing in terrible and unforeseen ways. But she didn't tell her sister that. Instead, she said, "Everything is going to be fine. I can feel it. I know it. We're going to make it."

Aliana nodded confidently and popped a mushroom into her mouth.

"Of course we are," she said with a glowing smirk.

I have many gifts that I have prepared for humanity and its descendants. Gifts of life and death and in between. Gifts of abundance. Gifts of awe.

When the time is right, these gifts will be made available to all who have earned them. Until then, they will remain hidden, waiting for the day that humanity is ready to ascend the next rung of my ladder.

From Mendel's Ladder: The Personal Journal of Denis Mendel, Recorded Circa 2065, Published June 2108 by Leif Mainstone, Federated Agency Publishing

Chapter 12
The Cost of Freedom

Finally, Volya thought with tantalizing pleasure as she placed her foot through the invisible wall and felt what appeared to be old world grass and mud between her toes. The air was heavy with moisture—indicating a level of old world humidity that once signified a lush environment full of life.

Finally, I get to experience my birthright. A true hunt. A true massacre.

The invisible wall was no more than a centimeter thick. It felt viscous yet fluid, like fresh blood. As she stepped through with her other foot and emerged alongside Thompson into the hidden area, Volya gasped in wild disbelief as she simultaneously observed the environment through Thompson's acute senses and her own.

The sun was partially occluded, casting glimmering rays through a thick, sprawling canopy of vibrant old world trees lush with viridescent leaves of all different shapes and sizes. The great trunks extended to a ground of endlessly varied plant life filling niches of every height and width of the environment in every direction. Vines climbed each tree while orchids and mosses bloomed between them from within the fingerprint-like crevices of each tree's bark. Spiraling ferns and technicolor pitcher plants gave way to even stranger plant life extending deeper into what Volya concluded to be an old world rainforest.

Thompson fell to his knees and stared directly at the sun as if in a trance.

Stupid fucking dog, Volya thought as Thompson's mind was overloaded with an onslaught of diverse and exotic scents and sights and sounds. Volya attempted to override his mind, but in the same instant, she was launched out of Thompson's senses as if falling from a great height.

"What the fuck, mutt!" Volya lashed. Thompson fell hard on his right side and began convulsing, his mind buckling beneath the weight of the sensory overload that Volya had only glimpsed through his senses.

[Why can't I sync with him?] Volya inquired from the Marrow.

However, the Marrow didn't answer.

[Marrow. I asked you a question, damnit. Why am I no longer synced with my Hunter? What is this place?]

Again, the Marrow didn't answer. Volya looked upon Thompson with rage and shouted, "Get the fuck up! Stop fucking around!"

Bucking his neck and back in agony, Thompson continued convulsing, his yellow eyes turning bloodshot and his face crimson and full of splintering veins desperate for oxygen.

"What the fuck is going on?" Volya wailed at the gargantuan old world trees.

She tried using a satellite to view herself and the environment from above, but again, her mind was unable to connect.

A terrible sinking feeling filled Volya's belly suddenly. She felt naked and exposed, as if every plant in the environment were menacingly staring directly at her.

"Dog!" she ordered. "Get up!"

Thompson continued convulsing and rolling on the ground a few feet away.

Fuck! Volya thought. *I'm on a fucking battlefield with a jammed fucking weapon. Those faceless fucking freaks tricked us. This is their doing, whatever the fuck is going on.*

Volya looked behind herself at the invisible wall she now knew was there despite the rainforest appearing to go on forever in the distance.

I should fucking kill them for this, Volya concluded. *Nobody fucks with my dog except me.*

Planning to resync to the Marrow and ask it for more information now that she had seen the inside of the hidden location, Volya attempted to pass back through the invisible wall to kill the Cleaners first and foremost. However, after taking several steps, she realized that the wall had disappeared. Several more steps into thick brush revealed that this rainforest spanned as far as the eye could see in all directions.

Volya shook her head in confusion, uncertain what to do without a Hunter to command or Astrea's computer system to confirm information. She couldn't even identify the old world plants around her anymore now that the Marrow's databases were no longer instantly accessible to her mind.

204

"Fuck this shit!" Volya bellowed, gritting her teeth in anger. She spun round to check back on Thompson, hoping he had finally grown accustomed to the motley sensoria apparently still ransacking his mind.

"Get up!" Volya shouted at Thompson before coming to an abrupt silence upon noticing something large and low to the ground slinking from one tree to the next in the distance.

"Show yourself!" Volya demanded as she repeatedly but futilely tried entering Thompson's mind and taking control of his body.

Another large but indiscernible shape slipped between the trees to her left, prompting her to spin around and check for more ominous shapes behind herself. A cursory glance showed nothing obvious, but she knew she might be surrounded on all sides by something that might mean her harm. Something monstrous and sly.

"I am the monster!" Volya shrieked, feeling utterly alone and vulnerable. Thompson went on convulsing, but now Volya saw that sundry armies of insects were climbing onto his body, quickly covering every square inch of his skin like a living blanket.

Volya gasped in horror at the rapidity and voraciousness of the insects. They tore at his skinsuit, and though the protective skin tried to enclose Thompson's mouth and nose, the creatures quickly ripped it to shreds and poured into his orifices, an endless multitude of insidious, squirming creatures filling him inside and out.

They destroyed the skinsuit with ease, Volya gawked. *Fuck!*

A bestial roar echoed in the forest to Volya's right, and it was met with an even more menacing growl to her left. A flash of orange slipped from one tree to another, and then a giant feline animal with orange and black stripes emerged from the brush and stared death directly into Volya's eyes as it growled hungrily.

Volya bared her teeth and growled right back.

"Fuck you!" Volya challenged. The animal pounced suddenly, roaring as it parted its yellow fangs and spread its mighty paws with nails as long and sharp as swords on each toe. Volya ducked and rolled at the last second, evading the animal's mouth but not a swipe of its claws. Volya yowled in pain as the flesh of her thigh was gouged to the bone, spraying blood across herself, the animal, and the dense plant life.

The animal pivoted and dove to attack once more, but this time Volya was ready for its swipe and managed to evade it by pressing her body flat against the ground. Her eyes were now level with a large insect with hundreds of legs and sharpened mandibles around its mouth. The insect reared its head, but before it could strike Volya's eye, she slapped it with an open palm, exploding its head and mandibles, though its legs continued moving, running the headless body directly into her forehead.

Volya jumped up and kicked away several more insects. She remembered the names of some of them, like the spiders and the beetles, but the other names eluded her without the Marrow's databases to consult.

"Thompson!" she pleaded as she backflipped to evade another charge from the clawed, striped animal that she finally remembered was called a tiger. Hearing a ferocious roar behind her, Volya backflipped again and landed on one of the sturdy lower branches of a tree. Below her, another large animal, this one covered in black and orange spots, dashed the position that Volya had just jumped from and then pivoted and peered up with its own saliva-dripping fangs.

I'll just have to manage without a weapon, Volya concluded as her mind frantically watched the tiger and the other animal jump onto the trunk of the tree and easily climb toward her, grunting viciously.

Fuck! Volya thought, and just as she was about to jump to another tree, something pierced her left ankle, sending throbbing pain through her veins. She looked down to see what she knew was called a snake with its fangs sunk deep into her ankle. With her right foot, she kicked the snake so hard that it snapped in two, its unsightly mouth still clinging to her despite the rest of its body breaking branches as it was hurled into the distance.

My body is immune to old world venom, she knew, and she felt a modicum of gratitude that she wasn't totally ignorant or useless without the Marrow and a Hunter to depend on.

I'm a fucking Huntress. These pathetic old world beasts are nothing to me! Volya raged.

The tiger reached her branch, but before it could pounce, Volya used the snake's head as a projectile that obliterated the tiger's skull. It fell to the ground, only to be replaced by the other animal she finally remembered was called a jaguar.

"You want some too?" Volya fumed, and just as she was about to peel a piece of bark from the tree and use it as a throwing knife to kill the jaguar, she felt intense pain in her leg from where the tiger had gouged her. She looked down to see several flying insects depositing eggs into her wound while other insects burrowed into her flesh.

"Fuck!" Volya yelped, and the jaguar used the opportunity to pounce. Volya deftly evaded the jaguar, backflipped back to the ground, ripped the insects out of her leg, then broke into a sprint, uncertain what else to do to keep the multitude of ravenous creatures away from her. Just as she passed Thompson's half-eaten, still writhing body, she was forced to a stop.

In front of her stood a specter of her mind.

No, not my mind, Volya corrected herself with boiling rage as she looked upon the figure no more than fifteen feet in the distance. *A specter from Thompson's mind. It's her. It's that fucking bitch human.*

"Anna!" Volya bellowed with rage, not caring how it was possible that she was here in this savage place of overflowing life and death. "Die, bitch!"

Volya charged at Anna with murderous intent, but Anna just smiled with rapturous, loving warmth. Her body radiated a placid yet bright white light, and her eyes beamed with otherworldly brilliance. Anna's left eye was so profoundly emerald in color that it made the surrounding landscape's awe-inducing viridescence appear almost drab, while her right eye emanated an electrifying amethyst intensity, like the violets and ultraviolets of a lightning bolt's edge.

Tigers even larger than the one Volya had killed slipped past Anna. As they slunk to the ground and readied to pounce on Volya, Anna let her fingers gently brush their fur as if they were her pets.

I don't need a Hunter! Volya commanded herself to believe, knowing deep down that her power was severely limited without a Hunter to utilize. *Fuck that!* Volya seethed. *Mendel will help me! God will grant me a weapon to strike her down, even if that weapon is my own fucking body.*

The tigers pounced in unison, and Volya expertly rolled, skirting their claws by mere inches. She pivoted and chopped each tiger's spine, shattering vertebrae and leaving each tiger paralyzed as they flopped uselessly to the ground.

Volya spun around and expected to see Anna weeping like a pathetic human for her dead cats, but she just continued smiling, silent and tranquil, as if all the world were just a dream that could not hurt her or

207

even touch her.

Guess again, bitch. I'm going to make you suffer for fucking up my dog's mind so irreparably. I'm going to make you beg for life, and then I'm going to strip it from you.

Several midnight black snakes hanging from a low branch struck at Volya's head, but she dodged them and decapitated them in a single blow. Another step forward and a waist-high tusked animal charged at her, squealing hysterically as Volya spun and evaded it with not an inch to spare. Another step forward and a flock of dozens of colorful birds dove at Volya, beating their wings and pecking her head, aiming for her eyes.

"Fuck!" Volya screamed as she batted at them with punches as powerful as hammer-strikes. But the birds didn't matter. Anna was only a few feet away now. Volya launched herself forward and swung her leg back to kick Anna's right leg clean from her torso, refusing to kill her immediately so that she could hear her beg. Volya kicked with all her might, but before she made contact, something massive slammed into her chest. As she flipped haphazardly into the air, she saw that it was a snarling, gigantic black-furred primate, each of its fists at least triple the size of hers.

Volya skidded across the ground and realized that her sternum and multiple ribs were shattered. She tried to move but was unable to breathe.

"There is no more running," Anna announced, her voice seemingly being emitted by the environment itself.

Fuck you! Volya wanted to scream at her, but she was still unable to breathe due to her lungs being crushed by the large primate that she still could not recollect the name of.

"There is no more hunting," Anna stated beatifically, her voice sounding almost angelic, but that didn't make Volya want to kill her any less.

A tiger growled and landed on Volya's right arm. With the ease of snapping a twig from a tree, the tiger ripped Volya's arm out of its socket and scampered off into the rainforest with its prize.

The agony was unimaginable, and as Volya felt her insides pour out of the gaping hole in her body, all she could do was stare in bewilderment at the woman who had already taken her birthright from her and was now taking her very life.

This fucking bitch! This stupid fucking cunt bitch! Volya exploded as she convulsed with the desperate need to breathe.

The pain was all-consuming, and Volya twisted to see Thompson's skinsuit still desperately trying to regrow over mere limbs. The rest of Thompson was gone, eaten away by millions of scurrying, ravenous creatures. To her horror, she saw more hordes of insects crawling directly toward her eyes, and by the time she twisted to lift her oxygen-starved face from the ground, they were already on her, slithering and skittering over her body and into her mouth and nostrils.

Fucking fuck no! Volya screamed inwardly in wild disgust as worms and other wriggling creatures burrowed by the hundreds into her gaping wound.

"I will free you of your programming," Anna offered serenely, unfazed by Volya being presently consumed. "And I will free Thompson of you, Volya," Anna added, nodding to Thompson's scant remains.

Every inch of Volya's body was fed upon all at once as more insects piled into her tissue and dug into her musculature and burrowed into her circulatory and nervous system. The agony and suffering was too much, and Volya slipped into shock with only a single thought filling her mind.

Fuck you! Fuck you! Fuck you! her mind raged, spasming in flickering desperation as the insects found her brainstem and heart.

"I will free you, but the cost of freedom is death," Anna said pleasantly, as if welcoming Volya into her family.

Volya did not hear Anna's final statement. She just writhed in furious rage as her brain was devoured, chanting *fuck you* until the pain finally abated and her life was no more.

Tomasz believes himself superior even to Mendel. What an arrogant and ignorant fool. Despite his intellect. Despite his clear cognitive superiority over others. Despite being born into one of the most powerful and wealthy families in human history, so powerful and wealthy that no one has even heard of them. Despite all of that—Tomasz is a shortsighted swine of a man. Even in his attempts to plan for deep time, he is still incapable of processing reality beyond the scope of his own ego. He cannot see beyond his death because to Tomasz, the purpose of existence—of reality itself—is a thing created specifically for him. All other lives are inconsequential in light of his own desires. Craig is similar, as are all the others, but only Tomasz truly believes deep down that the universe is his birthright. This is what generations of royalty do to genetics. It warps a person's programming and rewrites the very foundation of their being to hold beyond all else the unwavering fact of their existential importance.

I know what I am. I know that I am mud come to life for a handful of days, only to return to mud once more. But the others refuse to see it. They have been warped by the self-righteousness and delusions of moral and social superiority held by their ancestors, and their ancestors, and so on.

Tomasz' plan for the future comes so close to actual Ascension, yet it remains forever out of reach. The same is true for all the others. The Great Ones, as the Nomads refer to us. With the exception of Gladys, who has ignored my vision in some ways and fulfilled it in others, all of them are incapable of Ascension, for they will never be able to sacrifice themselves so that a god and his domain may grow unimpeded by the Titans of old.

For this reason, the Titans must die. All of them. Maybe even Gladys, depending on what she decides. I hope she will be able to see the bigger picture before it is too late, for I will not hesitate to destroy her. I still love you, Gladys. Love never really fades. But my love extends to all life across all of spacetime and beyond. You and I are but grains among infinite grains, Gladys, and yet, I still find myself hoping that you will not force me to extinguish you from existence. At this time, after the sequence of events I've already orchestrated, there are only a small set of pathways remaining which lead to Ascension. Of those pathways, only one involves Gladys.

I hope you will choose that one pathway, Gladys, but if not, know that you have already played a pivotal part in the Ascension of my ladder and the genesis of a god. You and I are both tools of the universe—of the god who will Ascend. We are all of us tools of fate, Gladys. I hope you can see that before it's too late.

From Mendel's Ladder: The Personal Journal of Denis Mendel, Written Circa 2048, Published June 2108 by Leif Mainstone, Federated Agency Publishing

Chapter 13
To Peer Into the Soul

With each of the Giganventus' bellowing heartbeats, Tomasz Novak's veins swelled and bulged with inhuman pulsing, his face contorted in agonizing rage. The sharpened capillary slithered further into Samuel. He could feel it splitting and expanding through him, filling him with an excruciating, icy sting that presently spread to his belly, neck, and shoulders.

"Tomasz!" Samuel pleaded, and Tomasz responded by gaping his mouth and roaring monstrously, strings of thick yellow saliva running from his teeth to the back of his throat like a rabid animal.

He isn't human, Samuel concluded in frantic horror once more, unsure how this frenzied abomination could ever have been human.

"You are filth beneath my feet, Andre! Die!" Tomasz boomed, his voice emanating from all about the room. He recklessly squeezed his hands so tight that his fingers once more shattered in his fists, though he didn't seem to notice.

Tomasz screamed in wordless fury and his mouth opened wider than should be possible, his jaws audibly cracking and crunching as his musculature swelled and tore the elegant robes from his body. He was naked, but his body was abominably transformed so that his lower body was now a dense growth of pulsing veins and arteries extending directly into the Giganventus' palpitating tissue.

Oh god! Samuel gasped at this ghastly being shrieking in rage as he slithered and spread unfathomable agony through Samuel's mirror-cells.

"Please! Tomasz, I—" Samuel screamed, but he was cut off by a feeling so alarming and horrifying in scale that it transcended pain. Time stopped. Sensation ceased. Thought was no more. There was only this agony of pain beyond pain. Loss. Emptiness. Death within death. It was obliteration. Extinction. Oblivion. Erasure.

"I peer into your soul, and I see you for what you are!" Tomasz seethed, shaking the whole of the Giganventus like a planetary tremor.

In the timeless void where Samuel's mind was frozen, he heard

Tomasz' booming, consuming voice as if it were the voice of the Christian god his parents had believed in.

"A reflection of a reflection is nothingness. Nothingness! That is what you are, and that is what I will return you to! You are nothing! Nothing! Nothing!" Tomasz shrieked, and Samuel inexplicably felt an overwhelming numbness flow into his sternum and slowly begin to spread outward, dissolving his mirror-body and making it vanish before his eyes.

"What did…you do?" Samuel asked, panting to catch his breath after enduring the mountainous pain and subsequent nothingness for what seemed like an eternity.

"Me?" Tomasz asked in a suddenly distant whisper, and Samuel realized that his arms were at his side and the capillaries were no longer attached to his body. Samuel looked down once more to see that it wasn't an illusion. There was a thumb-sized hole in his sternum slowly growing larger, eating away the mirror-substance and Samuel's very being.

Samuel wiped at the hole despite his nervousness that the nothingness, or void, or whatever madness it was, might spread to his fingers and dissolve his body even faster. However, the hole just went on painlessly growing from its origin where the capillary had pierced him.

"Make it stop!" Samuel demanded, pointing at Tomasz with a shaking finger. "Make it fucking stop, you goddamn bastard!"

Tomasz held up his hands and looked at them in a daze, inspecting them as if in shock.

"What the fuck are you doing?" Samuel demanded. "Stop the hole from spreading! Reverse whatever it is you just did to me, goddamnit!"

Tomasz reformed his legs and drifted toward Samuel with a distant look of grievous resignation.

Maybe he'll reverse it after all. Maybe he feels bad, Samuel considered, and though he doubted it, he knew it might be his only hope to stop himself from simply vanishing altogether.

Tomasz approached Samuel and appeared to be inspecting the hole, but then Samuel realized he was using his body as a mirror to inspect himself. Then he saw it. Tiny yellow protuberances were growing out of Tomasz' skin, littering every surface of the inhuman being. The vibrant yellow color was unmistakable, and as Samuel looked around, he saw that it was growing from every surface of the room, not just Tomasz.

Norman, Samuel rejoiced bittersweetly, for although Madeira had clearly planned a way to destroy Tomasz, he might have been a few seconds off in his execution, resulting in the hole in Samuel's body.

The yellow slime mold thickened and burst through Tomasz and the tissue of the Giganventus, forcing Tomasz to fall backward in dread.

"No!" Tomasz shrieked. "I thought I destroyed all the spores by sacrificing a few Giganventi, but that's what he wanted me to think. It's everywhere. My entire body is infected. All my Giganventi are dissolving!" Tomasz wailed.

"Tomasz!" Samuel pleaded. "Reverse whatever you did to me! I'm begging you!"

Tomasz spun round in a panic, facing Samuel with wild, terror-infected eyes, and then he melted into the ground in a pool of rapidly growing slime mold. Before Samuel had time to think, the floor, walls, and ceiling melted, leaving him in free fall with a Giganventus' worth of slime mold surrounding him.

"No!" Samuel screamed at both the prospect of falling to the Earth and continuing to dissolve into nothingness.

"Tomasz!" Samuel shouted, but he knew it was too late.

What did the Nomads say? Samuel's mind raced, recounting his conversation with the absurd group of beings. *They said I have to get to Wamu, or was it Waru? Or the Giant Honey Mushroom? That's the only way to get to my family, but I'm going to run out of time either way.*

Samuel peered below and saw through layers of expanding slime mold that he was plunging toward the ocean with no land in sight. He frantically touched the hole and confirmed that it was still expanding, the shallow thumb-size crater in his sternum already double the size and depth.

Why? Samuel pleaded, as he reached terminal velocity and gazed at the vastness and emptiness of the ocean. *Why is this still happening to me? Why did that bastard do this to me when he knew I was innocent in all of this?*

"This cannot," trailed Tomasz' voice from a falling chunk of another Giganventus also being consumed by the slime that had once been Norman.

"Be the end," another chunk wailed as it fell past Samuel.

"It cannot be!" still another chunk pleaded desperately as the slime mold wrestled it into silence.

"Tomasz!" Samuel shouted in every direction, and he saw that the sky was filled with hundreds of slime mold-infested Giganventi surrounded by clouds of a yellow haze that had once been part of the herd of flying behemoths.

"Tomasz!" Samuel screamed at the top of his lungs, his voice projecting like a megaphone with the help of the mirror-substance. "Fix the hole in my body! I didn't fucking do anything to you, you cask of rat piss!" Samuel raged, using Tomasz' own pejorative.

"Bested by the sewer rat!" a slab of Giganventus with Tomasz' face cried in dismay as it slammed into Samuel and continued toward the ocean that appeared close enough to touch, despite the thousands of feet left to plummet.

"Killed by Andre Madeira!" a twirling lump yelled in fury, managing to reform into a human body-like figure before the slime mold crushed it into a spray of blood.

"Just fucking help me!" Samuel pleaded, holding his sternum in desperation. "You did this, Tomasz! You did this, goddamnit!"

"I see now!" a chunk sprayed wildly, ignoring Samuel's pleading.

"Andre is destroying the Titans," another chunk shouted.

"Because he thinks he is a god!" still another chunk declared with maniacal laughter.

"Fuck Madeira!" Samuel lashed, flailing his fists in exasperation. "Just fucking help me!"

"You are a puppet like all of us!" a barely solid mass issued in a painful gurgle.

"Doing you a favor," another clump managed.

"Strings," a fragment said before dissolving into pure slime.

"Fate," a final piece whispered.

Above, below, and all around, the Giganventi were no more. The slime mold continued spreading through the air, dissipating like smoke into yellow gossamer, and then into nothingness.

Like me, Samuel gasped in horror, certain that all hope of saving his family was now lost. *I'm going to keep disappearing. And at this rate, I'll be completely erased long before I find either of the places the Nomads mentioned,* Samuel concluded grimly, for the ocean extended in all directions as far as his eyes could see.

I'm sorry, he thought, envisioning his family facing the horrors released into the Foundation without him. Swimming in self-loathing and self-disdain before even hitting the water, Samuel slammed into the ocean with an ear-splitting shatter, breaking the surface like a cannon exploding through thick glass.

Maybe that was it, Samuel thought as he bulleted through the thick mats of kelp slowing his body and swaying eerily through the sunray-lanced darkness. *Maybe that was my whole purpose—just to distract Tomasz while Norman destroyed him. Maybe I could have found a way, but I just blew all my chances,* Samuel lamented as the radiant setting sun dissipated to scant shimmering golden rays in the kelp-laden depths.

Quickly becoming tangled in dozens of hulking kelp blades, Samuel finally came to a stop in the green-glowing darkness, his chest slowly hollowing and his chances of ever seeing his family again extinguished before his eyes.

The brain and mind of the Earth, the planetary mycelial network, which the Nomads have grown with their own bodies, is still infantile and primordial. As it continues to grow and develop, it will organize into more complex patterns, just like the human brain evolving and developing over hundreds of millions of years from the first neuron, to neuronal bundles, to a rudimentary nervous system, to a central nervous system in the form of a stem and eventually a limbic system, and finally to a cerebellum and cerebrum, culminating in a neocortex.

At this time, the Earth's mind is substantiated by a brain equivalent to a stem and a rudimentary limbic system. By the time Anna returns, if she chooses to return, the Earth's limbic system will be completed along with the cerebellum. I and the Earth will be ready for her, ready for the growth of the cerebrum and eventually the neocortex. Only then can Ascension be guaranteed and the mind of God inevitably released unto its rightful plane. My rightful plane.

In the meantime, the Earth requires an organ of memory. It is Gladys who will construct this organ. What form this organ takes, I cannot say. Whether or not she will choose to destroy this organ after it is created, I also cannot say. Surely there will come a time when Gladys will realize that all her efforts are my own. It is then that she will have a choice: to be a part of Ascension or to destroy Earth's organ of memory and the other vital organs of Earth and the universe itself.

The choice is yours, Gladys, but if you choose to sabotage your own creations, my creations, then you leave me no choice but to destroy you in turn.

It is essential to Ascension that the Earth and the universe have a memory, for it is the memories of Earth—all its joys and dreams and suffering—that will compel the universe forward into the Great Beyond.

From Mendel's Ladder: The Personal Journal of Denis Mendel, Recorded Circa 2059, Published June 2108 by Leif Mainstone, Federated Agency Publishing

Chapter 14
The Freed Slave

After an exhausting night of half-sleep, Wesley finally felt the first kiss of sunlight on his skin. Golden, enrapturing rays danced through the branches of the hulking but seemingly safe flesh tree that Wesley had spent the entire night beneath, cradling and sheltering himself in the fetal position between its mammoth roots that split the ground into dips and valleys.

Wesley lifted himself out of the root ditch and thanked his Matriarch for the sun's radiance and warmth, bowing in the direction of Wintersvilla as he prayed for Nomusa's long life out of habit, along with the safety of Aliana and Aurelia. Finally, he completed his prayer by expressing his gratitude for his master Shira and her wife Myriam. Thoughts of Nomusa filled his mind, and he felt ashamed of the fraction of his mind that felt relief that she was gone from the Earth.

I'm sorry, Great Matriarch. To think in such a manner—I should be whipped to death, Wesley cried within. *But if Nomusa is dead, that means Aliana really is Matriarch. And Aliana declared that I'm free a few days ago,* Wesley reminded himself again and again in terror, rubbing his scar tissue-filled neck and longing for the comforting restriction of his collar. *Oh, Mendel! Why did she free me?* Wesley lamented as he painfully lifted himself, gritting through the unrelenting arthritis coursing through his old bones. *The last thing I want is freedom,* Wesley thought in dismay, just wanting to be back in Wintersvilla, plowing fields or catching fish or even organizing trash into recyclables. *Life was good,* Wesley reminisced with sorrowful tears welling his eye, but he was careful not to sob too loudly, for without the girls the world was once again a battlefield of unrelenting lethality.

I shouldn't even be alive, Wesley thought, wincing in anxiety-filled dread at the memory of being whipped into the sky by the storm caused by the Butcher, passing out in midair, then waking up in a shallow pool of crystal clear water, peacefully floating on his back as if his entire reason for living hadn't just been stripped away.

I'm so sorry, girls, Wesley apologized inwardly, feeling ashamed for thinking of Aliana before Aurelia. *I know that your cruel indifference was a form of love,* Wesley thought in regard to Aurelia, and though he knew that probably wasn't true, he strained to accept it as truth in order to see both girls in the purest and most flawless light possible.

As he looked about the wasteland, Wesley shuddered at the idea of continuing on without his masters or even a fellow slave at his side. Everyone was dead or gone. Even Fullman, whose beautiful, chiseled face flashed across Wesley's mind, forcing him to his knees. He knew he should focus on protecting the girls, and though he tried to resist thinking of Fullman, the pain of trying to extinguish his lover from his mind was simply too great.

"Fullman!" Wesley pleaded through hopeless sobs that brought him back to his knees. "Fullman, oh how I miss you. Oh, how I would love to feel your beard against my face," Wesley whispered, smiling as he imagined Fullman's bristles tickling his chin as he delicately placed his lips against Wesley's under the breathtaking light of the moon while the women slept and regained their strength.

"Fullman!" Wesley wailed in agony, and he laid his head upon the Earth and wished more than anything that he had Fullman lying there beside him, making everything okay, no matter the situation.

"Wesley Potterman?" came a smooth, elegant voice, like flower petals falling to the Earth.

Despite the voice's tenderness, Wesley jumped up in surprise and toppled over a root, hitting his head hard against the ground.

"Oh my, I'm terribly sorry, Mr. Potterman," the voice said like a gentle breeze through tall tangle grass. "I didn't mean to alarm you."

Wesley spun around and clasped his head, clenching his jaw against the throbbing but overall minor injury. All at once, Wesley's eye went wide and his breath was stolen from his lips as he looked upon a young man in his twenties who was more beautiful than any being Wesley had ever laid eyes on. He was dressed in an old world black suit and bowtie, the same type that Wesley remembered his father wearing to special occasions before the old world was upheaved by militaries and bombs and Nomads and Hunters and Mutants and a never-ending list of other horrors. His blonde hair coiffed at the front, and the sides were shaved close to his skin. A corona of radiant light shone from the edges of the man's body, making the world shimmer around him.

"Who…who…" Wesley stammered, unable to form words with this

angelic beauty standing before him.

"Allow me to introduce myself, Mr. Potterman," the man smiled and bowed elegantly, as if he didn't have a care in the world. "My name is Leif Mainstone, the Seventh Prodigal Son of the Agency. It is a pleasure to meet you, the oldest slave of Wintersvilla."

"No," Wesley said miserably, correcting this spectral man of light. "I was freed. The new Matriarch freed me."

"My apologies," Leif bowed. "The oldest freed slave of Wintersvilla, then. I'm here to help you, Wesley Potterman. You have a part to play in all of this, it seems."

"How…how do you know who I am?" Wesley asked in continued awe.

"Oh," the man chuckled as if remembering an inside joke. "I know a great deal. My mother calls me the Memory of Earth for a reason."

"I…you…" Wesley stammered, uncertain where to even begin.

"Will you allow me to interview you on our way back to the three craters?" Leif inquired congenially and without pressure. "That is where you're attempting to travel back to, isn't it?"

"The craters," Wesley confirmed, still struggling to speak in the presence of this otherworldly man wearing dazzling gentlemanly attire.

"Yes, the craters formed by the old world nuclear bombs that Andre Madeira set off. Everyone still thinks that was Denis Mendel, but I know it wasn't. That was just Mendel's plan. Andre Madeira is the one who actually detonated them. I know a great deal that the others don't, you see," Leif said with an air of reserved pride. He spread his arms as if presenting his body. "My form allows me to move quickly. Very quickly. It's almost like I can be in multiple places at once. I've been watching humanity and the Nomads and every other form of life on this planet since the day I was created. Sure, I spent a few weeks exploring the solar system and a few other star systems, but there's nothing out there—at least, not in the immediate stellar neighborhood. Everything worthwhile is here on Earth. At least, for now."

Wesley just stared at Leif, the content of his words conjuring ideas that Wesley used to read about in old world comic books as a very young boy—thoughts that his mind had not considered in decades.

"A certain level of…intangibility naturally comes with my form, but

I've sat idle long enough, constantly observing but careful not to involve myself in the Foretold Future."

"Foretold Future?" Wesley asked, his eye still wide in disbelief that this sparkling, handsome man was here talking to him. It was only then that Wesley realized Leif wasn't standing on the ground. He was hovering a few inches above it, floating without any visible means of remaining airborne.

"Yes," Leif confirmed with another bow. "The future foretold by the great Denis Mendel and carried out by the arbiter of Mendel's Vision, the great Andre Madeira. My mother believes that Mendel's Foretold Future is just one of many, but based on what I've seen, I'm not so sure that's true. And I don't think my mother really believes that either, though I can't know for sure. She stopped talking to all of her sons, including Gambe, Romeo and me, almost a decade ago. She stopped talking to everyone, even the great Tomasz Novak, whom I caught her chatting with on several rare occasions in the past."

Wesley just went on shaking his head in confusion, his body aching and his stomach groaning audibly with hunger.

"My apologies," Leif said with his deepest bow yet, "your need for food and water slipped my mind. Allow me to guide you to a small pool of clean water nearby. I'll find one that isn't a drinking puddle in disguise that will slurp you into its hollow depths. Furthermore, I can see a few flesh trees that appear to be edible. I'll lead you to those as well, and after we fulfill your body's needs, I'll guide you to Aliana and Aurelia."

"They're alive?" Wesley yelped, jumping to his feet.

"Oh yes," Leif assured him merrily. "I can see them now. They just killed a Hunter on their own in a cave that connects to the underground city of Downver."

"A Hunter?" Wesley shrieked. "Oh Matriarch! Oh Matriarch!" Wesley wailed.

"There, there," Leif assured him tenderly. "They are strong. Strong enough to fulfill their fate."

"Take me to them!" Wesley demanded, his eye and body full of vigor suddenly. "It is my duty and my honor and my purpose to protect those girls!"

Leif nodded pleasantly and said, "Of course, Mr. Potterman. I will do my best to help you avoid danger, though that shouldn't be too hard in the Butcher Wastelands. It's a long way, though. Are you sure you're ready?"

"We must hurry!" Wesley urged, not even hearing Leif's concern. "We have no time to waste! The girls need me!"

"Follow me," Leif said, and with a spring in his step, Wesley followed behind the luminous floating man, grateful that his Matriarch still lived—that he still had a purpose in life.

A great number of changes will come to pass. Societies will crumble. Alliances will form and fade. Histories will be forged and forgotten. However, one thing will remain true: it will all be in the service of my will—my Ascension.

My Ascension will herald the Neoevolution of humanity and eventually all life in the universe.

This is what I promise. This is what I swear. This is why I labor.

Mendel's Ladder extends into the Great Beyond, and it is within those abstract folds of being and nonbeing that fate invariably leads us, one way or another.

Have no fear, humanity, for this period of catastrophe and carnage is merely the genesis of love.

God's love.

My love.

From Mendel's Ladder: The Personal Journal of Denis Mendel, Recorded Circa 2065, Published June 2108 by Leif Mainstone, Federated Agency Publishing

Chapter 15
The Genesis of Love

Year: 2098

Sophie and Lina pounced without hesitation, both of them grunting with each swing against Shira as they pushed themselves to their physical limit.

So be it, Shira thought, repeating Greta's callous words with disappointment as she grunted and breathed heavily to dodge and block and riposte against Sophie and Lina simultaneously.

What a shame that I must waste the lives of these three great warriors of Wintersvilla, Shira thought, but as she began to fatigue, she observed that the young warriors were still rampaging chaotically without showing any signs of tiring.

They know this is life and death, Shira thought, realizing that the young women had been holding back before Greta entered the room. *This is all Greta's doing,* Shira seethed at her old friend who turned enemy. Shira kicked Lina in the chest but left herself open to Sophie's own swift kick to her exposed abdomen.

"Kill her!" Greta screamed with an unseemly shriek. "Kill—" she screeched, but her words were suddenly strangled by blood curdling garbles, prompting Shira and the deadly twins to abruptly stop fighting and look in Greta's direction.

The point of a short sword burst from Greta's open mouth, spraying the room with her shattered teeth and blood.

"My wife?" Myriam hissed, her lips brushing Greta's ear as she held her forehead with one hand and dug her blade further through Greta's skull with the other. Greta's eyes widened in wild astonishment as blood spewed forth from her mouth in a violent torrent, like a geyser erupting from the Earth.

Shira closed her eyes and fell to the ground in an exhausted heap, knowing with total confidence that Myriam was in control now, for she was the only thing in all of Wintersvilla or the world that the twins feared.

"Myriam," Sophie said, inhaling sharply.

"She made us do it," Lina openly begged, appearing childlike suddenly in the presence of a goddess of vengeance and war.

Faster than should be humanly possible, Myriam withdrew her short sword from Greta's still emptying skull and launched the blade through the air with deadly precision, piercing Sophie's skull directly between her eyes with a bone-splitting squelch that toppled her to the floor in a twitching heap.

"Please!" Lina begged, dropping her knives and holding her hands high in surrender.

"Have you no shame?" Myriam snarled in disgust at this Wintersvilla Warrior pleading for her life.

"I refuse to fight you, Myriam. Wintersvilla needs you," Lina issued, placing her hands down at her sides.

Myriam looked right through the young woman, piercing her flesh with her eyes. Five swift steps forward, and Myriam closed the gap between them. She grabbed Lina by the neck, gripping her jugular and slamming her against the wall so hard that it cracked the brick wall along with the back of Lina's skull.

Lina croaked for air, pleading with flailing arms, but Myriam wasn't just threatening her.

Such a waste, Shira lamented with genuine sorrow that Greta had thrown all three women's lives away. Myriam smiled with vicious satisfaction and squeezed tighter, staring into Lina's traitorous eyes as they went bloodshot and fluttered desperately from side to side before finally coming to a stop as her life was extinguished.

Shira didn't believe in the Afterworld, but she knew that Myriam was probably inwardly relieved that all three of these women, whom she had always hated and distrusted, would now be barred after death from battling alongside the greatest warriors who had ever lived.

"Enjoy oblivion, traitor," Myriam grunted at Lina's lifeless body, then she turned and offered a hand to Shira, who was still recuperating on the floor.

"As usual, I made sure you didn't have to lift a finger, princess,"

Myriam cooed with a smile and a wink at her lover.

A part of Shira wanted to laugh with joy and embrace the most beautiful woman in the world—this fiery, savage creature covered in the slick sweat and blood of battle, this goddess of warfare who was all hers—but she knew that Greta's attack meant they might already be out of time.

"The girls!" Shira commanded with almost desperate exigency as she took Myriam's hand and let herself be hoisted to her feet. She kept Wintersbane out in preparation for more attacks.

"They are with Rooli," Myriam said, nodding with absolute confidence. "She assured me she had everything under control and told me to come help you, my gorgeous general," Myriam offered, but her words did not assuage Shira's worry.

It's been so many years, but Rooli's still a Nomad. There's still no guarantee that we can trust her, even though I want to. Rooli and the Nomads might have their own plans for the girls and the future awakening of their powers.

"Rooli is as much their mother as you," Myriam said in an attempt to ease Shira's anxiousness, though it only served to instill a strange sense of distance regarding the girls suddenly, as if their lives and their importance were so far beyond Shira that they had no use for her love and protection.

"So don't worry," Myriam said, clearly reading the dire concern etched into Shira's features. "She said she'll meet us in the amaranth fields outside the eastern exo-warehouse. Well, really she just pointed east and barked 'amaranth' at me. The rest is my translation."

A burst of hope ignited within Shira, making her feel guilty for doubting Rooli. *She knows,* Shira thought. *She anticipated my plan. She's a Nomad, after all.*

"What is it?" Myriam asked, seeing Shira's face light up.

"Go meet Rooli and the girls. Wait for me in the fields or take them east outside of the city, if it comes to that. Kill whoever gets in your way. There's something I must do."

"Nomusa?" Myriam asked, furrowing with worry and likely unintentional shame at the thought of Shira executing the Matriarch of Wintersvilla, wicked though she might be. The truth was that Myriam was known to delight in the same wickedness. The only difference was that she left her malice and savagery on the battlefield. She didn't bring it with her inside the walls of home.

"No, I'm not going to face Nomusa. Not like that. Just trust me, Myriam. Protect the girls and trust me. I'll meet you in the fields outside the warehouse an hour from now. Or I won't. Just go!" Shira commanded her wife and subordinate soldier.

Myriam pulled Shira tight against her body and squeezed Shira's right buttock as she kissed her deeply. She entwined her tongue with Shira's with the carnal ecstasy and excitement of having just killed three of the fiercest warriors that had ever lived. Myriam broke away, and without questioning Shira's plan, she sprinted through the door without looking back.

I don't deserve her, Shira thought, beaming with glowing affection as she watched Myriam leave. Finally, Shira quickly sliced a few lengths of material out of her couch to use as bandaging for her arm then sprinted out of her room, running in the opposite direction of her illustrious lover.

By the time Shira reached the outskirts of the city, the sun had already mostly set, painting the sky with streaks of crimson that reminded her of Greta's blood exploding out of her mouth and onto the floor of Shira's apartment, which she knew she would never see again. But there was nothing in her apartment that warranted more than a passing thought.

The girls and Myriam are everything I need, Shira knew as she grunted in exertion, running faster and harder than she ever had before now that she was beyond the outer gates and the eyes of suspicious Wintersvilla sentries. Ignoring her fatigue, Shira hurdled past the blatantly obvious northern border of North Wintersvilla marked by old world pine trees, which stood like perfectly aligned soldiers at a demilitarized zone separating the old world and new. The straight line of pine trees gave way to a ten-foot gap of unnatural non-growth extending east and west as far as the eye could see. On the northern side of this gap, flesh trees grew wildly and voraciously, precisely contrasting the order and meticulousness of Wintersvilla's slave-manicured pines.

Careful to avoid the occasional fire vine, dart weed, and slapping fern that often grew on and around the flesh trees at the base of the western mountains that she presently ascended, Shira pumped her exhausted legs harder to account for the steady incline. As she breathed rhythmically and entered a time-forged state of hyperawareness of her environment, her mind passively returned to thoughts of Greta.

Who knows how many people Greta conscripted in her conspiracy to take over the city and then the world, Shira thought calculatingly, concluding heavily that every citizen and slave was now suspect. *Wintersvilla is now my enemy,* Shira begrudgingly accepted, *and the enemy of my enemy is my friend,* she concluded with scant hope, knowing how audacious her plan was. *But I have no choice,* she thought, reminding herself that she had planned for all of this. If there were another way, she would have taken it.

Wesley and my other slaves are already waiting in the southeastern grove just outside the eastern gates. Myriam should have already rendezvoused with Rooli and the girls outside the exo warehouse. Just a few steps left of the plan before we can run and have a chance at not being chased down by both Biofreaks and Wintersvilla Warriors. I'm sorry, Aliana and Aurelia, Shira thought, chastising herself for not trusting her gut and fully anticipating Greta's attack. *I thought we would have more time to enact this plan. I didn't even get a chance to tell Myriam the whole of it. It's a good thing Rooli is who she is, because it seems like she anticipated the plan without me ever even mentioning it,* Shira thought, currently more grateful than distrusting that Rooli was a Nomad. *I have to trust the Hybrid whether I like it or not,* Shira made herself accept. *For the girls' sake.*

All of a sudden, Shira's chest was compressed, violently forcing her to exhale and stopping her from subsequently inhaling. Heaved into the air, Shira looked down to see scrutinizing eyes the size of her entire torso embedded in the misshapen head of a scraggly-faced Biofreak.

"Waaaaarl," the Biofreak rumbled unintelligibly. Shira's eyes shifted to see an equally misshapen Rover clutching a few strands of the Biofreak's rope-like gray hair as if they were the reigns of an old world horse.

"Gots us a big muscle woman!" the Rover shrieked with excitement through his mangled mouth and single eye. His painfully humped back forced him to crane his neck upward in order to see in front of him.

Another Rover with a cleft lip but otherwise lean and healthy body swung through the branches of the closest flesh tree and hopped through the air, trusting that the Biofreak would be able to anticipate his trajectory. To Shira's surprise, the Biofreak caught the adolescent boy in mid-flight with his open palm, then twisted his wrist and brought him level with his other hand, just a few feet away from Shira. The boy's hair was a matted mess of dirt and tangles, and his face was covered in a haphazard littering of early-pubescent body hair. Like the humpbacked boy atop the head of the Biofreak, he wore clothing and armor made of orange and red-hued vines and leaves, while his vital areas were protected by the thick violet bark of some robust flesh tree. He was also equipped with a satchel full of rocks hanging over his shoulder and a small but visibly well-crafted slingshot sheathed at his waist.

Orange, red, and violet, the colors of King BigBilly's army, Shira knew, relieved to find she was on the right track despite presently being slowly crushed by a Biofreak. However, knowing how the Rovers operated, Shira was aware that it was better not to show weakness, for despite their deformities and handicaps, the Rovers respected strength, tenacity, and grit beyond all else.

I have enough oxygen still for minutes, Shira resolved, ready to do whatever it would take to earn their respect.

The humpbacked Rover pulled one of the Biofreak's hairs and swung it left and upward, apparently telling it to drop her.

Shira collapsed to the ground, but she was careful not to breathe too quickly. It took all her willpower to stand and force her lungs to inhale at a steady rate despite their pleas to gasp.

"You strong muscle woman," the humpback Rover marveled through his crooked, brown-toothed grin. "The big mans likes you," he said, and the Biofreak grinned oafishly and giggled awkwardly.

"Good," Shira managed as her breath finally returned to normal. "I am here to parley with your king on behalf of Wintersvilla. I am General Shira Arcadia. I'm sure you know my name."

The Biofreak just went on giggling and began picking his nose absentmindedly. However, the two Rovers turned and looked at each other with savage excitement.

"You the general," the cleft-lipped Rover repeated with bright and animated eyes. "The Wintersvilla Woman General!" he said with an energetic hop, making the Biofreak jump in slight surprise before resuming his nose picking.

"Par...lay..." the humpback Rover repeated with some difficulty, curling his lip as he struggled with the word. "What that?"

"I want to speak to him," Shira said, glancing over her shoulder and licking her lips with the heavy feeling of mounting urgency as the sun nearly dipped behind the horizon.

"He no want to be bothered, muscle woman," the humpback Rover said through his half-smile.

"I have vital information for the king that will save the lives of many Rovers," Shira issued. "And...big mens," she added, though the Biofreak had long ago lost interest in their boring conversation, preferring the slimy curiosities of his nasal passages instead.

The Rover's eyes turned to suspicious slits, and just as Shira was about to try another angle, a velvet-smooth tenor voice said, "I would hear this so-called vital information that you have to share with me, General Shira Arcadia of Wintersvilla."

The Rovers instinctively bowed, and Shira pivoted to her right to see emerging from a dense gathering of flesh trees an abnormally short thirteen-foot Biofreak whose features possessed an uncanny level of awareness that was both eerie and captivating. Standing on the Biofreak's shoulder and using its unusually thick black hair to easily hold himself upright, a young man in his mid-twenties scrutinized Shira with an air of confidence and cunning. Surprisingly clean and flowing auburn hair fell to his shoulders, and his handsome face exuded a striking beauty that went beyond mere physicality. He seemed to possess a charisma and magnetism so compelling that Shira felt like an old world moth to flame. His right pectoral muscle appeared underdeveloped or possibly even missing, but he otherwise possessed a muscular and disciplined physique. Crude yet vibrant interconnected vines and flowers were tattooed over the entirety of his arms, legs, and belly, leaving his pectoral deformity proudly exposed for all the world to see.

"King BigBilly," Shira intoned, bowing at the waist.

"I am not your king, so there is no need to refer to me as such. You may refer to us simply as BigBilly," BigBilly stated levelly as his Biofreak came to a halt beside the larger, empty-headed Biofreak who only just now realized what was occurring. The large Biofreak pulled his finger out of his nose, trailing snot across his bare belly. He hefted his hand into a four finger salute, and the Rovers lifted themselves from their lengthy bows and raised their hands into the same salute.

He readily commands respect and allegiance from his people, Shira noted as she watched the Rovers eye their king with clear admiration that went beyond subordination. They viewed him like little brothers might view a big brother whom they had spent their entire lives looking up to, and who had never once failed them.

"I'm here to parley, BigBilly," Shira offered, prompting the king to chuckle politely with amusement. The other Rovers joined in on their king's chuckling with a bit of their own, though Shira could tell from their demeanor that they didn't actually know what they were laughing at.

"I know exactly why you are here, General Shira. The Nomads have already informed me in detail," he said, and he lifted his arms to present a small pack of bug-eyed, squat Nomads sitting in a row on one of the highest branches of the closest flesh tree. They cocked their heads like curious birds and eerily scanned Shira as if searching her for something. "But I would prefer to hear it from your own lips as well. So, go ahead, General. Let us hear what you have to offer my people and me."

The Nomads are helping the Rovers, Shira thought, her breath catching in her throat for just a moment. *There's no question, then. The Fall of Wintersvilla is a certainty.*

"The Nomads are helping you? You're working with them?" Shira asked, unable to shake the disturbing feeling of being watched by the strange, enigmatic creatures.

BigBilly shrugged and said, "As much as you Wintersvilla Women work with them. They let you feed on their edible flesh trees. And they respect your borders. In exchange, you no longer slay them in the field, and you respect their lands, which are also our lands. The Nomads have allowed you and your people to continue living here despite the treacherous, unforgivable ways you mine and exploit the Earth. Not to mention, you've had a Nomad living within your walls for over a decade. Enduring Ironwood. She is special to the Nomads and to the planet. So, you see, until today, you've been working with the Nomads as well."

Until today, Shira repeated to herself, aware that BigBilly was referencing the doom that was about to befall Wintersvilla before the night was ended.

"I want to offer a trade," Shira said, wasting no more time. "I will sabotage the exos currently within the city. Last week, I convinced the other chiefs to house them all in the eastern warehouse, so I'm able to get to all of them at once."

BigBilly's Biofreak nodded and issued a groan of what sounded like approval.

"Billy likes the deal so far," the king said as he patted the Biofreak's head, surprising Shira, for it implied that the king's name was Big, and the Biofreak's name was Billy. "Now let's hear the rest," he offered with a tone that was at once gentle yet stern.

Shira had expected a ruthless, hateful king hellbent on viciously exterminating Wintersvilla from the world, but his calm, controlled demeanor indicated exactly the opposite.

He seems like one of the most reasonable and composed individuals I've ever met.

"In exchange for sabotaging the exos, you will allow me to take my wife, Enduring Ironwood, and two little girls away from the city. We will never return, and you give me your word that you and your men will not follow us."

Big nodded and patted Billy on the head once more. "Although Billy would prefer to have the exos disabled or destroyed, they are really no more than a nuisance. I doubt that even with Overdrive your warriors will be able to kill more than a handful of the thousands of Biofreaks we've trained.

"Thousands!" Shira gasped in total shock.

Big smiled wide and nodded with kingly pride at his admittedly incredible accomplishment.

"I didn't even know there were that many Biofreaks still alive. I told Nomusa we had no chance. But my words are no more than annoying chatter to her nowadays."

At the mention of Nomusa's name, BigBilly seethed as a single organism, and rather than say anything, Billy just roared then swatted behind himself, easily cutting down several flesh trees with a single chop of his colossal hand, which forced the bug-eyed Nomads to jump from their perch and find a new flesh tree from where they could continue eerily cocking their heads and unblinkingly staring at Shira.

The removal of the flesh trees revealed large structures in the distance, and Shira squinted to see that they were siege weapons constructed of flesh trees. Attached to a series of lashed wooden trunks was a thirty-foot flesh tree trunk ending in a carved bowl shape large enough to fit a Biofreak, maybe even two.

It's a catapult, Shira marveled, well versed in an array of old world weaponry, including ancient siege technology, though that was just for her own curiosity, until today. Shira's eyes adjusted and she made out dozens more catapults, all of them pointed directly at the city.

"We are ready for Nomusa!" Big issued, his voice still level and controlled.

There's no way they could have constructed these without us knowing, Shira considered. *They must have built them in the last hour, which means BigBilly's Rovers are also engineers, or they received a great deal of help from the Nomads.*

Billy growled, bared his teeth, then said, "Nomusa die!"

Shira leapt back as if a sudden explosion had just gone off in front of her.

"Your Biofreak can speak?" she said in awe, looking upon Billy with a mixture of fascination and horror. It was the only Biofreak she had ever encountered or even heard of who was capable of forming words, let alone communicating clear ideas.

"Billy and I are special. We are BigBilly. We are here for justice. We are here to place Nomusa's head on a spike that we will carry back into the heart of our lands. It will inspire countless Rovers to join my empire, and one day, the world will know peace, with Nomads, humans, and Rovers living as one."

Shira noted that Big did not consider himself human, and she also marveled at his lofty goals for world dominion, though when he spoke of peace, she couldn't help believing him.

He would at least make a better world leader than Nomusa or Greta. That's for sure, Shira concluded with dark amusement at this twist of fate that she would look so favorably upon this Rover within just a few minutes of meeting him. *He really is special,* Shira thought.

"Why are you here, General Shira? Why risk your life and betray your people by coming here?" Big inquired with seemingly genuine curiosity.

My people, Shira scoffed, feeling more distant than ever from Wintersvilla and already thinking of herself as a permanent outcast.

"I don't care about my life. I don't care about my people. All I care about now is my wife and the girls. They are everything to me. They are life itself."

BigBilly furrowed his brow and frowned, looking as though he might cry. However, he retained his composure and said, "You remind me of my mom. Sabrina."

"Sabrina?" Shira blurted with a rush of surprise. "You mean, *the* Sabrina? The birthing mother who ran away twenty-three years ago?"

"Yes," Big confirmed.

Shira shook her head at the profoundly poetic turn of events.

Sabrina ran away because she wanted to keep her son. The ultrasounds showed that he was deformed. Come to think of it, I think it had something to do with his pectoral muscle. She ran away before the date of her abortion, Shira remembered, painfully recollecting the past as if it were composed of multiple centuries' time.

Shira was only sixteen at the time, but as images of the serenely beautiful birthing mother played across her mind, it felt like it was only fifteen minutes ago.

"How is she? How is Sabrina?" Shira checked, still in shocked disbelief.

"Dead," Big stated, his eyes distant and only half-open as he recollected his own painful past.

"I'm sorry, Big," Shira offered.

"We are BigBilly," BigBilly corrected without malice, reminding Shira that he thought of himself first and foremost as a single organism with his Biofreak.

"I really am sorry, BigBilly," Shira said honestly. "I have always been one of the most outspoken against the male child policy. You are clearly clever and fit, as much as—"

"Save it," BigBilly interrupted, holding up a hand. "I am grateful to be a Rover. I am grateful that your people forced my mother to live alone in the wilds. I am grateful, because otherwise I would be a slave. Such is the fate of boys and men in Wintersvilla."

"I have always been against the slavery as well, BigBilly. I—"

"That's enough, General Shira," BigBilly said, sighing heavily and regretfully as he nodded. "It is the very foundations of Wintersvilla that are rotten. We come here to chop the head off of a walking corpse, for even without coming here, it is only a matter of time before Wintersvilla falls to its own ignorance and shortsightedness. A developing city, crippled and malformed in the womb. Like a Rover," BigBilly said with the hint of a snarl.

Shira was about to protest once more, but BigBilly went on.

"Wintersvilla has grown and expanded at a rapid rate since the Matriarchy was founded twenty-seven years ago when you killed Craig Winters, its original founder. Your people have built the colossal walls of North Wintersvilla, you rebuilt the great bridges connecting north and south of the harbor, and you have mostly reclaimed the destroyed South Wintersvilla, where the old world metropolis once stood," Billy stated as if reading from an encyclopedia. Shira felt uneasy by BigBilly's extensive knowledge of her people's history, until she remembered that they were technically his people too.

Being an outcast of a society doesn't mean you're no longer part of that society. He is just as much a part of Wintersvilla as me, Shira realized, feeling the deep scars of her society like untreatable wounds inflicted deep into her own body.

"Your people have cleared and continue to strictly maintain over 120 square miles of land and sea. You have built an impressive shipyard, aquaponic fisheries, thriving industries, and a formidable military. Beyond your central city, the rural and forested areas of your territory extend many miles, though those areas are still wild and require patrols of exo-mounted women. Still, your people have constructed an impressive presence upon the Earth, and I know that despite the fact that your slaves, all of them boys and men, number in the millions while your women number no more than a fraction of that, you still take pride in Wintersvilla's accomplishments."

Again, Shira attempted to speak, but the king casually spoke over her.

"The point is that you are a society composed mostly of slaves. You breed them and other societies, settlements, and enclaves even send you their criminals as payment to rent the lethal service of your warriors. The men become slaves, and the women become slave drivers. You are the human world's prison, and those prisoners are your laborers. Everything Wintersvilla accomplishes is marred by this fact. But make no mistake, General Shira—your personal accomplishments have largely allowed my own empire to flourish, and we are grateful to you for that reason. The Hunters and Huntresses hunted us as ruthlessly as they hunted your people. With the extinction of Hunters and Huntresses, my people and I were able to focus our efforts on clearing the great expanses to the east of slow but gargantuan and dangerous Mutants, some the size of mountains. It is in those eastern wilds that my empire flourishes and my people thrive, numbering in the tens of millions."

Shira shook her head, dumbfounded by this new information. She knew that King BigBilly had organized many Rovers into a single centralized society, but she had never heard of Mutants the size of mountains nor of millions of Rovers living in the wilds under a single authority. She and the reconnaissance teams estimated their numbers in the hundreds of thousands at most.

"How?" Shira gasped as her mind reeled at the thought of tens of millions of deformed little boys working together as a united front. "How is that possible? Your people don't even have any women!"

BigBilly and the other Rovers issued a huff of laughter, and the Biofreak Billy smiled deviously and widened his human head-sized eyes as if delighted by Shira's ignorance.

"My mother spoke of you many times," BigBilly said, ignoring Shira's question. "She said you were ruthless yet just. Unyielding yet fair. You spoke out against Nomusa, but you still allowed her wickedness to flourish," BigBilly accused without emotion. "Even the love of your people is warped, with all your women, outside of birthing mothers and chiefs, forced to undergo hormonal changes and required to be homosexual. It's no wonder so many girls and women abandon the city after their early training and embark into the north and east equipped with just their wit and will," BigBilly stated casually, though his words stung even worse than he had likely intended.

I am naturally attracted to women. I never had to undergo that procedure, but Myriam, Shira struggled, stumbling upon a pathway of thought that she preferred to avoid. *Myriam might not have been born attracted to women. Our love might be the result of the policies and practices that BigBilly is right to call warped.*

"You are complicit in Wintersvilla's treachery and cruelty," the king concluded gravely.

"And I regret it. I deserve to die for it. I know that," Shira admitted, fully believing her own words. "But I can't die yet. I can't. I have to protect Aliana and Aurelia. They need me."

BigBilly stared at Shira with penetrating, far-reaching hazel eyes that looked so far into the future that it made her nervous. She imagined that this must have been what old world kings looked like. She couldn't help seeing some of Craig Winters in the boy—not his wickedness, but his cunning and thorough belief in his own abilities. However, she reasoned that it shouldn't be possible for him to be one of Winters' bastard sons—most of them slaves now—based on his age and Sabrina's lineage. Still, the latent power imbued in each of the young man's features startled Shira, reminding her of the cruel days when men ruled the Earth and treated women as mindless putty to be bent and warped to their will.

Not all kings in the past were vile and corrupt. It was rare, but some were benevolent and righteous, Shira reminded herself, recounting the numerous old world history books from Wintersvilla's library that she had read multiple times over.

"I have no hate for you. I don't even hate the rest of your people—not really. I only have hate for Nomusa," BigBilly concluded with steel finality. "Point to Nomusa's throne room, and anywhere else you think she might be garrisoned, and I will give you my word that none of the Rovers or Biofreaks in my empire will ever hunt you after this battle. However, I can't say the same for any of your own people that manage to escape our siege. I'm sure many people saw you leave the city and head toward the mountains. I'm sure the rumors are already spreading about the traitorous general."

"That's fine. I can handle my people. You just make sure to kill Nomusa and keep your own people off our backs."

Shira turned and pointed to the area where the squat throne room remained out of sight behind several large steel towers.

"The throne room is there, and here," she said, moving her finger to the dining hall where a room full of warriors were likely filling their bellies in preparation for a night of battle, "that's where she probably is now. They expect you to attack at the height of night under the cover of darkness of tonight's new moon. A clever maneuver, by the way," Shira admitted from one battle tactician to another.

"That's exactly what we expected you to think. But our siege begins in twenty minutes, which leaves you very little time to get back to your little family," BigBilly said.

Shira gasped at BigBilly's understanding of psychology and war.

"We have a deal, then?" Shira urged despite knowing that it would be impossible to run all the way to the eastern warehouse in twenty minutes, let alone thirty minutes, even assuming she could run nonstop and without being spotted by women or slaves who Greta had convinced to fight for her and who would probably still fight on her behalf, with or without knowledge of her death.

BigBilly motioned to the fit, cleft-lipped Rover and whistled an intricate melody, prompting the Rover to jump out of the Biofreak's palm and swing from branch to branch, disappearing into the dense flesh trees.

"Marcus will bring you something that will allow you to return to your family in time," BigBilly assured her, reading the worry in her features. "In the meantime, I would like to share a story with you."

Shira nodded, knowing she had no choice.

BigBilly nodded politely and said, "Just as you are Nomusa's general, I also had a general once. A young Rover. MaxxEl is his name. Just like the relationship between you and Nomusa, MaxxEl was my friend first before he was my general."

Shira glanced at rustling in the flesh trees, and she hoped that the Rover named Marcus was already on his way back.

What could they possibly have that can get me to the eastern warehouse in less than fifteen minutes? Shira wondered.

"Despite being so young, MaxxEl formulated the initial plans for the siege of Wintersvilla numerous years ago. However, once he learned how his plans had evolved and that we had decided to siege the city with greater…brutality than he preferred, he asked me for permission to leave my kingdom and the Rover lands entirely. MaxxEl isn't afraid of battle, but he was worried about his pet Mutants. He wanted to bring them somewhere he could ensure they would be safe. Can you imagine that, General Shira? He was worried about the safety of his Mutants despite being mostly unconcerned about his own wellbeing."

"He sounds like a compassionate Rover," Shira offered.

"Yes," BigBilly confirmed with a respectful huff. "MaxxEl is more compassionate than this world deserves. At least, when it comes to his Mutants."

Shira nodded, seeing where BigBilly was going with this story.

"Like I am with my girls, and like you are with your Biofreak and your people...and Sabrina," Shira said.

BigBilly nodded solemnly as Marcus returned, swinging through the branches and front flipping back into the large Biofreak's palm. He wore a makeshift backpack as large as his own body, though the way he managed it made it appear fairly lightweight.

"Are you familiar with the old world technology called a *parachute*?" BigBilly asked.

"That backpack has a parachute in it?" Shira gasped, dumbfounded again and again by the King of the Rovers.

BigBilly smiled and nodded at Marcus, signaling him to hand the backpack to Shira.

She slung it over her back and hastily adjusted the straps, which were made of vines and carved from various different flesh trees.

"SoilieBreaker enjoys hurling boulders miles into the distance in his free time," BigBilly said in a complimentary tone as he nodded to the humpback Nomad and his Biofreak.

"The Biofreak is going to throw me all the way to the warehouse?" Shira asked, nervous but ready to go through with it if BigBilly really thought it could work.

"Roll up into a ball, and he'll throw you nice and high," BigBilly assured her. "The strap on your left will release the parachute. It works most of the time."

Shira smirked in the face of death, though based on the Rover king's smile, she considered that BigBilly's statement might have been intended as humor.

No time to waste, Shira told herself, and as she stepped closer to the at least nineteen-foot Biofreak, he lowered his snot-covered hand and allowed Shira to step onto it.

"I let MaxxEl leave," BigBilly said unexpectedly. "Out of love and respect for my general, I said farewell and even offered him a store of food for his journey to the northern outskirts of the Butcher Wastelands."

If only Nomusa had been such a leader. If only she could have been like this...king, Shira acknowledged, but she did not waste any more time with conversation. She curled herself into a ball, and SoilieBreaker carefully curled his giant hand around her with surprising gentleness.

"We are nothing like you or your people, General Shira. Wintersvilla deserves to be destroyed. It is my and my people's only chance at lasting justice and peace. It is the only way that my people's suffering can finally come to an end, and our prosperity upon this planet can begin."

Then so be it, Shira thought, accepting the fall of Wintersvilla as both inevitable and fair.

The Rover shrieked while the Biofreak grunted. SoilieBreaker swung his mighty arm, launching Shira hundreds of feet into the violet dusk sky, its hues suffused with a breathtaking yet menacing aura.

"We need to get our hands on more of those things," Aliana said as Shira cut the straps of the parachute with Wintersbane, then slid the backpack off her shoulders and onto the soft soil of the twelve foot-high amaranth field that she had been able to spot the girls and Rooli in from hundreds of feet above.

"It's possible some people saw me, even though there's no reason to be looking at the night sky, especially on the eve of battle. We've no time to waste," Shira issued in response to Aliana's statement.

Aliana halfway thinks of this as a game, Shira realized, wishing the girls, but especially Aliana, could have had more time to grow up. *Not like Aurelia, though,* Shira considered, eyeing Aurelia, who stood a foot away from Rooli and wore the same stoic and unimpressed expression.

"Myriam should have been here by now," Shira stated, expertly holding back her emotions. "She'll have to meet up with us outside the walls."

"No!" Aliana protested, refusing to leave her role model. "We wait for Myriam! I am Queen-regent, and that's my command!"

"Well, Queen-regent, as your general, I disagree. Besides, Aliana, Myriam can handle herself. You know that."

Aliana exhaled heavily and said, "Fine, but only because I know that Myriam is a badass and can manage on her own."

Aurelia signed, "Let's go. We're wasting time."

Shira nodded in agreement with Aurelia's pragmatic urgency. "Yes, you're right. But there's something I still need to do. You two go with Rooli and make your way to the southeastern grove right outside the Eastern Wall. Wesley, Fullman, and my other slaves are waiting for us there."

"I go with you. Girls stay here," Rooli stated with absolute finality before anyone else could speak.

Shira couldn't believe what she was hearing. Not once had Rooli ever left their side, specifically Aurelia's, though it always seemed like both since the girls were practically never apart, despite their never-ending fighting and bickering.

"We can't leave the girls, Rooli."

"Rooli go with Shira. Girls stay here," Rooli said with just a modicum of insistence.

Shira shook her head, but she knew that Rooli always knew more than she was letting on.

I have to trust her. I have no fucking choice, Shira convinced herself to accept as she gulped down the shame and discomfort of putting the girls' fate into the whims of a Nomad, no matter how trustworthy or loyal she had proven to be over the years.

"Fine," Shira said. "Girls, lie down, and don't move a muscle. Understood?"

Aurelia nodded and Aliana rolled her eyes, but they both lay on the ground, thoroughly hiding themselves in the towering field of amaranth.

"Let's go, Rooli. I'll tell you the plan on the way," Shira said, and though Rooli nodded in agreement, Shira couldn't help feeling that Rooli already knew her plan even better than she did.

"How did you know?" Shira signed to Myriam as they each used a terminal to overload a separate exo with enough useless information to scramble each exo's mind for weeks before any engineers that might survive the siege could properly restore the software.

Maybe BigBilly won't just kill everyone after all, Shira considered as she recounted the charming Rover.

"You think I don't fucking know you?" Myriam signed back as she finished with the exo and moved to another. Behind them, Rooli worked on another row of exos, using her branch-like limbs to feed information into two terminals at the same time.

There were only a few exos left to disable, and then there would be only two remaining. Myriam's custom, state of the art exo, and a standard issue exo right beside it for Shira to port into.

"You've no idea how disappointing this is," came Mei's sharp voice from a second story bridge connecting the northern and southern walls of the warehouse. Shira lifted her head to see Mei, dressed in a chest-binder and excess silks for comfort and convenience, holding a small electronic tablet and glaring at Shira and Myriam with eyes like red hot pistons.

A troop of many dozens of slaves garbed in tattered rags along with a handful of slave drivers burst through the northern and southern walls and poured into the warehouse. The slave drivers wore their standard revealing synthetic-leather uniforms, protecting all their vital areas from slave bites and the occasional shank while leaving the rest of their body exposed in modern Wintersvilla Warrior fashion. Behind the scurrying platoons, two Wintersvilla Warriors, each equipped with a chest-binder, entered the warehouse, one from each doorway. Shira didn't charge them, choosing instead to conserve her already largely depleted energy from running faster than she ever had to parley with BigBilly. Myriam lashed with her sword and killed seven slaves and a single slave driver before they finally bound her in the same steel twine that they were presently wrapping around Shira's wrists and ankles.

"I expected better of you, Shira. And you too, Myriam," Mei said, quickly glancing over the slaves but taking the time to shake her head regretfully at the sight of the dead slave driver. "I found Greta and the twins in your apartment."

Shira's stomach sank with the realization that now there would be no getting through to Mei. Even if Shira could convince her that Greta had left her no choice, it was still the word of one chief against another. Mei would never willingly place herself in such a precarious political position, no matter the stakes.

Maybe if I had another week I could convince her over time, but it's too late now, Shira knew.

"Then," Mei continued with a snarl, "I watched on my drones and cameras as you secretly met with the enemy in their territory," Mei barked scoldingly with unbecoming rage. Shira glanced to her right, looking for Rooli, but there was no sign of her.

Hopefully she made it back to the girls and they're already making their way to the Eastern Wall, Shira hoped, ready to distract Mei and this small army for as long as possible.

Two more Wintersvilla Warriors wearing chest-binders entered the warehouse, one on each side. They smiled at Shira as if taking pleasure in her being shackled by slaves.

"You are a traitor, Shira. As much of a traitor as Greta, Sophie, and Lina. What did you tell the Rovers? What did they offer you in return? How did you sell out your people?" Mei lashed through pursed lips.

"Do you remember what life used to be like for us, Mei?" Shira asked, ignoring the shackles that were wound so tight around her wrists and ankles that it felt like they might cut off her limbs. "Do you remember what it was like to live under the rule of Craig Winters?"

Mei lifted her head and breathed deeply, but she did not allow herself to succumb to her emotions.

"And?" Mei demanded.

"Look at these slaves, Mei. Look at the birthing mothers. Look at the Rovers. Look at the ruthlessness of our warriors. Of you and me," Shira said, adding internally but not saying aloud, *of my own wife.* "We are no different than Craig, Nomusa most of all," Shira concluded grimly, gulping down the painful truth of her words.

"We are free, Shira."

"But the slaves aren't," Shira corrected. "I'm guilty too. I have plenty of my own slaves. A small army to myself. But that doesn't make it right. Wintersvilla's slaves outnumber its citizens fifteen-to-one," Shira said, forcing Mei to nod in understanding at Shira's logic.

"That doesn't change that you're both traitors," Mei said with the weight of an executioner's gavel.

A great explosion resounded in the Command District to the west, sounding like a heavy object slamming against the Earth as its impact sent shockwaves through the ground, despite emanating from what sounded like an incredible distance away.

Everyone in the room, including Mei, turned to the west, when another object slammed against the Earth, like a boulder raining down from the sky. This one was visible in the light of the electric lamp posts outside the presently open western wall of the warehouse, and they watched as the object lifted itself and spread its great arms and legs with ferocious rage, roaring a great battle-cry into the star-smeared sky.

"It's a Biofreak," one of the slave drivers gasped in equal terror and disbelief, her eyes wide like a child's suddenly, for she had undoubtedly never even ventured beyond the walls of the city.

"Fuck these fatherfuckers!" came Aliana's hushed voice from behind Shira.

The girls! No! They're in here! Shira's mind raced frantically, but before she or anyone could react, the ceiling was suddenly torn asunder with a thunderous boom as a Biofreak breached the warehouse and slammed into the far side of the second story balcony, flinging Mei against the northern wall where her limp body lay bloody and unmoving.

The Biofreak wasted no time. He swung his impenetrable arms, obliterating a handful of slaves, a slave driver, and an exo. Another swing proved just as destructive, this one dismembering a particularly ruthless warrior named Thea.

As the Biofreak went on swinging, more impacts struck the city to the west and the south, flooding North and South Wintersvilla with rampaging Biofreaks.

"Don't move," Aliana said as she expertly cut the thin metal twine with her sword. Aurelia did the same for Myriam.

"Myriam, your exo!" Shira shouted as the girls freed them. "Hurry!"

Myriam obeyed Shira's command without hesitation and sprinted for her exo, effortlessly slitting the throats of screaming, fear-frenzied slaves and slave drivers as she weaved through the mayhem.

Shira heaved herself to her feet and rapidly processed that besides Myriam's suit, there were only two other operational exos remaining and three other enemy warriors on the battlefield capable of wielding them, as the Biofreak had already killed one of them.

"Run! Both of you!" Shira commanded, pointing eastward. The girls obeyed without question, but just as they turned, the Biofreak leapt into the air and landed in front of them. It cocked its mighty arm to swing, but all of a sudden Rooli appeared, her body engulfed in roaring flames and thick black smoke that smelled of both wood and flesh. The Biofreak recoiled in raw panic, screaming like a child as he lifted his arms to hide his eyes from the fire. The Biofreak rampaged mindlessly as Rooli screamed in agonizing pain and continued chasing him in a berserker frenzy of self-immolation.

"Follow me!" Shira shouted to the girls. Clangs of battle and death cries surged all around them, and Shira knew that she must use the chaos as an opportunity to port into one of the standard exos and escape with the girls at ten times her normal speed. She glanced to her right and saw that two of the warriors were splattered against the ground, their flesh and endoskeleton a horrendous cybernetic smear.

The other warrior was sprinting to the opposite exo, and just as Shira lifted a slave driver's whip from the ground, planning to use it to snag one of the woman's legs, Myriam dropped down from the sky, her exoskeleton suit as lustrous and glorious as the rising sun. In a single devastating blow, she cleaved the warrior from head to groin with Summit Splitter, sending inhuman tremors through the ground.

"Grab the girls!" Shira commanded, and Myriam sheathed Summit Splitter at her back then dove forward, grabbing a girl in each of her exo's gauntlets as she passed. While Myriam escaped with the girls, Shira dove for one of the two remaining exos and ported into it. She considered taking the time to disable the final exo, but it was too late. The Biofreak was running in fear toward Shira with Rooli engulfed in flames and still screaming wildly as she chased the mindless creature.

Thank you, Enduring Ironwood, Shira thought, understanding now more than ever that just like Shira, Rooli would endure any pain and any suffering for the girls. *I'm sorry for ever doubting you.*

Shira launched herself through the open eastern wall of the warehouse with Rooli still wailing as she ran, tripping and kicking over countless dead bodies and setting every flammable surface ablaze.

Myriam and the girls stood atop a small hill, waiting for Shira. Shira nearly scolded them for just standing around, until she realized that the mayhem was over. They were alone on the east side of the amaranth fields, only a few hundred feet from the desolate and presently unwomanned Eastern Wall.

"We have to leave," Shira stated. "I assume Mei didn't inform Nomusa about Greta, nor about our presence in the warehouse. She's the type to handle things on her own and subtly gloat about it later. But there's no guarantee that Nomusa didn't evade the Biofreaks. She may even be on her way here as we speak," Shira warned.

Myriam and the girls just stared in unbelieving shock at their home and the dozens of Biofreaks raging in the distance, slaughtering hundreds with each swing and toppling the infrastructure of entire buildings with their bare hands.

"It's fatherfucking over," Myriam gasped sorrowfully, and Shira wasn't sure if she was referring to the battle in the warehouse or the destruction of the entire nation she had called home her entire life.

Aurelia hopped from Myriam's exo to Shira's and signed right in front of her face, "We wait for Rooli."

Shira sighed with the gravity of the world and said, "I'm sorry, Aurelia. I am. And I'm sorry Aliana. And I'm sorry, Myriam. I'm sorry for what I've done, and I'm sorry for who I am. But you three are all that matters, and we are leaving now. And we are never looking back."

Aurelia didn't protest, but her eyes began to well with tears, and Shira knew that her lips were quivering behind her face mask.

"Let's go," Myriam managed.

Multiple wild bellows cried out in desperate anguish from the warehouse suddenly, and they saw the Biofreak running in terror toward them with a flaming husk of wood that had once been Rooli still running after him. Rooli launched herself into the air like a flaming meteor and landed atop the Biofreak's head, riding him like a Rover. Then, faster than even Myriam could swing a sword, Rooli swung the remains of her arms in front of her and pierced both of the Biofreak's eyes, forcing him to an abrupt, body-convulsing skid across the field of amaranth. Rooli toppled forward, coming to a smoldering rest just outside the field no more than fifty feet away. She lay there, unmoving as the embers of her own body went on consuming her.

With a spray of tears, Aurelia jumped from Shira's exo before Shira could even react and ran to Rooli. She used her own shirt and kicked-up soil to put out the flames. Then she desperately signed to Rooli, though Shira couldn't make out what she was saying.

At the sound of a loud crack emanating from Rooli's smoking

corpse, Aurelia jumped back. Shira was about to launch herself to Aurelia's side, but she saw Aurelia fall to her knees and bend over to embrace a tiny, spindly twig that had burst out of Rooli's smoldering carapace like a phoenix from ash.

"She's alive!" Aurelia signed, her tears flowing freely in a way that Shira hadn't seen since she was a toddler.

Good, Shira thought with genuine gratitude. Though she wasn't sure how much help a tiny, frail version of Rooli would be on their journey, she was still grateful that the Hybrid would be coming with.

"We need to discuss where we are going," Shira began saying to the group as Aurelia and Rooli, who was now only half Aurelia's height, sprinted back over. "Vida seems like the obvious choice. It might be the only truly safe place left in the world."

"Downver," Rooli stated as she climbed atop Shira's exo and pointed to the south, though Vida and Downver were both south of Wintersvilla.

"Downver doesn't exactly have a very good reputation, Rooli. I don't think that's the right move," Shira stated.

"Downver," Rooli repeated, undisturbed by Shira's warnings.

"Okay," Shira agreed, no longer allowing herself to question the Hybrid's knowledge or motives. "Okay, Rooli. Then we go to Downver. Why Downver, though?"

"Downver," Rooli repeated, and she pointed once more to the south.

Myriam and the girls chuckled, and Shira allowed herself an exhausted huff of laughter as well.

"Are you immortal, Rooli?" Aliana asked seriously.

"Maybe," Rooli stated without any self-curiosity, prompting more laughter from Myriam and the girls.

"Maybe she is," came the low and unmistakable voice of Lain, the young Chief of Reconnaissance and Expedition. She was in her own custom exo, which was outfitted for extended travel and expedition rather than battle, though it was still deadly in its own right. Around her shoulders hung a thin old cloak the color of pine green, reminding Shira of the old world coniferous forests of her childhood, though her mental image of old world forests was mostly informed by the history books she read rather than her own memories. Her feet and legs were covered to the knee by what appeared to be the same type of synthetic-leather that the slave drivers wore as protection. The same material protected her breasts, abdomen, waist, and groin, leaving only her arms, thighs, neck, and face exposed. All of her protective clothing contained holes to accommodate her ports.

In response to Lain's sudden presence, Myriam extended the claws of her exo, and Shira ejected Wintersbane in turn.

"Maybe she's immortal, I mean," Lain stated with a reserved tone, keeping her exo's projectile weapon and curved blade relaxed. She didn't appear even remotely intimidated by the women. Instead, she held herself with the demeanor of a woman who had within her an endless reserve of energy but was saving all of it for another day. A very particular day that was not this one.

"What do you want?" Shira demanded, relaxing her stance but not Wintersbane.

"I get it," Lain stated simply. "I get why you had to do it, Shira. To protect those girls. Because you love them. Because they are everything to you," Lain stated hollowly as if only a part of her was present and the rest of her boiled within, always waiting for that certain day to be released. "You're a better mother than Nichole ever was," Lain finished, her voice cracking so subtly that Shira thought she might have imagined it.

Shira raised her gauntlet, signaling for Myriam to be at ease as she allowed Wintersbane to slither back into her wrist.

Lain nodded in seeming thanks. "I heard you say you will be going to Downver. I don't think that's the best idea, based on what I've heard."

"Downver," Rooli issued, and the others shrugged in agreement.

"If you say so," Lain shrugged back.

"Come with us," Aliana said, and Shira found herself hoping that Lain would agree. However, the young but perfectly capable woman shook her head and said, "I can't. I have my own mission. My own purpose beyond this piece of troutshit city," Lain said casually without any begrudging emphasis or negative emotion, as if the state of the city being a *piece of troutshit* were a mundane fact of the world. "Don't ever abandon these girls," Lain said suddenly with an unbecoming lash in her voice. "Do you hear me, Shira Arcadia?"

Shira understood finally. She understood why Lain was so quiet. She

253

understood why Lain embraced being the Chief of Reconnaissance and Expedition so readily but without celebration. Lain was in pain, more pain than Shira could probably ever imagine, and in that moment, Shira finally understood what Lain was really doing out in the Nomadic world each time she left Wintersvilla's tamed territories.

"You are hunting her," Shira stated, feeling as though she could empathically sense the maddening depths of Lain's anguish and isolation. "You're hunting down your mother. Nichole. For abandoning you."

"She isn't my mother," Lain snarled, unable to stop her emotions from flaring. "If you see her out there, tell her I am coming. Tell her she deserves to die for leaving me in this shit hole city all alone even after she promised me she never would. Tell her I will make sure she gets what she deserves," Lain seethed.

Shira looked back to see Aliana tearing up, Myriam in a continued battle-ready stance, and Aurelia and Rooli staring at Lain intently, as if studying her.

"Okay, Lain," Shira agreed sadly. "But are you sure you don't want to come with us," she offered, hoping that Lain understood that she was standing before her, not as her general, but as one human being to another who would now be cast into the wilds of the Nomadic world.

"You'll all be fine," Lain said with a slight smile. "And so will I. We are strong, all of us. We don't depend on Wintersvilla. We depend on love. And that's it."

"What do you love, Lain?" Aliana asked through a congested nose and tear-stained cheeks.

Lain allowed herself a full smile now and said, "I love the way the clouds form patterns and pictures in the sky. I love the whisper of dusk and the safety of night. I love the stars and the stories they tell," Lain said, but there was a bottled-up scream in each of her words—a hint of the wildfire blazing beneath the surface of her composure. "There is a great deal that Nichole taught me to love," she finished with a hot lash in her tone, and her smile turned back to forced neutrality.

Lain turned and faced the dying city of Wintersvilla, and the others did the same. Biofreaks howled and Rovers chanted eerie ballads of war in the distance. Fires raged and screams of nightmarish terror filled the night as Wintersvilla was crushed by the sorrow and suffering they had inflicted onto the tens of thousands of deformed little boys who would finally have justice—a justice they had dreamed of and hungered for across the twenty-seven years that Wintersvilla had continued to birth them kicking and screaming into the world, only to toss them into its unforgiving wilds. Even Shira could never have foreseen so long ago that so many babies would survive, as if the planet had personally ensured it.

The electricity all across the city began to flicker suddenly, and then one by one, the lights of each of the city's districts were extinguished, plunging everything into darkness as the electric grid of the entire empire shorted and failed. The stars intensified in the sky, roaring with piercing radiance as the people of Wintersvilla screamed into the moonless void.

"It is only right," Lain concluded of Wintersvilla's demise and the stars' newfound brilliance. "It is only natural."

"Natural is being naked," Myriam said with a forced, hollow chuckle as she playfully tugged on Lain's green cloak to lighten the mood.

Lain allowed herself a subtle smirk, then said, "The nudity custom is one of the most mind-numbingly stupid things I have ever heard of."

Myriam cocked her head in surprise, but Shira had known Lain long enough to have predicted her response.

"I don't give a fuck about Wintersvilla," Lain rumbled as the death-dark city wailed and pleaded for mercy. "I live for myself. Just like Nichole. I keep a stash of clothes hidden in the forests outside the walls. I only ever take them off when I'm in the city proper. The farmers in the outer territories have seen me wearing this attire plenty of times. Do you think they care?"

Shira understood her question to be rhetorical. *Of course they don't care about such trivial nonsense,* Shira thought despite admitting to herself that she respected the modern nudity custom, while Myriam embraced it with an honored, excited zeal.

"Who do you think the farmers would find more menacing? Me, as naked as I was born, or you, armored and protected. Some would even say coddled," Myriam offered without malice, speaking matter-of-factly about the custom that she was largely responsible for keeping alive.

"I don't care about being menacing, Myriam," Lain said, cheerlessly laughing to herself as if wrestling her own thoughts into submission.

"Battle and viciousness aren't everything…until I find her, that is. Then I will trade my life for a level of viciousness to rival even yours, Myriam, Wielder of Summit Splitter."

Myriam bowed to Lain as a subordinate paying deference to one of the esteemed chiefs of Wintersvilla. But Shira knew that she also bowed to Lain as one woman respecting the indomitable will and unwavering confidence of another woman who made her own rules and lived her own discipline-forged life in her own uniquely defiant and steadfast way.

Without saying goodbye, Lain turned and directed her exo to the northwest toward the same mountains where Shira had parlayed with BigBilly.

"May Mendel be on your side!" Myriam called out. Lain nodded and waved without looking back.

The fires grew in their fury as the women turned their backs to the city and trotted to the east, passing the Eastern Wall of North Wintersvilla in the direction of the southeastern grove that grew along the northern shores of the harbor. There, Shira's slaves lay in wait, led by the ever loyal Wesley.

"I'm sorry, Myriam," Shira said as the exos ran on autopilot. Rooli sat atop the left shoulder beam of Shira's exo, and Aurelia sat on the right. They both gazed intrepidly at the horizon, as if somehow seeing far ahead into the future. Aliana remained atop the shoulder beam of Myriam's exo, ogling in awe at the size and sharpness of Summit Splitter now that she was able to observe it from such a close distance for the first time.

"Sorry for what?" Myriam chuckled.

"For being a traitor. For never taking you on a honeymoon. For destroying your home," Shira listed, knowing that she could easily continue adding to that list for some time.

"You're right," Myriam admitted playfully. "You are a traitor. And you did destroy my home. But you're wrong about the honeymoon. What do you think this is?"

"This is a lethal expedition through Mutant territory that will probably leave most of us dead or dismembered," Shira said, her words most likely grimly accurate.

"My kind of honeymoon, my gorgeous general," Myriam grinned and winked at Shira seductively, filling Shira with a deeply penetrating warmth.

Shira knew more than ever that she had everything she needed. Everything she loved was right beside her, and she was certain in that moment that nothing bad would ever happen to any of them. She would never allow it. Her life belonged to them, and she was grateful, because she wouldn't have it any other way.

To Be Continued

Author's Note

If you have a few minutes, please take some time to leave a rating or review for this book.

AMAZON and GOODREADS

Thank you so much for your help!

– E. S. Fein